Sandpebbles

"Poetic beauty, sassy humor, genuine struggles of the human heart. *Sandpebbles* kept me enthralled from cover to cover."

—Patsy Clairmont

AUTHOR OF *MENDING YOUR HEART IN A BROKEN WORLD*

"Hickman is a great talent. Her wisdom shines from the pages, as does her compassion. *Sandpebbles* is a gift to treasure."

—T. Davis Bunn

"What a great story! Patricia Hickman's writing touches the heart while it delights the senses. Beautiful!"

—Lawana Blackwell

AUTHOR OF *THE GRESHAM CHRONICLES* AND *TALES OF LONDON*

"Captivating and insightful, *Sandpebbles* unveils the profound beauty of people's need for one another."

—Deborah Raney

AUTHOR OF *BENEATH A SOUTHERN SKY* AND *A VOW TO CHERISH*

"As a new widow, I want to put this book into the hands of as many people as possible and say, 'If you really want to understand the journey of grief, read this!' This book will minister to hearts and lives."

—Stephanie Grace Whitson

AUTHOR AND CHRISTY AWARD FINALIST

"Patricia Hickman's contemplative style is poignant and poetic with deep insights into the hearts of her characters. A keeper to be read again and again."

—Terri Blackstock

AUTHOR OF THE NEWPOINTE 911 SERIES

"*Sandpebbles* is lyrical and funny, haunting and true."

—Deborah Bedford

AUTHOR OF *A ROSE BY THE DOOR*

"With her unique voice, warm humor, and rich insights into everything from pain and loss to single parenthood and new love, Patricia Hickman has given us another treasure."

—Gayle Roper

AUTHOR OF *SUMMER SHADOWS, SPRING RAIN*

"Beautiful prose, charming setting, and likeable, well-developed characters. Well done."

—Lisa Samson

BEST-SELLING AUTHOR OF *CHURCH LADIES*

The Women of Faith Fiction Club presents

Sandpebbles

By Patricia Hickman

W Publishing Group™

www.wpublishinggroup.com

A Division of Thomas Nelson, Inc.
www.ThomasNelson.com

Published by W Publishing Group, a division of Thomas Nelson Company, P.O. Box 141000, Nashville, Tennessee, 37214, in association with the literary agency of Alive Communications, Inc., 7680 Goddard Street, Suite 200, Colorado Springs, Colorado, 80920.

ISBN 0-8499-4300-0

Printed in the United States of America

02 03 04 05 PHX 9 8 7 6 5 4 3 2 1

TO JESSICA NICOLE HICKMAN
who loved dance, music, butterflies, and daisies.

9-21-1980
4-27-2001

While my memories of you, my angel girl, are rent by the pain of separation, I know that we are only a whisper apart until the day our Savior reunites us. I found this scripture written by your own hand on your nightstand, and I know you really meant it: *"Do nothing out of selfish ambition or vain conceit, but in humility consider others better than yourselves. Each of you should look not only to your own interests, but also to the interest of others."* (Philippians 2:3–4) This was your beacon, and it is still shining today.

One

NOT LETTING GO IS MY DOWNFALL. I CAN THINK OF at least three lives I saved because of it and at least two lives I wrecked. Case in point: Whenever my husband Joe and I saw an accident, I leaped from the car, checked the victims' vitals, and directed traffic until the local cops and EMS team arrived.

Be that as it may, succumbing to this same inner mechanism is why I held a gun on two thugs and rescued my baby-sitter, Yolanda, from what would have been possible torture. It was not a real gun.

A year and a half after Joe's death I drove home from Gum's Food Mart loaded down with ears of corn and shrimp for a seafood boil near the ocean. My boy, Mason, expected me to punctually pick him up from his Grandpa's and chauffeur him to his baseball game. My late habits at the newspaper office triggered occasional tardiness. He tended to get miffed about my weak timekeeping. So I almost missed seeing Yolanda at the Hep-Ur-Sef coin-op car wash because I exceeded the speed limit. But in an oblique sort of manner, I saw the spray wand lift and lower above Yolanda's VW Beetle. Then the whole hose contraption went haywire. Suds fountained in the air as the hose spewed in circles and made cobralike gyrations that caught my eye and caused my foot to hit the brake.

That is when I saw the thugs. One wielded a terrorizing blade. According to the ten o'clock news that night, the wayward boys had escaped from a jail in New Jersey, stolen a car, and made it all the way to our town of Candle Cove, North Carolina—a mistake they will most surely never make again. We are tight here. Whatever they intended to do with Yolanda never came to light. Before they could wrestle her away from the Beetle, my tires squealed to a dead stop right in front of them. Grenades of corn pitched throughout my SUV and I remember whisking away husk hairs for a solid month from the upholstery and carpet, a fact that irked me for the longest time. Mason had dropped his black water pistol onto the floor of the car. With both hands, I gripped it tight through the open window. I hid the plastic cap that holds in the water with my thumbs. "Put up your hands! I'm the police!"

Yolanda whitened and tried to speak even though one of the brutes had his filthy hand clamped over her sweet teenage mouth.

Both of the men were so surprised they froze, and the one with a knife threw it down. I called May at the police station on my cellular and she sent our two cops, Harold Gleason and Bobby White, over right away. (They were having jalapeño bagels at the nearby Lighthouse Java Mill.) I ordered the criminals to lie facedown on the pavement and Yolanda ran shrieking out into the street to flag down Harold and Bobby. Harold held them at bay while Bobby cuffed them and read them their rights. Harold said he wanted to swear at me for succumbing to my mechanism only to endanger the life of two helpless women, one being myself. But I had already stepped aside to retch into the Hep-Ur-Sef trash container.

Yolanda cried and ran up the bill on her parents' cellular phone, calling first her mother, her father who was away in Pittsburgh on business, her orthodontist, and her best friend in the whole eleventh grade. She hugged me and bawled on my shoulder so hard I had to tear myself away to run and fetch Mason, who by that time paced in front of his grandfather's house, tapping the tip of his bat against the walk, irate as mad bees. Even though I had rescued his lifelong babysitter, he was angry enough that he spilled out disconnected phrases that seemed to combust at the end with incensed grunts. The slightest infraction on my part, in his ten-year-old estimation, was worthy of castigation.

That is why I took him to Virginia every spring to visit his father's grave, to leave flowers, and to help Mason forgive me.

Six months later, the second anniversary of Joe's death rolled around, and Mason and I drove all the way up to northern Virginia to visit his daddy's grave. Neither of us wanted to stay behind in Virginia, or return to North Carolina. The trees along I-95 were not greening yet, and that disappointed Mason. Ten-year-old boys like him see sunsets and blooming trees and grow up to be men who can cry. Mason's daddy could not cry, and I believed that was what caused his death.

I thought that Joe's death would end my life. Even when Bobby and Harold showed up at my door stiff as soldiers with the news of Joe's passing, I had said just that very thing—"Dear God, my life is over!" But instead of ending me, Joe's accident left me opened up and walking around. Yet if I attempted the most menial tasks, I felt a paralysis slip over my mind. The most insignificant incidents reminded me of my Joe, like the time I opened a tool drawer out in the garage and found it stuffed with bank slips and gas receipts. I thought I had cleared away all of the clutter that reminded me of his pack rat tendencies, but right next to a ratchet and a box of matches lay more of his addiction to disorder. I cried for days. For hours every night after I sent Mason to bed, I cleared out every possible cranny in the house where Joe might have tossed a piece of this or that, even poring through his shoeboxes filled with tax returns until his clutter was eradicated and every inch of our house cleared of the-history-of-us. After the Nights of Eradication, I worked to close the windows of my soul and bar the attic of my mind.

It was the very worst thing I could do.

During our summer, we are the sun children of the Sound Country, not a long distance from the ferry that tools tourists out to Ocracoke Island or from any number of the fishing villages that dot the decaying womb of upper coastal North Carolina. Candle Cove draws beachcombers and business opportunities but not always both trades at once. Winter does not kiss us with heated passion the way it plays to its mistresses of the low country and Florida. Damp winters sluice the Sound people with blankets of firmament so thick the sky is one with the fog beneath our feet.

Summer is where we prefer to live. Mason wanted to cross the threshold to the inland with its thickets of live oak and find it green, not plain—not allowing the wind to howl through the naked tree limbs, brittle beggars undressed in the fields. Winter makes its home up north, but it plants its feet in the Carolinas, enough to chill the field and to blow snow across the upper decks of the mountains and leave a tinsel of cold upon the Atlantic side. Mentally I had painted our little piece of heaven green, just as I painted my mother alive. "Soon, Mason, we'll have us a good spring."

We saw the "Welcome to North Carolina" sign as we left Virginia behind, but the crossing of thresholds had lost its sheen. When too much change comes to your door, you grow anxious around thresholds.

I had learned to watch Mason without him knowing it. He sat with the passenger shoulder safety belt twisted behind him. Mason complained of seat straps too high for short kids. He never minded the height issue until fifth grade. But now he attached all of his worth to it, as though it were his defining trait. Within every comment from a grade-school imbecile—and every class has one—he found hidden meaning between what was said and what was implied.

My observances of Mason were as covert as all of the things that kept me a step ahead of him, like the furtive ways that a mother watches her boy so he won't complain she's smothering him. I catalogued a mental collection of a mother's snapshots into little significant files like "Mason when he is angry with me" and "Mason when he daydreams." I thirsted for the tender and rare moments right now, the sight of things that stole my breath and gave me pause. You learn to look for beauty in the fragile lace of life when other things in your world come unthreaded.

Mason remained transfixed on the ebbing color that stained the horizon, as though he were sucking the color out of the sky himself. A mélange of orange and cinnamon firmament floated just above the mountains, a marker for where the sun had just kissed the sky before bed. He traced the cloud shape onto the surface of the car window. Or perhaps he drew something else. I don't know why I give every action a meaning. It's just the thing a writer does when she sees something mysterious.

"This is North Carolina," he said, "not South."

"Right, Professor. North comes before South."

"Not if you're coming from Florida."

"Let's stop here tonight. Then tomorrow morning we'll have only three hours left until we reach Candle Cove."

"Grandpa's looking for us."

"I told him it might be tomorrow."

A LaQuinta sign the color of orange and cinnamon floated above the interstate. It advertised a special for families.

"Free breakfast. Let's stop here." I braked.

"Continental. That's not real breakfast."

"We have continental every morning: cold cereal, frozen waffles, toast."

"Ask if we can check the pillows first. I hate pillows that are overpuffed," he said

"Overpuffed isn't a word. Unless you're saying it as two words." We drove over a speed bump and past the flashing vacancy sign.

Mason slid his finger up and down the bridge of his nose in a manner that followed the inward curve of the bridge to the upturned and rounded curves that housed his trademark Longfellow nostrils. Whenever anger shot up his spine, those same nostrils flared and he looked pug-nosed.

"I hope the dog and cat are all right. Hercules always acts psychotic after he's been at the Pet Spa," I said.

"Johnson acts psychotic every day. Cats are all psychotic."

But none as off-the-wall as Johnson who had feline phobias such as a fear of walking on sand—he would mince onto the sand, shake his paw, and turn and run back up to the cottage. Only he didn't like the cottage either, and I swore he had agoraphobia or whatever you call that thing when you just want to stay in all of the time. "You know you love Johnson, Mason. You ought to. He's gotten too old to give away."

"A needy family still might take him. For a rug."

"This LaQuinta looks new. Maybe we'll get a new room. Toss my shoes over here, will you?"

"I'd rather pick up Hercules tonight. He's nervous without me." Mason slid my sneakers toward me with the side of his foot.

"He'll be fine one more night. Anyway, the Pet Spa closes at seven, I think. We have to wait until tomorrow to check him out anyway. This is like a three-day weekend for me. If Gloria keeps her word about it, that is." Gloria Hammer, my assistant at the Candle Cove *Sentinel*, had promised to keep the presses rolling in my absence from the weekly newspaper. I had never used my degree until after Joe died so I chose a business that seemed to line up with my journalism major, forgetting I might have needed a few courses on small business administration. I purchased the *Sentinel* as a safety net after Joe's death. Instead, it consumed our money as if we had carved a hole beneath the little downtown bank and plugged it with a vacuum. "Your last day of spring break. No cooking, no making the beds."

"We don't make the beds now. This place looks Mexican. See if they have a Taco Bell, Mom."

"You wait here, Mason. I'll get a key to check a room."

"And don't forget to check the pillows." He yelled "overpuffed" through the glass.

I crossed the asphalt beneath the registration overhang and glanced at Mason, but he stared down at the floor, stared as though he needed to count how many caramel corns had dropped to the floor between northern Virginia and North Carolina. He had grown more argumentative over the last few weeks, more as we packed away the office where Joe had kept his law files. And even more so when we swept away the veil of snow from the grave site where two years ago we had laid Joe to rest.

The night clerk was a Southerner who had developed a sonorous Midwestern elocution. I knew that because I could still hear the mountains in his vowels whenever he said, "Please take advantage of our free breakfast that starts at dawn."

"I notice a large bus parked out back. Is that a seniors' tour or a youth group?" I wanted peace all night.

"Neither. It's a basketball team from Florida."

I held the key card a foot away.

"They're a good bunch of young ladies."

"Oh, ladies' basketball." I always thought it strange to call those young girls "ladies," and imagined them with enormous handkerchief-stuffed black leather handbags with brass latches. I remembered Mason's request but felt too silly to ask about the pillows. "I need to check out the room first. But I'm sure it's fine. If I don't come back, it means I took the room."

The clerk picked up the phone but answered me tacitly, lifted his head and pinched his forehead until both eyebrows beetled, black antennae spreading over dark insect eyes.

I steered the car around the lot, slowly ascending the hills of speed bumps and following the red arrows the clerk had scrawled on a hotel map. "You can check out the pillows yourself, Mason."

"I wish I was already home. It was dumb to plant Daddy so far away."

"His family comes from Virginia, Mason. Your dad grew up there." Mason followed me up the little rear porch dimly illumined by the muted yellow courtesy light, and then tramped ahead to be the first inside.

"Virginia is too cold. My fingers almost froze up and cracked off."

"I think we enter through that doorway. Then down the hall is the elevator."

"You don't listen to anything I say."

"Mason, I'm tired."

"You look it."

We rode the elevator up to the second floor without a word exchanged between us. The door opened to a hallway decorated with quiet red carpet. Electric candlesticks cast a soft ambiance. I fiddled with a luggage strap and then said to him, "I know for a fact I haven't said anything to make you mad at me. I think you're tired."

Mason turned his rounded koala face from me, as if to keep me from studying the way his eyes lilted, slumberous at the corners. "You don't miss him as much as I do. If you did—"

An older man, his years frozen around his eyes, stopped to look at us two doors down. We vanished from the stranger's reproving stare and locked the door behind us.

"Mason, I just took a road trip halfway up a nation just so we could visit your daddy's grave."

"You didn't cry."

"Maybe I'm cried out. Folks get cried out. Tear ducts empty. It's not unnatural." A weird bareness rose up inside of me. I felt naked, my insides twisted open by a ten-year-old corkscrew.

"Why does his name on the grave thingy look so cold anyway? I feel like I want to cry, or I'm supposed to but it's not coming out. I waited for you to start, right when you put those plastic daisies in the stone vase. But you never cried, Momma."

"I see what you mean. I need a soda. You fill the ice bucket and I'll get the drinks."

I swore that Mason and I had talked out Joe's boating accident. Heaven knew the rest of Candle Cove had talked it to death. Mason's gut-thundering honesty shined up nice on some days but on others left me without any energy.

When Joe died, he had left enough of the aroma of manhood on Mason to make him wish for it, but the scent had faded. Mason ran in dogged circles in search of his dad, in search of a face that would tell him what God looked like.

Mason handed me the overnight case and then gutted his duffel bag, a bombed-out explosion of boy's underwear and game cartridges. He dumped both bags near the bathroom door and then scuttled downstairs to lock up the car, marching almost in cadence, the chivalrous male. On some days, he faked it so well, so near ultimate maleness that I believed Mason needed no more than just me. Just us; that was all we needed. I pressed a tissue against my eyes. The cold made them moist.

Sunrise had come too early, especially since I had allowed Mason to rent an in-room movie at nine the night before and break open the microwave popcorn deposited onto a tray by the maid. After an hour or so of driving, I initiated conversation to suppress the sleep demons that turned my eyelids to lead.

"For lunch, let's have a root beer float and toast it just like when your daddy did on that day up at Ocean City. It was your birthday, I believe. I'll bet your daddy would like that."

"Should we wait until we get home and invite Grandpa? Will we be home by then or did you mean along the way?" Mason had encircled the calendar day in red crayon and scribbled three initials—DDD—for the "day Dad died." He laid the calendar on the seat between us open to the month of March, the tenth day.

I might have noticed an important calendar notation made earlier on my way out of town, but I didn't even give it a glance. That is what caused all of the trouble. "We might be home by then but I have work waiting at home. I have to stop and pick up some extras for the cottage, too. Grandpa's invited a pastor to preach either next week or the week after. Or, I guess he's an evangelist. But for the life of me I can't remember if it was next Sunday or not. Whatever. Dad acts like he needs the break, anyway." My father had pastored Candle Cove Presbyterian for twenty-seven years without a real vacation.

"Grandpa wants to go fishing, like he thinks I like it."

"If you don't want to fish, tell him."

"I'd hurt his feelings."

"Grandpa's been told worse things than that, Mason. Pastors hear everything." I felt as though I were slipping back into my old flannel bathrobe as we passed by the familiar towns such as Brinkleyville and Glenview.

"When we go away and then go home, I'm glad to get away, but gladder to get back home," I said.

A rabbit raced alongside the SUV, slightly ahead of us, its legs stretching behind it so extreme in gait, it seemed to fly. Mason eyed it and squinted like a wishful huntsman. He drew an invisible gun, made a cocking sound with his tongue, and then yelled, "Blam, blam!"

"I'll bet you're ready to get back in school after a break."

"I hate school." He blurted it out as though he knew it would annoy me.

"Boys like to say that, right? It's something you're supposed to say when you're a guy. I wonder if you really mean it, though."

"Of course I mean it." He fired his invisible bullets again. A satisfaction spread across his face as though he didn't see the long legs split a sea of grass and vanish, but rather lurch in a moment of surprise, a stain of red forming at the heart, a jerk, and then a collapse.

"When I kept up with my school work, I mean, when I was your age, I liked school. I never hated it when I had it all together, had my GPA up."

"We don't call it a GPA. Just grades. I make the grades, but I still hate it."

"Hating it has to be a male thing."

"All my friends hate it." He scanned the passing field for more wildlife.

A rotary movement caught my eye, a twenty-something-foot-tall mug that rotated above a hamburger stand. "It's a sign, Mason."

"I'll get my shoes on." He said it like a television jingle.

"Good. I'll make the list for Dad." I parked us right outside the takeout window. "Dad's secretary forgets so many little things, especially since Mother died. I don't know why that is. He should pay me a salary for all I have to do to keep Thelma straight."

Mason carried the tray of cheeseburgers, onion rings, and root beer to a red Formica table with chrome legs. "We never take this long to get home."

"I don't know what you mean." I emptied the tray, arranged the food, and then handed the tray to a passing waitress.

"You were in a hurry to get to the cemetery, to Daddy's grave. But you're taking longer to get home."

"I hadn't noticed."

"We've been in the car like forever."

"Drat, they put ketchup on my burger," I said.

"I need to sign up for baseball season this weekend. Tomorrow morning."

I drew in a breath and sighed. "You didn't tell me."

He broke our communal glare with an irritating retort. "I did. Mom, you forgot. Again."

"So we'll get up in the morning and do it. Mason, you exaggerate about me as though you have to parade all of my flaws out in front of the world. I'm not a bad mother."

"I need new pads, cleats, pants. Everything's too small. If I have to wear those pants another year, maybe I won't play. "

"We'll get the baseball gear. Don't make me feel like a louse, as though I'm going to make you go to practice with your rear end hanging out."

"If you don't want to go, Grandpa can take me."

"I said I'd take you. I'll be right back. I can't eat this with ketchup." I returned the burger to the front-counter attendant, who sighed and ferried the sandwich into a suspiciously hidden-from-sight kitchen. Mason sat with his back to me. When he wanted something, he always made me feel inadequate, a loose thread on his shoulder.

We finished lunch without sharing many more words. I made a list of things, certain Dad had forgotten them.

The sky clouded an iron gray painted with winter shades that darkened the nimbostratus layer and its ragged skirts. But the quiet aroma of spring left a far hint of complaint in the air, as though winter had stayed beyond its welcome. I shifted and it caused Mason to stand and clear away the litter. He shuffled the trash into a rubber bin and walked alone to the SUV.

He crawled into the middle seat behind me. The rest of the trip, he slept. A tinny rhythm emanated from his earphones. They curved around his neck like a stethoscope. I turned off his cassette player. As we drew nearer to Candle Cove, to Pamlico's teeming universe, I felt something slipping from me. The cemetery visit left me feeling as though I swam the journey home with anchors tied to both feet.

I once believed that North Carolina offered a comfortable lap for errant souls like Joe. But the ocean beyond the estuaries and further, on past the archipelago of islands adorning the eastern shores like a bridal tiara, was unforgiving. It swallowed up too much. You can only be swallowed once by water if you don't pull yourself out fast enough. It was no way for Joe to leave the world, in my opinion. I wanted significance in my marriage—banners I could wave around and say, "Joe and me, we made it." But he left all hope on the bottom of the sea with the fish and the sand. Sand pebbles make for weak touchstones, shifting, hiding, and changing places until the world forgets you once made footprints.

Joe left little behind in the way of a legacy, except a disputed piece of land and a cat. I hate cats, although I am cautious to never make mention of it in the *Sentinel.* I could lose subscriptions. My loathing for cats had more to do with the acquiring of my last name, a stylish name for a writer, according to some of my writer friends. When I said my vows to Joe, I acquired a cat and a good literary name. Once I considered the name a lucky amulet for a writer, although my prose never bubbled close to the abilities of the writer's circle I admire—the Candle Cove Inksters. It is believed that genius flourishes in remote pockets of the Carolinas, but seldom in Candle Cove. I know of at least one irritating genius who ran with the Inksters, but I wanted nothing to do with her. Sarai Gillman was a Wilmington grad who poured coffee up at the Lighthouse Java Mill by day. The girl's wand-shaped shadow flickered against a stained window shade every evening as she fashioned plots that she never shared, even with the Inksters. But also perched in the window were cats. Cattails sashayed back and forth in the girl's window, little metronomes keeping time to the ticking of the keys, the cadence of thought shaped into words by her. The very idea of the creatures jumbled in a mass around that writer's feet repulsed me; all that thrumming those animals do annoys me, as though their motor is forever idling. I know that Inkster has an overage of cats by the silky filaments that cling to her T-shirts and the jagged claw marks along the hem of her uniform: Caucasian-pink knit slacks tattooed with an embroidered lighthouse on the front pocket. But since Joe died, I've wanted nothing to do with cats—especially the aged family tomcat, Johnson, that coils around my feet every evening when I water the potted geraniums that droop along the three sage-green shelves above my kitchen sink. But that doesn't mean I neglect him. My antipathy for cat lovers I acquired much earlier. But as I said, I'll sell them a newspaper.

Joe adopted Johnson when we dated. Johnson hated my golden retriever, Hercules, the puppy I bought for Mason when he turned three. After Mason's birthday party that year, we relegated Hercules to a backyard pen simply as a means of quelling the constant feud between cat and dog. It is mysterious the way the animals mirrored their owners. I argued with Joe at the slightest provocation in hopes I could help him grow. I was always honorable in my motives.

It was all my fault for falling for lawyerly charisma in the first place.

Joe Longfellow had hooked me from the start. My initial hunch that he would ultimately draw me in by his devices against my better judgment came when I first took notice of the sound of his voice. I kept myself from men like him by cataloguing male voices into a secret system I shared with no one, save my best friend, Dinah Buckworth, who hosts a local radio show called "In the Kitchen with Dinah." I was proofing a college paper I had just roughed out while at the study of my parents' beach cottage. Stumped by one elusive fact, I had phoned the venerable law offices of Blakely and Chase in Wilmington for one loaded detail, only to wind up with the after-hours answering machine. Joe Longfellow had just passed his bar and made use of his afternoons by researching cases for Blakely and Chase. Blakely had asked Joe to provide the message for their answering machine. I phoned in for a meager thread of research for a postbacc paper. Joe Longfellow's dazzling pitch explained the firm's law specialty, that thing they did for the banking industry as transactional attorneys. Immediately, I placed him on the farthest spectrum of my male voice scale, a scarlet ten with conjuring, albeit, troublesome tendencies that marked his deep vibrato with a subtle trace of jagged machismo—a slight touch of it, but nonetheless, enough to sound the siren. I possessed in my midtwenties a weak splinter of craving that seldom hooked me with the wrong man, but on occasion pricked me in all of my vulnerable places. It was a dreadful chink in my ideology; a gene for which neither of my parents accepted blame.

Joe's voice had had such an effect on me. Instantly pricked, I had left a brief message, but called back ten minutes later to inform "the voice" that I would pick up the information the following day. In person.

My mother, Julia Norville, had a premonition about him, even though she took no store in premonitions. She called those shudders of portent that afflict maternal instinct her "discerning quakes"—a slight tremor that stole her breath and nothing more. Mother quaked only twice for my sake—once when through a dot-com Web site I bought a used Tercel that gave out after one year and, second, when I met Joe Longfellow.

"He's not of your moral fiber," she had said, but how she knew that I never knew.

"Mason, we're home."

Candle Cove sat as a breath along the Atlantic, a phosphorescent crescent of light at the end of the day. A pallid shard of daylight flickered, engulfed by the curtain of rain that followed us home.

"Don't forget the dog, Mom."

As if I would. "After we unpack, we'll pick him up. And Johnson." I remembered the root beer stand again. We had wandered into and back out of the roadside stand without ever acknowledging the anniversary of Joe's death, without toasting root beers, as though numbed by the calendar date. Mason dragged his gear to the house, put his key into the twenty-year-old keyhole, and vanished into the dusky entry. The sky let go of the rain and it washed the dust from the SUV, ran into the gutters, flushed down into the waterway, and out into the ocean.

The untoasted moment left me feeling unpardoned and unfinished. I would step inside and ask Mason's forgiveness if he even so much as hinted at the infraction. If he forgot, then I would pick up the dog and cat, and go to bed tacit and incomplete. That is what you do when your life is a wreck.

Two

MASON PULLED A QUILT OUT OF THE FAMILY TRUNK that masqueraded as a coffee table and tented up a cozy hiding place on top of the sofa where he curled up with Hercules. The cat paced out on the deck, done with his business and whining miserably to get back inside. His tail was ringed with charcoal and bent like the flagpole of a defeated foe.

I cradled chlorine cleanser under one arm like the Princess of Hygiene. "You stay here and relax, Mason, and I'll be right back."

I drove to Dad's seaside place where I would make a checklist for the cottage. I could clean it on Monday. That would be soon enough to prepare the place for any guests.

I passed Dad's house on the way to the cottage. His home, lit low like the whispered blush of a monastery, was tucked into a copse of trees. A tangle of hardwoods and yellowed palms, a product of Florida transplants that clashed with native trees, cosseted the pale green bungalow. Every Friday since I could remember, James Norville shut himself away from the fray of committees and hospital visits to lay the finishing touches to the Sunday morning message. His preaching books encircled his comfortable chair: a *Strong's Concordance*, a newsmagazine or two, and a handbook of biblical history. A dim study light illuminated the soft veil of window sheers that rustled whenever the floor vent warmed the room. Later, I would call and tell him we made it back all right. But for now I imagined him with an afghan draping his lap, planted next to his mother's old upright radio that had not played a single hymn since the days of "The Old Time Gospel Hour." My mother's miniature dachshund, Arnie, would lie on the braided rug with its chin and face pressed against Dad's woolly house slippers. The dachshund developed white chin whiskers in its later years, a phenomenon Dad called "Arnie's beard." I would not transgress to disturb such a scene. I drove to the cottage a mile away.

The cottage windows revealed an illumined kitchen. A movement inside the cottage startled me. A shadow crossed the lace curtains hung one summer by my mother and me in the old place. Twice I glanced down at the calendar day circled by Mason. It occurred to me that Mason's broad red strokes might be hiding other things, such as a note about a visiting pastor, and yet I plowed into the sandy back garden without so much as an inspection of my own orderly records.

Three additional human shapes appeared inside behind the lacy sheers, smaller bodies wildly moving through the kitchen, nymphlike shadows dancing against my mother's sacred window. I elevated myself from the red leather seat of the Mustang once driven by Joe. The sounds muffled by the closed-up nature of the house in its winter state had a natural quality; not like the noise of intruders, but the abiding familiarity of ownership.

I approached the house from the kitchen side, a rear entrance with a yawning two-level deck. The ocean roared and slapped at the shore, digging saltwater talons into the sand as the tide shrank and flexed into frilled gills of spray and grasping waves. I entered the rear deck from the wooden steps that Dad and I had stained blue-gray to accent the ocean hues of the cottage. Through the windows, I saw her: a blond-haired woman scoured the twin sinks and chattered with several children, one of which clung to her shirttail. Dad never hired a housekeeper, never would have paid hired help to clean the cottage when he could call me.

My trip away with Mason must have convinced him I needed a break. I tapped on the rear-door window as I hid the cleanser inside the deepest pocket of my Windbreaker.

I startled the woman. A young girl sidled behind the woman's hips, a kittenish yelp emanating from her soft triangular mouth. The blonde looked to be in her late twenties, the gleam of youth melding with the chic of maturity. I returned her faint smile, but felt the woman intercepted my concern. She opened the door with one hand. In the other, she clutched one of my mother's old aprons.

"May I help you?"

Her question annoyed me. "This is my father's cottage. I've been out of town and dropped by to check on the place."

"Oh, are you Marcia?"

"March. Like this month, the month of March."

"I like that name. Charlotte, go and bring your brothers and sister in here to meet Ms. Norville."

Charlotte flew, her arms and fingertips draped with wings made of felt, gold braid, and a translucent fabric, wings that fluttered behind her, primitive and fashioned by an unrestrained imagination.

"March Longfellow. Norville was my maiden name." I followed the blonde goddess into the kitchen, careful to close the door to keep out the chill of the ocean wind.

"I'm pleased to meet you. I'm Ruth Arnett. Your father told you Pastor Colin Arnett was coming, I hope."

"That's this weekend, then?" I felt my mother's opinions alight all over me, scrutinizing my tone and intent. I reconstructed the sentence. "Welcome to Candle Cove. I'll do everything I can to make you comfortable." I sounded mechanical, like a flight attendant droning her spiel over the intercom. But the unparalleled scrutiny of Julia Norville lived inside of me, eliciting the proper response.

"I feel as though we've made you uncomfortable. I don't believe you were told about us. I know Colin. He won't want to be a bother, but sometimes when the men do all of the planning, well, not all of the details get ironed out. Please, all I have are some cold drinks until Colin returns from the store. Let me fix you something."

"No, I don't need a thing. My father doesn't usually handle the details of visitors. I've always done that. I usually ask the ladies at church to bring meals by for visiting ministers. I must have written down the wrong date, is all. I hope you know it isn't like me at all." I changed directions, not wanting to sound grasping. "Reverend Arnett doesn't need to stock the pantry. I can make a few phone calls tonight and you'll have dinners on the way by tomorrow night, home cooked. Our ladies are really good cooks too. Breakfast items we leave here in the cottage for you, if that's all right. Or we can set up an account for you at Millie's if you prefer a hot cooked breakfast. Millie's pancakes are popular."

"No, goodness no. I already feel as though we've imposed enough. Your father was kind enough to consent to our joining Colin at the last minute. That's why he volunteered to run for groceries. I do all of the cooking, so I'm used to that, although Charlotte here is turning out to be quite the kitchen helper herself."

The winged child smiled, her hair white and poking out of a ponytail holder in damp spikes.

"Colin called Reverend Norville last night, thought the kids and myself would like a seaside visit. It's been a hectic year. I've been working on my dissertation."

"I'm just thinking of finishing my master's myself," I said, although it sounded down the ladder from Ruth Arnett's dissertation. "I write, though. I guess I don't have much use for a doctorate unless I decide to teach college.

"I didn't know you wrote, Ms. Norville."

I didn't correct her this time. "I own a small newspaper here in Candle Cove. Sometimes I write travel articles for the *Charlotte Observer*, too. But that's just a little freelance work on the side I do for a friend. Helps to pay the bills." The newspaper had yet to meet budget or clear a profit, but I kept that bit of sour news to myself.

"It's so pretty here. We drove here in the rain. But we arrived in time to see the sunset and it's beyond what the postcards around here can portray. If ever we have the time, I want to visit the Outer Banks. But I don't know how you get out to those islands. By plane, I guess."

"Or ferry. Roanoke Island has festivals; you might try Roanoke first. Or Ocracoke Island."

"But I don't like a lot of tourists. I'm looking for solace." Ruth lightened her tone as though she longed for peace at this very instant.

"Pamlico Sound is perfect, then."

Two little boys made the flight down the staircase in only six steps.

"Troy and Luke, mind yourselves and come in here and meet Reverend Norville's daughter."

"Nice to meet you boys." I waved at them knowing how children in this day and age are less prone to shake a hand.

Ruth Arnett rinsed out the sinks and wiped down the tiled countertops as she spoke. It made me uneasy.

"I actually carried over some cleaning supplies," I told her and half-turned as though I might go back out to the car to fetch them. "If you all want to go to dinner, I'll have the place dusted and ready before you return. I don't know how Dad and I crossed wires, but I'd like to make it up to you."

"The cottage is already in really nice shape, and you weren't expecting the whole Arnett clan, so I insist—you don't need to do a thing. I've had my mind so buried in books; really, a little domestic duty is a welcome change. Colin's bringing back barbecue. I hope I sent him to a good place. We found this little dive as we drove down this road that parallels the beach. Dives have the best food, we've found."

"JoJo's Barbecue, I'll bet. Plenty enough of a dive, if that's what you like."

"You should join us."

"I can't. I left my ten-year-old asleep on the sofa with the dog."

"You have a child, March. Maybe he can come play with the kids this weekend."

"He would like that. I have to get him signed up for baseball practice tomorrow morning. We'll see how tomorrow goes."

"And don't worry about breakfast. Colin's picking up milk and cereal for the kids. We'll be just fine with that."

"I should go, then. Glad we could meet. Maybe I'll meet Reverend Arnett tomorrow. You all have a good night's rest."

"Thank you, Ms. Norville."

Two headlights flooded the kitchen, then dimmed next to the Mustang. Ruth waved through the window to Colin Arnett.

"Daddy's back with the food," said Charlotte. "Luke, you and Troy go wash your faces and hands right this minute."

Troy grimaced, unwilling to bend to his sister's dictates.

"That's a good idea," said Ruth. "I haven't seen Rachel. Ms. Norville, I'll be right back. Seems like the youngest is always the last one down."

"Four children." I counted them.

Ruth bounded up the stairs, her long legs wrapped in black knit and punctuated at her narrow feet by Nikes. She sprinted like a runner. I tried to imagine my mother in clingy knit but couldn't. Ruth Arnett had failed to adopt the wrappings of a clergyman's family. No floral frocks off the KMart blue-light-specials bin, no Payless Shoes enclosing her delicate toes. Just the lightly girded style that makes the few size-two women in the world look to-the-nines when scarcely wearing a thing.

Colin Arnett banged the rear door with his knee.

"I'll get it!" Charlotte ran past and nearly tripped on a loose ruffle around her hem. She twisted the brass knob with both hands. "I hope you got me chicken, Daddy!"

"Charlotte, grab this bag under my arm. I'm just about to drop it, honey," Colin said.

The girl, who looked to be an eight-year-old, hefted the bag of milk but swaggered under the weight of the gallon jug.

I reached for the milk. "I can help."

"I have it." Charlotte lifted her wings and thrust the milk carton onto the countertop.

"Charlotte lives under the mistaken impression she's in charge." Colin set the other bags next to the milk. "Just like her mother. Hi, I'm Colin Arnett." He held up his hand crooked to one side with his thumb pointing up at the ceiling as though he felt comfortable holding a calligrapher's pen.

He had long fingers, curved at the tips. He seemed well practiced in ordinariness. My father's poise when he introduced himself held a mystery about it. I remember how awestruck I'd felt as a girl about the word *Reverend* carefully placed in front of James Norville's name. It was the way he said it, with careful enunciation, plummy with a bit of starch. Colin Arnett said his name insouciantly, like a bohemian in Greenwich Village.

"I'm Reverend Norville's daughter. I've been away or else I would have stocked the pantry for you. I hope you're not inconvenienced."

"Your father told me you were gone away on a trip. I'm here a day early and bringing five more than he expected. I'm glad to pick up a few things. Hope this barbecue place has food as good as it smells."

"I can put all of that away for you," I said.

"No, please. Ruth will manage and she doesn't mind. Charlotte, you and your brothers go pick up your toys. You left them all over the downstairs parlor."

"We haven't entertained an evangelist in a while. I've made friends over the years with evangelists and their families. The road can be wearying with all of those motels. When my mother and dad bought this place, they wanted it to be a refuge for traveling ministers. I hope you find it peaceful here."

"Actually, I'm a pastor. I haven't had to dwell for long summers in the caves of Motel 6s. Your father and I met at a ministers' meeting last year and we've corresponded ever since."

"Dad loves to write letters."

"Almost a thing of the past, I'm afraid. It's unique to find a fellow minister who is willing to pen a letter. You find out more about a person when he writes than if you're having a telephone conversation. Or e-mail."

"I guess that's true."

The boys ran through the kitchen and disappeared into the downstairs bedroom. Ruth had dressed them in robes and slippers.

"Your tribe is hungry," I said.

Colin left his jacket atop a table where my mother once cultivated violets. When he turned his back to me, I placed it on the hall tree.

"They've been restless. I've been careful not to share the purpose of our visit here. It's too early. But it's as though they sense a change. Children are more insightful than we give them credit for." When he moved, it was with balance, like a man practiced at tennis or any sport that required agility in a small quadrangle of space.

I transported the gallon of milk to the refrigerator. "I'm not altogether following you, but as I said, I've been away."

"I can't imagine moving away from our home near Lake Norman. My wife spent so many hours decorating the place. It has her touch all over it."

I lifted a pint of slaw from one of the brown bags. Then I stood with it pressed against my stomach, forgetting my domestic obligations in order to try and decipher the coded language of this city minister.

"When your father's steering committee first called, well, it just didn't seem plausible. But they were so persistent. I have a lot of admiration for tenacity in a church committee."

"I don't know anything about a steering committee, Reverend Arnett. I'm close to my father and he would tell me about any changes. Does he know why you're here? I certainly don't."

"Your father is a thorough planner, Ms. Longfellow. He explained to me his desire to retire a year ago. But I never saw myself as the one to take his place."

"My father isn't old enough to retire. He's in his prime and his congregation would never stand for it."

"He hasn't told you." He leaned against the countertop. He had gray eyes, studious, and they studied me. "Then I have no business telling you. This is terrible."

"My mother and father built this church from nothing, gave birth to it as though it were their own child. They spent up all of their savings just so the new church would not founder under the weight of a salary." I felt my nostrils flare, just like Mason's.

Ruth waited at the foot of the stairs. "Colin?"

"I've made a mess of things, Ruth," he told her.

"What did you do?"

"Reverend Norville hasn't shared the news of his retirement with his daughter."

"Colin, no. Ms. Norville, I'm afraid we've intruded on your life tonight. You must think of us as awful people. Charlotte, go back into the parlor with Rachel and the boys." She rushed them out of the room much the way my mother used to send me out of my father's study.

"Dad would not retire without telling me. Reverend Arnett, you don't understand how it is between us."

"I do. Your father speaks highly of you, Marcia."

"March."

"Like the month, Colin." Ruth gathered up four small drinking cups.

"I feel I should call him tonight," said Colin. "If he doesn't mind, perhaps you and I can pay him a visit together, Ms. Longfellow."

"I'll drop by on my way home. I should leave anyway. My son is at home alone. I'm sorry if I've messed up your evening. You all seem to have misunderstood about this matter with the church. But I'll get to the bottom of it. I do look forward to hearing your message on Sunday, Reverend. And I will send the ladies over tomorrow with hot meals."

"That isn't necessary, March," said Colin.

"It's what I do here."

I hurried to Dad's place. I lingered out on the porch and rehearsed what to say. All of his hints about retirement, if they were hints, lined up, but somehow I had never connected the dots. He had invited me to bring Mason over the day before we left for Virginia. Mason and I dropped by, but I cleaned his bathroom floors while he ground peppercorns for a salad. When he talked about fatigue, I suggested he give his secretary, Thelma, more hours or hire her an assistant. I insisted I would drop by his house on Fridays and do his deep cleaning. On Monday, I said, I could fax a list of tasks to Thelma just as my mother once made up the Monday list. He sat in his chair and read the rest of the day.

Reverend James Norville opened his door. "You're home. I was just about to phone you and see if you all made it back all right. You've picked up your dog, I guess." He never asked about the cat, but I knew why. Dad hated hearing about money spent on family pets, and caring for Johnson equaled what it would cost to finance a small island.

I put my arms around him and kissed the side of his face. "I just came from the cottage. It's full of people." I walked past him. "But you already know that, I guess. I'm sorry I wasn't here to let them in. Did I misunderstand you about the date or, well, it doesn't matter now."

"You met Colin Arnett, then."

"And his wife. Is she a young thing or what? I guess those four kids keep her skinny and anorexic looking."

"Ruth is not his wife."

"Sure, she's his wife. Ruth Arnett. She introduced herself. Caters to her husband like nobody I've ever seen. Kind of poured into that little knit thing she wore, but if I were a size two . . . you were making ham and eggs for dinner?" The carton of eggs lay open on the kitchen island, an efficient package of cholesterol. The vacuum-packed ham lay beside it. "You should come to my place, Dad. I'll make us both something else, something substantial. Pasta, maybe, or lentil soup and French bread."

"I don't call lentil soup substantial. Colin Arnett's wife, Eva, died four years ago of cancer."

"Then who is Ruth Arnett?"

"Colin's sister. She moved in with them after Eva died. Being the only two old widow men at the ministers' state council last year, he and I became friends. We've written back and forth some."

"He told me. I wouldn't call him an old widow man."

"Just me."

"Not you either." I closed up the eggs and put them back in the refrigerator.

"I plan to eat that."

"Soup and salad. That's what we need tonight."

"I'm glad you came by." He retrieved the eggs. "If you want to go back and get Mason, I'll cook for all of us tonight. But you make the biscuits. Mine taste like plaster of Paris."

"Mason won't eat pork, Dad. Kids are funny these days."

"They'd rather eat pulverized chicken fried in a vat and served by a clown."

"I should call Mason, wake him."

"Let me go and bring him back. That way you could start the biscuits." Dad reached for his hat.

"No, Dad." I put down the phone. "I don't want Mason to hear us talking about Colin Arnett."

He let out a breath. "I tried to get together with you and tell you. Kind of like stopping a runaway train."

"All this time I thought it was a misunderstanding. You can't retire. What a silly notion! You'll have no income and the church people, well, they'd not allow it."

"I have a small retirement saved, March. Your mother and I planned for this."

"Not enough. In five years you'd have a good retirement. And there's the school project. Half the congregation didn't want that school but you convinced them we needed one. They'll shut it down if you leave."

"The school is stable. Phil is adding a sixth grade next year. Just in time for Mason."

"Colin Arnett has different ways than you."

"Make those cheese biscuits. It's been a good bit since I had cheese biscuits."

"He doesn't go by a title, just says, 'Call me Colin,' and you know what the board will do when they hear that. They'll not want this man. He's not conservative enough."

"You've known him five minutes and already he's a liberal."

"Not a liberal. His ways are not as conservative as yours."

"March, I know your whole life is wrapped up in the church. I haven't made any decisions, though, and neither has Colin. He doesn't want the job and we've set no date."

"I'm glad to hear that." I foraged for biscuit mix.

"The only reason he came was to get away. He's taken a little country church of fifty people and grown it to more than a thousand. He thought a trip to the ocean would do him good, give him time to think."

"Candle Cove Presbyterian is large enough for the size of the town." I felt as though it shrank as I spoke. I sprayed diluted bleach along the top of the countertop to counteract the faint smell of bacon grease.

"He's a go-getter, a real man of vision."

"He wears Nikes, for heaven's sakes."

"I've been thinking of switching, myself." He stared at his own two feet.

"Nikes don't go with polyester."

"Oh, before I forget, your mother-in-law called while you were gone. I guess you haven't had time to check your answering machine."

The silence between us was close to tangible. Dad turned his back to me and swayed as though he mentally sang a hymn.

"She's such a greedy woman, Dad. You know I don't want to talk to her."

"I take it you didn't visit her in Virginia."

"She has no business contacting me."

"Anyway, I've done my bit by telling you she called. Don't shoot the messenger."

I pilfered through the pantry. "You're out of biscuit mix, Dad."

"No, you're looking in the wrong place. It's under the kitchen sink."

"You shouldn't put food products next to cleansers and mop buckets." I dragged out a bottle of mop detergent, two scouring pads, and a soap pad and organized them into a plastic pail.

"I moved the mop bucket to the back on purpose. It was in the way."

"You're turning this house into a bunker." My mother had once said it would happen if she were to land in heaven ahead of my father.

"You treat me like a visitor in my own house. I feel as though I'm conversing with a drill sergeant. Not my daughter."

I pulled out a pen and paper to add to Monday's list the need to reorganize Dad's kitchen.

"Mrs. Longfellow sounds so dismal, March. To hear her talk, you're just not listening to her side of things."

"As usual, she said too much. Someone needs to hang a sign on Joan Longfellow that says 'Warning—she overshares.'"

"She's really worried about the family estate."

"Dad, Joe wanted Mason to have that five acres in Virginia. To hear Joan babble on you'd think I was breaking up a set of museum crystal or something. Mason is a Longfellow too."

"The land has family buried in it."

"I'm not having them dug up, for Pete's sake! My husband is buried there, too, but she doesn't seem to distinguish the connection."

"Family burial plots are sacred. You know how the old families in our church feel about that little church cemetery."

"You want to tell Mason he has to give up his inheritance from his father, you do it, then."

"You're jumping to conclusions, March. I just think you should be easier with this woman, more sensitive. Coddle her, maybe. Assure her that Joe's part of the estate hasn't fallen into enemy territory."

"I'll not coddle a greedy, grasping woman. She acts as though I sank Joe's boat myself."

"Grief makes you act like someone you're not sometimes."

"Will wonders never cease? I found the biscuit mix, Dad."

A set of heavy knuckles pounded the door frame. "Someone's at the door, March. You want to get it, or should I?"

"Oh, I hope it's not that Colin Arnett. I'm not in the mood for him."

"It's him." Dad squinted to see the top of a man's head through the small window above the peephole in the sash door.

I scooped up my purse, in no mood to iron things out. Colin Arnett was probably one of those smooth take-charge types who envisioned setting me down and calming my brow just before he coaxed me into his way of thinking. Men like him could not fathom people like me who quietly held together the works for years without intrusive help from outsiders. "You talk to him, then. And be sure you tell him you haven't made up your mind, that you might have been hasty in calling him in the first place."

"You should write it all down. I can just read it to him, like a script."

"I'm going upstairs to call Mason." Aggressive tactics called for evasive measures. I stepped over Mother's rug in the entry, but kept my back to the door. When Dad opened it, I didn't want to make eye contact with Colin Arnett. My eyes would give away the fact that I had talked about him. Eyes always give away our secrets. He would jump to conclusions and believe I had disparaged him, which I had not.

The porch slats out front squeaked beneath male weight.

"March," Dad yelled from the entry. "It isn't Colin at all. It's Jerry Brevity. I think he saw your car in the driveway."

Jerry Brevity exterminated rats for the families that lived near the water, especially those families who lived near the Intracoastal Waterway.

"Keep your voice down. I can see how you confused Jerry's giant rat truck for the Arnett SUV." I tried to become one with the ficus tree at the foot of the stairs.

"Jerry's been asking around about you."

"Tell him I don't have time to talk, Dad."

"Why don't you like him?"

"His bulb's a little dim, that's all." I whispered now and waved my hands at Dad to release me.

I heard the door open but turned the circular corner on the staircase. Jerry Brevity had asked me last week to join him for pie and coffee at the Lighthouse. I took Mason bowling instead. Jerry gave off a chemical tang that reminded me of citronella.

Jerry had parked his truck behind the Mustang. The rat atop his truck advertised his trade. The giant rat curled on its back with *X*s for eyes appeared to be placed at the curb for me, a rodent offering much like Johnson leaves at the back door when I scold him.

I took the stairs two at a time and entered my father's bedroom. He still had not removed Mother's fussy Priscilla curtains, but the lace comforter was folded and placed in a corner of the room. Mother's quilts lay folded in not-so-tidy angles at the foot of the bed. Stacks of books rose like columns on the nightstands that flanked the headboard. The old books and Dad's rubbing ointment made the room smell like the lobby of the Airfresh Inn, the local retirement home. I would come Wednesday after I finished the weekly edition, clean this room, and restore it to its natural condition.

It is what I do.

Good morning, Candle Cove, and wake up to the Saturday journal of "In the Kitchen with Dinah," a weekend edition of this week's highlights. Dinah reveals her secret recipe for hummingbird cake that will tickle your rib cage with only half the calories. . . .

The radio alarm next to my bed blared, the town trumpet ruling over Saturday, insensate to the fact that I had not had a day off in at least twelve months. Dinah's drawling and catarrhal voice oozed from the taped version of her daily weekday show.

"Mom, I can't find my glove." Mason clattered outside my bedroom door.

"This can't be Saturday." My legs stuck straight out, stiff. The flat sheet enshrouded my right calf.

"Here it is. I found it." Mason appeared in the doorway. "You're not dressed."

"It won't take long. I can't see. By George, I knew it would happen! I've gone stark blind." I groped around me.

"You have your Lone Ranger on your face."

I pulled the sleep mask down beneath my chin. "I don't smell coffee. Shouldn't I smell coffee?"

"I think you forgot to set the timer. We have to leave in fifteen minutes. I can call Grandpa if you can't move any faster."

"I'm up, Mason, for crying out loud!" Dinah Buckworth sounded overly cheery. I hit the off button on the radio. "You go and fish out all of your gear while I dress."

"I put it in the car already."

"You can make me some coffee then." He walked out of the room. I whispered, "Please."

The phone rang. Mason answered it in the kitchen. He said, "sure thing" a few times and then hung up. "Mom, it was a lady named Ruth. She has kids and they want me to come play with them this afternoon. They're at Grandpa's cottage."

"Mason, you should have called me to the phone."

"She said she wanted to talk to me."

"I think we have plans this afternoon. We're doing something with Dinah and her girls."

"The Buckworths are mean. Come on, let's go!" His hands quivered like springs. "Want me to call a cab?"

I sat on the edge of the bed. The night before, I had arranged the meals for the Arnetts and mentally qualified that act as the end of my obligation. On Sunday, I would greet them, duty fulfilled and obligation discharged. Then I would bid them farewell. The thought of Ruth Arnett percolating about the cottage as though she feathered the little Arnett nest sent me into a quasi-neurosis. Mason could visit with the Arnett brood for half an hour and then I would offer up an excuse to cut us free.

I turned the spindle to open the wooden blinds. The trees budded outside my window, a yellow-green pattern against gray bark and the fading gray of morning. I wanted spring to come, to pass through my walls, a little splendor without so much change. Joe had given me a life's worth of adjustments. Today I only needed a splash of color and the sight of a baseball diamond studded with little boys. Tomorrow I would like to manage a quiet Sunday the color of faded grass. Let God lavish his brush strokes with deeper hues elsewhere on the planet. I only needed a watercolor wash and a whisper of his attention. Even a late spring would not bother me one iota. Winter lingered as a quiet guest.

"Mason, let's throw together a picnic lunch. Later, I mean. Once we're finished at the park."

"And take it to the cottage. I hope this lady has boys. All of the best boys have moved away from our neighborhood. We never move. We just let everyone else move away from us and leave us at the mercy of the Buckworth girls. I'm glad we got invited. You'd be glad too if you'd just think about us not having enough boys around."

He ran out and climbed into the Mustang. He never heard me raise a note of complaint or say I only intended to include just the two of us in our afternoon agenda. I scrunched into a pair of faded denims and joined my boy who had obligated me with the very family I had intended to avoid. I did not know how to train him in the fine craft of putting up defensive little walls.

A ring of people surrounded the baseball park, Southern men who wore ball caps and mothers engaged in baby chat and diaper dialogue. We parked in the only empty space next to an SUV so large I couldn't see around it. I would not let Mason step out until the dust settled. I slipped the car keys into a cloth bag and handed Mason a bottle of chilled water.

"We don't need bottled water today. Just to be on time with pants that fit." Mason's eyes could not be seen at all. He hid the upper half of his face beneath the brim of his cap.

"We're not late, Mason. So you can stop pouting. And don't worry about your trousers. You're not playing until next week so blue jeans are fine today, so don't make me out to be the guilty party in all of this."

He pulled the cap down further over his eyes.

"Let's go, then." I said it above my emotions to show him that I remained in charge.

The assemblage of automobiles acted as coals in the sun. The park air already felt warm, a distant hint of the Southern heat that, by April's end, would gather the parents into the few shaded areas that bordered the baseball diamond.

"March, over here!"

Dinah Buckworth waved from the metal bleachers.

"Mason, here's your money. Go join Dinah's girls in the T-shirt line."

"I don't want the Buckworths on my team. Dinah's girls fight all the time and give knuckle bruises. Nobody wants to admit they've been knuckle-bruised by a Buckworth."

I unscrewed the lid on my Diet Coke and waved at Dinah. "We made it!" Even though Dinah sat two feet away, I yelled due to the fact that getting a ten-year-old boy off to baseball practice on time seemed worthy of at least a brief outburst of euphoria. "Looks like they're just getting started. I overslept." I clambered up onto the bleacher. It was hot against my posterior and caused me to lift and sit lightly.

"You should wear your hat, March. Too much sun messes up your smile." Dinah moved over a space.

"I don't know what the sun has to do with my smile."

"If you take a good look at Rena Foley's senior picture you'll see what I mean. She had that drop-dead-on-the-ground-I'm-beautiful smile back then. Now she's spent so much time tanning, her smile just sort of freezes. There's no brilliance in that." Rena had been the high-school prom queen. Not all of them keep their bloom.

"That's not the sun, Dinah. That's plastic surgery."

"Have you noticed anything else different about her lately?"

"Not especially."

"It's as though, and I'm not a shrink, mind you, but I'd say Rena is a little shy a bulb in her attic and not at all the together little cheerleader she once seemed cut out to be. Not altogether whacked out, mind you. More like—eccentric." Dinah rubbed sunblock on her elbow.

"Eccentric? Angst-ridden. But not eccentric."

"You and your words. Can I say eccentric if I want? You sound like some English teacher."

"Dinah, I'm not correcting your grammar. It's about the right choice of the word. Like you pick the right garlic for the right pasta. *Angst-ridden.* Drama, you want drama. I always say that's what's lacking in radio."

"Angst-ridden. Say, you know I woke up this morning with one of those epiphanies."

"There you have it. *Epiphany.* A perfectly good word."

"Dinah, old girl, I thought, you have to step up to home plate and take a few swings at life yourself. Then, I thought to myself, we need to take a road trip."

I filed down a splintered thumbnail.

"Like you hear women do at our time of life." Dinah kept ruminating on her epiphany and saying "our time of life" as though she delivered a eulogy. "First we map out our points of interest, but it's not like we're just wasting gas for antiques. We look up ancient Indian burial grounds, map the constellations and such. I couldn't find Orion if you held a gun on me and told me to do it or else. It's high time I explored the planet and figured out my existence and stuff like that."

"I can't see wasting a vacation milling around a burial place. I just did that, and it's no vacation."

"It's a spiritual trek. We just go to them, for whatever reason. A soul journey, but we pick who gets to go. But not Rena. Too eccentric."

I listened to Dinah's epiphanies at least once a month.

"I guess you and Mason must have gotten back last night. Janie said she saw the lights on down at your father's cottage. Your daddy must have company."

I scooted closer to Dinah to allow another mother some room. Her twins whispered to one another and waited in the shirt line behind Mason.

"Dad invited a minister to come up from Lake Norman. He's speaking tomorrow morning at church. He brought his family with him."

"Your daddy hasn't asked anyone to speak in a long time. I imagine he's ready for the break. You reckon he's playing around with the idea of retiring? My father waited too long and didn't get to enjoy his time on earth."

"Dad's fine. He enjoys his time on earth by working for the Lord, Dinah. He's been corresponding with this minister for a while. They're friends."

"Geraldine, you stay in line next to your sister," Dinah shouted from the bleachers. Dinah and her ex, Gerald, had disputed over the girl's name and then went round two when he pitched for the second daughter to be named after his father. "Claudia, stop tying up your shirt like that so the whole world can see your navel!"

"I have to go see them today. Pastor Arnett's sister invited Mason to drop by and play with the kids."

"He even brought his sister. I'd like to see where they're stuffing all of those people."

"He's a widower. His sister bunks with his two daughters. At the cottage, anyway. I don't know about their arrangements at home." I yelled at Mason, "Mason, get your shirt a size too large! They shrink."

"The minister's a widower."

"Right. Colin Arnett. You ought to come and hear him speak."

"Does he look preacherly?"

I thought of his tennis player's posture and the comfortable way he wore his own skin. "I don't know what you mean."

"Don't act like I'm insulting every minister on the planet. I mean, does he, well, have those provincial habits and J. C. Penney wardrobe and such?"

"I don't remember. I should have marched in and picked through his clothes, Dinah."

"So, you didn't get a good look at him?"

"I didn't have a reason to get a good look at him. I was only at the cottage to clean it up. I met him for an instant. Geraldine is punching that Aimes boy, Dinah. If Lucy Aimes sees that, she'll breathe fire."

"Geraldine, don't fight with the boys! I swear, March, if ever these girls marry off it'll be the day I walk on water."

"Who says they have to *marry off?"* Dinah made pawning off her girls to the first available man sound like an auction.

"I tried to get Gerald to spend a lot of time with them when they were small so they'd get along with men, not become like them."

"You've done right by them, Dinah. They need to stand on their own." I never told her what the hometown boys thought of her darling twins.

"After you spoke with this minister, I guess you decided you'd be better off with the rat man, Jerry Brevity."

"You just come right out of nowhere, Dinah, with your wild imaginings."

"Jerry's not so bad. At least we thought he wasn't so bad in high school."

I momentarily leave behind the image of Jerry in the industrial-green jumpsuit. "Rat Man. We never thought we'd be calling him that, not when he was the star quarterback for the CCHS Stingrays. Back then Candle Cove had so few stars."

"Jerry's a fine match, don't get me wrong. His house is paid for and it has this wonderful loft room upstairs. A body could set up a nice place to write and never come out again. Maybe he wouldn't mind if you seldom saw him."

"Maybe you need to set your sights on Jerry Brevity's loft. With the right equipment up there, you could broadcast your cooking show all the way to Raleigh."

"Dinah and the Rat Man. Sounds like a rock group."

"I hate it when you get off on talking about men, Dinah. You're too becoming to engage in desperate talk."

"I can't believe *you're* calling *me* desperate." When she was perturbed with me, she stared flatly ahead.

"I don't know why you would bring up Jerry Brevity or this Colin Arnett as though I were out hunting with my man net."

"March, your good looks have your brain all confuddled. One day you'll look in the mirror and see those little smile lines and there won't be a smile, just the lines."

"I'm not lonely, Dinah. I have Mason. Then there's Dad and the church."

"And Europe."

"Europe was Joe's dream."

Someone handed me the team's snack roster. I signed the parent rotation and handed it off to Dinah. A mother with a baby in a frontal sling turned to face Dinah and tell her that she tried her hummingbird cake and really liked it.

"I'm sorry, March. I'm an idiot and I can prove it. You're right. I've never seen you so happy. You were happy before marriage and you're happy once again. Not every woman has to have a man, and if anyone fits that category, it's you. I told you I'd stop trying to make you a match and here I am at it again."

"The kids are finished." I rose up and moved around the stooped back of the mother with the frontal sling. "I have to go pick up deli food. We're taking it to the cottage. Mason and I decided to take a picnic lunch over to the Arnetts."

"Cozy."

I saw the Buckworth twins approaching Mason from the rear so I yelled, "Mason, grab your gear." I cleared my throat to resume a certain amount of decorum. "Dinah, you have a good Saturday. Maybe we'll see you and the girls at church tomorrow."

"When I walk that church aisle next, I'll be carrying a bouquet."

"On the arm of the rat man," I said.

"You just like to meddle."

When my folks, James and Julia Norville, bought the cottage, some of the neighbors thought the young minister and his wife were being frivolous. James had inherited a little money from his father. He knew that he could send it off to a foreign mission or a shelter for young mothers. But it was only five thousand dollars, and he wanted to see the money used to encourage others. After he hit on the idea of providing a cottage for weary pastors and their wives, Mother worried that the purchase of a beach house might be misconstrued as self-serving, although it was their money, fair and square. When the money didn't cover the monthly mortgage payment, she took on extra baby-sitting just to pay the added expense.

One summer a minister lived at the cottage for a month after an overzealous church board had ousted him from a church he had founded. The division had started over the selection of new carpet and ended with the purchase of new baptismal curtains. I never met the minister but was aware that my mother carted hot meals out to him in the early evening, little trays of crab salsa and grilled salmon and cheese bread. Dad stayed at the cottage well into the night, climbing into bed with Mother after I had fallen asleep.

I never crossed paths with most of the clergy and only sometimes with the wives whose hearts mended at the Norville cottage. I served because I always did, because my father needed me. That is important.

After Mason slid his seat belt into place, the phone rang inside my purse. Dad called to see if Mason and I were dropping by the cottage this afternoon. I told him we were.

"So you're visiting the Arnetts. That's a bit of a surprise," he said.

"Mason and I are taking a picnic out to the Arnetts, Dad. It's a polite gesture. You're welcome to join us."

Dad declined. I heard him draw in a breath and then confess the real reason he called. "Joan called again. I'm becoming less adept at knowing what I should say to her."

"I didn't return her call because she's making a nuisance of herself. Eighty acres isn't enough for her, Dad."

Mason stared out the window. His silence proved his invisibility to the conversation.

"March, tell me what you want me to say to her." His voice sounded tinny over the phone.

"Even if she comes, I won't see her. The last time I saw her, she blamed me for things, well, you know what things, and tried to pressure me into giving up Joe's tract. It doesn't surprise me, Dad, but I don't care if she's headed for my house. Mason and I are visiting the Arnetts, so Joan can wait all alone. She should have called first."

"She's holed up in that ritzy hotel spending who knows what kind of money and she seems to be reaching out to you, March."

"I know she called, but she didn't connect like polite people connect. You know, like to say, I'm dropping by for a visit on such-and-such a day. How does this sound to you, yada-yada-yada. You don't just drop in uninvited. If she calls back, tell her we're gone for the day. Maybe she'll take the hint."

"What if she shoots the messenger?"

I ended the conversation.

"Mason, please do something for your mother. Here, take the phone. You call the cottage and ask Ruth Arnett if it's all right if we bring over the picnic." I pulled up to the curb at Ruby's Deli and Box Lunch Haven. Ruby had sewn new curtains from red-checkered tablecloths. Her high-school-age boys, Dillon and Frank, teetered on ladders tall enough to allow them to clean the windows top to bottom. A flock of sea gulls squawked at the guests gathered at the outdoor picnic tables.

"Hello, Mrs. Arnett, my mom wants to know if we can bring a picnic lunch when I come over." Mason cupped the receiver. "She says that would be great."

"Tell her we'll be at the cottage shortly, right after our order is ready."

Mason passed along the message and hung up.

"I'll just order at the takeout window," I said.

"If Grandma doesn't want us to have that land, I don't want it, Mom."

"Don't ever say things like that, Mason. Suppose a person decides he doesn't want you to have an education. You don't just lie down and throw away your education."

"You say Daddy left it to me. If the land in Virginia is mine and Grandma wants it, then I'll just give it back and stop all the fighting. You're always upset. Before Daddy died, you and Grandma never fought."

"Mason, at your age, you don't know everything. For your father's sake, I seldom said the things to your grandmother I wanted to say. It's really hard to explain. After your daddy died, it was like opening a wound too soon. All of your grandmother's anger came spilling out. Things I never even knew that she thought about me, now I'm hearing for the first time." I did not want him to know any of that. I opened the door hoping to close my mouth. Mason joined me at the takeout window. "I didn't want you to know any of this."

Mason looked like his daddy, the backward leaning stance with one foot poised toe-down behind the other heel. But he was less of Joe when it came to Longfellow philosophies. Joe, like the rest of the family, had always employed an overly thin-skinned approach in regard to his mother. I went along with him for a while. But the way she always had her hooks in Joe made me think less of him.

"Grandma must have bad feelings about me too, then."

"She loves you, Mason."

"But she doesn't want me to have my daddy's land, like, I'd never live in Virginia anyway."

"Maybe she knows that, and if we ever sell the land, well, then this hundred-year-old estate will lose a little part of the past. That's her fear. The past is very important to the Longfellows. But it's also a part of your daddy I want to preserve for you. When you're grown, you'll be glad I saved this tract for you." I felt as though less of what I said was actual reality. I wanted to say the right thing to a boy who warred on the side of conciliation but who might grow up to remember a mother that fought for his future. I wondered if this was less about Mason and more about what he might eventually think of me. The purity of my motives troubled me. "By the time you're a grown man you'll know what you want."

"I want a triple club with American cheese," said Mason.

Ruby, her big red hair glinting in the sun, smiled through the window.

"You ought not to have gone to all of this trouble," said Ruth Arnett. "I've never seen pickles so big, and this potato salad doesn't look store-bought, not at all."

"All the locals here frequent Ruby's Deli. Ruby and her sister make everything fresh in the morning. I've never been able to match her potato salad," I said.

Beyond the cottage, the Arnett children ran on the sand a few feet from the tide's edge. They all wore red department-store parkas as they flung rocks into the ocean and waited as if to see what the chilly waves would swap in return.

Ruth knelt and faced Mason with a look that said he was the only person in the room. "You must be Mason. If you want, you can join the kids. Charlotte is probably closest to your age."

"It looks like you have a lot of kids," said Mason.

"I don't have any. But I treat them like my own. My brother, Colin, and his wife wanted a large family." Ruth lifted herself without effort and addressed me. "It really disappointed Eva when she couldn't have any more children. But it didn't make sense to take any more risks after she found out about the cancer. Did I mention it was ovarian?"

Mason watched the Arnett children and fixedly stared after them as though he willed them to look over toward the cottage and see him.

I helped him out. "Mason, you go introduce yourself to the Arnett children. Invite them to join us for lunch. We can feed you kids on the deck. Plenty of seating out there if you think it's warm enough, Ruth." I opened a sack of paper plates.

"This is a treat for us. Colin's kids have always grown up around the mountains. After we saw how quickly we arrived right here at the ocean, we felt silly for not having come sooner. I don't guess you ever tire of the ocean."

"Never have."

"That's the best part about living in the Carolinas, people say. Mountains to the west and ocean to the east," Ruth said.

"And the nation's Capitol just to the north."

"I've been to Washington, D.C. Ever visited the Capitol during the cherry blossom festival, March?"

"No, I made the mistake of visiting D.C. in the middle of a protest. Some group upset about ecology. Streets blocked everywhere by police." Mason and I had traveled to the District of Columbia to see the Space Flight Museum. The Capitol was grayed over that day by a nasty spring rain, while the streets, in a heightened state of security, filled with D.C. police.

"Your father mentioned you've done some travel as a food critic."

"It gets me good deals when I travel. But I also run a small newspaper here in Candle Cove, the *Sentinel*. All the goings-on around Candle Cove can be summed up in a day; the Thursday edition. Everything else I do is freelance, food articles and travel pieces."

"After I'm finished with school, I want to know more about preparing food beyond the mundane. Our mother cooked meat and potatoes every night, meat loaf and such. When I see those cooking shows on television, I admit it intimidates me. I understand your mother was somewhat of an expert on cuisine." Her focus connected briefly with the shoreline.

"Julia Norville. My mother could have written her own cookbooks but she only cooked for us and the visitors to our cottage."

"Such a shame we missed out on that. I know you miss her."

"I guess your mother and father are still around."

"They are. Getting on in years, but still a little involved in their church. Mother and Daddy retired in Texas, near Galveston."

"Then you've seen your share of the ocean."

"Yes, but not as pretty as here, obviously. But I'm glad Colin's children can be here. Colin's so busy at the church, our parents usually have to come to see us." Ruth inhaled as though she could still smell the Gulf of Mexico. "When Eva was alive she made certain they all had at least one little trip a year just to get away. Colin tends to work himself to death. I don't know if he works smart, necessarily. But he certainly works hard."

"My father takes his vacations inside of a book."

"Colin loves that about your father. Reverend Norville recommended so many books, Colin can't read them all. He loves collecting them, I think just to swap them out with other ministers."

I had not come to the cottage to grow to like Ruth Arnett. I opened the kitchen door. "Mason, you all come to lunch."

He ran out ahead of the pack, the noon sun burnishing his crown as though someone had dipped him in butter.

"I guess Reverend Arnett is at the church," I said.

"Colin found an open-air restaurant down the beach on his morning run. Said they had these grass huts covering the tables and chairs. No one was about, so he took his Bible down along with his notes to prepare for tomorrow. I find him studying outdoors quite a lot, so he's apt to disappear into the landscape here as well."

"I hope you like these sandwiches, Ruth." I plucked each sandwich from the bag and peeled away the butcher paper. "I had them made up plain—no lettuce, no tomato—for your children. But ours are loaded. Ruby makes her own bread. Be sure and take home some of her foccacia."

"I hear a phone ringing. Oh, you must have one in your purse." Ruth pointed gently at my handbag.

I took the call out on the front porch.

Dad's tone was flat. "March, I told your mother-in-law you were away for the afternoon. Joan has checked in at the Concord Suites, but she insisted on finding out when you'll be back home. If you call her, it might give me some peace for a good little bit." His smooth, lacustrine pitch punctuated the sentence with a ripple of worry.

"She's a vulture."

"I have her number at the Concord."

"I'll meet her there. But don't tell her, please, Dad. Mason can stay here and visit for a while with the Arnetts."

"So you're having a picnic. That's nice of you, March."

"Nothing more than I always do for you and your guests."

"Colin, he's a nice man."

"When you say that, like you keep saying that to me, I'm sure you aren't implying anything by it."

"I wouldn't do that, you're right. I think you should know that Colin is sensitive about his Eva. He talks about her in present tense. Death is something that some people get over. Others don't. Colin's never gotten over Eva." His television made intermittent sounds as he rummaged for entertainment. "In other words, you're safe from human intrusion," he said.

I did not tell him how annoying I found his comment. "I should go, Dad."

"Bring me by one of those sandwiches from Ruby's, if you have the time."

"I'll drop one by on the way back from the hotel."

We divided the large poor boys each into three sandwiches and passed them out to the children. Charlotte rested her hands on the tabletop. After she nudged her brothers and sisters to bow for grace, I noticed her left hand held no symmetry with her right hand. The thumb was a rounded stump, her fingers small and malformed like tiny baby carrots harvested too early. Mason introduced Charlotte to me.

"Charlotte's eight," he said. "She might move here. She likes baseball."

I overheard a gentle sigh from Ruth's direction. She did not look Charlotte's way.

Four

JOAN LONGFELLOW TORE THE TOP OFF THE SWEETENER packet as though she saw through it or past it. Somehow her hands finished the task without her full attention. I waited in the Concord's lobby behind a potted palm, a tall tropical tree encircled at the roots by bromeliads with centers so red they seemed to lay open, wounded. Joan sat right next to the plate-glass window. Her manner at the Concord Grille drew eyes. I knew without a doubt that the way she wore her money on her face had less to do with money and more with the fact that she was a Barton—not the Oklahoma Bartons but the Virginia Bartons, the Clara Barton of the Red Cross Bartons. And somewhere in there were General Lee and Turkey Trot, but Joan never wanted to be associated with Indians. She often pointed out that Turkey Trot, the big park near the Potomac, changed hands several times. Her family purchased it from the Indians, she would always say. I would not say that her family outright donated the land as a park, but sometime before the charitable donation, they farmed on it. Joe never understood it completely. When Joan dies, most of what is the truth will die with her.

She nested in front of the Concord Grille window, I felt, so that no one passing by might miss her. From the corner of Lantern Street and Fourth, I saw that hat, stiff felt with a wide brim that tilted to one side. The color fizzled somewhere between hibiscus red and crimson. It contrasted with her Lanzoni pumps and the knee-length sport jacket. While another woman might appear uncomfortable seated alone in a restaurant, Joan exuded a broker's air about her, as though she anticipated at any moment that an important coterie of polished chums would appear. Her movements became a pattern. She checked her watch, turned over the wine list to see the choices, and then examined the appetizers on the menu. I witnessed her ritual three times before I collected enough courage to approach her.

Joan's hat tilted back and then up, which caused the attached plume to wave hypnotically; it drew me into her magic web as if she understood her own power while I fell helpless to it. I stopped behind her in order to form an opening line.

"I apologize I didn't call first before coming into town," said Joan.

I saw her eyes looking at me in the glass in front of her.

"No need to apologize," I said. My intent was to say, "You should have called first, of course."

Joan maintained her focal point through the vitreous wall that secured her like a protected egg. The fine hotel, the doting waiter, and polished windows—all of it encompassed her security and her power.

"If you try the crab canapés, have them made up fresh," said Joan. "You have to watch the crab in North Carolina. It isn't like the Maryland crab. They don't know how to season it here, either."

"I had a sandwich from Ruby's." I pretended to enjoy being common around Joan.

"I've come all this way. You may as well join me."

I pulled out a chair at the farthest arc of the circular table. My fingers rested atop the chair back. I sighed and then politely took a seat.

"How's my grandson? He isn't with you, I see."

"Mason is playing with friends. Dad invited a minister in for the weekend. He brought his family along. They're all at the cottage."

The waiter filled my water glass and delivered an iced tea to me on a paper doily. "I can bring Mason by tomorrow afternoon, if he wants to come."

"He can swim in the pool here at the hotel."

I pretended to like her idea. "Mason might like that."

"I went by Joe's grave. Someone's redecorated it." Her voice lowered and thickened but she made her comment while looking past me into the street. I squeezed lemon into my tea.

Joan tapped at the tabletop, quiet for a moment as though she mentally took aim with her arrow. "You'd think that if someone were going to decorate the grave, they'd tell me about it. Or ask me if I'd like to come and help. It's our custom to attend the decorations as a family."

"You have some purpose for visiting us, Joan. I'd like to hear what that might be."

"Joe used to tell me when you all dated, 'that March is a really direct girl.' He thought I'd like that about you."

"If this is about Mason's inheritance—"

"Sometimes, it's as though Joe is still alive. Just like our land lives inside us."

"Mason's a Longfellow, too."

"You always hated Virginia. If I thought we could keep it all together, like a family, I'd not worry about it."

"When Mason's an adult he'll decide, then, on his own. I've told him about the family legacy. I can't do any more than that with a ten-year-old boy." *And,* I thought, *I won't allow you to hang that land around his neck like a weight, like being a Longfellow was a noose around his daddy's neck.* "Joe didn't do everything right, but he left the land to Mason."

"I won't hear anything disparaging about Joe."

"Don't presume you will." I pushed away the water glass, not wanting any part of this luncheon.

"He was a tender young man. I always knew he cared about me. He didn't hide his feelings like his daddy, Ronald. I think Ronald thought it wasn't manly, but he never understood Joe like I did."

"But Joe had his flaws, Joan." I muted my words. I lived in this town. "I didn't see them at first, either. He had his way of making me believe what I wanted to believe about him. But I fell in love with someone that didn't exist. The last morning I saw him, I didn't even know him anymore."

"He knew you didn't love him. That became his insecurity." She heightened her tone and spoke in an ingratiating manner as though Joe might overhear and be proud of her. "And the downright end of him."

I looked at my watch. "Don't be ridiculous! You didn't know him any better than me. And you stop all of this critical blame laying, accusing me of sending Joe out into that storm or the same as!"

"It didn't come out of *my* mouth."

"I won't let you tie me into one of your corners. Not with lies. Reality is what exists in spite of what we believe." At least that is what Julia said into my mind right then.

"You use it to bite people, March." Her slender fingers lifted and made a clenched fist that she used to lightly rap the tabletop, once for each overly enunciated word.

What that woman could cause to run through my head I could never repeat! The way she tried to tie me up in her despotic bag and throw me onto the highway of her twisted opinions as though I would mewl for mercy made me physically ill. She obviously underestimated how fast on my feet I could be. "You irk me, that's what!"

"The thought of him going into that ocean alone, like a man devoid of love, depresses me." She pulled out a bottle of pills and demonstrated her need for prescription medications. She popped a couple and downed them with wine.

"Joe knew I loved him. His insecurity consumed him long before I ever met him." I crooned "long" and then realized I sounded just like her. I put my face in my hands. Either I was morphing into a Longfellow or some distant gene encoded with bellicose insanity had finally reared its ugly head.

"Any woman with her head on straight could have helped Joe find his way."

The waiter appeared again, although he stood three feet away.

A vise around her vocal chords could not have silenced her. Not an ounce of energy remained in me. I felt my little rubber raft deflating right smack in the middle of her tumultuous diatribe. "Joan, I think you've come a long way for nothing. I'll not sit here and allow you to tie my heart in knots and leave me feeling guilty because it makes you feel better about yourself." I hate myself when I cry.

She laid a finishing touch of gentility to her reply. "I promised Ronald I'd not feud with you and here we are at it."

"Assure Ronald that it only lasted for a moment." I rose and left the Concord Grille. Without glancing up, I minced past the polished plate glass. I pulled away when the doting waiter attempted to accommodate me, and turned my back to the red felt hat that hid a woman and her cold plate of insecurities.

It rankled me to know that if it were not for me and the procession of notorious faces from his daughter's past my father might be sitting in his red easy chair having an otherwise quiet Saturday afternoon.

"Can we not talk about this—say, save it for a day we want to fully ruin?" I asked him.

"Remember Ruth and Naomi." When Dad used his Bible analogies, it deflated me.

"I can't be Ruth to Joan, Dad."

"Let me finish. Ruth's humility is the example I'm trying to unearth. I'm not blind to Joan. I'm only suggesting you emulate Ruth. We all should emulate Ruth."

"Women like Joan dominate, like she dominated Joe. Like she would dominate Mason and me if I allowed it. You just can't play the humility card around Joan, Dad. She's a usurper. If I give in, then Mason loses all rights to his inheritance. I can't let her win."

"It's about winning, then," he said.

"Rights. It's about rights, but not mine. Joe wanted it this way." I pasted a cardboard frame around a photograph of Dad and Mother. "This church album is almost finished. I made it sort of like a pictorial diary from the day you and Mother started the church until now."

A lone man stood as a ghost in one photo, an old black-and-white snapshot I rescued from one of the many shoe boxes in the attic. The man, Avery Woodard, had a broom in one hand and a box that said "kick in" in the other. His mother was a Lumbee Indian; the Lumbees descended from the Cheraw that inhabited North Carolina for more than two hundred years. Avery's father was a drunkard. Some said Avery's father beat his wife during her pregnancy and that caused Avery's deformity. Others said his father beat Avery before he was big enough to stand up for himself and that ruined him and bowed his back. Young boys teased Avery whenever he walked downtown with his cane. Local men had fun with Avery, playing tricks on him at the only barbershop in Candle Cove back before the first salon took over all of the local haircuts. One man told Avery to lie back in the barber chair so that he could give him a shampoo. Avery hobbled around town for months with red hair. The red color accentuated the spike of cowlick at his forehead. For the longest time, the flat-faced boys along Brindle Street called him Rooster.

Dad paid him five dollars every time he swept the walks around the church. He fashioned a shoebox with a leather strap that Avery hung around his neck. Avery used the box to beg for money. "Kick in," he would say.

Dad smiled when he saw Avery's crooked frame, his gaunt face staring out from the album page. "Old Avery. Sometimes when I go for a cup of coffee or a haircut, I expect to see him all over again pushing that broom up Main Street."

"Rona Guggenheim, one of the Inksters, says she knows for a fact

Avery's ghost chased some kids down Brindle Street last October. But her writing is so mystical I think it's made her weird."

Dad made an *L* around Avery's photograph with his right hand.

I held up a sepia photograph, the edges slightly curled and scalloped. "Here's Collette Russell. I scarcely remember her; kind of a stick-looking woman with poppy-seed eyes. She started the first baby nursery." I snipped the white edges from the photo to fit it into a smaller mat.

"She's passed on too," said Dad.

"Lot of memories from church. If I get this finished tonight, I'll display it tomorrow at the church social."

"You want Colin Arnett to see it, I guess."

I closed up the album. "Not Colin especially. I don't know what he has to do with our church album."

"Nothing. That's your point, I guess."

"I don't have a point. I started this album a year ago, long before I ever met the Arnetts. You look flushed."

"I feel fine. I believe I'll go visit the cottage. I can bring Mason home, if you want," he said.

"Sure. I'll make some pasta before I go. Or if you want, you can eat with us."

"Pasta here sounds fine. I plan to read a little tonight, maybe watch an old movie, go to bed early. Don't need company for that." Dad had placed the soup cans and tomato sauce cans inside three different cabinets. I stacked them into two rows while I searched for the pasta and garlic.

"I guess you haven't met Arnett's children," I said.

"Not yet. He picked up the keys here while they waited at the seafoam-green cottage."

"Colin's daughter, Charlotte, she's a special girl," I said.

"Her hand was deformed from birth."

"I meant special, like she has a creative nature. That's all."

"I can't help but notice how children like that have great buckets of wisdom, something innate, as though before they were born they basked in the presence of God." Dad's words almost smelled of thunder when he talked about God.

"For crying out loud; linguini's in the broom closet!"

"It's all right. I moved the broom to the garage. It's my new system."

"So the garlic must be in the attic."

"That wouldn't make sense at all, March."

Phyllis Murray canceled her Saturday hot meal for the Arnetts. Her youngest, Gregory, came down ill. She apologized three times after she finally reached me at Dad's place as I was making spaghetti sauce. Mason and I made up a basket of chicken-salad sandwiches, macaroni salad, and brownies including extra helpings for ourselves since I had no inclination to eat the spaghetti I had cooked for Dad. I took M&Ms and put them on top of the brownies for Colin's children. It was such a nurturing gesture, but his kids were beginning to have that effect on me. Especially that little doll, Charlotte.

We pulled up to the cottage with the afternoon sky as blue as larkspurs. "We're here," I said. The cottage's architecture was from the Arts and Crafts era. I knew about its architecture only because my mother would say that to the pastors' wives who flounced through the cottage on one of Mother's tours. She had asked my father to paint it sea green six years ago, to match the ocean, she had said. But Dad never could squeeze in the time. He drove up one day to see Mother hefting a large can of seafoam-green paint onto a ladder. The white trim matched the sea gulls, she had told him, knowing he might not realize the why of the color, while the "algae-blue" shutters contrasted with the deep furls in the ocean waves. I kept geraniums in her flower boxes for several years until travel assignments ate up my summers.

Mason and I gathered up all of the Rubbermaid containers too large for the picnic basket. We balanced them, our arms loaded, all the way up to the deck.

"Your teacher called today," I said.

"I'll carry in the sweet iced tea." Mason pressed down the screen door latch. Then he stepped back onto the deck with no intention of sharing the facts of his lackadaisical work habits with strangers.

"I'd appreciate it, Mason, if you'd give me an explanation."

"Tell me what she said, first."

"Mrs. Wagner's message mentioned 'concerns about Mason's grades.'"

His bony shoulders lifted, then ebbed along with a sigh. He carried the iced tea back around to the cottage deck.

Ruth had opened all of the blinds, lifted them up as high as blinds would go. The windows on the west side of the house reflected the late afternoon sun while the east side emitted shadows from the ephemeral day. Mounds of Mexican heather sprouted leaves as green as watermelon rind along a brick border that wound from the front walk to the rear of the house. A group of empty clay pots lay heaped near the deck, yawning for lack of attention, pining for a departed mistress to return and fill them.

Ruth met Mason at the door. Her arms wrapped around him, slender long fingers cupping the back of his head like an old friend. Mason lifted the pitcher up to her. At once, Charlotte appeared and grasped Mason's forearm with her good hand. They leaped from the third step onto the sand and raced to meet the tide.

"March, you must be weary of all of this running back and forth," said Ruth. Her feet moved across the wood deck in Birkenstocks and thick, oatmeal-colored socks.

"Phyllis Murray's son is sick. I'm afraid it's chicken salad tonight. Phyllis is a much better cook, too."

"Then I insist you join us. No need to run back home and cook all over again. Besides, chicken salad is perfect for this time of year. Time to put away sweaters and heavy foods."

"Don't worry about us. I made enough for us too. It's at the house, though. I'm putting Mason to bed early. He's a difficult one to get up on Sunday."

"All kids are like that. Imagine four heads to comb on Sunday."

I couldn't imagine. "Here's the macaroni salad in this tub. I'll bring in the rest if you can take the salad." I retrieved the picnic basket and met her in the kitchen.

Colin finally made an appearance from the sanctum of his studies and took the basket from me. "All of the meal carting has given Ruth a nice break," he said.

Ruth filled four plastic cups with milk.

"We look forward to your message. Several from the congregation have called to ask me about you," I said. It was true, one call setting off the curiosity of another probing member, to another, and then another. I could scarcely tell them everything. It was not my place. But neither could I lie. That would not have been Christian.

Colin averted his gaze. When he crossed his arms, he mulled over my words and injected an ambiguous silence between us.

I had spoken with several women who consoled me by saying that no man could replace James Norville, and the thought of any man so much as standing in my father's shadow was just a big farce. But Colin did not need to be privy to any of our private affairs. "A little variety is good for them," I said. I think I inserted a little laugh.

Troy and Luke plowed through the kitchen with sand buckets for helmets. They bore a starfish in each hand, beach tokens their aunt must have picked up for them at a tourist shop. Starfish seldom make an appearance on our shores. When they do, early-to-rise vacationers snatch them at once.

"Colin filled me in on your situation," said Ruth.

I stepped out of her way so that she could arrange the food on the plates according to the dictates of a nitpicking brood.

"Your father explained about your husband's boating accident. God has really strengthened you, I can tell. After the death of a spouse, we know, it's so hard to rebound."

"Mason helps me to be strong." I realized how that sounded. "And God, of course."

"And I've been calling you Ms. Norville and you've been so patient with me, not correcting me. Longfellow is such an interesting name. And you're a writer. It must be a fascinating life to spend your summers traveling the coast and then writing about it." Ruth scooped her chicken salad onto a lettuce bed instead of bread.

"I mostly run my paper. But when I do pick up a travel piece, Mason travels pretty well. It gives me a chance to get him out of here, but at someone else's expense. Dad says you've built a thriving community church, Pastor Arnett."

"Colin is fine. "Pastor" sounds too formal."

"Some congregations really like it when you take their small flock and increase it several levels."

"I'm no magician. It's a spiritual matter, a matter of hungry hearts."

"That, I guess, and a growing populace. Take Candle Cove. We have a large influx of tourists, but our growth is seasonal. We can barely keep a coffee shop in business." He had a right to know the demographics of the matter. The least I could do was to tell him the facts of the matter.

"But you've become an offshoot of New Bern's growth. You have an untapped college population. The business community needs spiritual leadership injected into it." He counted it all off, tapping each perfectly curved fingertip. "That ethnic grocery store across the street from the deli is thriving. That's another unreached group. Growth is not always about numbers. It's about touching your community."

I felt as though he were trying to lure me into his classroom for dunce laymen.

"Colin, you can call in the children," said Ruth.

"The Latinos come to our bake sale every year," I said, and then wished to goodness it had not popped into my head. "I think we touch our community."

"Of course you do." Ruth had such a desire to be the bridge between any obvious divide. "All this church talk makes me dizzy."

Beyond the cottage, Charlotte held her pant legs up around her knees while the waves dampened her cotton hand-sewn top and pants. Colin threw open the door and yelled for her to back away from the water. The wind and sea absorbed his words. I watched him cup his hands to his mouth and yell twice more. Colin loved all of his children, but I imagined the thread that attached him to Charlotte trussed his words with pain. He was besotted with her, forever trying to keep her under his injured wing. I imagined Eva on her final breath handing him the duty of taking over her watch of Charlotte, anxious about her only alternative—that a solitary man had to fill the post of a multitasking mother.

"I'll send them back in. Mason and I need to go. If you want, Ruth, you can return the picnic basket to church in the morning."

"We'll see you then," said Ruth.

Mason finally looked up and noticed me waving my sweater amid the lilting heads of swaying oat grass. We waited while Charlotte skipped up the steps and twirled all the way into the cottage, a graceful pod returning to her protective tree.

I felt then that Colin would worry less over her if he would take her home where she belonged. Pain is best conciliated in the entrails of its own cave.

I was not sure if Mother had said that or I.

five

COLIN WALKED INTO CHURCH WITH HIS SISTER ON his arm as though he escorted her to the prom. Ruth Arnett was too sexy to stand beside her minister brother. I don't mean that she dressed indecently or exposed things that should not be exposed. While she lived all week in knit items appropriate for either vacuuming or a run on the beach, her Sunday ensemble could have come out of the Jackie Onassis museum. Not many women wear the colors of the sun well, but the fiery red radiated from Ruth.

Colin wore a navy turtleneck with a classic jacket, dark gray with thin slivers of blue thread that matched his turtleneck tastefully enough to say "I don't wear ties." My worries faded. If this turtleneck-clad offshoot from the casual nineties was my father's only excuse for retiring too early, I had no cause for alarm.

Ruth and Colin's children took up most of the front left pew. Rachel wore a necklace made from string and plastic beads that did not match her dress, and colored socks with white sandals. It looked as though the boys had dressed themselves. They both wore faded jeans. No self-respecting pastoral family sent their offspring to church in faded denim.

"Mrs. Longfellow, I made this for you," said Charlotte.

She was the first Arnett to call me by my real name.

She crossed the aisle to the right front pew where I sat with Mason every Sunday. Mason helped his grandfather distribute church bulletins in the lobby. We had no official children's program. All of the older people thought it best to teach the young ones to sit respectfully through the minister's message. Charlotte held up one of her origami creations, an elaborate white angel.

"Charlotte, this is beautiful. Maybe you should save it, though. I don't want to take your best work, and this looks like your very best," I said.

"Hang him in your kitchen window above your plants and he'll be with you through the storms." She placed the paper angel in my hand. She whispered on a breath as sweet as a cherry Lifesaver, "The ocean makes the storms around here, and this angel will blow them back. He told me that himself, but it's a secret."

I felt the limp flesh of her fingers against my wrist. The warmth of her skin against mine surprised me, although I don't know why I expected her misshapen hand to be cold. "I do have plants in my window. Mason must have told you."

"Boys don't talk about such things, Mrs. Longfellow," she said. "You just have that look about you of a plant lady like my mother." I was surprised again when she held her smallish nose close to my white sweater. "You have her same smell."

I felt Charlotte's arms go around me. The little girl held on to me as though both hands were whole. I've heard of accident victims who sensed a limb as whole again even after an amputation. It was as though I could close my eyes and count ten little appendages hooked around my upper arms. Before I could thank her, she pressed her cheek against my lips. Without a thought, I kissed her. "Thank you," I said.

"But you have to remember that angels just work for the man upstairs. Not us."

I laughed.

She joined Rachel on the front left pew. Before she sat down, she lifted herself up on her knees to smile at Mr. and Mrs. Caudle. Ruth leaned over to whisper something to all of Colin's children. Charlotte turned and seated herself. All of them sat up straight and looked up at their father. Colin opened his Bible and lifted a laptop to the podium. By the use of a remote control, he flashed a sermon outline onto the white screen, regarded it for a brief satisfied instant, and then turned it off. Behind me, Lorraine Bedinsky emitted a faint gasp. Whether she thought it a sacrilege to use computers in the church, or was satisfactorily impressed, I could not say. I read the elders' minds, though.

Later when the sanctuary grew warm right in the hot center of Colin's Sunday morning message, Ruth peeled off the blazing orange-red jacket and laid it across her lap. This innocent action exposed her tanned shoulders and I thought Mrs. Caudle would elbow her husband's rib cage sore. The Caudles occupied the second pew to the left every Sunday, a pew they had paid for during the pew drive of the eighties. That accounted for the polished brass plaque on one end engraved with the name CAUDLE. But this vantage point gave Mr. Caudle a birds-eye view of Ruth Arnett's perfect shoulders. Dad stepped gingerly up the steps to the platform, made a half-turn, and gazed appraisingly over the congregation. For the entire life of his pulpit ministry, he had ascended the stage with the assurance of a wizened old college professor. I remember a candlelight Thanksgiving service when he had not noticed a loose button as he dressed that morning, two buttons down on his suit coat. It dangled from two threads like a loose eye. My mother noticed it first. She could look more perceivably appalled than any woman in the church. As he opened his spiral notepad, his right hand traveled up the breadth of his coat, moved up and down on the button as though he plucked the strings of a cello, and then quickly laid hold of the offending member. Those who saw it craned their heads, turkeys in a lineup. With one hand, he plucked the loose button from the coat, held it up for all to see, and made an object lesson of it, some sort of analogy how one unattended sin could distract from the fabric of our lives. Every person in attendance but my mother and myself praised his wit and courage for showing up for a holiday observance ready to sacrificc his appearance for a point well-driven.

Mother knew the truth, the way my father awoke on Thanksgiving morning, his thoughts riveted to one crystal revelation that he fiercely harbored until he released it from his notes and delivered it to the congregants. He had no more noticed that button than he would acknowledge the agony on my mother's face.

A seasonal storm had settled all up and down the East Coast and, while our Carolina brethren up in the mountains woke up to six inches of snow, Candle Cove braced for the chilly rain. Our numbers were down in spite of the announcement about the visiting speaker and the rumors that Reverend Norville was hinting at finding his own replacement. Dad looked out over the sparsely filled pews and said, "In spite of the gloomy weather, Candle Cove Presbyterian has a spark of sunshine this morning." He read a list of Colin's accomplishments to the chilled congregates. Colin crossed his legs first one way and then the next.

I pulled out a pair of eyeglasses I use only for reading and opened my Bible as though somehow I had previewed and endorsed the sermon's text from Colin's notes.

Mr. Caudle spread himself against the pew while his wife whispered something to him. If Ruth heard Mrs. Caudle's nasal, asthmatic idioms, she made absolutely no indication but kept her eyes on her brother.

Lorraine Bedinsky sighed again.

Several more families entered from the rear wearing dark raincoats that shimmered with the effects of the East Coast storm front. A woman, dressed slatternly, entered from the rear. None of us had seen her before, not around the New Bern mission when we dropped off our clothing bundles, nor around the soup kitchen where we flocked every Thanksgiving Eve. While Dad capped off his introduction,

Colin lifted his crossed leg to plant both feet against the crimson carpet. I do not know if leaving the platform followed proper etiquette, but he left the platform. Dad's gaze lifted above his spectacles. A modest sprinkle of serenity dimpled the corners of his eyes. Instead of introducing Colin, he lengthened his preface and explained how he and Colin had first met. But, with transparent stares aplenty, all of us followed Colin to the rear of the church.

The woman had a stooped posture. Some condition had left the right side of her face in a contorted smile, although her eyes had ceased to smile in juxtaposition to the rest of her.

"Welcome," was all that Colin said. He placed a soft grip on her wrist and pointed toward his sister. The visitor allowed him to escort her to the front.

Lorraine leaned toward me to ask if Colin knew this woman.

I shrugged. All I knew of Colin Arnett was what Dad had shared over the last twenty-four hours.

Ruth and the children lifted in unison, as though moving to the pew's end was part of the morning's orchestration.

The sky hurled rain against all the windows as though it had waited for this one bent-in-two woman to enter the sanctuary.

As for Colin, he seated the woman next to Charlotte and took his place again on one of the platform thrones.

Dad, his usual polite baritone drawing every eye, announced, "It is my pleasure to introduce Pastor Colin Arnett."

I have heard of congregations that applaud but we at Candle Cove Presbyterian do not assemble to applaud any more than we gather to sway as some are given to do during the offertory. Some feel that if we so much as tap a toe, by the very act of music combined with movement we lead the children into outward displays inappropriate for a solemn assembly.

If Colin noticed the hushed welcome, the hint of polite smile that peppered the sanctuary, he returned nothing in the way of a gesture. I expected him to launch the colored computer thingy he had put together for his sermon outline. Instead, he bowed his head and whatever he prayed, he shared only with God and none of us. That elicited another sigh from Lorraine, although the Caudles kept their heads bowed without so much as a flutter of an eyelash.

Colin concluded his prayer and then introduced his sister and his children. While Rachel, Troy, and Luke turned their heads to only peep at the people behind them, Charlotte turned effusively around in her seat and waved her undersized hand.

The Caudles' fixed stares took on a domino effect. Eyes flew open from the front to the rear of the sanctuary. I could sense the fascination with the child's hand from the farthest pew as if she had hypnotized them. Mrs. Caudle pulled out a stick of spearmint gum, unwrapped it, and handed it to Charlotte as though the child had the pew jitters that seize children on occasion.

Colin thanked my father for inviting him to speak. But every perfectly timed polite gesture from this city preacher sent pangs of annoyance through me. And every anxious posture shift I made in my pew elicited a harrumph from Fern Michaels. I returned my attention to my open Bible.

Colin, more succinct than when he spoke in casual conversation, said, "In keeping with my promise to my own children not to bore them to death, I'd like to invite all of the children to come to the front of the sanctuary."

Charlotte slid from her seat while her brothers and sister inched to the seat's edge without truly committing.

"If you like stories, I'll tell you all a story." Colin knelt at the platform's edge as though all of the children from our church had already responded. He obviously did not realize the tenacious discipline exacted from every exhausted parent to train offspring to sit like little soldiers upon the pews.

I did have enough sympathy for the man to finally nudge Mason out of his seat. From every pew, the children fell into a procession down the aisle to the area in front of the communion table. Colin glanced toward me and I nodded my head ever so slightly as though I held the release code over all of the offspring of our esteemed families. I had never counted the heads of all of the children, so it surprised me to see thirty heads lined up across the front. Colin drew them in closer, more in a cluster in front of him, and from that point on it was as though his cognizance of every present adult disappeared from his mind. Mason moved toward the front of the pack and sat cross-legged next to Charlotte.

Colin led them in a song accompanied by hand motions. His singing voice differed from his everyday talking voice, a rich, stentorian baritone that settled into a euphonious miracle of a sound as he led them into the chorus. But I did not give Dad the satisfaction of a glance. After the song, he brought out a gold pocket watch. He told a story of his grandfather's watch and how his grandfather passed it on to him. Somehow he tied all of that in with how our faith is like gold passed on from the grownup to the child. After another sort of finale song, Colin sent them back to their seats.

The woman with the bowed back pulled a tissue from her purse and dabbed her eyes, although I did not sense the need for tears.

Behind me, Lorraine sniffed.

Mrs. Caudle uncrossed her arms and fiddled with an offering envelope.

Lightning carved barbed blue fire across the sky and the sanctuary cooled a degree or two.

Nothing that followed could be blamed on me, although I felt my father shoot one too many of his glances my way after the morning service. If two women had made egg salad that morning for the church social to follow, then six more followed suit. Under the cabinet that housed fifty pounds or more of coffee and sugar, I pulled out the large metal bowl that had served no less than five hundred pounds of egg salad over the last twenty-five years. I was up to my elbows in egg salad, consolidating it, topping it off with parsley and paprika. It had not been my job to escort the royal family around to the dining hall. All they had to do was follow the crowd from the sanctuary to the fellowship hall. As Colin called for the final prayer, I slipped out along with the other ladies who led the food committee and prepared for the hungry. By the time my father led them to the back of the building, the line outside the doorway was already three deep. Dad led the Arnetts to a circular table and gestured for Wanda Albemarle to serve them all iced tea and lemonade. "March," he said in front of everyone, "if you and several of the ladies could prepare a plate of food for the Arnetts first, it would help them on their way."

I had duly escorted every visiting minister through the buffet line more times than I could count, but making eye contact with Colin Arnett agitated me. So I removed my apron embroidered by the Tea and Scriptures club, folded it over one arm, and breezed past him to mutter, "Pastor Arnett, if you all will follow me, then you can fill your plates as you desire." I had noticed the way that Ruth, out at the cottage, had pecked around her food, ignoring the meat and going straight for the potatoes and corn. In my estimation, she was a polite vegetarian. It was a simple fact that I did not know how to feed the woman. Dad glared at me.

Colin watched his family fill their plates. He put a few items on his plate but never really looked at his food.

"Good day to be inside," said Fern Michaels.

"Indeed," I said.

She winked at me. Somehow I failed to understand the nature of it. Yesterday, during a phone call, she had mentioned her loyalty to my father as pastor. I thanked her. It was innocent.

After first routing the seniors through the line followed by the families and then the singles, I handed my apron to Wanda. "I'll go and see if the Arnetts want seconds," I said. *Before my father blows a gasket,* I thought.

"Oh, they're already gone," said Wanda, and then she added with a degree of indignation, "The pastor ate almost nothing and then had that sister of his round up the whole kit-and-kaboodle and off they went. Maybe they don't like our food."

"Wanda, you keep the line moving. I'll be back in a minute."

Several people told me that Dad had retired to the pastor's study. I found him at his desk with a plate of partially eaten chicken wings. His chair back faced me and he sat looking out at the rain. Thelma laid the offering report on his desk and excused herself.

"I feel as though I'm part of some conspiracy," I said.

"And you've come to confess," he said.

"I mean, against me. Not that I've instigated one."

A row of tightly closed hyacinth and daffodils, little embryonic orbs, banged against the glass like windshield wiper blades.

"Dad, I fail to see how you can be mad at me. All weekend I've run loosey-goosey to cater to the Arnett family, mind you, in spite of the fact that you forgot to clue me in on their arrival. I assume you had me arrange this whole social today to benefit them. Then they up and disappear as though we've insulted them."

"And you, of course, warmed them with your charm."

"Like always."

The clock ticked in syncopation to his steady breathing.

"We have a hundred people to feed, Dad. Surely Pastor Arnett understands that I have other duties to fulfill and can't tend to his every whim."

"He does. For the record, he said nothing about your lack of attention. I've never met a more gracious guest."

Lightning brightened the office. I closed the drapes.

"Some of the families are under the impression that Colin came to—how did they put it—steal my job. That wording wouldn't have originated with you, I guess."

"Of course not. At least, if some of them said that, I would have just said nothing at all. It isn't my place to discuss church matters." The one or two phone calls I made on Saturday night in no way should have been misconstrued as divisive. I only answered truthfully the few things I knew about the man. Innocent, innocent words, in my estimation.

"March, you know this church needs you and I've needed you. But with a stronger man at the helm—"

"There is no stronger man, Dad, than you."

"I've always loved to see myself through your eyes. But I think you should know, I like Colin because he reminds me of myself twenty years ago. I've faded a bit."

"Mother wouldn't allow such talk." All of this nilly-natter about fading left me feeling unsettled, as though the ground eroded beneath me while the church walls creaked, threatening to collapse.

"She'd agree with me."

"And you should have let me fill your plate. I'll get rid of these chicken wings and bring you some salad."

"March, will you please just sit and listen? Forget what's on the menu for once and listen to me."

Suffice it to say I hated it when he sat me down as though I were twelve all over again.

"Colin Arnett received some horrible news this morning. In spite of it, he managed to deliver a timely message that we all needed to hear—at least, I needed to hear it."

"I haven't criticized his message."

"When he took over that little church in Lake Norman, he had one man on his side, a man who accepted the position as his first board member and his best friend. Through all of the changes Colin brought, he never left Colin's side. That friend died this morning. Some heart condition, to hear Colin tell it. But Colin took the platform in spite of the weight around his neck. He's got more character in his little finger than most people have head to toe, March."

"Dad, I didn't know about his friend."

"I know. But you need to know something else. Colin turned down our pastorate. To tell you the truth, I'm heartsick over the whole thing. I've seen steering committees search for three years and not come across a single candidate of Colin Arnett's caliber."

"You think I ran him off."

"Wild horses couldn't run him off if he felt this was the right place. But you certainly didn't welcome the man, either. I've never seen so many steely-eyed stares coming from a congregation. A godly love, that's what the whole place lacked this morning."

We sat, both of us, listening to the clock and the thunder.

"We showed that out-of-towner where to hit the road, I guess," said Fern.

She and three other women wiped out casserole dishes near the pass-through to the kitchen.

"There's our dear March," said Grace Caudle. "We'll not let a Charlotte man come in here and tell us how to run our church."

It sounded like a line from a fifties sitcom.

"Grace, I don't think Pastor Arnett came here to tell us anything. Dad invited him. They've known one another for a year. Could it be you're all imagining things about him?"

"I only know what you told me," said Fern to me.

"This whole business of me telling things around the church is getting out of hand. I don't know anything about Colin. He's a decent enough man, I guess." I helped Fern set out the clean dishes so the owners could claim them.

"It's how you say it, March," said Grace. "Like how you just said he was decent, but you had a sort of question in your voice about the whole thing, like you didn't really believe what your own mouth said."

"Grace, you're imagining things."

"I heard it too, that questioning," said Fern. Her lips had a beak-ish look, pursed and ready to peck. "March, is this man trying to take your father's place or not?"

"Fern, I'm not at liberty to discuss my father's business."

"There's that dubious tone again." Grace stacked the twentieth foam plate on her tower and asked a deacon to come and tote the left-overs to the garbage pail. "March, Fern and I, we've been around a long time. Don't think we don't know a pushover when we see one. And you're just that sweet pushover. This Arnett fellow might blind you, but he can't blind us."

I could not tell them my father had searched for over a year for his own replacement. "If Reverend James Norville trusts the man, perhaps you should offer the same trust."

Fern harrumphed all the way to the kitchen.

"I just want to know if anyone in particular, certainly not either of you, but are you aware of anyone making anything in the way of a rude comment to Pastor Arnett?" I asked.

Grace spoke first. "We're the pillars of the Presbyterians, Hal and I. We offered our kind and gracious appreciation of his message."

"And told him how no man would ever replace our own Reverend Norville," said Fern. Both of them all but turned up at the toes and laughed.

"But we weren't the only ones." Grace changed aprons. After she tossed the soiled one in the laundry bin, she said, "Everyone showed support. Reverend Norville should feel very secure in his position."

Fern adjusted the rabbit brooch at her shoulder, a rhinestone hare with ruby eyes that appeared to bleed whenever she moved. She looked leporine herself the way her eyes twitched. "All done. Time for choir rehearsal."

It occurred to me that Colin Arnett must have felt that he sat among vultures. Several groups had formed around the dining hall, husbands and wives, elder members who joined the quiet talk, wide-eyed and shaking their heads as though they had all weathered a larger storm than the one moving up the coast.

Bill Simmons, a board member, approached me. "March, we're so sorry we couldn't attract this Colin Arnett to our church. We'll form an official steering committee and take the weight of the search off of your father. He was so hopeful of finding his own replacement."

The church organist struck up a progression of chords out in the sanctuary that sounded like a spirit song at a baseball park. Choir rehearsal started at two o' clock on Sunday afternoons. Several stragglers left the dining hall clutching a hymnal against their chests. The thunder became distant, a far-off clanging of pots in heaven.

Showers of blessing, Showers of blessing we need;
Mercy drops round us are falling, But for the showers we plead.

Before I went to bed that night, I finally rounded up a pen and wrote in my long-neglected journal:

Even as I write, I cannot recall the meaning of mercy, its dictionary meaning. If I find a place for it in my journal, first of all, I shall have to look it up. I am a stickler for just the right word with just the right meaning. The word "mercy" is misunderstood because it is so overused in church circles. Like other words such as "grace" and "love."

I want to compose a letter to Colin Arnett and his family and thank them for the gracious love they showed to us this weekend. It will cover a multitude of sins if I choose just the right words. I want to find a place for "mercy." It seems so appropriate.

THE TWO-SIDED COTTAGE-STYLE BUILDING THAT housed the *Sentinel* was also Julia–Norville green. My business neighbor, Eric's Tropical Pets, had signed the lease only six months ago to take over when Bette's Doggie Treats had gone belly up. (Little canine snacks in the shape of Bette Midler from her pre–Divine Madness days had little impact on Candle Cove, even though we do love dogs here.) Eric left a sticky note on my door that read: *I have a missing iguana. Eric*

My assistant, Gloria Hammer, had arrived ahead of me. I could see her blouse pressed against the upper portion of the plate-glass door, her arms over her head. Since her body had a fourteen-year-old's trunk, she looked adolescent in the glass, a teenage girl lightly balanced on the ladder, small-chested in a T-shirt designed for a boy. I tapped the glass.

"Hold on. I'm installing the bell." She said it as though I was waiting for an answer. She graduated from high school seven years ago, but still had the look of one of those olive-skinned seniors who never has to wear makeup. Gloria repaired small appliances for laughs, a skill she had picked up from her Ecuadoran grandfather. Our coffeepot had seen two repairs, the last of which, she declared, would make it a lifer. On our slowest day, Thursday, Gloria would compile a list of gadgets we needed to make our workdays easier, and then she would proceed to invent the most economical plan for implementing the new widget. Every Monday, I edited the obituaries, prepared for the city council meeting, and listened to the pinging chorus of Gloria's thrumming cosmos.

Her feet moved down the stepladder like a firefighter's, toned calves leading her on to her next experience. "Welcome home," she said through the glass. "Your mother-in-law is in town." She opened the door as though she were handing me the trapeze bar. Most of her hair was pulled back into a ponytail, but little stubborn ringlets the color of auburn and fire made a halo around her forehead.

"If she came by here, I don't want to know."

"No, I saw her at the Lighthouse Java Mill this morning."

"This is important, Gloria. If her car looked all packed down, like, packed to leave, that is a good thing. But if she looked more like 'Hey, I'm just grabbing some coffee before I plot ways to stay and haunt my ex-daughter-in-law,' well, that is something different entirely."

"But if she is only here for the weekend, her car wouldn't look packed down, but might have a bag or two in the trunk. And I couldn't just say, 'Hey, Mrs. Longfellow, looks like a two-bag weekend.'"

"Joan never has a two-bagger weekend."

"Then I haven't a clue as to how to check the woman's vitals."

"Joan likes to get an early start when she travels. If she's staying to shop, you won't catch sight of her until the mall opens."

"Then, you're safe. She was at the Java Mill at six."

I breathed a sigh of relief and penciled in Mason's baseball practice on the calendar.

"Coffee's ready."

Gloria had already filled my ceramic mug and left it next to my keyboard.

"You forgot the cardboard," I said.

"I don't think cardboard placed where you put your lips is sanitary."

"Cardboard is good, Gloria. It keeps my coffee hot. They make cardboard from trees. It's organic so it can touch where my lips touch."

"Mrs. Pickles left her daughter's wedding announcement in the night drop."

"It's about time someone gave Eleanor a reprieve from that hideous name."

"Bad enough Mrs. Pickles is known for her prize-winning canned pickles and tomatoes." Gloria erased last week's edition from the white grease board. "We need to make Thursday's paper seem like the Spring Edition, as though we were thinking about the season in advance. I could take some shots of the fashion show at Bernie's. All of the families who have high-school daughters parading down Bernie's runway will buy us out."

"Good idea. Oh, Eric's missing an iguana," I said.

"Life was calmer when the doggie treat lady was next door."

"Once the little lizard sees that we don't leave food lying around, it will go back home to Eric. If it's here, that is. By now, it could be in the causeway."

"I think they eat cardboard," said Gloria.

The bill sorter pinged.

"I didn't know anything was due today," I said.

"Eric owes you rent. I set the bill minder to do both—remind you of paying and billing. Oh, and that editor friend of yours from Charlotte left a message. Something about a new seafood place in Gastonia."

"That's code for catfish house," I said. "If it's not near the ocean, it can't be seafood."

"Gastonia. That must be in the mountains."

"No. Other side of Charlotte. I told Brady I don't do catfish houses. The Carolinas are full of these perfect bed-and-breakfast places—you eat, you go to bed in another century, you wake up with breakfast at your door. Catfish is so eighties. Women read my articles. They don't want something from a deep-fryer vat."

Gloria roughed out the front page on the white board. "I guess Mason had some qualms about going back to Virginia."

"When I promised we wouldn't go out to the Longfellow estate, he was okay with it, really."

"If ever I have kids, I want them to like visiting their grandparents."

"So Phil isn't ready yet, I guess?"

"Neither of us is ready. It would be like kids having kids." She never liked to talk about the fact that she and Phil had been trying to get pregnant for four years.

One of Gloria's gadgets flashed a tiny red light, meaning low battery or some such. "Having you for a mom and Phil for a dad would be kind of like having the Disneys for parents. That's not so bad, Gloria."

"We're not mature enough."

Eric waved at us through the door. Gloria beckoned him in. Eric Weinstein looked like a long, deflated balloon, a thin frame curved at the spine. His nervous hands appeared homeless if he did not have something to hold. He handed Gloria the rent and then relit his cigarette. The envelope had ashy residue around the seal.

"Always on time," said Gloria. She did not mean to make a dimple on one cheek when she smiled at Eric. But I always suspected she knew of his crush on her. "Find your iguana?"

"I've looked every place an iguana might hide. Fritz will look for the warmest place and just stay there and wait for the flies to come to him. He isn't aggressive or anything. Sort of a lazy iguana. I think that's why I haven't sold him."

"Eric, I don't think people know if the iguana is lazy unless you tell them," said Gloria.

Eric paused. He always fished for ways to elongate the conversation with Gloria.

"Thanks for bringing by the rent," I said. "We'll keep a lookout for Fritz."

"'Bye, then." Eric strolled out, moving light as air, as if the weak indoor currents propelled him.

"I think you torture him on purpose," I said.

"Finally, he leaves. If I torture him, March, it's by my very presence. Not one single thing do I say to lead him on."

"Of course—it's your breathtaking presence."

"It's a curse."

"Or that hint of twinkle in your brown eyes, that look that says, 'go ahead and salivate, Eric, but I'm far beyond your grasp.'"

"Look, the man can see I'm married. Men like him levitate to women like me because we're safe. With me, he never has to face rejection just because he's, well, Eric Weinstein."

"Gravitate. I think I'll turn up the heater in the bathroom." The weather idled between the dead end of winter and the mouth of spring. The circulation room, the place where our three hired retirees bundled the papers before delivery, smelled earthy, as though Gloria had just watered all of the potted plants. I figured Gloria must have moved the plant cart out and away because it angled several inches away from the wall near the bathroom. Wylie and Brendan Poe, the brothers who manned the print shop, never showed up before nine on Monday. A pile of soil caught my eye. One of the large clay pots lay on its side with jagged triangular tears in the begonia leaves.

"Gloria, maybe you should call Eric," I said. I looked inside the bathroom. The big dragon opened its mouth and hissed. Its saurian tail wrapped around the base of the toilet. The pea-colored hide hung loose around its stomach. I closed the door.

A camera dangled from one of Gloria's hands as she phoned Eric.

Eric and two high-school boys entered with a length of rope. While Eric looped the rope over the iguana's head, the boys wrestled with its trunk.

Gloria took a photo of all of us standing around the beast. It made page two of the upcoming *Sentinel*, right between the city pound's pet-of-the-week column and Doris Idlewild's recipe for corn relish.

By the lunch hour, we had written the copy for the stories that had trickled in over the weekend, typeset them, and set up the obits, the weddings, the divorces, and, of course, ended with Eric's iguana. By two, Gloria and I shared a submarine sandwich and watched the downtowners, other small business owners who milled around the square during the lunch hour. Every Monday, several women from the bakery held a paperback swap under the large oak in the dead center of town. Leon and Edward Seam, two brothers who run a small law office, conversed with a carpenter. It was rumored they planned a facelift on the law office.

"So I guess you and Mason will be off on another beach excursion soon."

"We have only three miniature bottles in our sand collection," I said. "High time we added another." Mason and I schemed to collect sand from almost every beach in the world. Joe called it ambitious. We collected our first bottle of sand from nearby Myrtle Beach, the second from Candle Cove, and then the last one from Ocean City. Mason picked up several catalogues from the Travel Hut at our small beachside mall. He found a lagoon in Cancún he wanted to visit, deep-blue water, scuba diving, and white sand. We had yet to collect truly white sand. To the Ocean City bottle, Mason had added three small pebbles that sat atop the bottled sand until three months ago when one of them disappeared. I jostled the sand around but never found the third black pebble. "I think Mason is going through some things," I said.

"He's missing his dad."

"Always that. He acts mad at me a lot of the time. Lately, anyway."

"They probably sent you some grief material after Joe died, I guess."

"So he might still be going through the anger phase. Is that what you mean?"

"Joe died so abruptly. Maybe Mason's still trying to pull all of it together."

"Makes two of us."

She gave me one of those piteous sympathy gazes I had grown to dislike. "I guess visiting the cemetery left you feeling a little melancholy, too."

"You know how that crazy lunatic from Georgia drove up here just to shoot someone because he was mad at his girlfriend?"

"That loon from Macon?"

"Yes, the Macon loon. He killed that poor old man who lived his whole life just to open an ice cream shop in Myrtle Beach. That old guy got up that morning thinking that all he had to do was heat up the fudge and chop the walnuts. It was a lousy way to go. But I'd like to get a phone call from the police one day, a call from the chief of police to let me know that they finally got a confession from Joe's killer, that Joe didn't just veer into the high seas and dump himself overboard. But that a loon from Macon who was mad at his girlfriend hijacked Joe's boat. That Joe died fighting. I just want to know that Joe died fighting. You know that shooter had a bandage over his nose when they led him up the steps to the jail. That old man died fighting. Took a crowbar to that gunman."

"Joe's boat dumped over during high winds. What are the chances some loon from Macon would find Joe, mug him, and dump him into the ocean?"

"It's not even plausible, Gloria. I just said, 'I wish,' that's all."

"Mason believes it was an accident, March. Can't you just leave it at that?"

"I hope Mason believes it. But he hasn't been himself. He was too eager to help pack away Joe's office at the house. I wanted to put the rest of his dad's stuff up in the attic with his other things. But I had to stop Mason from carting it all out to the curb. Just lately, he acts as though he's mad at Joe."

"That doesn't mean he suspects anything other than the truth—it was an accident. He's just mad at his father for leaving. And you don't have any proof of anything other than an accident either."

"Just that he left me broke. That the insurance company took a long time to settle. That Joe's firm went belly up three months after his funeral."

"They say that auction was fabulous." Gloria said it gently, as though she was not sure I wanted to hear it. "Those attorneys must have had high tastes. All we need is just one of those mahogany desks to give this place the sprucing up it needs. I wish they would've had the decency to offer you a piece of it or a part of the auction revenues."

"Not possible. The bank got it all. I carted a box of Joe's stuff out one day, the stuff I really wanted for sentimental purposes. Pictures and bookends I had bought for his office myself. I stopped and asked a security guard what he thought happened. He said to me, 'Too many chiefs. Not enough Indians.' I think Joe and his partners wanted too much too fast. But Joe never listened to me. He always wanted to prove to his family he could measure up. He made me feel as though they were his real family."

Doris Idlewild opened the front door. In one hand she carried a brown bag from the deli. In the other, she toted her large purse that always looked weighted down with a bowling ball. "Don't tell me you two were really attacked by a vicious animal—" she whispered the remainder of her sentence, "from next door?"

"Sorry, Doris. You'll have to buy the weekly to get the full story," said Gloria.

"I have to wait until Thursday?" She looked disappointed.

Gloria nodded.

Doris glanced ahead as though overtaken by an afterthought. "You got my corn relish recipe?"

"We did and it's already on page two," I said.

"Oh, fine, then. Got to run, girls."

"Gloria, you're so hard, making poor Doris wait until Thursday. By then she'll have us taming Godzilla."

"What a nice idea. Eric's lizard was kind of a Godzilla. Maybe we should change the headline."

"We'll look silly. It was bad enough I agreed to stand next to that scaly Fritz, but now it will look as though I had some part in wrestling it out of my bathroom."

"How is that silly?" Gloria gathered up our deli wrappers, but saved the leftover lettuce—the loose part untouched by mayo—for her compost bin.

"Silly as in we don't have anything better to do around the *Sentinel* than to wrestle iguanas. Like we're not a serious newspaper."

"Of course, we're a serious newspaper. Didn't we give Doris Idlewild's corn relish recipe second page? A frivolous newspaper would have given it front page news along with the iguana story."

"But if we nix the whole iguana story and use an AP clip of the president overseas, well, that's what a serious newspaper would do on page two. We need more world news."

"Not so. Don't you remember when the snapping turtle stopped traffic across that bridge in New Orleans? The *New York Times* picked it up. To outscoop the big guys, you have to be in the right place at the right time."

"An alligator, Gloria, not a snapping turtle. If we had wrestled an alligator, well, that is newsworthy—two domesticated suburbanites face off with an alligator. That's not a pet-store lizard story."

"March, that iguana is all of six feet long. He's no gecko."

I put the cup to my lips but pulled it away when the now frigid coffee touched my mouth. "I think I'll make a fresh pot."

"If you want to pull the story, March, then pull it. It's your newspaper." Gloria heaved the sigh of a martyr. She swiveled her chair all the way around and, after hand-pressing the wrinkles from her cotton skirt, she took our deli trash around to the small kitchenette in the corner of the newsroom. I heard the sound she makes when she digs through her tool drawer.

"Okay, I won't pull the story." I yelled it so she could not later say that I never said it. "Maybe it is good human interest for us after all."

The clink-clank drawer-shuffle noise stopped.

On my desk, a group shot of me and a few friends from Chapel Hill including Brady Gallagher, the travel editor for the *Charlotte Observer*, had faded. Brady was the only member of our little group with whom I had kept close communicado.

Next to the college snapshot, Joe stared at me from the framed wooden photo just above my desk pad. Behind him, the mast of his boat furled against the wind. I snapped the photo the day he christened it with a bottle of champagne. Both he and Mason had taken the maiden voyage of the *Sparticus* around the beach and up to Wilmington.

I tipped the frame forward and lay the photo facedown. Sometimes when I looked straight into his eyes, soft orbs of dark green that looked free from care, I relived the worst of times.

Like the worst day of our marriage.

If the bank had not called that morning about the overdue car payment we might not have had such a terrible fight. Someone had called Joe from the office when I returned that morning from taking Mason to school. Otherwise, when I sauntered into the kitchen with a sack of Lighthouse bagels, he might have already been on his way to the office. I sliced the bagels, toasted them, and buttered his on one side since he'd never developed a taste for cream cheese. Before I could hand it to him on a plate, the phone rang again. I answered it that time. The woman from the bank had a punctilious manner, as well she should, but had it been one of the girls I went to high school with, I might have really wanted to bean Joe for not mailing the payment. I had specifically remembered the way he had asked me for my share of the house payment a week early, as though he were ahead of things. A year before, I had opened a separate bank account due to the fact that he had a bad habit of laying his little automatic teller machine slips all over the place until he got a pink slip in the mail telling him he was overdrawn. Since the pink slips made me feel as though his bad banking habits were a reflection on my character, I opened my own account so that I would never get a pink slip with my name on it. When I paid him early for the house payment, I thought he was paying all of it early, the house, the car, the electric bill. But here was the bank woman asking why the car payment was ninety days past due.

That is what caused the fight between us. I railed on and on about his responsibility to Mason and to me. He swore that he thought he had made the payment, but could not cough up the proof. Then he grew peaceful. Joe never finished his buttered bagel, but left the house. We had not kissed in several days and perhaps that was the very thing that clouded the whole reel of my memory with guilt. His secretary told the police that he had come in to work happier than she had seen him in days. When he left for lunch, he never returned. The office staff thought he had met with the firm's biggest client, United Nations Bank. None of the staff knew that Joe had lost the account a week prior and spent his days carrying on as though he still possessed a good lawyer-client relationship with them. Only his partners knew. Joe had taken cash for one bill to pay another bill, believing the large check to be imminent from United Nations. But I never thought that he had stopped kissing me, or making love, just that I had not initiated it myself as a punishment for his incompetence.

Never did I mean for him to think that I would never kiss him again. But as the reality of our bankruptcy surfaced, my desire to solidify our relationship with an alm of affection drowned under swells of anger. Joe's happy gaze mocked me. He knew things that he did not bother to share with me.

But realizing he had not touched me, when he knew it would be the last time, really lit my fuse. Big time.

Maybe tomorrow I would move the photo to my top drawer. By week's end, to the bottom drawer.

Gloria walked in. She clutched the newly developed picture of us and Eric's iguana. Her gaze took an oblique dive left of where she stood and she saw Joe's photo facedown. "You need a new picture for your desk? I have a nice one for you."

My shoulders rolled forward. I reached for Joe's framed snapshot and sat it back up again. I couldn't replace him with a lizard. Joe still lived among us and made me feel as culpable as ever.

Seven

I SHOULD HAVE SENSED SOMETHING SOUR IN THE Monday afternoon air when I pulled up to the baseball park with Mason. We parked next to the truck with the upside-down rat attached to the top. Jerry Brevity gathered Mason's team around the bleachers left of the concession stand. The Salamanders gathered into a huddle while he passed out team shirts and caps.

"The rat man is our coach—no way! He drives that stupid truck. All the other teams will make fun. And he smells like Grandpa's closet." Mason slapped his glove against his leg to make either a small cloud of dust or a statement.

"I had nothing to do with it, Mason."

"Grandpa should have coached. I told him, but he never did nothing about it."

"*Anything* about it. Grandpa can't keep up with you boys, Mason, and run the church. Don't you go and make Dad feel guilty. If Jerry's the coach, then I want you to respect him as such." Jerry waved at us. "Besides, Jerry doesn't have anything better to do. Grandpa has church matters to think about."

"'Salamanders' is a stupid name, anyway. They don't have teeth or claws. You can't win if you're an amphibian."

"People used to think salamanders were magical."

"But they're not. They have those stupid little legs and you can't tell if they're a lizard or a fish. It's like they can't make up their minds."

"You kids voted on the name."

"It was the Buckworth twins that did it. They had just enough pull with some of the wimps, like, if they didn't vote for their name, then later they might get a fist in the face. No guy wants to be known as the kid beat up by a Buckworth girl."

"If you want to play ball this year, then don't walk—run! Get up to those bleachers, Mason. Run, now, or I'll march you back to the parking lot and we'll go home! You run!"

Mason ran. His head bobbed part of the way, an agitated jerk that somehow, in his mind, gave him the final say. When he reached Jerry Brevity, he tossed me a glance as though he wanted to let me in on the fact that he plotted his moment of vengeance.

Finally, the row of Bradford pear trees that surrounded the field had turned a milky pink and shed petals around the boundary of the playing field in a soft snowy trail of strewn blooms. Visitors to North Carolina sometimes mistake the trees for cherry trees or some other fruit tree when the truth is that the trees produce no fruit at all. Not pears, not anything; just blossoms that fall away to reveal the perfectly pear-shaped foliage that looks as though an elfin arborist slipped into the fields at night to create paper-doll symmetry.

Jerry had a standard coach's posture: always arms akimbo with his right thumb tucked into his front pocket. Even when he traveled house-to-house, he carried himself like a coach, knit slacks tight against his derriere with a crisp white shirt tucked just so the curve of the tail made a smile on his backside. To hear Mason describe Jerry Brevity, one would imagine the rodent exterminator with poison canister in hand, a smarmy lurker with missing teeth. But Jerry managed his life with such precision, his first imperfect wife left him in search of a less exacting paradigm.

"March, I missed you at your dad's place the other evening," he said.

"Oh, you were there?"

"I saw your Mustang. You must have been upstairs, or some such. Say, I noticed those—what do you call those little road signs?—bandit signs, stuck in the ground out along the roadside and saw your son's league needed a coach. Thought you all might use a little help."

Mason lifted his glove and placed it on his head. He emitted a deep sigh, just loud enough to make Jerry glance and then look back at me.

"Can never get enough good coaches," I said.

"Your Mason, your little guy here's a sharp player. We'll have us a good time, won't we, little buddy?" He rubbed Mason's head, but Mason moved away from him.

I heard a trill from inside my handbag. "Pardon me. Phone call."

Jerry called the Salamanders into a huddle.

I seated myself next to Gladys Martin, who must have carpooled with Dinah. I saw no sign of my best friend— just the Buckworth girls spinning near first base and grinding their heels into the dirt.

Brady Gallagher phoned to remind me that I forgot to return his phone call. Gloria had left the note from him right atop my desk with *Charlotte Observer* underlined as though I could not remember.

I did not remember.

"I'm sorry, Brady. You wouldn't believe what happened today," I said.

"One guess. You trapped a dragon in your bathroom and it's making headlines."

"Gloria."

"You work her too many hours. I like that."

"I told her to go home."

"And you think we only have catfish houses in Charlotte. We have real seafood."

"As usual, Gloria keeps no secrets."

"But you were right. It was a catfish house. That's what I like about you, March. You're pure class. You want seafood—I'll give you good seafood. Write down 'LaVecchia's.'" He waited, somehow knowing that I scribbled it down.

"With a *k?*"

Brady spelled it for me. "I'd like this piece by next Monday."

"Mason and I could take a trip down Friday night."

"You're a pro."

"Anything else?"

"That piece you did last year on Ocean City—Fred liked it."

"I'm pretty sure it was over two years ago."

"He thinks you should do more travel pieces. Fred's outlined a new column concept called 'The Barefoot Traveler'."

"Sounds big, Brady. Like something you'd save for yourself."

"I've got bigger fish to fry. Maybe I'll tell you about it when I don't have so many ears around. Besides, you know I'm a soft touch for friends." He hesitated. When I did not respond with wild appreciation, he said, "Fred wants to give the customer a wider travel scope. Not just North Carolina and catfish houses, but more of the South—from D.C. to Florida."

It sounded like a more rigorous schedule, but a temptation. "Brady, I genuinely love the idea, but I have a son, and a newspaper to run."

"You'll have a budget, an expense account. Maybe an expense account. We'll grow into that stuff, you know. You'll fly. If this column takes off, say in three months, you'd get a raise. You could do it on weekends at first—take the boy with you. We'd use your lovely face in some touristy pose, say with a nice pair of shades, you sort of glancing over the rims. If you're good enough, we're talking syndication. I thought since you could use the money, you'd want to have first shot."

"We're fine with money." I moved away from the team moms. None of them needed to know I was nearly destitute.

"But you could be better."

Mason swung at air. He choked the bat and pounded home plate with it a couple of times. I could tell he was preoccupied with Jerry Brevity. The dust on the plate rose like steam.

"I'll let you know, " I said.

"Monday. I need to know by then."

"Maybe a little more time than that."

"Fred wants to move on it. You know how he can be."

"Okay, Monday."

Gladys Martin and two other mothers raised their brows and smiled at me, sort of a deliberate invitation to join them, I assumed. I ambled up the metal bleachers. Gladys moved to one side and offered me the awkward middle position between them.

"March, I was just saying, well, all of us are talking about you. Hope your ears aren't burning. We've watched you with Mason, with your business, well, everything. Not every woman could hold up as well as you have."

"We're doing fine, Gladys." Except for the town *Sentinel* that managed to pay its managing editor/owner a mere subsidy of a salary, but why go into that?

"We just want you to know that you're admired. That's all," said Gladys.

"I've had good moral support. My dad's been, well, pretty unbelievable."

"But you're strong, March, you little warrior-mother, you." Gladys could have stood her words atop a white picket fence and they would have been no less saccharine or less obvious to those seated around us. Several other mothers shifted and turned to look at me, the warrior princess. My mouth felt dry inside, unable to press a credible smile into my resistant cheeks.

Joan Cramden handed me a rice cereal marshmallow treat.

Flattery caused me to falter over my words. "Look, I really don't think I warrant accolades." I finally pieced together a cognizant thought. "Things happen and you either get up the next day and face whatever life throws you, or you just stay in bed." *Some days, I'd rather stay in bed.* But I didn't say that, any more than I would blurt out the details about the nights I lay with my head on the pillow softly moistening the linen fabric I once shared with Joe. No one wants to know the real truth about how suddenly pain can enter a person's life, knife through her heart, and leave her bleeding without a single visible scar.

"Still, you are just a dream of a trooper." Joan brushed lint off of my shoulder.

She did not want to know the truth, believe me. Once a soccer mom had commented about the flower bed in front of our house that was bountiful with blooms, and I mechanically pointed out how the perennials sent to us for Joe's funeral had become the flower bed. She fell silent and I realized no one could take facts like that in quick pill form. *It's a lovely flower bed. Yes, they're straight from the funeral parlor.*

Mason bunted. I knew he hated to bunt. His scowl could be seen from space.

The baseball moms continued in their misconstrued worship of March Longfellow. I remained staid, saying little in return. It isn't that I try to prove anything to these friends of mine, or be falsely strong. It's just that when the facts of your life have gone from normal to dark, no one wants to hear about the dark. So you fall silent about the painful things and talk about the things that are more palatable to the general populace.

That is how you keep your friends.

Doris opened an orange soda and gave it to me.

A salt breeze floated past and it cooled our skin.

"Nice of Jerry Brevity to coach for our kids," said Joan.

"It seems to me that if he'd stop tooling around Candle Cove with that dead rat on top of his truck, he'd do better for himself," said Gladys.

"That's how he picks up extra business." Doris acted informed about Jerry, as though she had picked through his underwear drawer or something.

"I don't mean more rodent business. More—other kinds of business. Like, he's eligible and all, but who wants to be seen riding around with a hundred-pound rat?" Gladys stared after Jerry as though he were a wasted container of man.

Doris said, "I don't guess you should care, Gladys. You're fifteen years with number two."

I think Gladys mouthed, "Not me."

"Jerry just blew his whistle. Water break, girls," I said, ready to put a period on the chatter.

Two of the moms carted chilled bottled waters down to home plate.

"Thanks, ladies, for the rice treat and the orange drink." I sidled between the two of them and melded into the throng of parents.

We watched the boys polish off the cold bottled waters. Doris passed out the rest of the marshmallow snacks to them, but Mason turned his down. He and Jerry conversed a few feet away from the parents. Mason smiled at me, direct, like he sent me some son-to-mother signal. Jerry nodded and patted Mason's head. Jerry turned around and caught my eye. I met them along the baseline between home and first.

"Mason here has a fine idea," said Jerry.

Mason and I exchanged glances. I thought he smirked, but I could not be certain.

"He said that we should all go out for dinner and then an ice cream cone. I suggested Dooley's. They have those great outdoor tables, little umbrellas like you women like. It's a nice warm evening."

Several excuses flew through my mind. But because Mason had set up this whole evening with Jerry Brevity he would never back me up. "Mason, you have homework. And you know we have that teacher meeting tomorrow." I thought the hint of revealing his scholastic indiscretions might deter him.

"She didn't give us homework, Mom. We can go." Mason's sappy buoyancy as he leaned against his bat typified some little con artist.

"We'll make it an early dinner, March. They have the Early-Bird specials, too."

"And ice cream," Mason kept interjecting until I wanted to throttle him. "You know how you like ice cream, Mom." In spite of Mason's self-proclaimed loathing for the town exterminator, he managed a sentimental smile that warmed just like the glimmer of sunlight in Jerry's eyes seemed manipulated.

"I have a good idea, too," I said, being certain to avoid Mason's gaze. "I'll follow you there, Jerry. But Mason here can ride with you in your truck. Jerry, Mason's been saying for the longest how he would like a ride in Brevity's rat truck." Instead of waiting for an answer, I made my way toward the Mustang. "See you there." It would take a day to scrub the exterminator's scent off Mason. It would be worth it.

Sybil Ettering started the Inksters, and if she never published a line of prose in her life, she would go to her grave with one byline—as the founder. Her gravestone might say—"Founder of the Inksters"—and anyone who read it might look at it and wonder about it. Sybil sat with Sue Bonadett and Glenda Wiggins in the far corner of Dooley's. The three of them sipped beers and tossed peanut hulls onto the floor (which was not only allowed but recommended because the oils enriched the wood floor's finish).

If I could have stopped Mason and Jerry at the door, I would have steered them over to Sonnet's for fish and chips. I had not seen the Inksters in two months. The thought that I might be seen on what appeared to be a date with the rodent man who walked so familiarly beside my son, and both of them wearing matching peach Salamanders T-shirts, made me feel as though something inched the floor from under my sneakers. I told myself that dragging behind in Jerry's shadow was my only hesitation and not the fact that I had not written a thing in several weeks. The shining glass windows that encircled the dining room mirrored the three of us, bugs under a microscope. I wanted to pay Jerry to walk a few steps ahead of us and then sit two tables away, but Sybil already bore a hole through us. Sue stopped her glass at her lips. A smile formed and I saw her hand pat Glenda's leg. Jerry approached them first.

"Must be ladies' night out, and a finer group of ladies I've never seen!" said Jerry. Everyone in town knew that he and Sybil's husband, Bernie, played side by side on the same bowling league.

"Look at the three of you. Jerry, you must be coaching Mason's team." Sybil never looked at Jerry the whole time she spoke, but kept staring at me. She had glued on her sort of splayed-looking lashes that parted like starfish prongs. Sybil's fingers, adorned with her ring collection, made her fingers look like little sausages wrapped and stuffed with pawn-shop jewelry.

I wanted to explain the platonic nature of my dinner with Jerry, but the translation was vague and lost in my anxiety. "Mason just finished baseball practice. Jerry's joining us for a bite to eat."

"We've been missing you, March, at group critique. Sue here has just finished her twentieth poem," said Sybil.

"Why, Sue, I never knew you to be a poem writer," said Jerry.

I heard Mason whisper "poet." I could not invent a punishment to equal the misery on his face.

Sue's timidity was her aura. "I finally got the nerve to write about my divorce. It's been a very cleansing experience." She always looked back at Sybil when she spoke, for approval or some other such affirmation to let her know she had made a valuable contribution to the conversation.

"March, I hope you've been practicing your creative webs. We'll get that little creative flow of yours going before you know it," said Sybil.

"I've come up with a few ideas," I flat out lied. "Mason and I have been so busy with just life, I haven't much time for development."

"March, your mind paints life in such grand strokes," said Glenda, making graceful swirls in the air with both hands. "You think in ways that sort of just—your ideas make money. For instance, I can't think of a thing that anybody would want to buy. But you come up with this little newspaper, and, next thing you know, everyone in town is reading your *Sentinel.*"

The *Sentinel's* profit margin could be scraped off the bottom of Glenda's shoe, but I did not bother to tell her that.

Sherry Dooley offered us a table. I asked Sybil about the next critique group and then tried to act interested.

"We've switched it back to my house," Sybil told us. "Glenda's having her floors relacquered. The fumes nearly killed us. Say, I don't know if you've heard about Sarai Gillman—you know the girl that pours coffee down at the Lighthouse ? She got her first nibble from a New York editor. It's the big time for her, I'd venture to say."

"Sarai Gillman heard from an actual editor, she did," said Glenda.

"She's a gifted girl," I said, not showing jealousy. "I never thought she would stay long here in Candle Cove. Sarai is so—I don't know—sophisticated in her thinking. She can just walk into a room and everyone knows she's not from around here."

"Now before you go, tell me the name of your new idea," said Sybil.

"It's a story about—angels," I said.

"She's going to be rich, Jerry. Better get her while she's poor," said Glenda.

Mason pulled at my hand.

I knew it would do no good to say, "Jerry and I are just friends." Not with this group.

Sherry Dooley led us outside to the red tablecloth-draped tables on the veranda. The tide ebbed into mirrored sheets that reflected the rose-and-yellow strips of sky strung out like a clothesline. Mason dropped his hat onto the seat and ran to climb onto the thick rail that overlooked the beach. I wondered how he might react to Brady's phone call from the *Charlotte Observer.* We would have to spend most weekends flying. I tried to imagine him at home with Dad or hefting his duffel bag through airport terminals. Before Mason climbed into his bed, I would tell him of Brady's offer but not admit that it was a temptation for me. Nevertheless,

I could not get the thought out of my head of how carefree I would feel sitting at a desk writing about places I had visited. "This is my favorite table, Sherry," said Jerry. He handed her a dollar.

"My pleasure. Janet will take your order, folks."

Four high-school boys sporting green-and-gold letter jackets collected around a corner table. Jerry returned a nod. Some summer past he had most likely coached their baseball team or played referee for the community soccer league.

"Jerry, you never coached full time. I'll bet you would have been a good coach," I said, speaking aloud what I had always privately wondered.

"My folks never encouraged me to go on to college. I guess that's the only reason. Never was much of a student, but I got good business sense. You know my ex always called me "the perfectionist." I do well for myself, March. Spend my summers coaching Little League. Work on my house some. Everything I want, I have." The last few words of his sentence wilted. A trace of melancholy rose in his eyes and he looked at me with a question in his face, as though he had asked me something and then waited for my reply.

"Mason, come take a look at the menu. You still have school in the morning and I don't want you up too late." I drew the conversation away to other things.

"I tell you, son, you just get anything you want, steak, what have you. I seldom get to pick up the tab for a hungry boy." Jerry pushed a menu toward him.

Mason and I had not had a steak since before Joe's death. Joe was the family carnivore. Mason sat on the edge of his chair with his eyes planted on me as though he awaited a mother's verdict.

"Mason usually orders off the children's menu. Really, he can't eat a whole steak."

"Nonsense." Jerry flipped open the menu and pointed to Dooley's steak list. "Can't be hitting them out of the ballpark on French fries and chicken nuggets."

"Filet mignon," said Mason.

"There you go!" Jerry helped him select a loaded potato caked over with all sorts of Dooley toppings.

"Mason, let's split it, then," I said.

Jerry ordered two filets for the both of us and a porterhouse for himself. "Tell me about your little news operation, March. I guess I've seen your *Sentinel* in Wilmington, New Bern, and even along those little gas stations up around Raleigh."

"Still too early to say. I've picked up a new advertiser. Bill Hayden's Chevrolet." It sounded insignificant compared to the news Joe once came home boasting about.

Mason rolled his eyes and sort of deflated onto the tabletop.

"Seems like I've seen your office light on late at night. You burning the candle at both ends, I guess?"

"Tuesday nights. Mason sleeps at Grandpa's unless Yolanda is available to baby-sit. You remember her, don't you? Cute face, braces? Almost got kidnapped?"

"You almost got yourself killed," said Jerry.

"Anyway, we have to finalize our stories and make sure we're not leaving out Ed Finneman's special on dog food. He keeps threatening to take his business to Wilmington. Other nights Gloria stays late if the printer's acting like it does when it goes on the fritz. Our printer gives the guys fits. But Gloria has her way with the machinery. Liona's good enough to take notes for me on Mondays sometimes for the city council meeting, especially if Mason has Little-League practice."

"Ever play tennis up at the country club anymore?" He seemed to remember every small detail about my past, but I did not let on that it bothered me.

"Tennis? Not in a year." Three gulls flapped into the landing and collected near our feet. "Mason, don't feed them. It makes them aggressive," I said.

"You used to be pretty good at tennis, from what I remember."

"They have these funny ideas about dues at Randolph's Country

Club. Gee, do they have courts—the best. But you know, I don't miss all of the country club goings-on. You know, all of that who's-wearing-what and who's divorcing. Joe loved the club. So it's good I don't go. It would remind me too much of him. I don't even know how I got ushered into all of that—hoopla. Well, this all sounds pretentious. Club blather—it's not really what I'm into." I hoped Jerry would take the hint that I did not intend to go prancing into Randolph's all tennis skirted up and hanging on his arm as if we were the new couple.

"The city built those new courts up near the ballpark. If you want, I can swing a racket. Maybe this weekend we could meet for tennis."

"Jerry, thanks. But I just have too much going on with us, with Dad, work, my church. And since you are, in a manner, bringing it up—not that you are calling this an official date—but, sort of, you know, I just can't see myself in the dating circle again. Besides, Mason and I are going out of town this weekend. It's a travel assignment from a friend in Charlotte."

Mason sat up.

"I didn't know until just a while ago," I said to Mason. "Brady called while you were at practice."

"Is it a beach?" asked Mason.

"No, up around Charlotte," I said.

Mason pressed his face into his hands again on the table.

"It's a seafood place. So, it's not really a travel assignment, per se. More of a food critic's assignment. But freelancing for me can take on many forms. Maybe I'll have my plans all under one roof one day, be organized enough to have more help at the *Sentinel* so I have more time to write. Who knows? Is it getting chilly?"

"March, you sound as if you think you have to make up excuses for what you do. If you're a writer, just say it out like that—'I'm March Longfellow, the writer.' You don't have to chase rabbits all over creation trying to explain it."

Now he was advising me. Cute.

"I am a writer. But I don't know why I'm bothered about saying it. Maybe because I feel more like a Little League mom or the preacher's kid. Or Joe's wife. Or if I say I'm a writer, maybe someone will actually ask me to show them, say, something in writing. I feel like a fraud. Then all I have to show them is, sort of, a few odds and ends, here and there, the city council meeting or the report from the school board. And some people don't think you're a real writer unless you have your name on the front of a book. You take whatser-face, Sarai Gillman. When all of the Inksters are yammering on about what we all write in our various ways, you just see the level of interest go up when someone says her name. She's, to them, a real writer. But, say 'March Longfellow' and all of them, well, wink and elbow one another. They don't understand that running a newspaper takes a lot of time." All of my creative juices glug down with the bubble bath at night.

"Get out the gun. March Longfellow's hunting for wabbits."

"Jerry, don't try and do imitations. You sound Iranian."

"Your steaks will be right out, folks," said the waitress.

"The phone's ringing, Mom," said Mason.

The quick, almost emotionless voice on the other end of the line had to repeat the statement twice. "I'm sorry to inform you," was all that I understood.

"Mom, you look funny," said Mason.

"I'm sorry, Jerry. We have to go. Mason, honey, your grandpa's had a heart attack."

Jerry sighed, offered his sympathy, and ordered a beer.

Mason followed me out of the restaurant. I tried not to show watery eyes to him. "I knew his eating was going to get the better of him." I pressed a tissue against both eyes.

The drive to the hospital, past the hot dog stands, Leon's ABC store, and the ebbing tide along the Candle Bay faded into a listless horizon. I could not remember saying my good-byes to Jerry or somehow letting Mason know that everything would turn out, well, fine. I don't remember how we made it to the emergency room at

Holy Mary by the Sea Hospital with two foam boxes packed with steak and potato.

I had never seen my father hooked up to monitors and IVs. "Daddy, we're here," I said.

Before they had taken his wallet and belongings, he had pulled out a photo of my mother. He held it against his chest with his one free hand. It was an old picture of her standing out on the deck of the cottage as she painted it the color of the sea. "It's Julia, March. I think she misses me," he whispered.

"No, Dad. Not yet. It's a slow tide tonight."

Eight

OUR LITTLE HOSPITAL, HOLY MARY BY THE SEA, cared conscientiously for the bruised and those afflicted by infection. But by the first kiss of day, the local doctor issued the order that Dad should ride by ambulance to Raleigh. Dinah Buckworth drove behind the ambulance with Mason so that I could ride shotgun with Dad. Bill and Irene Simmons called those who could get away and ferried them by church van to Raleigh. Dinah weaved in and around the jarring host of motorists full throttle until the highways thinned of school buses and commuters idling toward New Bern or Jacksonville. The Presbyterians were no bigger than a filament of lint in her rearview mirror.

Dad's doctor proclaimed the surgery a success although Dad lay in his bed sluiced of color, a soldier winged by his own bullet. Three bypasses issued through his arteries to unclog all of the routes to a more agreeable tomorrow.

Since Tuesdays required so much of my attention at the newspaper office, my phone did not stop ringing the whole morning. I took Gloria's calls out in the hallway. She held together the weekly like the glue I knew her to be.

Fern and Leon Michaels doled out magazines to the church members gathered out in the lobby. Lorraine Bedinsky, engrossed in soap operas, knitted coasters beneath the overhead television. Grace Caudle dropped Hershey's Kisses in silver heaps around the lobby tables, as though by doing so she prevented fainting spells between breakfast and the lunch hour. The act caused a surge in aluminum foil wrappers balled up and dropped in all of the planters.

I stayed beside Dad, acting as custodian of the floral arrangement cards and the get-well greeting cards. The doctor taught him to place a pillow against his chest whenever he laughed. Only Bill Simmons elicited a flutter of laughter from Dad in his postoperative slouched-and-drained-of-life posture. It was the same old dialogue that older men all said to one another after a heart attack—"Some people will do anything for a vacation."

By the second day, the doctor told him he might find his appetite. He more than found it and gave us a shameless list of foods he wanted brought in.

"Dad, they just cleaned your pipes. Should you be clogging all the works back up again?" I asked.

"March, you know better than to try and convert me to that tasteless soup-o-mania lifestyle you call healthy eating. None of it appeals to me. If you have to live life in misery, then you may as well cave in and eat rocks. Now go and bring me a box of vanilla wafers."

"It's on the list, Dad. Mason's back at school today. I have to leave around noon in order to pick him up on time. Before I leave, I'll bring you a few things."

"Fine. If you don't wind your way back down to that paper office, Gloria will find 102 ways to take up the remaining office space with her gizmos."

Bill Simmons opened up a chess board. "I thought we could get caught up on my beating you again at chess, James." Bill had gained a lot of seniority as a systems analyst and took advantage of some time off with Dad.

"Bill, you always liked punishment. Set her up," said Dad. He cleared a *Moody* magazine off his tray. "I'm glad it's not raining today.

We've had such a parade of people driving back and forth, I'd feel terrible if they had to drive in bad weather. Bill, I want you to take over the midweek service, of course. March can get you a good book of devotions off my bookcase. Steal one by Oswald Chambers. Just don't read it verbatim. Too boring. At least try and, well, if you can teach—how are you at summarizing?"

I hoped Bill did not overhear my sigh. His penchant for leading board meetings overshadowed his ability to stir the hearts of spectators.

"You want me to try and preach?" Bill said with a near squeak in his voice.

"I'm well aware that you can't preach, Bill. But give it a go, if you can."

"James, I'll do my dead-level best."

"If you call the state office, they might have a young intern that can fill in Sunday. I'll be back week after next."

The head board member slid the chess pieces into place. He offered no more than a half nod. But then he emitted a sigh and arched one brow. "Week after next. I don't know, James, if that is wise."

"Dad, you just had triple bypass surgery. Maybe you should ask the doctor how soon you should be back in the pulpit," I said.

"Harry Weising up at Kannapolis had his quadruple bypass and in two weeks conducted a wedding, two funerals, and stepped back into the pulpit without so much as a blink. I'm in better shape than Harry. Let's flip to see who goes first." Dad faced his king and queen toward Bill.

"James, you go first."

"I don't need your sympathy, Bill. You go first."

"Dad, I don't know Harry Weising but I do know how stories circulate. I think I should call Colin Arnett. He knows our church now and considers you a friend. I'll bet he'd come if we ask," I said.

"Whose going to ask Colin Arnett? You?"

"Perhaps I should be the one." I still had not penned a letter to Colin with my grace-and-mercy speech and could now kick myself for the delay. So I mentally fashioned conciliatory speeches that might warm him up to visiting Candle Cove Presbyterian again.

"Colin is done with us, March. It would be in poor taste to call him back now."

"You say that as though something bad has passed between us. But Colin lost a friend Sunday. It distracted him, that's all. If I call and tell him you've just had triple bypass surgery, he'll come back."

"March, we've formed a steering committee. Don't trouble yourself about the matter. We'll find a candidate," said Bill.

"I'm not talking about a candidate. Only a fill-in guy."

"You don't ask a man who pastors a congregation of 1,005 and counting to fill in at a church of 110." Dad grunted. He lost a pawn to Bill.

"Although if you could get him to reconsider, March, well, we'd be the happiest church around," said Bill. "We have people willing to start a building fund, for once. Man like Arnett, he could steer us in ways we can only imagine." He moved another pawn forward.

"March is too busy, Bill. She's got this Charlotte paper after her now for a new travel column."

"Be sure and speak for me, Dad," I said. "I can't think for myself."

Bill had grown accustomed to our gentle sparring, but I made certain I punctuated each sentence with a wooden smile.

"Neither can I, March. That's why you always think for me." Dad placed his pawn in Bill's square and shoved the black pawn aside. "It's just the way we Norvilles are, Bill."

"I believe I'll hunt us down a cold drink. Don't touch that board, James. I have eyes in the back of my head," said Bill. He tiptoed out of the room.

"Colin Arnett lives in Lake Norman, Dad. This weekend I agreed to do a piece about a seafood restaurant in Charlotte. Not too far from Lake Norman. I'll just drop by. Piece of cake."

"So you plan to pay him a visit and, what, tell him things have warmed up in Candle Cove?"

"No. Here's what—first I'll request a meeting with him. I'll tell him our congregation might have felt a little blindsided this weekend. We didn't have a chance to show him our best side. I'll ask him will he simply give us another go." It sounded levelheaded to me.

"So we ask this man to whom we gave the cold shoulder this weekend to please reconsider coming here for a cut in pay and a congregation that is easily blindsided. My friendship with the man is the only reason he considered Candle Cove in the first place, March. We don't have much to offer Colin Arnett or anyone of his caliber."

"I beg to differ." Bill appeared with a canned drink in each hand.

"Bill, you know what I mean. We just tend to run a little behind here." Dad popped the top on his drink.

"March traipsing off to Lake Norman is like sending the ant off to bring back the whole banana farm." Bill moved another chess piece. He studied Dad's reaction, which was nothing at all.

"You can be negative about it or you can at the very least let me give it a try," I said.

"Maybe she's just the ant we need, James. Check." Bill stared right at my father.

"Check?" Dad seldom lost at chess. "Maybe we should have started with checkers. Next thing you know, I'll be keeping up with the soaps." Dad picked up the remote control. "Hand me a *TV Guide*, will you, March?"

Never did I intend to approach Colin Arnett with the pastorate of Candle Cove Presbyterian. I did not know him well enough to do that. Had I given the idea more thought, I might have returned to Bill Simmons and told him our scheme was a pretentious front for my worry that I was still being blamed for Colin's rejecting us. But as Dad lay attached to bleeping monitors, the urge to patch the hole that sucked life from James Norville's world hissed at me.

The night before, thoughts had trickled in as I tossed in bed nervous about Dad's heart. When I finally drifted off, I dreamed about saving my father. In the past year I had had this recurring dream, an emotional flight through a dreamscape of ocean hues. This was the same dream, although in the midst of it, nonsensical elements weaved through the main elements. Always, though, I flew in the dreams, but not as an angel. I had brittle translucent wings, fluttering dragonfly wings that were too small for my body. My weight pulled at the insect wings. I had moments I thought I would separate from them, and I could feel them fraying at the small hinge that attached them to my back. Instead of lifting above the arc of ocean that wrapped our cove, I struggled to stay above the tide and not plunge into the roiling bath of salt water. The sand pebbles appeared as boulders that dissolved into the water and allowed the tide to swallow up our cottage. The seafoam-green paint made oily splotches on the surface of the sea, and I could see my mother floating away on the surface while Joe's hand disappeared into the darkest middle of its raging torrent. But this time, my father sat atop the church roof with his Bible, held it close to his chest, and quoted Psalms. He seemed bothered by my attempts to lift him from the swirling church, but even more so when I left him atop it. When I could not raise him and felt my wings crumble into the tide, he looked at me and I understood his wordless assessment of me. His mantle of disenchantment cloaked me, and I fell to the shore beneath its saturated weight.

Brady Gallagher phoned me on my drive back to Candle Cove. His wife had left him two years ago when his long nights at the office offered her too much time on her hands to make fast friends with a neighbor who rescued her one too many times from her dysfunctional lawn mower. Brady persisted on coffee and doughnuts and vociferous meetings. When I ran into him again face to face as a journalist—three years after our graduation from Chapel Hill—the dark sunken spaces beneath his eyes prognosticated his pitted road ahead. Once a year he disappeared into the Rocky Mountains for a two-week stretch of fly fishing, only to return and allow the newspaper business to hook up to his tank of inventiveness and readily drain him of it.

"Brady, some things have changed," I said.

"You aren't coming. If I scared you away with that column, don't let that keep you from this one piece." He sipped coffee. I could hear the slight breeze he made as he breathed across the top of it and then allowed it to slip between his lips.

"My father just suffered a heart attack. But I am coming. I just don't know if I can give you an answer so quickly about the column now. Dad met a pastor from Lake Norman. If I can convince this minister to return to Candle Cove, it will be a weight off Dad. But I need to be around for Dad's recuperation from the surgery for a couple of weeks. The biggest chore will be to get him to stay in bed and rest."

"That's bad news about your father, March. If I can do anything at all, you let me know."

"We have a good support system at the church. This health matter with my father has thrown me a curve, that's all."

"If you need to be released from this weekend, I understand."

"Trust me. I'm coming. Colin Arnett's church is in Lake Norman somewhere; Cornelius, I think."

"LaVecchia's has a location in Cornelius. I don't know Colin Arnett, but then, I don't know many preachers, as a rule."

I pulled up Bill's notes that I scrawled inside my Palm Pilot. "Arnett pastors Church on the Lake on Catawba Street. Sounds like a yuppie church."

"I guess they have to have their own churches now. To each his own."

Dinah met me at the cottage. Whenever I begged, she would take time off from the caterer's business she operated out of her house to help me clean the beach house. She always said it was because she knew if she helped me she could have the use of it whenever she wanted. It could not have possibly been because we had seen one another through the worst of female disasters and lived to tell about it. We washed and folded linens and prepared the downstairs bedroom as though Colin Arnett might soon return. Mason ran with Hercules along a crisp row of shells washed ashore overnight.

"I made us a big old pitcher of sweet tea, March. Let's fix ourselves a cold glass and take it outside. The sun is so bright today," said Dinah. Twin heads bobbed down the shoreline. Dinah's girls carried seashells inside the tails of their shirts. They dumped them at Mason's feet and all of them knelt and picked through the pile to ferret out the good shells and toss away the broken or chipped ones.

Dinah arranged a few store-bought cookies on a platter, balanced our tea glasses in the center, and carried it all out onto the deck. "I don't guess I ever had a chance to meet this Colin Arnett. You seem different about him now, is all I know."

"I think that my father believes I ran him off."

"Is he right?"

"No. Not entirely so. But in a manner of speaking, I'm still guilty. Because in my heart I was cold to him, even if I didn't say everything I was thinking. At one point, I may have sounded defensive. My memory's a little fuzzy. The man caught me so off guard I didn't know what to say. Dad should have warned me about all of it. But maybe that's the whole point—maybe Dad did try to tell me and I wasn't willing to hear him out."

"You can leave Mason with me and I'll take him to the game on Saturday."

"The game. Oh, Dinah, here I just spilled all of this stuff about going to Lake Norman onto Mason and then wondered why he was so silent on the way over here. He thinks I treat him like everything is important except what he wants to do. He probably tried to tell me about his game and I just talked right over him."

"I do believe I've never met anyone busier than you, March."

"No one else will do what I do, Dinah. If I don't take care of us, no one will. I have to run the newspaper. And since Mom died, if I don't keep all of these volunteers organized at church, well, then, who else will do it?"

"If the ladies spring bazaar is canceled, then what? The end of civilization as we know it?" Dinah scraped away the chocolate cookie icing with her teeth.

"It's not specifically the bazaar, Dinah, or the newspaper deadlines, or the town council meetings. All of it is held together in so fragile a way by such few people."

"Delegate. Hand it off."

"I've tried. But no one seems to care about the inner workings of the church or the newspaper as much I do. So the work is only halfway done, as though the person trying to take my place is just going through the motions."

"If you're the only one who cares, then maybe what you're doing isn't so important."

"Tell that to my father."

"The long and short of it, then, is that you do it for your father."

I broke my cookie in two and laid one piece on the plate. "Dad had depended so much on my mother to keep their busy nest comfy and stocked, to maintain all of her organizational charts she kept so well in her head. When she died, I stepped into her shoes without so much as a 'hold it' or 'let me think about it.'"

"I guess your father asked you to take her place then."

"Not in so many words." I pretended to look for the children. Finally, I saw movement on the shore.

They shook the sand from their clothes and chased after the tide in their bare feet.

"I could never take Julia Norville's place," I said.

"Just all of her obligations."

Dinah irritated the truth out of me, the sand in my oyster shell. "What are you implying—that maybe I'm just trying to keep her alive?"

"I always said you were sharp as a tack, March Longfellow." She handed me a cardboard box. "Take a gander at this. You'll never guess what's inside."

"Mason, when I told you about this weekend, you didn't say anything at all about your game. I think we should talk about it."

"You wouldn't have listened, I figured, so why mention it." He had used silence to make his point and make me feel guilty.

"I care about your games, your practices, everything about you, Mason. In the same way my father has to be reminded about his obligations, it wouldn't hurt if you reminded me. I don't get angry with my father when I have to remind him that he is having dinner with us on a specific night or that he is picking you up from school when I have to stay late on Tuesdays."

He shrugged. "So Grandpa's coming home Friday from the hospital. That seems kind of quick."

"They send patients home sooner nowadays, and don't get off the subject. I think you prefer to pout instead of talking things out. That isn't a mature way to do things, Son."

"I don't pout. That's a baby thing."

"Mason, if you would have mentioned your game to me on the trip over, well, we might have had the chance to talk it out. I know you realize that this trip to Lake Norman is important for Grandpa's sake. But your game is just as important to me."

"Are you farming me out to the Buckworths?"

"What if I am?"

"If Grandpa's coming home, I'd rather stay with him. Maybe I could help him out, you know, bring him things when he needs it."

"I like that idea. Then you could ride with the Buckworths to your game. Don't sigh like that, it's only a ride. Once you arrive, you run off with your friends, your teammates. No harm in that. Unless you want Jerry Brevity to pick you up."

"I'll ride with the Buckworths."

"Just don't go off trying to fix me up with Coach Jerry again. I still have to take my revenge for that last maneuver of yours."

"Is Pastor Arnett taking Grandpa's place?"

"If Dad wants that to happen, I pray it happens. Mason, we have to trust Grandpa on a few issues and this is going to have to be one of them. I don't know if Pastor Arnett wants to come to Candle Cove. We're a small church. But if he agrees to come, then maybe it's high time Grandpa took more time for himself, did a little fishing." I felt a pang when I said it.

The phone rang. Gloria was doing battle with the printer.

I sighed and knew how Mason would react. "Let's swing by the office. Gloria needs my help."

Mason rolled the back of his head against the seat. He emitted a faint moan. I understood the meaning of it. He never got to go directly home from school, from baseball practice, from a trip to the beach. While the other children filed from church with their parents only to head out for Sunday dinner, we stayed behind to collect litter around the sanctuary and to visit with committee members who needed advice. When I was not at work, I was still at work because the *Sentinel* clasped onto me like a newborn. "I think I'll just call her back and ask if she and the fellows can handle the printer without me."

"I can play outside, then," said Mason.

"What a good idea. I'll throw you a few balls. Don't roll your eyes again. I know I throw like a girl."

The phone rang again.

"I won't answer it. Probably nothing."

After two more rings, I picked it up.

"March, you need to get down here. The whole computer system just crashed," said Gloria. She never had a frantic edge to her tone, but she did this time.

I apologized to Mason several times on the way to the *Sentinel.* Mason never said a word, but stared out of the window and shot at invisible rabbits. I wanted to shout at Joe for not being around to see it.

Nine

When Dinah had found the boxed diary, she held it out nine inches from her face, closed but with her thumb stroking the edges of the pages. Both of us had agreed we should not read it, that it would be unfair to trip without consent across the strings of a man's private soul. Dinah, had she found it while alone, might have allowed temptation to rule.

The journal lay undisturbed on the passenger's seat for over an hour on the way to Lake Norman until I stopped to buy gas and a soda. I opened to the latest entry while gasoline glugged rhythmically into the car tank. I surmised Colin must have penned it the day he disappeared down the beach to study.

Colin's diary read like a photographer's journal.

I prefer the westbound road at early morning. The sun at my back has not yet dominated the sky and the horizon bleeds only a little color, a whisper of the day. All is pale. Swallows are busy in the trees, little creatures with darkened wings that sing and sing into the quiet of my pale morning. It is a pure song, one as quiet as a dimple made by one sky-cooled raindrop upon a pond. Some rush into the day with blaring horns, all moments penciled into the minutes as though they had already happened, as though handed to us already spent. But I sip the morning when

I travel, at least the virgin part of day before I am overtaken by my will. Until I become like everyone else.

I closed it up and continued down the winding rural snake of road thinking about what else he must have tucked into the journal. Thoughts about death. And Eva.

Halfway between Candle Cove and Lake Norman a lonesome stillness settled over me. I stopped to buy peanuts at a farmer's stand on Andrew Jackson Highway only to load up on honey and pecans. A girl clad in a dress too old for her young frame, the farmer's daughter, poured me a cold cup of apple cider and invited me to sample her pecans. I sat on a barrel to sip the cider, and that is when the insatiable urge to read Colin Arnett's diary again overtook me. It was a shameful urge but one that adhered to me. I returned to the Mustang and retrieved the diary.

Not even the darkest tide of guilt could pull me away. I flipped through the often-touched pages until I found an entry he wrote about Eva.

It is my first night curling up against your pillow without you, the wretched lone spoon. Your smell upon the linens is like a bed of narcissus after rain, a common flower until it is placed upon your gentle wrist and turns to nectar. I beg that smell to stay, but feel desperate, as though it is fading from me as quickly as my last moment with you. I keep whispering your name hoping the angels might deliver my frantic message to heaven's portals to tell you I have died without you. Surely God will finish me so that I may leave earth's ragged, spinning orb and join you in a dance among the stars. Hateful bounds! I am the blackest soul given by God's own hand the kindest treasure, a shining beam of womanly daylight for too brief a moment. To me the blackest soul, undeserving of your sacred attentions, God granted this cherubic gift and then revoked it. . . .

His words took my breath, his love for Eva suffused with self-contempt. He finished out the page with two lines of poetry.

For oh, my soul found a Sunday wife. In the coal-black sky, and she bore angels! Dylan Thomas

My throat tightened and I thought I smelled narcissus. I snapped the book closed, and glanced around feeling as though the farmer's daughter minced by me, stared with accusing little bullet eyes, and shook her finger at me to shame me for intruding on a grieving man's private musings.

I had not earned the privilege of peering into Colin Arnett's quiet moments, but there I sat swallowing whole his inner voice, doused with a drink of farmer's cider.

I read some more until shame seized me and then I put it away and continued eastward toward Mecklenburg County and the buzzing hive of Charlotte.

I practiced looking at Colin without revealing my culpability.

For all my love of the ocean with its procession of gulls embroidering the sky like starched origami, I could as easily make my bed in the city, and especially the Queen City of Charlotte. If I had not fallen in love with the Sound, I might have hitched my star to Charlotte. She offered so much to those who could no more bear to leave the South than to go without air. All of the designer companies had flocked from the hub of Charlotte out to her suburbs in Lake Norman and Concord—Starbucks, Banana Republic, Ann Taylor—along with various chain restaurants like Spaghetti Warehouse with its period indoor trolley and, of course, Joe's Crab Shack. If I had not accepted the assignment, I might have been fickle in determining where I would eat dinner. For lunch, I would ask Brady's suggestion in hopes he might spring for the midday meal. I had mooched from Brady since college; cadged jobs from him, lunches, and anything I could get without officially calling it a date. It would have been like dating a brother.

I drove into the parking deck and ferried the stub inside to be sure he stamped it "paid." My mother would have disapproved of my power over Brady, although I never shared such things back then. I considered it senseless to add to her censure list.

Whenever Brady and I met up again, he and I chatted about everything from frat houses to the old weekend beach parties as openly as my mother once chatted over the fence about Tupperware. I kept pictures from college in a shoebox, three specifically with Brady stuck between all of us six girls on the same floor who ran amok on weekends. Over the years his ginger-jar shape had expanded, with the bottom half as round and encompassing as the moon. In the grainy photograph, you could still see his inhibited grin thinly stretching into his cheeks and his eyes gallivanting obliquely—a bashful soul's refusal to look straight into the camera lens.

Since he had signed on with the *Observer* after our little gang all graduated, over time I noticed that whenever I departed his office, he had a habit of loosening his tie. Then he hesitated as though his heart stood on end for an instant. That is when I walked away as if on cue. I could not give him a moment of eye contact or indicate I ever knew of his ancient infatuation with me. My fondness for Brady and his geekish inclinations never crossed the threshold to fulfill his Walter Mitty-ish fantasies.

The secretary ushered me into his office, a shared space cluttered along the walls with posters of food award winners and travel pieces for which Brady held an eclectic fondness. The *Charlotte Observer* was not of the size to have a true travel column but instead tossed a few dollars toward the Sunday travel section, Brady's first twenty hours of weekly commitment. He referred to his other twenty hours as the "other things" he wrote for the paper.

I found him seated at his desk; several paper cups sat like bumpers on a snooker table, each cup filled in varying degrees with cold coffee—the first coffee of the day interrupted during the morning meetings and accompanied by the editorial doughnut, the coffee he brought back from the meeting, and the just-before-lunch coffee, still warm. Yet, Brady might have balked if any secretary had attempted to wrest any of them away before the noon hour.

He kept stacks of articles situated around his desk categorized into the edited-pieces stack and the not-yet-jelled-pieces heap—usually mailed-in articles by freelancers that required such wide snatches of editorial attention that he sometimes left them to morph into fodder for the circular file.

"Good for you; you made it. Hope the traffic didn't tie you up. March, you look great. You've lost weight and I must have found it for you," he said.

"Interstate 277 was stacked all the way into town." I peeled off the kiwi-colored sweater and draped it on a chair back. "Your secretary said they've closed the café here in the building. You must be brown-bagging it." Brady and I always started out our conversations in a desultory fashion, leaping from one trifling topic to the next.

"Some of us guys around the office eat at Showmar's. They make the best gyros I've had. Too, I have a friend at the Duke Power building and sometimes he gets me in at their eatery. You have to know someone."

"Gyros. I haven't had a real one since Joe and I took Mason to Ocean City."

He gathered three foam cups from his desk and dropped them into his waste can.

"Here's a pen and paper. If you want, just give me the directions. I can find—what did you call it—Showmar's? I realize I'm here early. If I can reach Colin Arnett, maybe he can meet me at LaVecchia's tonight for dinner. "

"Kill two frogs with one wheel."

"In a manner of speaking."

"Melanie, I'm taking Ms. Longfellow out for a business luncheon," he said.

The secretary shrugged. Her pouf of bangs billowed in a frayed sort of flight against what curl she had tried to hot iron into place that morning.

"I can pay," I said.

"These tightwads can front me a lunch. Forget about it."

"Any more details about this, what you call it, Barefoot Traveler column?"

"No up-front budget. That's the bad news. But you live in beach city, so I figured if anyone could make it work, you could. We're a Knight Ridder paper, so we dig up all the syndicated stuff, the exotic, for nothing. But it's the pieces on regional places we lack because there is no actual budget per se. And we get a lot of garbage from the guys who take a buggy ride in South Carolina and send us what they think is the definitive Charleston story. But they're not writers. They'll never be writers. Not like you. They just want to have written. Sure, they're cheap, but I have to completely rewrite the mess they send to me. I might as well do it myself. With you living between Pamlico Sound and Myrtle Beach, you're the perfect candidate for 'The Barefoot Traveler.' The money comes in when you build an advertising base. Folks all up and down the coast need someone like you to plug their place—but not just any place. We want the unique, the quaint, the quirky, and lots of local color."

"So I really wouldn't be away from Mason."

"Not right away. Depends upon how fast you build a budget and your own travel stash. How far you travel is up to you. The way I figure it, you have enough material in your neck of the woods to launch this thing."

It intrigued me.

The dining room at Showmar's was a cross between old people who eat applesauce in Florida restaurants, and an East-Coast deli. Every table displayed plastic red-and-white flowers inside empty olive-oil bottles as ordinary as laboratory vials. Brady cajoled a waitress he knew into fitting us in ahead of the line of noonday office dwellers that waited in the lobby and out onto the sidewalk next to Tryon and First. She led us to a window table, and that suited Brady fine.

"You staying in Cornelius, I guess," he said.

"I didn't make reservations. It's Lake Norman. How busy can they be?"

"Depends. Lake Norman has its own traffic jams now. All those New Yorkers and New Jersey types have invaded, bringing traffic jams and New York pizza with them."

"I'll bet the old-line rural families like that, the farmers and locals."

"They hate it. You'll see these stretches of rural, undeveloped land squeezed between two major commercial zones, and lo and behold, Old Farmer Jones has stuck little homemade signs in the ground near the road that say NO MORE LAND GRABBING! But the developers land on them with a bag of money, and out goes the family legacy and in goes a new subdivision."

"And a LaVecchia's."

"Say, that's a good piece of news. You have to drive four and a half hours in your direction to get real seafood otherwise. Only other reason I know someone would drive that far is for love."

A few seconds passed. If I stared at his coffee cup long enough, perhaps he would stop sniffing around imaginary holes. "My father's had a heart attack. He wants this Colin Arnett to take his place. I . . . when he first came to town, I didn't realize what transpired between him and my father, and I sort of, well, I wasn't expecting him and I misunderstood the situation is all."

Brady laughed. "You ran him off."

"Not at all." The waitress took our order. "But the whole church was caught unaware and no one rolled out the red carpet. Candle Cove Presbyterian knows how to welcome a newcomer if given a proper introduction. I just want to invite Pastor Arnett back to give us a second chance."

"Tell me how Mason's doing."

"Great. Or good, I should say. Maybe on some days lousy. Missing a dad around the house, but we make do."

"Mason's a good kid. Boys like him rebound amazingly enough. It's the widow who worries me."

"I'm fine, Brady. First a month and then a year after the accident, I hit a slump. Joe's family had such odd ways of managing grief, and

I felt as though I had to run around propping everyone up the week of the funeral. They all thought I was a barracuda because I didn't shed a tear that week. But I felt as though weakening for even a moment would make me a target. You'd have to know the Longfellows intimately to understand."

"I'll pass. You mentioned her once, that mother-in-law person. I had one once, but don't get me started."

"One night, four weeks later, I fell apart. I was in my bedroom—our bedroom—alone. Then the gloom sort of passed, and I thought I'd be back on the path to sanity. A year later it hit again. I thought I was losing my mind."

"March, you never call me even though I tell you to call me if you need me. I've told you at least a thousand times to call. But you never do."

"Even you wouldn't want to see me in such a mess, Brady."

"Pastor Father couldn't console you." He said it with sympathy.

"Dad was his usual bowl of compassion. But I needed to express some things to Joe, and without an audience."

"It's best to get it out. Keeps them from having to throw the net over you. But all of that propping up isn't good either. What else are you propping up?"

"That's a good question." I hated it when Brady started digging up all of my emotions. But I never let on to the way he annoyed me like a finagling little brother.

"That's what your trip here is all about. More propping."

"Maybe it isn't propping. What if I say that I'm doctoring? That isn't the same thing."

"It could be."

"I just know that I have to try and repair something I loused up. Do you ever do that, Brady, just open your mouth fully believing the right thing is coming out? You think you're a crusader but instead you wind up the village idiot."

"My ex-wife might like to answer that for me."

"I'm haunted by my own words, Brady. It's as though I watch myself going through the motions of setting things straight, but it's all in slo-mo, and I have this sort of deep satisfaction that I've just conquered another mountain. Days later, or maybe a week passes, and I wake up to realize that instead I've set fire to the whole thing."

"Pyro March."

"This conversation isn't helping, Brady." After my confessional to "Father Brady," he knew more about me than I knew about myself. Brady had that affect on me, like when he used to drag me in front of the cheap beveled mirror nailed to my dorm-room wall and make me look. "March, this is you," he would say. "*You,* meet March." He forever accused me of holding my feelings inside. He was wrong, I would tell him. But he just kept standing behind me making me look. The waitress placed a warm ceramic plate in front of me loaded with the gyro, tomatoes, and a white sauce.

"You know a little lamb had to die for that, don't you?" Brady shook salt all over his burger and fries.

I stared at my own hands and then nodded. I was glad I had my back to the window. I wasn't in the mood for reading my reflection.

"Pass the ketchup, will you?" Brady inhaled his food, the human vacuum.

I checked into a hotel in quaint Cornelius, a Best Western with all the usual appurtenances of a Lake Norman village-chic look. The desk clerk told me I was only a block or two from LaVecchia's. Mason would be setting out a hot meal for himself and Dad, some casserole and dessert brought over by Phyllis Murray. I called Dad's place. Mason answered.

"Mason, it's me. Phyllis brought you dinner, I hope."

"She did. Something with macaroni. Grandpa hates macaroni."

"Dad's more than likely going to be grumpy, Mason. Do you know who is taking the pulpit tomorrow?"

"Someone's taking the pulpit?" A second or two passed before he responded. "Some man from South Carolina. Grandpa says he knows him."

"That is a relief. You staying home with Grandpa in the morning?"

"We're going to watch videos. Mrs. Murray brought over a whole sack of them from Video Mac's. But Grandpa can't laugh too hard. It makes his chest hurt. He's making us do a devotional. 'I'm the preacher,' he says, 'so I get to give it.'"

"Can Grandpa talk on the phone? I mean, does he feel up to it?"

Mason asked him. I heard a long sigh, as deep as the ocean ebbing only to recede and then muster a weak wave onto the shore. Dad took the phone. He said he had allowed Mason to bring Hercules, but Johnson remained at the house with his weekend supply dish overflowing. We spoke for a few moments until he tired of talking. I let him go, but sat with my hand wrapped around the receiver.

When I called the Arnetts, first the answering machine engaged. But Ruth Arnett swooped up the phone. I could almost see her blond ponytail and knit Capri pants.

"Ruth, guess who? It's me, March Longfellow."

There was a pause and I listened to the awkwardness of silence.

"Oh, Pastor Norville's daughter. Say, we felt so horrible about rushing off that Sunday, but Colin's closest friend had a sudden heart attack. I've not seen Colin so devastated. Not since Eva died, anyway."

"I understand. My father's just had a heart attack, too." I heard her take in air.

"I'll bet Colin doesn't even know," she said.

"I told Dad I'd tell him myself. The surgery went great, Ruth. Dad is back home. Mason is tending to him. They're like two old bachelors eating all the wrong things and watching television. But I'm in town doing a food piece for a local restaurant. I was hoping to have a chance to speak with Pastor Arnett, if he's around."

"He's out on the lake with Troy and Luke. They're trying to learn how to sail. I hope they don't wreck the thing. Boats make me nervous."

"Me too."

She gasped again.

"Don't give it a second thought," I said.

"Colin has the same thing happen to him. People make comments about death all the time without thinking about it. You don't think about loose words, do you, until it visits your own house?"

"I know I'm calling last minute, but if he could meet me tonight . . . You know about a restaurant called LaVecchia's?"

She breathed out an accommodating, "Uh huh."

"Maybe ask him if he could meet me around seven or so. That is, if you all don't mind parting with him an hour or two. I need to discuss a matter with him."

"I'll leave a note here on his note board. He always checks it when he comes home. I'm taking Charlotte and Rachel for haircuts. But I'll be back later, so it's no problem for me to stay with the kids. LaVecchia's just took the place of that other restaurant. I can't remember the name. But Colin has eaten there before. I've heard good things about their food. Where are you staying?"

"At a Best Western in the Cornelius area."

"You aren't far from us. You and your church were so hospitable. If you want, I could just fix dinner here. Why don't I do that?"

"I can't. I'm here on a food critic's assignment. The *Observer* is expecting something on LaVecchia's."

"You have such creative sources for your vocation. I can't write a letter. Better at math."

"I can't do math. See, it takes all kinds." I thanked her and hung up. I placed my knit tops on wooden hangers to allow the wrinkles to fall out and then decided to take a drive around the lake.

Although a manmade lake with five hundred miles of shoreline, Lake Norman has such a busy-harbor look about it, you can sit out on a pier with your feet in the water and dream of the ocean. Dog owners ran with their pets along the shoreline. The warm day brought out the Jet Skiers. Their spray shot up from the glittering horizon, tooling against the wind with the sound of a lawn mower beneath the rider. Sailboats dominated the lake; white, red, and blue sails winding across the water's surface, pleasure carriers skating on a mirror. A yellow sail billowed, tilted aft, and then led the small craft away from shore. A father assisted his children with the boom, but the distance prevented me from determining if it was Colin and the boys. I watched until they disappeared around the curving line of suburban beach.

I left only a small amount of time to shower and change. The *maitre d'* seated me at a round table near a wall of glass that looked out over a garden. A pianist played soft jazz.

I waited until the waiter visited my table three times.

I had not warned Colin that I was coming and knew it was silly to fume about being stood up. I tried to imagine what magnanimous event kept him from a simple courtesy call to me, the person who had used up two tanks of gas getting here. I fumed over that thought until the waiter bent over and asked, "Is there anything I can do to help?"

"I'm fine." My face reddened.

The sky darkened as it always does when the sun exits to leave the moon alone to monitor the night. I ordered the sesame seed-clustered tuna and ate alone.

Ten

IT WASN'T UNTIL I RETURNED TO THE BEST WESTERN that I finally got an explanation about Colin's awkward absence. The concierge forwarded a message to the phone in the room: an endless message by Colin explaining a long evening on the lake with the boys and how immeasurably terrible it was to hear about Dad's heart attack. He invited me to join Ruth and the children for the morning service with a promise to meet with me afterward.

If it had not been for the promise to Dad, I would have never made the drive to Colin's church.

At ten the next morning, I followed the Yellow Pages directions to Colin's church, Church on the Lake, and found the entry drive a bedded-down-the-center floral island, a fusion of perennials such as not-quite-open day lilies and candytuft. A velvet border of purple pansies ringed the curbed island flanked by spikes of snapdragon with yellow dew-filled mouths lifted to the sun.

I parked and followed a chattering group of couples and children through the glass door entry, a perfectly high wall of glass that set off the church entrance like the gates of heaven. Two couples greeted me, effusive and smiling, and stuffed a church bulletin into my hand along with a brochure that pictorially led the reader through the amalgam of activities offered throughout the week.

I wandered through the lobby and stood antlike in what Bill Simmons had branded the "banana tree grove." Everywhere my eye fell, signs of Colin's and Eva's diligence shone, especially in the animated clusters of people gathered outside the doors that led to the main sanctuary. Colin Arnett had never intended to pastor our church, I realized. His kindness was the pure cause of his coming; a pastorly gesture of the ministerial brotherhood, the code of consideration held among clergy.

I fingered the set of keys to the Mustang.

"March, you came. We feel so privileged," said Ruth. She wore an Ann Taylor pantsuit, a chic algae color with a silk blouse woven from a bright lime fabric. Next to her, my cream polyester suit seemed ordinary, a blue-light special, the peach blouse now more like a splayed salmon hue under the fluorescent lights.

"I was in town already. It isn't my intention to be any bother to you all, so please, I'll just take a seat in the back," I said. More than anything I wanted to avoid meaningless banter about being left to eat alone.

"You'll do no such thing. Colin's given me specifics about you, March. You're joining us for Sunday dinner after the morning service. We're all going out to the Mid-Town Café. It's a bar-and-grill sort of place right on the lake. They'll seat us outside right near the water if we ask. Ride with me and I'll bring you back here to your car later. Are you headed home today?"

"Yes. Mason has school tomorrow, and I really have to get back and take care of Dad. He has a lot of people checking on him, but I worry about Mason being there alone with him. Like what if something happened and Mason didn't know what to do?"

"Then I insist you join us for a bite to eat. Besides, last night you sounded as though you needed to speak with Colin."

I had changed my mind. "I did?"

"I already told him you indicated some purpose about this visit. Colin, he's so approachable, really. You should always feel you can talk to him about anything."

"Your church is so, well, big, and it has such elaborate flower beds."

"Eva designed all of the landscape islands and the beds around the church. Her fanaticism for perennials lives on. I want to show you her shade gardens out back. The elders' wives held some rummage sales and raised enough to turn that area into a prayer-and-meditation garden. It's a memorial to her."

"Eva sounds so much like my mother." Except for the fact that Eva did not reside in my thoughts, still trying to correct my mistakes.

"If you want to see Eva, Colin says, just look into Charlotte's eyes."

Ruth led me around the lobby that encircled the entire sanctuary. I might have wandered like a rodent in an endless maze on my own. We passed through two exit doors and walked out onto a stone walk, red stones embedded in the manicured lawn. Apple trees flanked the walk all the way to the shade garden. But someone knelt inside so we stopped. Wisteria vines covered an arbor and allowed a gentle effusion of sunlight to bathe the garden in a holy, weightless illumination.

"It's Colin," I whispered. A sound as still as a robin on a branch, and barely discernible as a man's stifled sob, caused Ruth to take my arm. We left the garden and found our way back into the sanctuary.

Pastor Colin Arnett took the platform ten minutes later. No one but me saw the damp piece of shredded grass tumble from the part of his pant leg where his knees had bent only a few moments before.

Colin had a subtle teaching manner, a commanding presence that kept all eyes glued to him. He had the gentle touch of a Southern accent that wrapped the perfectly selected phrases like soft butter warming his words before he fed them to us. He taught a message about Mary and Martha, two sisters who served Christ—one with her works and one with her heart.

"We can so intellectualize our faith until we feel as though our mission is that of a good-works club," he said. "But until we find that intimacy with him, that quiet place of uninterrupted passion and communion, we will never know him, but only about him. The travesty is in only knowing about him. For then we can convince our dry, parched souls that he is our friend, when instead, our relationship with him is no deeper than that of a once-met acquaintance. Compare an ocean to a rain puddle and you will find juxtaposed the depth of these two sisters' commitments to their Lord, and the vast chasm between them."

Ruth pressed a soft handkerchief into my hand. I dabbed my eyes. The pollen is unbearable this time of year.

In spite of the crowded lobby in the Mid-Town Café, Ruth led us past all of the waiting groups to the rear of the restaurant and out into a screened-in patio. A girl in white shorts and a knit top that revealed her tanned stomach chatted with Colin. She was the hostess. He patted her shoulder and called her by her first name. The scantily clad hostess guided us to a table that overlooked a dock on the lake.

"How's this?" Her gum popped in time to the eighties rock vibrating through the sound system.

"Perfect," said Ruth.

The Arnett children clambered for a seat near the window while the hostess placed coloring menus in front of each child.

Large sailing masts rose up, white canvasses that spread a table for colored red banners and flags that showed off family crests. Girls in bikini tops and shorts sunbathed on the yacht decks.

"The people fortunate enough to live on the lake like to drive their boats right up to this dock and lunch here," said Colin.

"Dressed like that?" I said. He and Ruth exchanged a glance.

"I live near the beach. We have the tourists who pop into the restaurants dressed as-is. But not in church. It seems disrespectful to come to church dressed like you're going to a clambake." I remembered young girls dressed exactly like this hostess—a sea of long, bare legs milling outside in the lobby of his church. "How do you handle that?"

"We can't clean them up first, make them look like us, and then lead them to the Lord. If we do that, we negate the entire grace message. Jesus showed the seeking heart love and acceptance and then told them to go and sin no more. We have to trust God to complete his work inside of them. That is why we have small group studies, to help them on their journey."

"March, here's your menu," said Ruth. "Share an appetizer with me. The potato skins are especially good."

Colin had been especially chummy with the young hostess, probably one of those methods to establish a relationship with her. I tried to imagine Phyllis Murray's reaction if I led Miss Tanned Stomach up our church aisle. "Let's get the potato skins, Ruth. What else is good?" I said.

She recommended several choices.

"Ruth, you order for me, please. I'd like to show March the dock," said Colin.

Ruth quelled the children's protests and their tinny pleas to accompany their father.

Colin walked toward the exit to the dock as though he knew I would follow.

"I guess order for me too, then," I said.

Colin waited against a rail atop a sort of bridge that led out to where the boat owners tied up their crafts. A school of two-foot-long carp, speckled orange and brown, shimmied beneath the dock to the other side where children tossed fish pellets into the water. The fish competed aggressively with the Canada geese that floated on the warm lake water. Colin dropped twenty-five cents into a coin-operated fish food dispenser and funneled the pellets into my hands. I managed to draw the attention of an otherwise lethargic catfish.

"I'm sorry we had to leave your church social so abruptly. You all had worked so hard to lay out such a nice meal for us." Colin took a few pellets out of my hand and dropped them onto the surface of the water.

"No, please. You had more important matters to attend to."

"Jonathan Henshaw helped me start this church. If the Lord had not sent him along, I might have given up at the starting gate."

That would be a rare sight, I thought.

"Eva and I tried to start Church on the Lake in a motel meeting room. Our first four weeks, not a soul showed up. Finally, Jonathan and his wife just walked in one day. He encouraged me and prayed for me continuously. He found us a better location. Just when we would be down to our last penny, he would throw another check in the offering plate and it would be just enough to pay the expenses. He and Martha were older than us. I know they had to grow accustomed to our young ways, but they helped us build the mature core we needed."

"Early on, my dad and mother experienced the same struggles. I suppose that's one of the zillions of things you and Dad have in common. I sometimes wonder if the folks who wander in and out of churches every Sunday ever stop to think that their privileges were paid by another's sacrifice?"

"Willingly paid. I spoke with your father this morning. Sounds like he's having a relaxing morning with Mason. And Hercules. Charlotte speaks of your dog as though he were human."

"Did he mention anything else?"

"Your father? He asked about you. I had to tell him I left you to eat alone. I'm sorry about the no-show last night. It was nice of you to offer dinner out. It would have been nice for a change."

I dropped the remaining pellets into the lake water. They separated and floated away, uneaten.

Charlotte wandered up to the door of the patio to watch us converse. She pressed her most delicate hand against the screen of the patio as though it would give her a better view of us.

I waved at her. "You have such a way with your children. Between you and Ruth, it's as though their mother's death has left no ill effect."

"Children tend to minimize grief. Then one day, when they are older, say in their teens, something small, like an aroma of perfume or a face that reminds them of their lost family member, will surface. They experience a delayed grief. But I've found Charlotte several times out in Eva's rose garden collecting fallen rose petals and grieving over her mother."

"And what about you?" I remembered the soft curve of his posture bent over a kneeling bench.

"You, of all people, must know," he said.

"I have a troubled sort of grief."

"There is another kind?"

"Joe's death was questionable."

"I guess your father has spared me such things."

"Joe's family helped him obtain his law degree, kept him in law school. I never fully understood all of his struggles until later. He started drinking. And confessing when he drank."

His interest in what I had to say softened his eyes. "You don't believe the accident story, then?"

"Honestly, I never know what I believe. Only what I want to believe for Mason's sake."

"Mason needs a positive image of his father worse than he needs the truth, then?"

I was not sure how he had backed me into this time of confession. I kept my answers short. "It's second best when I don't know the truth."

"Joe's family believes it was an accident, I guess."

I nodded. The carp appeared out of nowhere and sucked my fish pellets into their mouths like scaly vacuums skimming along the pollen-coated surface.

"Ruth is under the impression that you came here for a purpose other than a food critic's assignment."

I kept watching the carp, weighing whether or not to continue. "It wasn't an excuse, if that's what you mean. I take freelance assignments from time to time from Brady Gallagher. He's the travel editor for the *Charlotte Observer*. When I attended the University of North Carolina at Chapel Hill, he and I worked together on the campus paper. We've stayed in touch over the years. He's a good friend. We've seen one another through bad marriages." I had never said "bad marriages" aloud until now. Not in reference to my own, at any rate. This man was better than my father at digging all the rocks out of my ledges.

Colin humanely allowed the comment to pass.

The sun warmed the tops of my forearms and I felt them reddening although they appeared white as porcelain in the incandescent sunlight.

"You were here strictly here on business then. I do like that about you. You tend to business without getting so sidetracked." His whole face brightened, like he had found something about me he really liked.

I knew that Ruth must have had her fair share of corralling four children alone inside a restaurant, but his words calmed me and left me wanting to hear him speak again.

"You have to leave today, Ruth said."

"Dad needs me." I sounded like a recording I had played so many times, the tape frayed.

Colin never blurted out anything, but formed every word deliberately. "You aren't upset that I didn't accept your church's pastorate? I suppose I know the answer to that question. Strike that comment altogether."

"I'm sorry you didn't accept it. I believed it was my fault that you turned them down. But now I can see why you would never leave Church on the Lake. You belong to these people. Candle Cove Presbyterian was lucky to have someone of your caliber come and speak, let alone consider us as your future church. We are small-minded people, Colin, and I don't mean that to sound so critical. If it is, then I criticize myself with the rest of them. You are vision-minded. When you started Church on the Lake, you started with nothing. But you built the church with this vision of yours in mind. Your people grew with that vision. Just look at us, so ingrained in the past that any hint of change seems like a sacrilege. We sing from books that look like Bibles. So to remove them to free up minds for worship is like removing a sacred emblem of the past."

"I can make a recommendation. A man I've met on several occasions. Solid and likable. Someone a little less turbulent than me."

"You aren't turbulent. Inventive and turbulent are two different things entirely."

"He's a little older than me. Seminary trained and hymnal ingrained."

I dusted the fish-food particles from my palms.

"We better get back to Ruth and the kids," he said.

Now all four Arnett-shaped faces peered from the screened-in patio.

"You're certain you didn't want to speak to me about something? Eva used to tell me all the time I plowed ahead like a steamroller. I hope I come across as agreeable. That is my intent."

We exchanged smiles.

I felt more relaxed. "More than you know, Colin." I refused to expose my own steamroller nature a second time.

"Thanks for calling me Colin."

Colin delivered the children back home, certain that Rachel and Luke needed an afternoon nap. Ruth waited while I changed into traveling clothes inside the church's ladies room. She hugged me in typical Ruth fashion.

That is when I saw the diary tucked beneath a peanut bag on the front passenger seat. I retrieved it and handed it to her. "I almost forgot, Ruth. Colin left this in the cottage."

"He's torn up the house looking for it. He'll be happy to see it. I'll have to resist the temptation not to peek. Diaries are such a lure, aren't they?"

My smile felt wooden, but it was the best I could do. "Thank you for a wonderful lunch, Ruth. Maybe we can get together again sometime."

"I would not be surprised. Better run."

My telephone rang. Brady called to see how the meal at LaVecchia's turned out.

"A pleasing presentation with a surprise hint of cinnamon in the salmon coating."

"Not the food. Did you wrangle the minister? You know, did you have your way with him?"

"Brady, it wasn't like that at all. Colin Arnett is not about to leave a church he's sweated into being. My father had a brief mental lapse and that is all this crazy scheme amounted to. Colin Arnett is not going to leave here and move to Candle Cove."

"You didn't ask him. I can tell."

"I'm not going to ask him. He lives here in happiness with the ghost of his wife literally entombed in the wallpaper and landscaping."

"That troubles you more than anything, I'll bet."

Did it? "What if it does?"

"After all this time, March is smitten."

"Not smitten at all, Brady. Don't jump to conclusions. I'm tired. Don't make me say something I don't mean. I have this long drive ahead of me."

"Come stay at my place. You could get some shuteye and drive home early in the morning. In my guest room, of course. Everything above board, I promise."

"I'm ready for the solitude, if you catch my drift. I crave aloneness, Brady. Maybe that's why I'm a writer. I want an early start, before dark."

"It's almost three. Did you know that church has been over for hours in most places? Doesn't seem like an early start was in the plan." He was still implying things not because he believed them but possibly because he might have the slightest hint of hope that I would deny them altogether.

"I joined the Arnetts for lunch."

"This Colin Arnett, he invited you to lunch?"

"Only in a manner of speaking. Through his sister, Ruth, really."

"Something's in the air, March. I think you should have given this Arnett fellow more encouragement. Another invitation, perhaps, to visit your little church again."

"It's between him and my father. I have to get out of all of this church business. It's not my problem anymore. How I get myself all caught up in Dad's affairs, I'll never know."

"It's the Norville way."

"Have I ever said that?"

"You be safe."

"Thanks for the work, Brady."

He hung up.

The security guard circled the church parking lot in a squad car and watched me for a moment. Figuring I posed no immediate threat, I suppose, he disappeared to the other side of the church parking lot. Except for a few teacher-training classes and a gathering of youths, the church would remain quiet. Colin had never initiated the traditional evening service, another reason he would not fit into my father's provincial oxfords at Candle Cove Presbyterian.

A group of teenagers squealed past, scraped the curb with their tires, and then parked at a slant in a parking place. A youth leader dressed in shorts stepped out from the building and waved them all inside. One of them carried a pouch of drumsticks. They whooped and followed him into the building and disappeared. The lights illuminated the windows one at a time all along their path.

I sank into the quiet leather of the Mustang and turned on a classical station. Some disc jockey played Beethoven softly, a quiet prayer between artist and maker.

Road trips offer the best time to pray. God listened to me complain quietly. He is always good at listening, even when I am not exactly where he wants me. But when you don't know exactly where you are supposed to be, the difficulty is offering him a silent elongated moment to fill you in on the details. His plans are never what you expect.

Eleven

I CANNOT EXPLAIN WHY THE NORVILLE HOUSE, A bungalow that roared with femininity, potted geraniums and impatiens, a place that existed for a lover of both Maker and his earth, now embodied only half its soul. It is as though a house knows and understands loss and mourns it with a cavernous ache. The front porch had grayed a lamentable shade of pewter and anticipated never again the pad of Julia Norville's canvas-topped soles upon its weathered boards at the evening hour. She never believed in ghosts, so it took an act of my will to imagine her final momentary garden vigil before nightfall, the manner in which she surveyed her fulsome, triangle-shaped acre with a gardener's approval. I counted three cars, one parked along the curbless road my mother once complained lacked definition, and the other two parked side by side along the curving driveway that disappeared behind the bungalow.

I left all of my things in the Mustang except a crinkled brown paper bag, a bakery bag I hefted beneath one arm. Before the drive home, I'd run in at a grocery store bakery at the Cornelius end of Lake Norman and purchased a half-dozen French pastries.

A mahogany cane occupied the end table in the corner of Dad's living room, a reminder of the surgery and the new, solemn change upon his life. The doctor had borrowed veins from Dad's leg for the bypass, and the incisions left Dad hobbling around, unbearably sore, and unable to drive for three weeks. I heard the quiet intercourse between Dad and Mason in the small downstairs room, the old guest room into which Dinah and I had moved Dad's things before I left.

"Anyone home?" I yelled. "I'm back with the goods."

"Mom!" Mason hopped out into the living room missing a shoe. He wore a faded yellow shirt, no socks, and a Tar Heels cap turned backwards on his head.

Gloria slid out behind Mason holding a comb. "I found this under the bed." She held a thermometer in her other hand between her fingers like an orchestra baton.

"Dinah must have called," I said to Gloria. "I've never known you to play nursemaid."

"Her girls are at their dad's and she had to pick them up tonight. She slept over last night, though. I think Pastor Norville believes no one can take care of him except his darling daughter. Bandage check is done, and your father is so cranky about his chest dressing. Doesn't want me to touch anything, so I'll leave all that to Miss Ellie. I cleaned out the bathroom sink and the john, needless to say, in spite of his complaining."

Mason used his arms to lift himself up utilizing Mother's kitchen tabletop. "We haven't even combed our hair, and we've watched at least six videos and two old movies on TV—they stunk, but the videos were good. Grandpa and I have so much food in the refrigerator, you won't believe." Mason sidled up next to me to whisper, "I found out I hate John Wayne."

Phyllis Murray stirred a pot of missionary stew. "The meal's all done. Nothing too spicy, but everything more than filling."

"That nurse you got for Grandpa makes him take his pills," said Mason.

"Ellie." I set a few extra plates around the kitchen table.

"That's her. She's got bad breath and one gray tooth."

Dad called out. He sounded relieved to hear my voice.

"Don't set a place for me," Gloria whispered. "Phil made a pasta dinner for us tonight and besides, I think your father's had enough company for the day. The good reverend is a little on the cranky end of the continuum." She held open the creaky front door and allowed Phyllis to hurry past.

"If you've never tried them, I brought home six of those tube-looking pastries filled with cream—I forgot what they're called—you have to try at least one."

"Don't even let me see one." Gloria held the bag to her nose. "Too divine. Better hide them from your dad, or did you forget about his appetite for breaking the dietary rules? Nurse Ellie left a list of your dad's marching orders, when the next pill is due, and all of that. She told him he could have angel food cake when he badgered her about his sweets list. Does that sound right? Oh, and your pastor friend, Arnett, left a message on the answering machine."

"A message for me?"

"No, for your father." Gloria poised her face as she often did when she treaded softly—her skin erased of lines and her eyelids half-closed. "If you have anything to tell me about, you know, the Arnett guy coming to take your dad's place, well, it can wait if you're too tired. Or maybe it's too sensitive to discuss right at this moment. If so, I understand completely."

"No news. The trip was a water haul." The fact that Colin called surprised me.

"Guess I'll go. See you later. Mason, be sure you put to use that comb I found."

Out in the street, Phyllis beeped delicately on her horn and pulled away.

"See you in the morning, unless you need to stay home with your dad," said Gloria through a crack in the door. The neighbor's outside light came on.

"I'll be in. Be certain Avery knows he has doughnut duty in the morning."

Dad yelled out again.

"See you at seven-thirty, then." Gloria lit down the front-porch steps. Her heels never touched the concrete.

The flour canister, devoid of flour for six months, made the best stash for the cream horns or whatever they were that I should have known better than to buy. The entire kitchen smelled of cream cheese and powdered sugar. I fanned the oven door to hide the smell of pastry with the aroma of warmed pita bread.

Dad sat next to the bed in the wingback chair, the one reupholstered by my mother in a feminine featherstitched texture of royal blue and violet. My mother once nurtured a fondness for this room, the first always to point out the flush of early day and hue of warmth upon the sill. Dad sat trapped in the late afternoon shadows of my mother's morning room, a purple afghan over his knees. Several books lay perched on top of the guest bed's blue coverlet, books by Richard Foster, C. S. Lewis, and Dostoyevsky. Three different times he had started reading *The Brothers Karamazov* in the last six years. The book lay closed but with the bookmark moved halfway through the thick mass of pages.

"March, you're home. That nurse is annoying. I'd rather you do the bandages. And let's do keep Gloria at the newspaper office. She's happier in her own surroundings."

Hercules crept from the blue dusk of the darkest side of the room, a whisper of sentry in his gaze. He lowered his head and widened his cola-painted eyes until I could see the red rims, a sorrowful question in his face that asked if I could possibly assume his nervous post. Arnie lifted his prickly chin although he kept his back in the curved shape of Hercules' torso, as though the Golden still lay curled around him, protective and warming his cold Doxie bones.

"Gloria never does this. You're a privileged man."

"She doesn't do it because she's better off with those coffeepot projects. If I had a broken coffeepot, that's when I'd call Gloria."

"Colin Arnett's church is sizable."

Dad pressed his chest pillow against the stitches. "I don't feel human. God, help me to feel human again."

"I couldn't ask him, Dad. You were right. It was a useless trip."

His needle-bruised hand caressed Hercules's crown. "The Arnetts are good people. Can't say I've met a nicer family. So I had a stupid pipe dream. It didn't work and I can move on. I don't always know the ways of the Lord." The next part he said with no degree of delicacy, as though he said it just for me. "Letting go of what I don't know is the hardest part."

"It bothers me that Colin suspected I was there with an ulterior motive."

"I can't imagine him saying that. He would have been right, of course, but he'd never say it."

After playing Colin's words through my mind again, I could not say for certain that he had even implied such a thing.

"I heard Gloria say that he called," said Dad.

"First, then, we'll have a listen to what Pastor Arnett has to say. Phyllis made missionary stew. I'll fix us each a bowl and we can all eat on trays in here together. Mason, you take Hercules and Arnie for their walk and we'll eat right afterward."

Hercules slid around me to beat Mason to the door. Mason appeared small in the wide cavity of the bungalow's entry; boy-denim blue, yellow torn shirt, and hair-thin minutes having ticked by this weekend that ripened him in my absence. He rounded his shoulders before he set off at a dead run, rounded his knobby arm sockets as Joe used to do and, in an instant, filled the doorway with the tactile likeness of his father.

"Missionary stew. Haven't had a good bowl of that since Julia and I stopped at that little place on Ocracoke Island. Missionary stew and Ocracoke fig cake. Can you cook fig cake, March?"

"No fig cake, no missionary stew. I'll be right back, Dad." I left the door open so he could hear Colin's message. Hercules and Mason thundered out onto the grinning porch followed closely by Arnie the yapper. I always called it a grinning porch as a child—the smiling upper landing, the porch-step lower jaw, and the window eyes.

"We should go over your homework," I told him, but Mason would have to hear it later. He was leaping off the porch, followed by Hercules, while Arnie minced down the steps to dodder off behind them.

Colin said so little in his message that I found I listened and heard nothing at all. I replayed it. *"James, Colin, you old dog, you need a rest. I'll call you later about it."*

Dad coughed and then let out a tenuous moan.

"Coming with that missionary stew and angel food cake," I said.

"Angel food cake is for wimps."

"That's what we are, Dad. Wimps." I set his food on a TV tray next to his chair.

The sky darkened. A few stars appeared, the first of the evening's orchestral players to warm up the night sky with the cosmic purple of twilight. Mason returned with the dogs and the faint light of perspiration on his upper lip. He pulled his school satchel from behind the door and ran with it upstairs only to emerge with his face washed of most all of the dirt except the ring around his jaw that made him look like the man in the moon.

We ate the stew and the pita and even the creamy pastries that I never should have bought. After I helped Dad back into the guest bed, I closed his door. Mason headed upstairs with his torn shirt, happy to sleep with me one night in Grandpa's room.

I insisted he shower.

I tapped the small knob of the answering machine to lower the volume. Once more, I listened to Colin's message. He had a pleasing voice that raised no red flags, no dangerous levels of tide that could draw me under except for one small, battered flag that insisted that I had grown happy alone. It waved raggedly above the shipwreck of my heart as I worked maddeningly to keep my life nailed together. March, the happy wreck. My finger hovered above the erase button for a moment. I left the message on my father's recording after a deliberate inspection of my ability to let go. James Norville, a grown man, could decide on his own what to do with the man.

Ellie showed up at six the next morning, just as I pushed Arnie and Hercules through the doorway and out onto the lawn to do their business. She set to work on Dad, first making him stand and then coercing him into taking the first minute steps of the day. I turned my face so that he would not see my lips stretched down the corners of my jaw. The drill sergeant tactics pained him as they pained me.

"Feels like fire shooting from my thigh down to my ankle. This isn't necessary," he said.

Many patients loaned veins from both legs, the doctor had told him, and did he realize his fortunate situation of rehabilitating just the one leg? Reverend James Norville held to the bedpost, his forehead pressed against the womanly shape of the wood, and asked Ellie if they could wait a few days. When she made him take another slow step, I turned away.

Then it hit me—a strategy. I needed to use the same tactics to pull the paper out of the nonprofit bog. I wrote down a note or two between flipping flapjacks and pouring juice. I rarely had epiphanies. I brainstormed some more.

"Mason, you'll never believe this! I made pancakes." I yelled twice up the staircase until I heard the thud of sneakers on carpet. He started down the steps, ran back for his satchel and the lunchbox in desperate need of fumigation, and ran up to me with a red folder full of school work. "Monday folder. Sign please."

I pulled out the "keeper" side first. "Spelling is all right. Mason, you can spell anything; how could you miss 'abbreviate' and then get 'raucous' right?"

"Assessment tests start today. I need a good breakfast and two number two pencils. Sharpened," he said.

"I'll sharpen your pencils if you'll go back and clean that patch behind your ear. You could grow corn." I pulled out two pencils from the satchel and took them out into the garage where Dad had bolted a hand-cranked pencil sharpener to a workbench.

By the time Ellie got Dad to the breakfast table, it was time for Mason and me to leave. Ellie read my face. "Don't you worry about your father, March. Every day he'll get better and better. It takes time, and sometimes it comes by the inches."

Dad massaged the lines in his forehead. "Pick me up some of that good orange juice, will you, March? Gloria bought that pulp-free kind. It tastes like kerosene."

"Ellie, you have plenty of food. Just warm it and he'll eat it." I let Hercules and Arnie back inside. Hercules balanced a ham bone in his mouth, one he must have nursed all weekend; nothing remained of it except the shape of a Stone Age cylinder.

"Bring me a pad and pen, Ellie. I need to make my calls," said Dad.

I heard the nurse sigh.

Mornings were warmer now. Mason leaped from the car before I could pull him up to the dead center of the car line where the mother Nazi insisted we stop each morning. He did not kiss me and had not kissed me in the car line since the second week of school. With his back to me, he yelled "good-bye" and ran to catch up with a young boy I only knew as Tony.

Six cars filled the gravel lot in front of the *Sentinel*. Gloria paced back and forth in front of the door and passed out her signature collated-and-stapled notes to everyone. She waved through the window glass at me and then stepped away to let Lindle open the door for me.

"Here's the lady of leisure back from the big city," said Lindle. He scratched deep inside his ear with his right pinky finger and then vibrated it, as though he tried to soothe one of those exasperating allergy itches.

"I hope you don't mind working late, Lindle. We need every person on deck if we're going to try and outdo the Raleigh *Thrifty Nickel*. They're pitching a big gardening issue to all the retailers." I walked past Lindle and into the middle of Gloria's womb-shaped circle of employees. "Hardware stores, gardening centers, nurseries, even grocery stores are being hit up by that *Thrifty Nickel* sales guy." I snapped my fingers at Lindle. "What's his name?"

"Garth Allen. But I think it's a pseudonym to gain customers," answered Lindle.

"If we're going to match the competition, we have to stay a jump ahead with new ideas." I pulled out my notes and flicked away a dried glob of pancake batter.

All of them stared at me as though I had walked through the door with smallpox.

"Anybody got any new ideas?" Gloria whimpered.

"I'm tired just thinking about it." Shaunda yawned.

I picked up an agenda and started redlining the points Gloria had made that needed a finer edge and then crossed out the discussions that took away from productivity. My mind ticked like a racing stopwatch.

"What are you doing, March?" Gloria whispered.

"Frankly, I don't see the need for discussing why we need a better system for collecting dimes for every cup of coffee. To me, it's like discussing whether or not we need more sugar on the powdered doughnuts." I paid her the respect of whispering it back, although it seemed everyone was privy anyway. I seated myself in the only empty chair.

"No need to be snippity," said Gloria. Her Latino accent took over whenever she was perturbed, making her consonants spit.

"I think a dime a cup is more than reasonable, March," said Lindle.

Everyone agreed except Shaunda who kept checking inside her purse for gum.

"Visibility is everything, people. If we're going to sell more papers, we have to think like the big guys. Expand our market."

Gloria sighed.

Lindle scribbled some notes onto a spiral pad.

"So does this mean we have to pay for the coffee in the old coffee can or do we pay Gloria directly?" Shaunda asked.

"I think the system is fine just the way it is," said Brendan.

"You would," said Wylie. He flicked his brother in the back of the head with a finger-and-thumb maneuver.

Brendan took off his baseball cap and flogged Wylie's thin, anemic-looking arm.

"Guys, can we get serious?" I wanted to flog them myself.

Gloria spoke. "Come on, everybody. March is trying to rally us. Get us pumped up. You know, this reminds me of a movie. There were all these little paperboys trying to make a living, but the big newspaper guys wanted them to work harder, to squeeze more out of their pitiful, starved lives. It's like that. March is trying to stretch us." Gloria ended her speech with a flourish of her hand and gave the floor back to me.

"Thanks, Gloria," I said, miserable.

"Are we going to be big, like a real paper, because if we are, I'm in!" Shaunda radiated ambition.

I recollected less significant Monday meetings. We accomplished more the Monday before Christmas than we did on this day. "Coffee break, everyone."

Brendan and Wylie beat the women to the coffeepot while Shaunda kept saying, "I'm just so confused."

Gloria watched me slink over to my desk chair. "I'll get your coffee. Cardboard on the top just like you like it."

"Wait, don't get me anything, Gloria." I patted the chair next to my desk, the one usually sat in by little old ladies setting up yard-sale ads.

Gloria accommodated me. Her dark brows made crescents above her eyes, as though she could ever hide the concern from her face.

"I'm no good at this, this hard-nosed boss business. The *Sentinel* needs K rations and the lean-mean-fighting-machine bluster and I'm just serving up biscuits and gravy and patting everyone on the head."

"I don't know who told you all that nonsense, but you are good just the way you are. We don't want you to change. What would be the fun of that?" Gloria rested an olive-brown hand on top of mine.

"The bottom line tells me, Gloria. We're not making it. I practically live here and it's not helping. Nothing I do is helping."

Shaunda appeared with a cup of coffee. "This is for you, March. Brendan and Wylie paid for it and said it was their treat." She set the cup in front of me and walked away.

"It takes five years for a new business to see a profit. You told me that once. Why you would start being so hard on yourself now is beyond me," said Gloria.

"Starting over isn't easy, is it?"

"My grandfather, he came to this country and had to start over. He was thirty-five, not much younger than you."

"I've never told you my age."

"Now he owns three restaurants and a dry-cleaning business."

"I know this speech. You got this off of a movie, didn't you?" I stirred a packet of sweetener into my coffee.

"March, you are doing all the right things. Look at all of these people."

I did as she said and stared while the girls pushed the Poe brothers away from the coffee machine.

"You got this many people on payroll, and none of us have missed a paycheck."

Except me, I thought. "I need to apologize to everyone before they quit."

"No one is going to quit. We all love our jobs. We sort of like you. On most days." Gloria kissed me on the right side of my face.

Brendan tried to kiss Wylie, to mimic us, but got slapped.

I thanked Gloria and disappeared into the bathroom. I had to freshen up, put on my better countenance, as my mother once told me, so that I wouldn't look so much the wreck that I really was.

Twelve

DAD AND COLIN CHATTED AT LEAST ONCE A WEEK until Dad had wrangled a commitment from him to come and visit. Dad called to tell me I'd better make the cottage ready for company again. The anticipation in his voice even made me excited.

On the way to school, Mason made me swear that I would pick him up at the first bell. He never said that he wanted to see Charlotte, which would be like saying he wanted to play with a girl. But he made it clear he wanted to be at the cottage as soon as the Arnetts arrived.

Gloria took over the proofreading while I ran to check on Dad. Dad watched old Andy Griffith episodes and held his chest with a pillow when he laughed. Ellie tried to coax him up from the bed to take his walk but he groaned until I could not stand it anymore. She asked me if I wanted to help. As each day passed, the killer instinct inside of me receded exponentially. I could never be a physical therapist, no more than I could make the Poes act their age. I left Ellie to fend for herself.

I listened to the radio as I drove to the cottage. Dinah's daily show was on. She'd invited the high-school home-economics teacher as a visitor. They discussed flan and other things I happened to know that Dinah never cooked. I flipped to a Top 40s station and listened to a male voice crooning about something up on the roof. *Is that Neil Diamond?* I thought. I could not remember, and it annoyed me to no end.

I opened all of the cottage windows to allow in a salt breeze. The aroma of an impending summer filled the musty cottage with fresh airy breezes. Overhead the skies floated lazily like lace doilies on a table of blue. I inspected the tabletops for dust and then bounded upstairs to change out all of the linens. In one corner I saw what looked to be a doll so I scooped it up. She had tiny wings on the back; Charlotte's angel made by her own hands with twine and cardboard. The angel was left against the wall as though in the midst of a teddy-bear tea party. Turning it over, I thought about Charlotte's fascination with angels and realized that she must have deliberated often about heaven when her mind wandered to thoughts of her mother.

Suddenly the cottage looked aged. I must have freeze-framed it some time ago to make it always look as new and fresh as when Mother potted geraniums in all of the window boxes and watered the nodding caladiums along the walk. But walking into the cottage now had the same effect as if I had pulled an old postcard from an attic trunk. The Julia–Norville green had taken on a faded hue. Her pronouncements—in her genteel estimation, therapeutic—were forever embedded in my thoughts, but fading too. I recalled how she once boasted to another mother about the easy A's I made in all of my English courses. She had an approving smile at that moment. I'd frozen it in place.

The phone rang. "Hello, Gloria."

"You remember, I gather, that Tuesdays are all-nighters at the *Sentinel*," she said. I could almost see the dimple of sarcasm.

"I'm almost finished here." The name came to me. "James Taylor." I blurted it out and was met with a wrinkle of silence.

"Who?" she finally responded.

"The guy who sang 'Up on the Roof.' It was James Taylor, wasn't it?"

"That's old stuff. I get all them old guys mixed up. Does this have anything to do with Tuesday nights?"

"Or was it Cat Stevens? No, I'm right. It's James Taylor."

"Is this some sort of new therapy, or have I called the wrong number?"

"A flight of fancy, that's all. Seventy's throwback nostalgia silliness." I ended the conversation in a delicate manner wondering why the gentle music of the past was surfacing along with happier memories. It was like the good stuff popping above the surface after a shipwreck, large barrels filled with expensive commodities and free for the taking. I gathered up the guest linens before I closed up all the cottage windows again, just as the sun moved once more to turn the sky the color of the cottage walls.

Sea gulls squawked at me on the deck as I intruded on their day.

A couple walked along the shoreline while a Labrador retriever, brindled and aging, ran ahead of them. This couple had walked the beach most days since before I sharpened number-two pencils for my father on Sunday morning to leave in the pencil slots in the pews. Two matching candlesticks, they were, two faces glowing from the shoreline in infinite splendor. The sun upon their backs caused their images to shimmer. They appeared to dance in the froth and looked like James and Julia Norville. Although dancing had never been a part of their courtship, it offered a lively image.

I thought about Joe's death, leaned against the deck and tried to remember him as I remembered us on the good days. I drew a frame around us, without the negatives or the reproving way I judged him as I had been taught to disapprove of irresponsible behavior. It was how we Norvilles elicited a positive outcome. It is a strange thing to dialogue with a ghost. But if I say things to Joe in private that I never said in life, I find a grain of completion. I longed for a fine finishing point to us, one not thrust upon me by a man who picked a poor choice of days to sail out on a stormy ocean. I wanted to know, "Joe, why did you go away so quickly and leave me to breathe without you, to be both mother and dad to our boy when you know I am a wreck? You saw me at those club tennis matches pretending to be a woman on top, while earlier I sat out in the parking lot wondering how I fit into the elite mix of the life you wanted for us." I cried my private tears, ones I do not share, even with Mason. Not even with my father. It is a different flavor of pain even compared to my mother's passing. It is a bond of the gold band, the bond of vows.

The couple disappeared behind the curve of shoreline that dissolves into ocean. The shoreline that is ours became nothing but the pulse of the tide, the whisper of laughter from the past. The warm breeze that had filled our sound with a comfortable kiss upon our skin called like a siren, making me long for endless stretches of summer. But with each passing year I had become less and less of who I once was, as though parts of me were carried away by the tide. Earthly summers were never meant to linger eternal any more than the same exact sand pebbles were meant to linger on the shore.

At once, something hard and ancient knocked against my soul a deep, creaking thump against my heart. I looked beyond the deck to where my father once kept the old Ford, the doors locked fast with a rusted padlock, the lock that banged in the wind. The lock that forever entombed my pain. It came to me then. I had kept things locked up for too long.

Gloria, Shaunda, Lindle, the Poes and I had one of those eat-in choke-it-down box lunches from Ruby's. Lindle finalized all the ads while Shaunda polished up her stories. Gloria had all the proofreading completed by two o'clock, which gave me the time to help Lindle position the ads. Half an hour later Gloria shuffled me out the door to pick up Mason from school. Something in Gloria's gaze indicated a deeper motive although I could not always read her as well as she read me.

Mason waited by the curb, his mouth turned up at both corners as distinct as a slice of melon rind. He jumped into the car, his breath seemingly stolen. "I made an A!" He waved a spelling quiz under my nose.

We cheered.

"We're headed for the cottage, right?" he said.

"Nope. Tuesday crunch day."

"Could you drop me by? Are they here?'

"I don't know. No time to see, either. I'll bet your teacher is happy about your spelling grade."

"I'm happy, you're happy. Who cares about her? I want to see the Arnetts."

"Mason, let's go this weekend to Neuse River Days. You know how everyone in New Bern builds those crazy rafts and races them. So funny when one of them falls apart right in the middle of the race. We could go Friday right after I pick you up from school."

"And take the Arnetts?"

I turned on the left signal and headed toward the office.

He constructed a perfectly aimed sentence. "Does that mean we'll be eating at the office again tonight? You know those people who work for you are completely bonkers."

"I can drop you by Grandpa's."

"Or drop me by the cottage. I can fix it up and get it ready for company."

"Done already."

"You don't like him. I can always tell when you don't like someone. It's kind of obvious."

"I don't like who?"

"Pastor Arnett." Mason was digging.

"Must be a problem. Gloria's standing at the door waiting for me."

"Ruth Arnett likes you. She says it all the time, but not in just what she says. I can just tell."

One of us sighed. Or maybe both of us.

"I like her, too. I like Pastor Arnett. I like all of them, but I have a job, Mason. Lindle's getting takeout from Dooley's. Do you want to eat with us or with Grandpa?"

He did not answer.

Right as we walked in, we heard a sort of shrill yelp, like a piglet caught in the gate.

"What's wrong, Shaunda?" I asked.

"It's the waxer. It bit it again!" She spoke of the temperamental machine the galleys of copy are rolled through before they're placed on the layout page. When the gizmo does happen to work, it applies a thin layer of wax that adheres to the layout pages. But when it doesn't—which is most of the time—it globs a thick coat of wax on the entire sheet of copy. "It's ruined!" she exclaimed.

"Did you use the foot pedal?" Lindle asked.

"Of course!" She shrieked again.

Mason settled his book satchel and homework against a desk. I joined Shaunda in the back.

We both stared at the waxy hunk of paper as though we expected it to somehow draw breath and repair itself.

"It would have been ruined anyway," I said.

"I waxed it on the wrong side. Now I have to do it all over again. I hate this job! I hate it!" said Shaunda.

"Shaunda, you say that every Tuesday."

"I do hate it!"

"Has anyone seen my Exacto knife?" Gloria, who never lost a thing, was perpetually territorial about her desk and her tools: her Exacto knife, her rollers, her pica ruler. None of those things could be touched without threat of penalty. Gloria had marked them all with her name. Yet every Tuesday one piece disappeared, then just as mysteriously reappeared the next day.

"Real journalists don't have to do their own layout or fight with a waxer," muttered Shaunda.

"When you are, as you say, a "real journalist," Shaunda, you can hire someone else to do your layout. But for now, just redo the ad, please." I coaxed her back to the computer.

"March, did you return Jerry Brevity's call yesterday?" asked Gloria.

"I did not. Why do you ask?"

"He called again this morning." She said it flatly, as though she brushed crumbs from her fingertips.

"Tell him anything, that it's Tuesday. Say 'crunch day.' That's a power phrase, isn't it?"

"He wants to bring by dinner for everyone." Gloria helped Shaunda guide her story into position.

"If he's paying, I'll have a steak," said Lindle.

"I didn't know what to tell him," said Gloria.

"He's coming, then," I said.

Gloria's brows came together to answer for her in a wordless way while she stared at Shaunda's page.

Mason slapped his forehead.

The phone rang in a sequence of calls. Gloria placed three callers on hold. "Line two's for you. I'll get the others."

I mouthed "Jerry Brevity" to her in the form of a question.

"It's your dad."

The Poes made a chortling noise from the print shop like cowboys too long away from women.

"What's up?" I could hear Dad's breathing on the line.

"March, I'm not sure what I've just done. You know I'm muddled up with all of these pharmaceuticals and it's just got me all in a twinge. Colin Arnett just called and we, or at least, he discussed the *Sparticus* with me."

"Joe's boat? I don't get it."

"I thought he had already discussed the matter with you and it got all tipped over in my mind until I got off the phone. That is, I think I gave him permission to take her out of the garage. The more I think of it, the more I think I really did just that."

"Dad, no one's taken the *Sparticus* out since the accident."

"I thought he was asking to take you out in it, you know, as though he were running it by me."

"Not take her out *and* put her in the water. We don't even know if she's seaworthy."

"You've not heard a word from Colin Arnett about the *Sparticus*, then, I gather?"

"None whatsoever."

He was silent.

"Is he at the cottage now?" It irked me to no measure that Colin would ask Dad about the boat and not me.

"You know he's a good seaman himself. He wouldn't take her out if she weren't good for the trip."

"I'm going there right now."

"You'll be miffed at me, then."

"We'll discuss it later. Let's blame it on your medication for now." I hung up.

Gloria and Shaunda stared up at me.

"So I guess you'll be leaving," said Gloria.

"Can you finish up without me?"

"Problems back at the ranch?" Gloria's smile did not match her glazed-over look.

"Someone's trying to take the *Sparticus* out for a ride."

"Let's call the cops, Mom! Harold and Bobby will cuff them just like they did Yolanda's crooks." Mason looked as though he shifted back and forth waiting to get into the little boy's room.

"Woe to that poor slob," said Shaunda.

"He's not a crook. He's a friend of Dad's. Can you handle the waxer, Shaunda?" I asked.

"I know what I'm doing, I've started all over. It's the pedal that gets stuck. I have the hang of things," said Shaunda.

"And what do we tell Jerry Brevity?" asked Gloria.

"Enjoy dinner," I said.

"I'll set out the china," said Gloria.

Mason leaped out of the car when we arrived at the cottage and beat a path down to the garage.

We found the garage door standing open. Inside, we saw the sandaled intruder who sashayed into my past without so much as a blink or Mother-may-I. He inspected the sail cloth.

"What are you doing? Or should I say, welcome back, and then what are you doing?" I stayed in the doorway until our eyes met.

"March, you're here. I tried to call you at your place, but no answer. Your father gave us the thumbs-up, though. I found your family's boat. Nice vessel. Really nice. How long has your father had her?"

"I stored the boat here. After Joe's accident. It is my boat, that is, it was Joe's."

We stared for the space of time that lapses between ocean waves.

"March, I apologize. Here I am scrambling all over your sacred ground. Had I any idea, I would have never called in the first place."

"I don't think the *Sparticus* is seaworthy."

"She looks fit," said Colin.

"We could put her in the water. See what happens," said Mason.

I thought that by touching Mason's shoulder he would read my thoughts. Instead he looked at Colin, hopeful.

"We could wet her, but not unless your mother approves, my man."

"Please," said Mason.

"I don't think it's safe," I said.

Colin's girls appeared.

"We changed into our swimsuits, Daddy. Ready for a boat ride," said Charlotte.

If I didn't give in, I'd be a louse in Mason's eyes and the Arnett children's to boot. "I guess it's all right."

The way we had left the vessel lodged between two stacks of tires, Colin had to drag her out with his car hitch at an angle.

Colin stuck his head out the window and watched Mason's gestures. "Turn the wheel right," said Mason.

Colin had to pull up and back several times before hauling her out completely. He jumped out and crawled beneath the trailer to inspect the hull. He rubbed the surface from stern to aft with the wide expanse of his hands as though he rubbed down a wet mare. Along one long side, he examined a bruised-looking scratch. "Here's some damage. But it isn't deep," he said.

"Actually we did that putting her away. The boat went over in a storm. Joe didn't have on a life jacket. It was a weird accident. Joe went over, but the boat survived."

Colin went over the bruised scratch with a chamois. "Not bad at all. But I'll take her out by myself the first time."

"I think I should go with you," said Mason.

Charlotte looked disappointed.

"Maybe later. Mason, I'll come back for you if she behaves herself." Colin ran his fingers across Mason's straight row of bangs.

If Colin agitated him, Mason hid it well.

Colin hitched up the *Sparticus* and drove her out to the boat slip. We watched the vessel plop down into the water and slide into place as though it pleased her to be out of the dungeon. He caught my eyes lingering over the boat as though I willed it to sink.

"This is a bad idea," he said. "Isn't it?"

"You've already wet the hull. Go ahead and take her around the cove. If you sink, we'll call the Coast Guard."

We watched him push away and troll past the buoys. The sail snapped and then furled. Colin looked like cast bronze leaning out from the mast, following the direction of the masthead as it turned with his body.

"My daddy knows what he's doing," said Charlotte.

"We have a boat too," said Troy.

"See, Mom. It's working and not sinking," said Mason.

"I could have done it. I can sail, too," said Troy.

"No, you're not, Troy. You're not big enough," said Charlotte.

Her words stirred a brother's spite and it glowed from the rims of his basil-green eyes.

Colin disappeared around the curve of the shore, past the neighbor cottage. The neighbors waved at him from shore. He sailed around the cove and then turned back toward us.

I will always remember the painful "firsts" after Joe's death. The first time I went alone to the Lighthouse Java Mill. The first trip to the mall Christmas shopping without him. With every "first" came a new bath of tears that plunged me back into my cave to hide from everyone I knew and to hide my tears from Mason. To see the *Sparticus* floating again without Joe's guidance sent me teetering.

As the boat lapped toward us, I stood on the dock and from behind me felt Mason's arms go around my waist. I remember when Joe passed from us, Mason could hug me right around my hips. I turned and looked down at him, then bent near him, but not so far this time as in the past. He kissed my face.

"Are you all right?" I asked.

He nodded as though by trying to speak his lower lip might quiver or those strong male feelings he worked so hard to hold inside might tumble out.

"We'll put her up. Maybe this isn't the right time," I said.

"No, I want this, Mom. I want to ride in the *Sparticus* again and feel the wind, like I might feel Dad again."

"You are the wise one. If you want Pastor Arnett to take you out, then I think you should go," I said. I turned away from the lapping ocean.

"Dad taught me to sail. I know how, too," he said it to me but looked at Troy.

Colin returned to the dock and all of the children spilled into the boat. Mason passed out the life jackets and helped the boys strap on the vests.

Colin held out his hand to me.

"Not this time," I said.

Mason looked at Colin and then at me.

"I have to get back to the office. Today's a long day for the *Sentinel*," I said.

"Maybe next time then." Colin gave me a sort of hokey salute. "Mason can stay with us for a bit, I hope?"

"I'll come by for him later." I gave a little tilt of the head at Mason, a signal that said that everything was all right between us.

Joe's boy took charge of the vessel, telling the Arnett brood where to sit and how to act. I realized I had taken too long to bring the *Sparticus* out into the daylight again. But the farther I moved from the date of the accident, the more I wanted to deny time to anything that brought back its memory. Mason pulled out the captain's hat, the one Joe had worn the day we christened the boat. He tipped it back so the bill wouldn't hide his eyes.

"Careful now," I said.

They sailed away. For every wave that lifted them up and then down, the children squealed like baby seals. The sea played gently against the hull and toyed with the vessel like a father bouncing a child on his knee. With every lap of water that kissed the hull, I felt the beat of my own heart. I turned away, not wanting Mason to see my tears. Not because I wanted him to think I was burly, a bastion of motherhood, but because lately we had shared too many tears. When I cried he looked as though he were to blame. I loved him too much to allow my inherited cloak of guilt to fall upon his small boy shoulders. I wanted us to share something else instead. A launching of our hearts, a putting to sea the things of the past.

He waved from the bay until he became a glistening twinkle in a mother's eye.

Thirteen

DINAH IS THE QUEEN OF SPONTANEITY. SHE CALLED with her latest epiphany, a clambake she would host at the cottage on the very evening the *Sparticus* had been planted back in the sea.

"This is rather abrupt," I said.

"You know me."

"So your first location didn't pan out."

"I would have had to get permits, and you know how I despise red tape. At your cottage we have all those cooking pots of your mother's, which is as close to a clambake as Candle Cove gets anyway."

I tried to think like Dinah. "You need a guinea pig. I understand."

"Guests. I just need guests, and you have plenty. I'll bring lanterns, lots of paper lanterns and Frankie Avalon music. If I do this fifties style, then I could really pull in some new listeners. You know how you're always talking about spark and drama. This could send me into syndication. I'll cook clams, lobsters—hot-and-spicy red potatoes and corn cobettes. Lots of French bread."

"Heavenly. I'll bring the watermelon," I said.

"Plus homemade ice cream. I'll add that to the list. The girls can pull the ice cream maker out of the attic."

"You always pull a party out of the hat just when I need it," I said.

"You'll help me hang the lanterns then?"

I could see Gloria's half-guarded stare. "Can't. We're right on top of pub day. But Ruth can help. I'll join you both as soon as I can get away."

Ruth and Dinah spent the rest of the afternoon hanging Dinah's lanterns. Mason and I joined them at the end of the workday. Ruth helped Dinah dig out Mom's old steamer pot. I called Dad and promised to bring him a plate of Dinah's delectables if he promised to behave for Ellie. He had few questions as though he crept cautiously around the *Sparticus* issue. I decided to let him simmer in the brew of his own making for a while. Before hanging up, he made certain I had properly invited the Arnetts to Dinah's little shindig—as though we would party under their Lake Norman noses and toss protocol to the sea.

Before the sun set above the ocean, Ruth and I set the steam pot to boiling and shucked corn on the deck. Charlotte joined us. She cradled the corn next to her with her small hand while her good hand pulled down the husks. After we made a good pile of husks, Charlotte tore them into shreds and braided them. She formed a basket the size of an apple with a miniature handle.

Dinah arrived with her station wagon loaded with baskets of food, the ice cream freezer, and the twins. Colin, Mason, and Troy carted her things to the picnic table while the twins joined Charlotte on the deck. Troy chased Hercules out onto the beach. Mason soon followed. Charlotte continued weaving the husks, mesmerizing Dinah's girls with her magic.

"You won't even guess what I made, not in a million," said Dinah.

We all stared blankly.

"Ginger ale. Have you ever known anyone who could make homemade ginger ale? Not too many people, I'll bet." She wielded the bottle with a kitchen towel as though she held out fine wine.

Charlotte cheered, nakedly impressed, and then ran to flash her handmade wares at Dinah.

I pondered the small cost of a bottle of ginger ale against a person's time, but I kept it to myself.

Ruth broke up the corn, washed it, and placed it all in a large bowl. "The corn and potatoes are ready. Tell us what to do, Dinah. We are your clay."

"First place the potatoes in the steamer, put on a good tight-fitting lid. I'll let you know when to add the corn. Someone needs to help me wash these clams. They still have some sand in them. Then we'll clean the lobsters."

"They're alive!" Charlotte stared, squeamish, and twisted her face into a grimace.

Dinah held up a large container with the lobsters inside.

"I can't eat them. They look like huge bugs," said Charlotte.

"I'll eat yours," said Colin.

That satisfied her.

Ruth followed Dinah back into the kitchen. They set aside the corn and started to work on the clams.

"We have some table covers around here somewhere," I said. I ran upstairs and rummaged around the linen closet. I felt my heel tap against something. It was Charlotte's angel. I picked it up and bounded downstairs with tablecloths and the doll in my arms.

"You found her. I left her for you," said Charlotte.

"Thank you kindly, madam." I lifted the doll by the string attached to its back. It swung below my waist, a pendulum.

Dinah reappeared with a large bowl of clams. Ruth brought the lobster and helped Dinah find a nearby table.

I disappeared into the kitchen to make sweet tea for any person with no affinity for ginger ale.

Colin followed. "I visited your father this afternoon. He's on the mend."

"He's complaining more. He's better. Trying to rule the world from his bed, though. Ellie wants him to walk around more, but it makes him cross."

"I could take him some of this good food," he said.

"No need. I have to go by his place on the way home."

"Quick! Time to add the corn." Dinah stuck her head inside.

"Should we place the bread in the oven?" asked Ruth.

Colin passed them the corn while I dipped a few more slices of bread into the garlic butter.

Charlotte helped me toss the tablecloths over the wooden tables. She placed plastic plates and flatware along the table edge and spaced each place setting so equally apart, it gave the tabletop a measured appearance. We watched in awe while Dinah added the clams and lobsters to the boiling mix.

"What do you ladies do for fun in the winter?" asked Colin.

"Cook indoors?" Dinah shrugged.

"Sounds like church people," said Colin.

We joined hands around the table while Colin offered thanks. Dinah stepped away from the scene and used the boiling pot as her excuse to turn her back to us. After Colin's "amen," she dished up the lobster and clams like a New England chef. All of us salivated. Dinah set hot pepper sauces and seasonings around the tables. Then she pulled out a large container of her own coleslaw and set it at the end. "It's buffet. Dig in," she said.

Frankie Avalon crooned "Venus."

Dinah and Colin talked sports. She told him about the girls' athletic prowess, but not in a disparaging way as she did around the other team moms who all had sons. I saw a pride in her eyes, and felt amazed at Colin's adeptness at drawing her out.

"So you once lived in Maine?" he asked her.

Dinah typically took longer to settle down around new people. But Colin had a way with her. He invited to her attend the midweek service with the girls.

I knew she would decline.

"That's kind of you to ask," she said.

"Why don't you come?" he asked again, as though he asked her for the salt and pepper.

I turned away and pretended to check on my ten-year-old.

"Maybe I'll come," she said.

My lashes batted several times. I reached for the margarine without looking up at either of them. I avoided staring at her open-mouthed. She always had some humorous way of avoiding my invitations to darken the door of the church. If I looked at her even once, she would jinx the moment. Of that, I felt certain.

"All right, I will come," she finally said.

I saw Mason elbow one of the twins.

"What's wrong with that?" She looked straight at me.

I did not know whether to feel grateful or resentful that Colin had coaxed her into the portals of our sanctimonious halls with such ease. Dinah and Ruth set to work to collect the dishes and pass warm cloths to the children to wash their hands and faces.

I stood and offered to take the dishes from Ruth so she could focus on the dirty faces. Colin followed me into the kitchen. Before I could pull the watermelon from the refrigerator, Colin knelt, and brought it out as though it were the size of a baseball. He found a knife and sliced it open.

"It's best if you slice it up into the smaller pieces. Not my gift," he said.

"Colin, I have asked Dinah to church so many times but she's never wanted to hear such things."

"Eternity is written on the heart of every man."

"Not Dinah's. Or if it is, she hasn't broken the code. We'll see tomorrow night if she really comes."

"But you want her to come, March, don't you?"

"Of course I do. I'm just doubtful. That's all I'm saying."

"After we pass these out to the kids, you want to take a walk on the beach?" he asked.

"You don't like watermelon?" I asked.

"I just need a walk."

After we distributed the sliced melon, he placed a hand on my shoulder and gave me an odd sort of nod.

At once Dinah, Ruth, Charlotte, and Mason looked up at us.

I followed him off the deck like Hercules did when he galloped after Mason. Colin removed his sandals so that he could walk closer to water. He allowed the water to lap over his feet, sloshing through it, his pants rolled up to his knees. He walked several paces ahead of me, enough to cause me to have to speed up to catch up with him. I felt awkward, aware of at least a dozen eyes on my back. I refused to look back at them.

A shrimp boat made a serpentine path not many miles out. The crew lifted the nets as they prepared to bring it in for the day. Colin watched the vessel out in the harbor. He turned to me and said, "I made a mistake today. It haunts me. Once you told me that the *Sparticus* was Joe's boat, the one that took his life, I should have turned it all around. For you, especially. I get trapped within my own zeal sometimes."

"It happened too far away from shore. It's not as though I have to pass the same corner every day where the accident happened. But seeing the *Sparticus* again, I suppose it had the same effect as passing the dreaded corner. It is something I've been needing to do. Mason needed today to happen."

He apologized again.

"Colin, you shouldn't apologize. When I saw Mason's face as he climbed aboard, I knew that it was right. I've been selfish about my grief, as though it belonged only to me. Mason has to deal with Joe's death in his way, his boy way. I've never been adept at sharing pain. I say I'm doing that to protect him."

Colin hurled a shell into the ocean. It skipped once before the ocean swallowed it.

"Do you find that you play mind games with yourself?" I asked.

"I do, when missing Eva is unbearable." he said.

"I've blamed myself a lot. This is all different from what you go through, I realize, since we're facing different issues and all. I felt blind to what was going on inside of Joe. He wasn't one to tell me, you know, man thoughts."

"Ha-ha! What are man thoughts?"

"That's what I call them. Man thoughts. Men keep the thoughts to themselves that drag the life out of them, only it poisons their souls like a tainted well."

"This afternoon, when I looked at you looking at that boat, I replayed the times I used to pass by the hospital and finally started driving different routes just to not have to look at that place anymore. Then I would forget and drive past and weep, until the day I drove past and the pain just stayed inside without a tear to shed. Which is worse—well, I haven't decided. I don't know what I imagined about your husband's boat. Maybe I thought it was on the ocean floor and you were safe from seeing it." He processed that thought. "That sounded lame."

"You turned the day into a celebration. What's wrong with that? Do you know how long it's been since we opened the garage door and drove the pain away from the cottage and allowed ourselves to celebrate the world of the living again? Consider what you did today as a gift to my son. We conquered—something."

"It felt good. I like to see Mason smile. I like to see you smile."

"How were the nights for you? What I mean is, when the day was over and everything was quiet, and all of the well-wishers disappeared, were the nights hard?" I asked.

"Evil. Dark, although it got better to get through the evenings. Less dread as time passed. How about you?"

I remembered his diary. "It's difficult to put it into words, how when the night comes the pain flounces in and sits on your chest, no smaller than an elephant. Nights were the worst time to me."

He watched the lapping waves, soundless while the ocean resonated a song for eventide, and then said, "Oh, hateful night. I wrote about it."

"You are such poet at heart, Colin." I pretended to look far up the shoreline. If I looked at him directly, he would know for certain I had read his secret writings. The wind blew through his hair and made the sleeves of his chambray shirt billow. I didn't know if chambray had a smell, but I swore I could smell Colin's chambray and his man scent in the ocean breeze. It was not my right to do that, but I did it anyway.

"The night comes and you pull it over your head like a hateful blanket. And you lie in your uncomfortable solitude and aloneness while all of the splendor and joy and wonder of life have abandoned you, leaving you with an extra pillow on your bed and no head to lay on it. You want to hide away." Some days I craved the aloneness, but I even craved being alone sometimes when Joe was alive, and that was another reason to feel guilty. I was afraid someone would notice my insanity, my little bouts with neurosis, and turn me in. But I did not tell him that.

"I made the mistake of trying to date. It hadn't been a year since Eva's death. I was trying to fill up the void with another person as though I could fill up an Eva-sized hole in my heart. No one could measure up. I tended to romanticize her." While Colin had painted Eva more lovely, I had mornings when I had to look at Joe's picture until I recognized his face again.

Colin waved at the couple who lived in the next-door cottage.

I waved too and then confessed, "I tried to fill up my void with busyness. Still do. But when the quiet returns, I have to face the pictures and words that filled up that awful day. Over and over I hear that policeman say, 'He didn't make it.'"

"I once thought it was awful to think about Eva's flaws. It made me feel as though I desecrated her holy memory. Then I realized it was her flaws that made me love her."

Colin peeled away two years' worth of guilt off of my plastic façade with that one statement.

"All of it is sacred. Everything she touched."

"Colin, that's it! I know exactly what you mean." I started to remember. "I couldn't empty Joe's trash can and couldn't stop digging through it as though I'd find some part of him in it. Even the litter in his trash basket was sacred to me." It felt good to say that about Joe. Maybe I didn't hate him, just the way he had left me.

"It's better not to play the saint, to remember the bad along with all of the good, because it was the bad times that strengthened you as a couple."

Now he sounded like a pastor again.

We stopped and looked back at Mason and the other children who looked only an inch high in the sand.

"You have no idea how much this has helped me," I said. I felt downright dizzy with relief, baptized by Colin's confessions.

"You know what they're all thinking back there, don't you?" Colin said and I bit my lip into submission to suppress a silly smile. He finished his announcement. "That I've started something between us. They don't understand our mutual pain."

"Colin, no one can understand it but us. I'm glad we took this walk." Until now I had not found as much goodness in the soil of Joe's life as he had in Eva's. Too much of me clung to his flaws. "Sometimes I feel bitter, like I'm going to grow old a bitter old prune."

"Before the accident were you mad at him?"

Maybe a little more confession would lighten the load. "We fought and it was awful. His firm was on the brink of bankruptcy, but he never shared it with me. When he came home from work in a state of unsettling quietness, he would shrug off my questions. That left me mad at him. So much unresolved. Too much revealed after the fact. Then when our two cops showed up to tell me about the accident, I wanted to shout at Joe and then hold him again and tell him we could work anything out if he would just stay around long enough to let the sun come up again.

"Every day after that when the phone rang, more bad news would come and that would compound the pain of his death. But being kept in the dark about his problems was the deepest well of my grief."

I could not share any of this with Colin without feeling sucked back in time. It was my descent into the definitive valley; in that whistling moment when thoughts fly like gulls against the heart, the pain had spilled in, the beating of the tide against our protected cove, the leveling of my soul. The reason I was a wreck.

I found my bearing and continued. "And then there was the problem of his family. His mother, Joan, knew enough about us to take her little digs at me. I didn't handle it as well as I should. She's always implied I caused his death even though she doesn't admit he may have taken his own life." It was as though she had been looking her whole life to find someone to blame for Joe's problems and happily found me. We always had this friction between us, so when he died, what little good we had between us fell apart after the accident. She acted as though I drove Joe out into the storm. "Neither Mason nor I knew Joe had taken the *Sparticus* out that day. He always invited at least Mason. It was the last time he would push me out of his life. But no one could prove he took his own life. That remains the million-dollar question."

"Did the insurance company investigate?"

"They might have but Joe's partner had neglected to pay the premium for several months. No insurance, no investigation. I'm convinced Joe thought Mason and I would have that policy for security, but his partner was in deep trouble too. Seems nobody talked much around the firm about problems."

"I'm sorry. Did he keep a journal?"

"It was always business as usual with Joe."

Colin looked at me, and I felt transparent and fragile, a piece of broken glass washed ashore that he had found and turned over and over to examine. My father as a pastor could always see into my soul, but Colin stripped me of all my armor.

"Shall we go back? The cottage has become a pin dot," he said.

I saw that he was right. "Here comes Hercules." The dog bounded toward us at a maniacal pace. Fast on his tail were the Buckworth twins. They squealed, their fondness for pursuit turning their mouths red. One had a kite, and they looked intent on tying the string to Hercules's tail.

"Dinah has her hands full with those two," said Colin.

"She does well. Dinah has made many friends in the community and established this cooking show out of a small catering business."

"You seem to be close friends."

"We grew up together. Her family moved here from Maine when she was thirteen years old. From that point on, we were like sisters. We're both as much a part of Candle Cove as the sand is the shoreline."

Colin picked up a handful of sand. "You know what is so amazing about this stuff?" He stooped and allowed the water to wash away all but a few translucent particles on the ball of his hand. He held up the granule to what little remained of the sun before the sky closed up its shop. "Who would have thought that God would use such small things to hold back the tide?"

We watched the Buckworths continue on their spree. Mason ran past, one hand brushing against me. He yelled for the girls to leave his dog alone. Colin laughed, and it sounded like rain on cracked ground.

Fourteen

WITH PUB DAY AHEAD OF US, I DRAGGED MYSELF INTO the bathroom as fast as my numb little feet would carry me the next morning, which was Wednesday—pub day, church night, but with a nice little caveat—Colin would be preaching, or as he called it, "teaching."

Before I roused Mason, I examined our sand bottle collection on the small stand in the bathroom. The bottle that had once held three small onyx stones now only held two. It reminded me of the unsaid words between Joe and me and all I had divulged to Colin. Maybe it was just my imagination and I was barking up the wrong tree, but if Mason had removed the third stone from our memory bottle, I might be able to get him to talk about it. If we, Mason and I, were going to be better than his father and me at talking things out, maybe bringing up the memory bottle would help.

I rapped at Mason's door again. "I hope you're up. I made your lunch." I heard the whispery, early groans of just-waking boy. "I want to talk to you," I said.

He invited me into the room, stumbled across the rag rug made by my mother, and breathed out a mumbled question that not even the U.S. Naval Intelligence could decipher.

I stood over his empty bed, baffled at how a tucked-in boy could awaken with his sheets twisted into ropes that barely covered his chunky frame.

"What did I do?" He yawned and balanced his not-yet-awake body against his bookcase.

"You're not in trouble, Mason. It's nothing, really. I know it's early and all. You'll think this is stupid. But do you know what happened to the third stone in our bottle?"

He leaned against his bookcase and backhandedly twirled the propeller on a model plane.

"Am I losing my mind, or did we have three stones in here?"

"Is this a trick question?" he asked.

"So you don't know about the stone? Not that it's a big issue. Let's don't make this a big issue. I'm going somewhere with all of this. Bear with me."

He shrugged and crashed the plane into his coverlet.

"Okay, I'll say it like this. We made this memory bottle in Ocean City. Sand from the beach, right?"

He nodded, but with his head lowered he stared up at me as though I were stupid.

"Then you, not me, dropped three little black stones into the bottle with the sand. One for Mason, you said. One for Daddy and one for Mommy."

"I need to get ready for school, okay?"

"Now, someone removed a stone. Let's say it's the Daddy stone. Would that be right?"

"I guess." He shrugged and took a step toward his closet door.

"It's supposed to be okay or something if we talk about your dad's death. Just like it was all right for you to take a ride in the *Sparticus.*"

He took the bottle from my hand. "A memory bottle was a stupid idea. Daddy even said it was a bad idea."

"I believe he called it 'ambitious.' But it was our idea and therefore good. Just a memory. Nothing more," I said.

"It isn't a good memory anymore." He tossed the bottle into his waste can.

"For me it is." I retrieved it.

"You didn't even want us to take a ride in the *Sparticus*. It made you mad."

"Not mad. Sad and mad are two different things entirely. Everyone deals with grief differently."

"I wanted to get in the boat yesterday. But when you stayed behind, I felt bad."

"You shouldn't, Mason."

"I hate the way I feel sometimes," he said. He lifted the model plane by the body, gently this time, and placed it on his bookcase. Then he dragged out his bag of marbles, held the velvet pouch by the bottom, and shook them out onto the bed. He picked through them until he found a small black onyx stone. He held it out to me. "I couldn't throw it away."

I saw tears form around the rims of his eyes. I cried with him and we allowed the tears. "I knew we could talk about this, Son. It's okay to be mad, I swear it. I get mad too. We don't know whether to toss out all our memories of Daddy or put them on display." I was just as confused about my feelings as Mason, but we sat ourselves down and had the finest of talks. I helped him find socks, and then we fixed his lunch for school and somehow made it before the late bell.

He ran past the Nazi car-line mother and then twirled like a quarterback faking a right, then going for the pass. "Mom, wait!" he shouted and I hit the brake.

My automatic window came down in maternal obedience. "What did you forget, love?"

He yanked open the passenger door and clambered to my side of the car. With his most extravagant embrace, he grabbed my face and sloshed me with the most wonderful and joyous kiss a boy could ever give his mother. "I love you, Mom!" He scrambled out past the bewildered Nazi mother and into the school building founded by his grandfather.

"Did you see that?" I said it to the bewildered Nazi as I grabbed for the Kleenex box.

She waved me on, but managed a smile.

Hal Caudle rang the church bell that evening as he had done on so many Wednesday nights, and many more Sunday mornings, and every New Year's Eve. I remember those New Years when he set a chair beneath the rope of the bell. One by one we children were each allowed to ring the bell. Grace Caudle said it was our way of telling the village "Jesus loves you; Jesus loves you." I always remember her standing beside Hal in navy polyester, the hornet brooch at her breast, and the earrings that matched exactly. I remember the glisten of love in her eyes for Hal. To her and Hal and their friends at the church, tradition was their way of touching God, even if at a safe distance.

Mason and I took our place up front. We heard a breath of whispers around us, but more heightened than usual. The sound seemed to come from the back to the front. That is when I saw Dinah and the girls taking a seat on the back pew for the first time. Dinah caught my eye for a moment and then dug through her purse as if she looked for something lost.

Change comes slowly in Candle Cove. Something as small as seeing a new face in church threw every little planet off its orbit. Cobwebs could form in the window just above where my father stood for so many years, but it was so subtle that it might go unnoticed until the web formed a pattern. There was a crack in the window's wood that now ran from the top of the window frame to the bottom, but since it happened over time no one noticed. I thought about the platform that would not hold my father's notes on this night or the old worn Bible, but the notes of a younger man. All at once, every particle in the building seemed to deteriorate in front of me, shifting as slowly as the orbit of the earth. I felt as though I deteriorated, slowly dissolving into the pew, but what was incremental had become exponential. I complained about my bad feet, my receding gums, and the twinges in my right shoulder. But I accepted it as a natural part of life.

The old air conditioner revived and blew the cobwebs, but not away.

It reminded me of the verse in the scriptures that says that even though outwardly we are wasting away, yet inwardly we are being renewed day by day. I wondered if anyone around me was aware of the renewal thing or just going for the wasting away aspect of it. Or if the deterioration had become so commonplace perhaps the thought of inward change was more unsettling than the idea of wasting away.

Hal and Grace dispensed with the ringing of the bell and marched up the aisle with Bill and Irene Simmons and the Michaels. They paraded up the aisle, penguins that never noticed the crack in the window, the cobwebs, or my bad feet. They did not see the age spots that appeared upon the hands of the bell ringers. Their expectations were small—that this night would mirror the church services of Wednesdays past.

Grace placed her handbag next to Lorraine Bedinsky and said, "I don't like the new gardener they hired to clip the church hedges. He has a bleary-eyed look about him."

"I'm glad you brought it up. I wasn't going to say anything," said Lorraine.

"He doesn't look old enough to be trimming the church hedges. That's the long and short of it," said Hal.

"How old does he have to be?" asked Lorraine.

"Old enough to reach." Hal adjusted his wallet in his back pocket. Then he stretched his hands over his head and made a clipping motion with his hands.

The women laughed.

All of them set to talking about the next church social and egg salad.

I felt as though I had been here before, as if aliens had picked me up and forced me to live the same day over and over. All at once, I wanted to step into the future or the past or anywhere but here and any time but now. I had spent too much time thinking about time travel and Joe's accident. I had to lay it down, put aside the fear of change invading my cloistered little universe, and stop deteriorating in front of the ones who loved me.

Lorraine Bedinsky pointed at Colin with her nose and whispered to Grace, "He thinks we're sort of clubby, doesn't he?"

Fern tapped me on the shoulder. "I went to see your father today. He's looking perky again. Got that rose bloom in his cheeks. Would not surprise me *at all* to see him back in the pulpit in two shakes."

Bill Simmons took his place next to Hal. "Let's not rush things, Fern. Pastor Norville has to mend. Things like this can't be hurried along."

Lorraine turned back to Fern and in her desultory manner launched into her egg-salad diatribe.

Hal sat back in his seat so only Bill could hear. His eyes had a dim color that reminded me of a fish that sat on the bottom of the ocean growing old and fat while the plankton fell into its mouth. The top of his head had lost all of its bald-man's sheen and looked like an old peacock that had lost its plumes. "Are we going to lose our pastor, Bill?" Old people like him do not know how well practiced they are in loud whispering.

The women glanced up and then looked away, looked at me.

I turned away from them and nodded toward the front so that I could avert Mason's curious gaze.

Colin ascended the platform. He delivered a message that lasted no longer than twenty-five minutes, yet was weighty with content. Even Lorraine later alluded to the "fine, fine message."

As every person gathered in the rear of the church, Mason tugged at my blouse.

"What is it?" I asked.

"Go talk to him before he leaves." Mason had combed the front of his hair up in a straight swoop that looked exactly like a young shock of wheat.

"Whom should I talk to?"

"Pastor Arnett."

"We have plenty of time to talk to them."

"Charlotte told me they're leaving tonight."

"They don't want to stay another night?"

"They're already packed. Pastor Arnett has a lot of work to do back in Lake Norman. The car is loaded."

"We'll go and say good-bye to them then."

"I don't want to say good-bye. You can talk to them and ask them to stay. Grandpa's sick. He told me about his retirement. They can move here and you can ask them to come."

We stood in line and it almost looked like a receiving line, as though we were accepting the new pastor and his family. I overheard Bill and Colin talking. A piece of paper was pressed into Bill's hand. He did not wait to open it. I peered around Grace and Hal and caught a glimpse of a name and phone number. Colin had made his recommendation to Bill.

Mason and I finally shook Colin and Ruth's hand.

"March, I want to thank you and Mason for your hospitality. You've learned well from your mother," said Colin.

"We have really grown to love your family," said Ruth.

While we continued to exchange pleasantries, I felt Mason's occasional tug at my blouse. Colin and Ruth led the children out across the dark parking lot. It was as if Mason, by the act of his will, tried to propel me toward them.

I stood glued to the asphalt and waved.

Colin strapped the last child into the backseat, turned, and walked toward me.

"Here's your chance!" Mason ran back up the steps and disappeared into the church.

Colin and I stood under the Wednesday moon. He shook my hand but held it a little longer.

"If you don't mind my asking, where were you when they told you about Joe?"

I didn't know what to say. Nothing came to mind. He turned away, embarrassed.

"In the bathroom cleaning out the sink." I blurted it out. I wish that I had made up something such as I was in the hospital visiting the sick. Or I was at the church. Anything but cleaning the sink. Now he would have this anemic image all the way back to Lake Norman of me shaking chlorine cleanser out into the sink. I had heard of women who had had premonitions about the loss of a loved one just as my mother had once had them. But nothing about the day had warned me what was about to happen. It was raining. Lightning flashed, and I imagined Joe seated at his desk working another Saturday to build his practice, then dragging home another briefcase of work and sitting with his back to me. Nothing told me in advance the day was over before the sun set.

Colin must have noticed my embarrassment. "Ha-ha." It was a nervous laugh, not cruel.

"Is that funny?" I asked.

"I think you're funny. The way you say things. That's all."

He shook my hand again and headed for his tank-sized SUV.

I thought of Colin's journal and how he gleaned moments and thoughts into a collective assessment of who he and Eva were as a couple. I stood out under the glow of the yellow parking-lot lights that looked like antique lamps and imagined. I visualized a little cloud hovering above my seldom-touched diary. It made me wonder in a hopeful way what good I might pull from the story of Joe and me. I had tried to erase us, but it only hurt worse, like flogging the air and hitting myself. Because I could still see us in Mason's eyes and we looked handsome and hopeful, all intelligence and freckles in the package of a boy.

Colin had molded each morsel of pain and shaped it into a metaphor that would help those around him consume it and be encouraged by it. While my life was forever on troll mode, Colin always moved with the wind at his back, never in the doldrums. He sailed off in splendor while the rest of us waved and cheered from shore effusively praising the magnificence of his courage.

To his poetic query, I had nothing more to say than I was cleaning the sink. "Ha ha, hoo boy, what a laugh!" I thought I was alone. (But what would be the chances of that?)

"Mom, are you okay?" Mason peeked out of the church doorway.

"I'm good, Son. Really."

He rested against the doorway and it seemed to me my mother had even painted the doorjamb.

I dredged up my thoughts about Joe's last day. We had pancakes. We had not had pancakes since the Christmas before, and I put blueberries in them just the way he liked them. He thanked me and there was this moment when he kissed my face, and then I turned toward him and we really kissed. He tasted like blueberries and both of us thought that was funny.

We had touched. I saw it and knew it was true.

The taillights of the Arnett SUV flashed red. The vehicle came to an abrupt halt. The side door flew open. Out flew the loveliest butterfly, her blond hair flying behind her, gold tresses falling around her shoulders in the sweetest aroma of little girl.

"Wait, we forgot, we forgot!" said Charlotte. She threw her arms around me, and I felt the presence of her hands wrapping around me.

"What did we forget?"

"Our angel hug," she said.

"You never told me about an angel hug," I said.

"Are they back?" Mason was fully outside now, under the exposed yellow light bulb above the door.

"Just for angel hugs," I said.

"Oh," he said it as though our girlish demonstration of emotion disgusted him.

I bent down and Charlotte kissed me right on the mouth.

"You be good and don't forget to pray," said Charlotte. She ran and disappeared into the car with her wings fluttering behind her.

They pulled out of the parking lot, their bumper a quarter-inch from scraping the sloped exit of the church parking lot. I watched until the taillights became distant, like a rescue flare at sea.

I said good-bye to Bill and Irene Simmons.

"Sounds like a good one." Bill held up the paper given to him by Colin.

"I want nothing to do with it," I said, and both of us laughed. I stepped back in to the church to turn off all the lights, a job my father had commandeered for years. The cobwebs disappeared with the dimming of the lights, and yet there was that scent of desuetude that settles on old churches. It is a sweet scent, like old bee boxes out in the field that have ripened with the aroma of honeycomb and the renewal of life every spring. Yet the musty ache of old pews cried for something new.

"Ready to go, Mom? I have practice tomorrow. Can you remember this time?"

"I'll remember, Mason. Let's go see your grandpa."

On the way home, Mason sang an unfamiliar song.

"What is that?" I asked.

"A song I learned."

"Then sing it."

He did.

"Interesting rhythm," I said.

He swayed back and forth and turned the dashboard into a set of drums.

"Where did you learn it?"

"Pastor Arnett."

"He is a good one to know new songs."

fifteen

GLORIA BOLTED THROUGH THE POES AND STOOD IN the middle of the floor. "The test was bluc!"

Shaunda lifted up a rounded fist and cheered, "We have liftoff, people!"

"What test? Did Gloria have to take her driver's test again?" asked Lindle.

I had read it all for the past few days in Gloria's face. The tired eyes, the pasty complexion. "Are we pregnant?"

"We are!" She hugged me.

The Poes bought her morning coffee and doughnuts. Shaunda left little pink and blue candies in a dish for her.

Thursday was slack day at the *Sentinel.*

Shaunda took a call from her friend at the courthouse. "News on Yolanda's criminals, March. Their attorney took a waiver of speedy trial, so there's a continuum."

"Continuance?" I asked.

"That's right. The trial is delayed." Shaunda typed up the story.

"I'm just ready for it to be over and done with," I said.

Gloria pulled out the layout pages and stripped them so that we could use them again. Lindle gathered up the waxed ads, filed the ones that we would use again the following week, and stuck the rest in a scratch-paper file. Nothing was ever thrown away. I sat at my desk and issued paychecks, as always semimonthly, and caught up on the bookkeeping I neglected all week.

"Gloria, would you mind if I check on my father? He seemed a little down last night."

"We're all under control," she said.

If anything had a pulse in Candle Cove, it was the *Sentinel.* While Monday through Tuesday led up to Wednesday's pub day, Thursday began the process all over again. Wylie and Brendan puttered around the print room and swept paper from the floor to prepare for the next print run, while Shaunda made appointments with school board members and the local schoolteacher, Tyler Klutts, who had decided to run for mayor—a fact that annoyed the incumbent, Fred Joiner.

Gloria took over the bookkeeping in a proprietary fashion, and I stepped away feeling incongruous with the day. I turned and left.

I found Dad out on the porch. He ate eggs and toast but complained raggedly. His hair, once clipped to the scalp, now grew in wisps that touched his collar with points of gray. Even with a warmer May, he buttoned long sleeves at his wrist, I assumed to hide the bruises from the intravenous tubes. His laugh pillow lay behind him against the wall as though he had not needed it for days.

"These aren't real eggs, you know. She thinks I don't know that this isn't genuine food. They'll find it causes cancer, and then the hens will be back in production again working double-time."

"Dad, can you never have eggs again?"

"I will if I want."

"If you don't mind, I'd like to go through those boxes I put up in your attic a couple of years ago. Joe's boxes."

He shrugged and tamped the noneggs into an empty soup can.

The attic had a window at one end, a circular pane of glass that allowed light to flood the otherwise darkened rafters. Beneath it was my grandmother's trunk graced at one end by three cardbaord boxes. On the cardboard side Dinah and I had marked it simply "Joe."

On the other side of the trunk, I saw a wooden pallet my father had fashioned with castors. In the early ministry years, he'd taught himself to repair our old Oldsmobile. He used the pallet to slide under the Oldsmobile to examine the underbelly.

It made a perfect dolly for one of Joe's heavier boxes, so I dragged it down and ferried it over to the attic opening and then slid the box down the ladder.

Dad was staring beyond the rail when I pushed the box over the threshold and out onto the porch.

Ellie held up the soup can with two fingers as though she held up a dirty sock and dropped it into a trash bag.

"I'd like two eggs over easy and toast with butter. And bacon if we have any," he said.

She argued with him.

"Please, Warden," he argued back, "just a simple breakfast with real butter and salt. That's all I ask."

"Go ahead, Ellie. But no salt, no butter, certainly no bacon," I said.

After she disappeared, he waved his cane at the neighbor's yard. "Clyde Janway's let his grass grow up. Must be off at his fishing cabin in Asheville. We once cut each other's grass when the other took a vacation."

"I don't remember Clyde ever cutting our grass," I said.

"Good people, the Janways."

"I think I'll go through this box."

"Looking for anything in particular?"

"If I were, it'd be a miracle to find it. At the time, just looking at his things all the time sent me into a nosedive, so Dinah and Mason helped me box it all up. We packed away all of Joe's junk like madwomen tossing every little piece down to his paper clips into boxes. I thought I might find a few things of his that would be more personal. You know, like a journal."

Dad drifted back to his world, a trait more common since his surgery. He was self-absorbed with any facet steered by James Norville: the church, his diet, his provincial circle of friends. "Bill Simmons called this morning. The board is contacting the minister that Colin suggested, " he said.

"Aha! This is the stuff Joe'd kept in his desk. You can tell the secretary boxed up this one."

"I forget where this minister graduated, but he's highly credentialed and open to the idea of living near the ocean. At least that is what Colin told Bill. He's writing his dissertation."

I pulled out Joe's leather desk calendar and a pen set. Mason might want the pen set unless he thought it looked too old-mannish. I remembered when all of the attorneys gave pen sets to one another at Christmas. Joe's set appeared brand-new, a brown faux marble sort of finish with a gold brass clip and a velvet lining in the box the color of egg yolk. It clashed with his gray desk set, or at least he might have said that at some point. For the life of me I could not remember.

"Everyone, all of the ministers, make videos now. Bill says this minister, Matthew Vandiver, is overnighting his video. What do you make of it?"

"I suppose he is sending a video of himself preaching or teaching, Dad."

"It doesn't seem natural. You aim a camera in my face and I go as wooden as a hobby horse." He disappeared inside his thoughts for a moment, his eyes wide like a doll's eyes and his mouth frozen in a smile.

"I wonder if this means something. All of Joe's desk thingamabobs look new."

"Excuse me, brothers, but we need to do another take for the video. We know you won't mind." Dad mimicked a broadcaster's voice, although he was lousy at it. He sounded more like Norman Vincent Peale on valium.

"Colin's church has a video camera in the balcony. They give videos to visitors. You just take a little ticket to the information booth after the service and they give you a free video of one of the services."

"Not Colin. He never sent us a video."

"Not to keep getting off the subject, but does it seem odd that all of Joe's office supplies are brand new? Look at this package of paper clips. Never opened. A letter opener that is still in the case. Is this a clue, or am I making something out of nothing?"

Ellie set Dad's eggs on the TV tray next to him. "Eggs over easy, toast with something on it, but I won't say exactly what it is or you'll start in on me again."

Dad thanked her in his most strained it-pains-me-to-say-this tone.

"I'll be back later with some dinner, Reverend Norville. Have a good day, March," she said.

After she pulled away, Dad said, "It's a shame she and I have to assume such an adversarial role. She is an otherwise nice woman."

"Back to me and my world. You've counseled people for years, Dad. The fact that Joe did not use his office supplies, would that be a red flag?"

"March, you've never practiced letting go of the past." He ate his eggs.

"I liked it better when you ignored me."

"You can't make God cough up all of the answers, line them all out just to please human curiosity. When God seems silent, it's possible he is trying to coax us into trusting him."

"I wouldn't call what I want to know human curiosity, Dad. Mom died too soon, but at least you knew the day was inevitable. When death pounces suddenly, it's like the aftermath of a bomb. You have to lift up stones and look underneath to find answers. I am not trying to find all of life's answers—just this one."

"Assume the worst; commit it to God." He sighed over his eggs and then placed a napkin on top of them.

"Admit it. You're crabby because it's hard to let go of your pulpit. So there you have it. The nut doesn't fall far from the tree."

A teenage boy motored up dragging a gleaming green trailer behind him. He backed a riding mower off the trailer and cut Clyde Janway's grass.

Dad studied his technique with a critical eye. The entire lawn was cut and edged in ten minutes.

"His blade is too low. Clyde won't like that chopped off-to-the-cuticle look. He should have hired a man with a push mower."

Arnie slumped around from the side of the house dragging his belly in the grass. Every step the low-slung pooch leaped to make the climb up to the porch punctuated his age, just as my father's inching gait accented his injured carriage. Dad yanked off the napkin, set the plate of remaining egg yolk on the porch, and allowed the dachshund to lick the surface clean. "Gloria tells me you've had some travel opportunities. You didn't tell me you have more travel assignments in the wings. What else don't I know?" he asked with a hint of pity, a man pulled out of the fight of life and told to sit in a corner.

I scooted the china dish from under Arnie's gluttonous tongue to rescue the Blue Willow heirloom.

"I'd hate to think you were turning down job prospects because of me." He drew up his lips like he did when he grew introspective. "Not that you did it because of me, but I'd hate to think you might."

"The timing isn't right, but I do have an offer of sorts. I could make the job as big as I want it to be or just let nothing happen. I never seem to have definitive offers, you know the kind that change everything, and your neighbors suddenly see you moving into the swanky end of town."

"You've held down the fort since your mother passed. It's time you had a life separate from mine. Maybe you could let this thing enlarge, as you say. You deserve a little swank, March. Nothing says you have to settle for the crumbs. I chose to make the church my life. I didn't choose that for you."

"The church is my life, too. Mason is my life. You, Mason, the

Sentinel. Period. And don't act like I've lost who I am just because I'm looking out after you."

"See! I knew it was because of me."

"Okay, maybe it's about you. You and everybody else. I can't just start hopping planes and leaving Mason or the newspaper behind. I've got people depending on me."

"I ask God every day, don't let me become a burden to my daughter. I can get along without you, in spite of what you may think."

"Would you look at this! Here's an entry in Joe's calendar. He always had nice handwriting. Did I ever tell him that, I wonder? He penciled in a few lunch appointments set up for the week after the accident."

"That would be a good sign."

"No, I'm afraid not. Not one business meeting. No court dates. In other words, if someone called him for lunch, he accepted it. But he didn't pursue anything legal or lawyerly. Not that it's any great surprise. I don't know why I did all this digging through his stuff. I keep holding out for a little grain of something I can give to Mason when he grows up and pieces his Dad's accident together."

"Maybe he won't. Not everyone wants to know the hard facts." Dad cupped his hands over his knees. He did that his whole life as a way of saying this conversation is beginning to bore me.

"Or maybe I just did all of this for me." *Mothers do that,* I thought. Make decisions out of selfish motives and then try and attach our motives to something as noble as *I'm doing this for the child.*

"Mason told me you and Colin took a walk on the beach."

"We talked about Joe and Eva, if that's what you want to know. We knew everyone gawking from the cottage would make something of it, but there was nothing to it. Believe me when I say that Colin is long gone. But it has nothing to do with me this time. Not that I was the cause of him not coming for good to Candle Cove the first time. Or returning. He didn't come because of me, Dad, but because of his friendship with you. You already know that, I gather, so don't look so smug. But I was hospitable, that's all I'm trying to say. So my hands are, as you say, clean in regard to Colin Arnett."

"You know why I like him? His faith has clarity," said Dad.

"I agree with that. Colin is everything I would like to be as a person of faith. While I lollygag along complaining as I go, he sprints ahead. You're right. He has clarity. Good choice of words. But I don't know what the big difference is between us. You know, like the *big* difference, the part of his armor that makes him so all-fired victorious."

Dad removed his spectacles and cleaned them. If he knew the answer, he did not say. "That little Charlotte has a way of winding her way into your heart," he said.

"She's a charmer."

"Bill Simmons would give away the church treasury to get that family in our midst. I somehow missed the mark in bringing them here. But who isn't glad they didn't get the chance to know them? They make everyone they meet feel refreshed. He may not be our new pastor, but somehow he touched all of our lives even if God didn't give him to us fully."

"He has his flaws. He fears death. Not that he's said anything. But he dotes on his family as though he is always spreading his large eagle wings to keep them close to the nest. Especially Charlotte."

"You don't fear death?"

"It's not death I fear, but the valley. You know as in the Twenty-third Psalm. When someone falls ill, or finances sag, or if you lose your job, you simply struggle to climb out. But when death comes this close, you move into the valley but you never see the moving van come back to take you out. You wonder if God still hears you when you speak to him or if he is tuned in to the pounding of your heart. You wonder if you will gather strength to take the next breath or the next step. Literally take the next step and walk into the next day. That's my biggest fear. Making it each day through the valley. We don't walk alone. But when I watch Colin, I envy his joy. He says it is not his own. But how does that translate to me?"

"You, Colin, and me, we've all walked through the same valley, March. But the reason the shadows are so deeply dark is that the light behind it is so joyously brilliant." His brows lifted. He was proud of the metaphor.

"I'm going to take this box and put it back upstairs. I don't know what I was thinking."

"Fine. Clutter up my house."

"If you don't mind, that is. There are no answers in this box. Maybe I need to have another talk with Colin. After we speak, I feel better." I pressed the old pieces of packing tape back onto the seams of the box and hefted it back down the hall and up the attic ladder. I stood in the light of the circular window and watched the sun caress Joe's boxes with a soft light.

"I really loved you, Joe. We never held one another long enough when we embraced. In our final year together, we didn't kiss in that lingering way. We never had the chance to say how we felt because we were always so busy. I'm listening now." Two wrens fought outside the window, causing the fruit-tree branch to lift and quiver. Joe and I had battled like those birds, fighting for turf, instead of for our love for one another. Twin tears spilled out, streaked down my face, and dampened my blouse. "If I've held on to you too tightly these last two empty years, it is because I am still waiting to hear what you never felt you could say. Maybe it's time I left those silent wishes up here in the attic." I now understood why some believed in the myth of ghosts in the rafters. "Good-bye, Joe. You've taught me a lot."

I left to pick up Mason from school.

We stopped at Ginger's for a quick meal of Cantonese chicken and rice. Thelma, Dad's secretary, phoned me on the cellular.

"March, I hate to phone you in the middle of all of your work, but we received a request for a hospital visit and Bill Simmons is off at a bowling tournament."

I could not for the life of me remember who might be in the local hospital.

"She's a cancer patient. I wouldn't take her a food basket although her family might appreciate it. Her name is Victoria Lane."

"I don't know any Lanes."

"Her dear sweet hubby picked us out of the Yellow Pages."

"She might be expecting a pastor, Thelma."

"Her husband says she wants to talk to someone about God."

"Mason is with me. Hospitals are a bore to children."

I was drowned out by the sound of preschoolers parading past Thelma's desk for afternoon recess and cookie break.

"You'll find her at Holy Mary by the Sea in that little pigeonhole of a cancer ward." She gave me the room number and paused as though I wrote it down on the steering wheel.

"Might she prefer the Baptists? They have a whole mime skit thingy for the sick." Channel 6 once came out and filmed them. It was a big production.

"Your daddy's done this so much, I figured you'd probably know by heart what to say. Ask Jennifer Cantalona at the volunteer's front desk for a Gideon's Bible if you don't have a spare on you."

Mason sighed when I told him where we were going. We debated about him being dropped off at a friend's house until I saw his school satchel exploding with assignments.

"I guess you know my answer," I said.

Mason did his math out in the waiting room. I sat outside the cancer ward in the hall and waited for the words to come to me, not recalling a single cognizant thing my father ever said to a dying person. *Why me, God? I'm as useless as a gnat.*

Sixteen

THE LANE FAMILY ACTUALLY CONSISTED OF THREE families. As many times as Mr. Lane defined his family to me, his ex-wife's portion—three teenagers with hair the color of corn—and Victoria's family, I never shuffled the deck in exactly the same manner every time. Two sisters, freckled and running their fingers through long tangles of hair that blazed into natural red curls, took frequent nicotine trips to the stairwell to light up. Victoria's skin tone indicated she might have once possessed the family red mane too, but all that remained were burnished filaments of sparse brows above her lashless eyes.

"Do I know you?" she asked.

Herb Lane stepped away from his wife's bedside and tramped toward me double-time with his hand extended.

"I'm March. One of you must have called Thelma at Candle Cove Presbyterian."

"You don't look like a preacher," said Victoria. She looked me over with blue eyes, intense as gas flames.

"I'm Herb, Vicki's husband. We only called an hour ago. You must have a sound dispatch system."

"Thelma. She's all we have," I said.

Herb dusted off the chair beside her bed and stepped away in hopes I decoded his gangly body language.

"I didn't know about your diet, Mrs. Lane," I explained. "Or I might have brought a fruit basket."

Behind me was a shuffling of feet, and the room emptied.

"I want to talk about Jesus, church, and my cancer," she said.

"My father is actually our pastor. He's recuperating from surgery. You can call me March."

She invited me to call her Vicki.

"I wrote down all of my questions. You should know I am dying, and this is all new to me. Dying and Jesus are new, I mean."

"What do you know about him? Jesus, that is."

Two Baptists at work had prayed with her and led her in prayer after her collapse from a brain tumor. I knew the Baptists in town to be fairly thorough.

"Maybe we should start with your questions, then," I said.

Vicki smoothed the paper in front of her that looked to be written on a grocery-list pad. "How do I know if I'm going to heaven?"

I knew that one by heart. Vicki had a Bible on her nightstand, placed in the room by the Gideons. I fumbled through the crisp pages and was greatly relieved when I opened to Romans. "That if thou shalt confess with thy mouth the Lord Jesus and shall believe in thine heart that God hath raised him from the dead, thou shalt be saved."

She scribbled on the pad.

Some kind person had left a bookmark in the back of the Bible printed with scripture references. God had sent in reinforcements. I turned to the book of John and read: "Let not your heart be troubled: ye believe in God, believe also in me. In my Father's house are many mansions: if it were not so, I would have told you. I go to prepare a place for you. And if I go and prepare a place for you, I will come again and receive you unto myself; that where I am, there ye may be also."

Right about now, James Norville would have pulled some really crisp and neat apologetics out of his knapsack of spirituality. I hoped she didn't see me fidgeting. Standing for years in my father's shadow did not qualify me for evangelism. I took another glance at the bookmark and then read: "If we confess our sins, he is faithful and just to forgive us our sins, and to cleanse us from all unrighteousness."

Vicki's fingers stopped moving. She rested her chin on her chest with eyes shut tight. Her monitor beeped steadily. My heart bumped against my chest to see if I was still alive.

She opened one eye. "I'm ready, then. Tell me what to say," she whispered as though we stood in the lighted bowels of a cathedral.

I leaned against the side of her bed with my elbows planted in the linens and my forehead against my clasped fingers. "Repeat after me, Vicki." I prayed a silent prayer. *God, I feel like an idiot. I'm so inadequate it's laughable. Could you please fill in the blanks for this woman?*

Gloria and Shaunda left a message. They photographed the fungus in the school gym, an incomprehensible photo, Shaunda said, of the janitor pointing at what looked to be scattered potting soil. Gloria's note said she would use a lot of adjectives for the piece, but the photo was nixed. The two of them went off to Dooley's for fish and chips and near beer, Gloria's pregnant-person substitute for her favorite summer beverage.

Lindle was at the Pontiac dealership selling the owner, Freddy Lydel (accent on the "LIE") on a full-page ad, Shaunda's note said.

Mason had finished his homework at the hospital. He and Dad sat out on the front porch straightening out the contents of Dad's tackle box while I ran back to the office to edit the LaVecchia's piece.

I had overused the words *delectable* and *satisfying* so I described the fish as "a phenomenal yet understated dish with a nutty kick and a heavenly cloud of garlic potatoes." The phone rang.

"Colin." I may have said it with a sort of animal-in-the-headlights astonishment.

His words possessed a discomfited nuance. His secretary, or some office clerk, spoke in the background. He answered her with a dismissive tone.

"How are you?" I asked.

"I've been thinking that perhaps we should try and hook up again."

"Hook up?"

"Meet."

"As in?"

"Meet."

"Mason loves playing with your kids. We'd love to have you all down again. Should I call Bill for you and arrange another service?"

"No Bill. No kids. No church. Just us. What I'm trying to say is, will you consider seeing me, but not with our families present?"

I did not know that Colin had room for such thoughts. "Colin, is this what it sounds like?"

"I'm trying to ask you out. But then there's the distance equation to figure out. We have a guest house at the church. Really, it's the old parsonage, but a nice cottage sort of house. Quaint, some say." He muttered something about not being well practiced at courtship.

"I am without a thing to say. We're just so different. You're like brass and jazz. I'm like old dusty organ keys." I don't think I said what I intended, but he caught me so off guard with his *let's get together* discourse.

"Oh, no, I disagree. You're really innovative."

I felt as though I was fishing for words of approval, so I opted for comedy. "Are you sure you have the right number?"

He had a laugh that pealed clear and concise all the way from Lake Norman.

Before I could answer with any sort of intelligibility, I argued with myself about my current situation. I had found my rhythm finally, I told myself. I knew what to do when I awoke and what to plan for the next day. In the big picture all I could see was distance and tension thrown into the mix if we tried to merge Longfellows and Arnetts. And then there was the matter of Eva. I could never live up to her perfect persona.

Someone tapped at the plate-glass door. It was locked, a practice of mine when I worked alone. If I answered it, I could stall. "Colin, hold on a teeny moment. Someone's at the door." I left the phone off the cradle and the line open.

Jerry Brevity smiled at me through the plate glass. He looked freshly showered and he had ditched the rat-man uniform for a nice polo and a pair of khaki slacks. I opened the door to him. He looked like a nicely aged version of the strapping high school quarterback.

"March, let's go get a burger. The yacht club is having a parade out near the pier. We can take chairs and buy a sack of burgers and have us a picnic while the boats parade by. Supposed to be a nice sunset. I know how you like sunsets."

It was true about me. Jerry was so observant of my every move, of every whim. He knew my flaws but saw them as (how did he put it?) sparks in the embers.

"I would love to go, Jerry. How nice that you thought of it." I said it overly loud.

"I'll put the top down on the Jeep." He strode back outside with almost leaping steps.

"Colin, are you there?"

There was an undeniable pause. "Yes, I'm here."

"I have a date. Well, it's nothing really. There is this boat parade. Our equivalent of the Disney parade, only with dime sparklers instead of a fireworks display."

"You don't have to explain. I realize you have a busy social life, March."

His diplomacy unsettled me. Not even a spark of antipathy. I felt guilty and conflicted. I tried to convince myself I would have joined Jerry anyway.

Colin apologized for disturbing my evening and then hung up.

"What was that all about?" Gloria and Shaunda had slipped in through the side entrance. They stood grinning at me.

"You've been standing there a while, I gather," I said.

"Colin called you again?" Gloria put away the camera case.

"Was that preacher asking you out? You know you'd make a good preacher's wife, March. You know the ropes. Me, I'd be lousing things up, getting into trouble," said Shaunda.

"Don't look now, but Jerry Brevity's waiting right outside with the top down on that bright red fancy Jeep of his. And that look in his eye says he's got his net out," said Gloria.

"I don't blame you, March. That Arnett, he has too many kids for my tastes." Shaunda locked up her desk drawer.

"Tell me you don't have a date with Jerry." Gloria sat backwards in the chair next to my desk to face me.

"Jerry's a respected business owner. Practical man," I said. "He's solvent."

"Safe," said Gloria.

"We're going to the yacht club's parade. Burgers and fries and nothing more." I closed up my purse with a rapid snap and stood to leave.

"Maybe you passed up good wine for near beer," said Gloria.

"I think you're making the right decision, March. Tell that preacher he needs to go find hisself a nursemaid." Shaunda stacked her notes into a tray.

"I thought you two were gone for the day," I said.

"Long-distance relationships never work anyway." Shaunda nudged Gloria out the door. They greeted Jerry and then left for the night.

I locked up my desk and the front door.

"We better hurry if we're going to catch the sunset," said Jerry.

He smelled of clean laundry and deodorant soap. His back sank against the seat and melded with the comfortable curve of leather. The lines of tanned skin around his eyes and mouth blended well with his surroundings, a comfy sofa of a guy you could never toss out for sentimental reasons.

But when I slunk into the Jeep, I felt lousy, like that left-out feeling when I'd been home for a week with the flu. Or like I'd just thrown out brisket for egg salad. Jerry smiled at me, crinkling the corners of his eyes, but all I could return was a musteline grin. I was climbing into the carriage of the town exterminator, not that his profession wasn't keenly needed in a township near the ocean. But when I sat next to him, I had no curiosity about the man, whether he smelled like chambray or wrote like Dylan Thomas. Jerry was Jerry, six feet of former athlete strung together by a past eminence. Jerry was no more than who he once was, and even minus that. His own existence was eclipsed by a few years of illustriousness. A legend who had faded with less importance than an old set of encyclopedias. His only claim to fame now was that he could say he knew me.

We motored away from the *Sentinel* toward the pier and the glow of sky along the horizon. Gulls lulled in the breeze as though drawn onto the fabric of gold-and-pink sky with gray *conte* crayons.

The office phone rang again, a distant chirring muffled by plate glass.

"You want to answer it?" he asked.

I could see the yellow light of the phone line blinking through the window, a wounded lightning bug.

"No. If it's important enough, anyone who knows me knows my mobile number." Whether or not Colin possessed the other phone number, I could not remember.

Jerry chauffeured us away and I felt a deep and sickening panic. My head felt as though it were swelling with the ether of anxiety. I gripped the seat and donned a pair of black sunglasses while my hair blew around my face in unbecoming tentacles. The visor in front of me was down and I saw my own face in its mirror, a reckless Medusa. Jerry rattled through the cove all the way to the pier while I turned stone silent.

Someone had erected a lemonade stand next to the Kiwanis Club's burger-and-dog shack. Jerry ordered a sack of burgers and fries with two lemonades. We set up our chairs and a camp table close to the shoreline. I bought grilled ears of corn including an extra to take home to Mason who always ran to the corn stand at the county fair each fall.

"I forgot to mail my article to Brady Gallagher," I said.

"For the *Charlotte Observer?* We can swing by the post office on the way back to your car," he said.

"Not to worry. I'll just fax it to him. It will be waiting for him when he comes in tomorrow morning."

"I wish my secretary, Adele, had your efficiency," he said.

A boat horn sounded on the bay. Children assembled along the ebbing water. Their sparklers made neon squiggles in the air.

"Someone like you could sure increase effectiveness at Brevity's Exterminating. You could drop that newspaper business, all of the pinching pennies, and have yourself a steady little income working for old Jerry. There's a lot to be said for security, March."

"I'm not a secretary, Jerry. I employ one, though."

The sun melted away, a big lemon drop.

He doled out the paper-wrapped burgers.

I waved with exaggeration toward the string of boats. "Oh, will you look at Harry and Clara Monoghan's *Miss Ursula!* They've decorated her sort of Calypso style with stuffed parrots. Surely they got them from some party supply. I mean, they wouldn't use dead birds, would they?" The lemonade circulated over my tongue in swirls of undissolved sugar granules.

Miss Ursula led the boat parade. Harry Monoghan wore a grass skirt over Bermuda shorts. He swung around the mast and shouted at the land-bound spectators.

"Harry's been nipping down at Dooley's," said Jerry.

"Look who we found, Sue!" Sybil Ettering juggled a lawn chair and a miniature ice chest.

Jerry sat forward but did not stand to greet them. "Well, it's our writers-in-residence in the flesh! Ladies, take a load off. Join us."

I acknowledged Sybil and Sue but glanced away when they paired us up with their gazes.

"March, it surprises me to find you among the landlubbers this year," said Sybil. The way she said "landlubbers" sounded unnatural.

"I heard you took the *Sparticus* out for a trip or some such." Sybil handed a ten to Sue and sent her for food and drink.

"March, you should have told me. I would have helped you decorate her and enter her in the parade," said Jerry.

"I don't belong to the yacht club anymore," I said.

"You're a veteran, March. Wing Bester would have let you in for old times' sake." Jerry pulled out a second burger.

Sybil had an epiphany. "Think how much that would encourage everyone to see you floating along all dolled up in your boat. Reminiscent of the days when you were voted in as Queen Pamlico."

"Did you take her out alone?" Jerry asked.

"I still remember that paddle-boat ferry with all of you girls in Southern belle gowns and parasols. You looked like crocuses blooming along the harbor. Bernie and I were still young marrieds in those days," Sybil gushed.

"I didn't know you could sail the *Sparticus.* Will wonders never cease?" Jerry found the large sack of fries.

"I was never Queen Pamlico, Sybil. You're confusing me with Dinah."

"You and Mason must have had a good time putting her back into the water," said Jerry.

"It was a whole group that went. Right, March?" Sybil set up two chairs and squeezed into one of them.

I was still trying to figure out how Sybil knew about the *Sparticus.* While Jerry zoned in on the bit of news about Colin and the *Sparticus,* Sybil spilled my private life out like a gossip scout for the *National Enquirer.*

"Couldn't have been more than seven or eight or she'd be over the limit. You have to watch your body limits or the Coast Guard will nab you quick," said Jerry.

Sue yelled at Sybil to find out her condiment preferences.

"Excuse me." Sybil lifted herself out of the chair and traveled laboriously across the sand, her sheer floral blouse billowing like a perfumed scarf.

"I didn't take her out, Jerry."

"Mason, then?"

"My father invited a visiting pastor into his pulpit. He and his family stayed in the cottage. They sort of found her out in the garage."

He pulled back the wrapper on burger number two, but then froze. "I hope they were sensitive to your feelings."

"Mason took to the sailing right off, like we should have tried it sooner. So I'm glad it happened. He's been a different boy ever since, like we're talking about things more openly now."

Jerry choked down a bite and looked sophomoric doing it. He rushed to interject himself into the conversation. "I'm glad you told me. I've been thinking you and I need to be more open about a few things."

I felt a swell of things I didn't want to hear billowing toward me.

"Ms. Longfellow, is that you?"

Two red-haired women stood blocking the evening sun.

"You're Vicki's sisters," I said.

"It is her," said one of the sisters.

"We don't know what to say, but you did a lot for our sister," said the other. "I'm Carla and this is Simone."

We shook hands. Simone flicked a cigarette butt into the sand next to her and ground it into the sand with her heel. I introduced them to Jerry.

"Nice to meet you, Jerry." Simone gripped his hand, an athletic handshake for such a petite female.

"Your wife came to visit our sister today at Holy Mary by the Sea, and she just was the best person anyone could have sent. Here we don't know you all from Adam, but she just came anyway," said Carla.

"Jerry and I are friends. We're not married," I said.

"For now." He placed his hand atop mine on the lawn-chair arm, curled his fingers around mine, and squeezed out some vague Morse code as though he cued me to counter his obscure proposal with girlish wild abandon.

"Do you mind telling me how long Vicki has to live?" I asked.

"A week. Maybe two. She's already hung around two months longer than the doctor predicted." Simone dabbed her eyes with the back of her hand.

"She's only two years older than me, and I'm thirty-nine," said Carla.

"It just goes to show you. I guess we better run. We saw the lights from the hospital window and thought we'd take a break." Simone pressed a light-up button on her watch face.

"This is such a small world. Thank you for stopping to say hello. And I was really glad I helped your sister." I decided not to divulge how worried I was that I would botch up things between Vicki and Almighty God. Somehow, in spite of my inadequacies, God reached through and reeled her in.

"Candle Cove is the most darling place. I can see why Herb and Vicki bought a house here on the water. It's like the end of the map, the last place you stand just before the climb to heaven." Carla's voice broke.

Simone lit two cigarettes and handed one to Carla.

"She just won't stop talking about God and all that stuff you told her. I hope you can come back. Bye, now," said Simone.

They walked away from us.

Jerry and I stared at the boat parade that was halfway finished by the time we looked up.

"The last stop before heaven. I never thought of Candle Cove like that," said Jerry. He turned away to listen to baseball scores on another man's radio.

"Jerry, are you familiar with Dylan Thomas?" I asked.

"Didn't he play for the Dodgers in the sixties? Nah, I'm mixing him up with another guy."

Sybil and Sue joined us and handed us each a funnel cake.

"Oh, we almost missed the whole thing standing in those awful lines," said Sue.

"You'd think there was nothing else to do here." Sybil laughed, her bottom lip coated in powdered sugar.

I watched Vicki's sisters walk, sandals in hand, all the way down the shore. I thanked God for filling in the places I may have left out.

Jerry chatted up my counseling skills and other things he really knew nothing about. I could feel him trying to draw me in as his good points ebbed from sight. The way he slipped in that little bit about marriage irked me to no end.

Someone set off Roman candles and a small fireworks display on the peninsula's shore. Fireballs erupted like blazing spheres lifting above the harbor, drawing a line from our cove to the sky as though it connected our lives to things not seen.

The phone vibrated inside my purse. I fished it out and walked away from our little banquet to find a quiet patch of sand.

"I've had the most goshawful day, March." Dinah was breathless.

"Are you at home?" I asked.

"I've brought the girls down to your daddy's pier to fish."

"You all missed the best yacht parade. Someone even sprang for a fireworks display."

"That's just the kind of crowd I need to avoid right now. How can I show my face after the worst show ever? Tell me you didn't hear the broadcast today?"

"The crab thingy. I'm sorry. I forgot."

"Clambake. The show was terrible, and I just can't go out in public. Syndication is a laugh where I'm concerned. I'm going to hurl the master tape out into the ocean and pray it's eaten by something with a slow digestive system."

"You want me to come out to the pier, I guess."

"I could use a shoulder to cry on," she said.

"I have to go," I whispered to Jerry.

He dropped me off at the *Sentinel* although he lingered at the door for something as encouraging as a kiss from me.

"Thanks for the picnic," I said.

He held my hand, lingered over it, his eyes a flicker of puerile hope in the yawning moonlight. The calloused fingers, sticky from a night out on the harbor, would not let go.

"If I don't hurry, I won't have time to fax my article. I have a friend in need or we could go for coffee. Besides, I've got to pick up Mason before he completely wears out my father." I kissed Jerry on the side of his face and disappeared inside my office.

I felt his eyes examine me through the window, begging for me to look at him and offer him the wee glance of hope he had been attempting to dredge out of me for all these past months. If I did so, it would be a lie. I kept my face from the window, turning it to the soft glow of Gloria's blinking nightlights decorating the wall near my desk.

It appeared Brady Gallagher had left his fax machine on all night. The article flowed in and out without a hitch. I drove as fast as possible and picked up Mason. We joined Dinah and the girls down on Dad's pier.

The twins coerced Mason into dragging out his grandfather's choice fishing gear. He led them to the edge of the small dock prattling like an old fishing pro about his treasury of lures newly acquired from Dad. They imagined sharks and manatees in the dark opal of the cove and how they would capture one and wrangle it to shore.

Dinah and I walked along the shoreline. Couples who had gathered earlier to ritually observe the sun sizzling into the ocean looked cloaked and dark in the twilight.

"I think you're being too hard on yourself. Shaunda said she caught your broadcast today and it sounded chic and eclectic. Those were her exact words," I said.

"She's being kind, March. It's the worst one I've ever done. I sounded like a complete fraud. I've never been to real cooking school, you know, just sort of fly by the seat of my pants. I sounded like some single mother trying to invent a job for herself. I can't say it enough how I just don't like being me today."

"I like you, Dinah, and I think you're just the best cooking-show host, and the best mother, single or not."

"If I could figure out exactly what makes me tick, I'd not go after a whale with the butter sauce and wind up looking like the biggest fool ever. Only I have to pick a career that magnifies all of my flaws and parades them out in front of the whole entire world."

"Candle Cove is not the entire world, and a hometown cooking show does not put you on parade."

"It's my entire world."

"I know. I know. I live in the same world, and know what it feels like to be scrutinized. That's when we turn on the song and dance, right, Di? Just so we feel accepted? We spend half our life spinning our wheels and asking open-ended questions to which none of us knows the answer. Like 'why am I here?' Maybe we've all gotten good at faking it just because we can't answer those hard questions."

"Are we really good at faking it, March?'

Suddenly every couple barely visible along the shoreline looked pink and still, as though each person had matched up with a star in a constellation and formed a parallel universe.

"See the corner where that dock used to be, March?"

I saw a corner post, dark and lifted above the wake where a dock had once been. I nodded.

"That's me on that corner. I used to hold up my life just like that post before the elements washed away the whole upper dock. Now it's as though I'm still standing alone with the tide beating against me. I stand there strong, as though anyone is going to notice. But all the while I'm wondering what happened to the meaning of me. I can't remember why I'm still standing in the harbor while the tide turns my insides into soggy splinters."

"See that other corner, Dinah? Well, that one is me, and there we both stand holding up nothing. You, the former Queen of Pamlico, and me the queen of nil. Our lives have worn away from us somehow. But we are still standing, and there is a lot to be said for a monument."

"Do people see us as a monument or do we just look abandoned, two fools standing in the fray while the world beats against us?"

"Well, that's something, Dinah!"

"I always thought I would account for something, March. Tell me what to do."

I didn't know what to tell myself, let alone Dinah. Here I had wrapped up all of my life in church and work and family but possessed not a single answer for my friend, my sister.

The moon appeared and cast a net of green across the lifting froth.

"Colin called today."

"Is he coming back?"

"He asked me to visit him in Lake Norman. All of the wrong things paraded through my mind, such as "What if he's just feeling sympathy for me?" What if when I get there, he just wants to set me on his pastoral couch and pick my brain apart? But he didn't say any of that, and I just sounded like a ninny, that's what."

"And you went out with Jerry Brevity instead?"

"I used Jerry. I swear to goodness, Dinah, it was the worst thing I've ever done."

"You make every change that comes your way sound like a disaster."

"I do, don't I?" I said.

"Call him back. Plead a brief moment of insanity."

"If I do, what if I realize it was the worst mistake in the world and then our children have gotten, well, accustomed to the idea of maybe, well, a family forming between us?"

"He only invited you to dinner."

"You're right. I'm making this the Titanic."

We heard a squeal from the dock. Mason and one of the twins tugged at the line while the bow bent toward the water.

Dinah and I ran toward them.

"We've caught something huge!" Mason yelled, then grunted as he lifted the rod. He inched the nylon thread back into the reel.

"It's a whale!" one of the twins shrieked.

"I wish I had my camera," said Dinah.

"Grab the net, people!" Mason yelled again, the man in charge of Moby Dick. .

One of the girls grabbed the fishing net and scooted next to him on her stomach. She scooped the hideous-looking fish into the net. Dinah helped her lift it to the dock.

"It's a catfish." Mason was not impressed. Sea catfish were not considered game fish by the locals.

"But a really big one," I said.

"I'd rather catch a stingray," he said.

The fish's gills undulated out as the creature gasped for water.

I suggested that Mason throw it back.

He and the girls flopped it over on its back, careful to watch out for the sharp fins and whiskers.

Dinah and I returned to the cottage to make tea.

"Is there something you're hanging onto, March?" she asked.

"That's an odd thing to say."

"You just always seem to be blowing off perfectly good invitations."

"Does it seem like that? Or am I just taking longer to weigh things? When I first met Joe, he left me thunderstruck. He was a man without imperfections. But that was my perception of him. I was wrong. When I look at Colin and I don't see any flaws, I'm paralyzed. Trust me, I lie awake thinking about the unseen dark side of a perfect man."

"You won't unearth any flaws sitting here in Candle Cove. You know he has them, though."

"Don't you think men are better at hiding them than we are?"

Dinah cackled.

"Then I see how he's taken over his family. Colin's such a good father. He's good to his sister."

"You know we've had our victories, March, and without the aid of a man. Maybe Colin's just one of those people who genuinely has his act together. I have my days like that. But explain why I grapple with this empty pang inside of me even when I've had a good day."

"It's the God space, Dinah. Every human has one, my father says."

"You know I don't like religious talk. Besides, you never shove your ideas down my throat. That's what I love about you."

She grinned, but I did not feel like acting inane, blowing off the moment.

"I'm not talking about religion. But I've had this workaholic mind-set about church and God, as though by filling up every minute of every day with toil and effort I'm earning points with my Maker." I suddenly felt a need to find a still place.

"But, March, you're the most religious person I know, besides your dad, and he's ready for sainthood."

So was the Apostle Paul, I thought. But God struck him down with a blinding light long before he qualified for sainthood.

"Let's don't ruin the night with our single-woman blues." She held up her tea glass. "A toast to us."

We toasted and then walked out onto the deck to wave the kids back up to the cottage. The moon had taken over the sky and given it a melancholy cast. No fireworks pointed toward the heavens to give us answers.

I would find a quiet place, I told myself, somewhere at the edge of the earth where the only distractions were the whispers of marsh grass and the sand pebbles washing from the shore. God is unambiguous in those quiet coves.

Seventeen

"IF WE COULD JUST HAVE IT A LITTLE QUIET IN HERE, everybody!" In a blinding flash of cowardice, I cut my eyes down at the office linoleum. On Monday Gloria and I had spent an hour before everyone else arrived deciding that the *Sentinel's* second-quarter earnings were redder than Mrs. Pickle's tomato preserves.

"When will I breathe life into this dead body of a newspaper, Gloria? Tell me I'm doing the right thing."

Her face softened with Job's patience as she cut out a fresh new cardboard cover for my coffee cup. "You know you're doing the right thing. Candle Cove needs its own paper."

We heard the sound of slamming doors. Some of the staff had arrived, but with every nimble body that sashayed through the door I felt another weight tossed into the scale.

The Poes' humming annoyed me. Shaunda, with her gum-smacking, drove me over the edge, and even Lindle's nervous fluttering back and forth to fill my coffee cup made me wish for a sedative.

"I'm sorry. Just go do what you do and I'll be fine," I said to them.

Gloria and I pored over the stories that had potential for the front page. A swarm of bees had invaded the mayor's office, a fact that had triple significance in an election year, and had the incumbent and his opponent parlaying accusations back in forth in veiled figures of speech as though the plague of bees had apocalyptic significance.

The New Bern Chamber of Commerce had faxed the data for the Neuse River Days: the homemade raft races, New Bern's version of Junkyard Wars—nail together the most disorderly jumble of scrap lumber, discarded tires, anything that floats, and enter it in a race. Then there were the petting zoos, moon walks, a couple of craft stands, and a mishmash of games set up beneath the spreading oaks along the river to take your mind off of the heat. Gloria streamlined the facts into a two-column piece.

"You work miracles, Gloria," I said, but she did not radiate as usual.

Shaunda interjected her weekend story about the winners of the tennis tournament. "Also six seniors received state scholarships. I'm out of here," she said. She grabbed a cup of coffee to go and headed for the high school to take photos of the scholars.

I phoned Dad and described the weekend pulpit substitute: an aging Presbyterian army chaplain with a nervous hand and a tendency to misplace his eyeglasses in the middle of his sermon.

"That is a good thing, March. It will encourage the church to be swift about finding a new man," he said.

"Line two. It's Brady. Can you take it?" Gloria refilled my now-empty cup and hers with dark Jamaican coffee.

I finished church business with Dad and took the call.

"March, this is the best piece we've ever printed. I can't say enough about your style. Well, you actually have one. Bill says there is no shadow of doubt you could find syndication as a travel columnist."

I sprinkled sugar into my cup.

"I have the perfect piece for you, and you won't travel far from home. A two-page spread on the Pamlico Sound, but the hook is the pirate history. You'll sample food, visit the B&B's, the inns and cottages along the islands, the boat tours, but play up the history about Blackbeard, the sunken ships, so forth and so on."

The need to get away and find a quiet place to think enticed me. "I'll do it."

"Good. That was easy."

"I'm needing some time to be by myself, like when you do the trout-fishing disappearing act."

"How soon?"

"As soon as we're ready to go to press here, I'll leave it with Gloria and head for Ocracoke Island. Expenses paid, I hope."

"Covered. But try and work out a few deals from the locals in exchange for your mentioning their business."

"I'm no good at that, Brady. No one ever catches my vision for swap-outs until it's too late."

"You'll try."

I hung up the phone and called Gloria aside. "Would it make sense to take a travel story assignment in the midst of our sinking ship?" I whispered it to her.

"Stop saying that. You know once we get the paper to bed, you're a free woman. You need the money. Go, go."

Between the hysteria of Tuesday's news day and Lindle's paranoia that he might lose the Gum's Food Mart account, I could not gather facts for the trip until Wednesday afternoon.

"Gloria, do you remember the ghost story piece out of Raleigh? Were there any pirate ghosts, or are they all strictly out of colonial America?"

"We have a paranormal file. I'll riffle through it and see if I find any pirates floating around." Gloria devoured deviled eggs from Ruby's and chocolate macadamia nuts from Beach's Nut House, her first visible craving.

"I want you to be in charge while I'm away," I told her.

Gloria kept her eyes on the notepad in front of her and left wide gaps of silence between her sentences. She stepped away from her desk and moved past me to straighten clutter around the copier and to clear away empty Frito bags left behind by the Poe brothers. If she saw me watching her, it might have accounted for the way she kept her back to me.

I had juggled the workload so long, it did not occur to me that dumping my juggling act on her might feel as though I was laying a pregnant elephant in her already pregnant lap. "You don't want to be in charge, I understand."

"No, you believe in me. I can do it."

"I shouldn't go to Ocracoke right now. The timing is bad," I said.

"You're the owner. You can do whatever you want."

"If I go, I'll be putting pressure on you, and you're having morning sickness and this is just wrong on my part."

She turned and leaned against the painted credenza. To see her straight on made her look thin, instead of the sideways silhouette with the slight hint of a bowling ball emerging from her abdomen.

"You're trying to tell me something."

Gloria burst into tears.

"Let's go for pastries at the Lighthouse. You ride with me." I guided her out away from everyone else.

The Poes stared at her from the doorway of the print room, their mouths two *o*'s.

"Back in a minute. Hold down the fort," I said to Shaunda.

Sarai had lit vanilla candles on every table, an aroma that blended with the fresh hot bagels. We bought the bagels and coffee and picked a secluded table far from the ears of the elderly newspaper readers.

"Gloria, if you're stressed over the responsibilities or maybe it's the numbers, you know it's only our second year," I said.

"We made payroll by a thin hair." She blew her nose and spoke, her words trembling between hiccups. "I keep wanting to encourage you, but this is my first time to know so much about the place I work for. I'm no good at this." She scraped an overabundance of cream cheese from her bagel with a plastic knife.

"Of course you're good at this. You're great! You're the downright queen of great. If this job is a burden to you, I just wish you'd told me sooner. This isn't fair, and what with you in your motherly condition and all. I swear I'm blind to all of these maternal hormonal things. It's been a while since I had my baby. I'm not insensitive,

Gloria. Just distracted. I'm the most distracted person you know. Now you know the truth about me. Can you still like me?"

Her laughed sounded gurgly, coated with phlegm. "Look at me blubbering like a hormonal weakling. I know we can do this, March. We'll have to juggle a few things. If it doesn't make you nervous, then far be it from me to worry for both of us."

"Who said it didn't make me nervous?"

"No arguments about this either—I'm buying your lunch today for all of this nonsense I've put you through. And I think you should take your trip, and I'll manage for you. Poe brothers and all. I don't want you to worry about us. I'm just feeling pregnant. That's all."

"It's my job to worry for the both of us, Gloria. You take care of you, Phil, and the baby."

"When you leave, it's as though things slow down. No one wants to listen to me."

"You're hereby promoted as my official assistant. I'll announce it to everyone so they'll know that what you say goes."

The color came back into her face.

"If my travel is affecting you, I want to know. I realize my job at the *Sentinel* is a twenty-four-seven job," I said.

"You have to pay the bills too," she said.

Sarai filled our cups again.

"I can't fathom what we'll do when I go into labor."

"You better call me. I'll be right there with you."

"That's not what I mean. Shaunda has her head all in the clouds about New York; Lindle is no manager. Too disorganized. The Poe brothers are out of the question."

"I won't travel the whole month of your due date."

She looked relieved.

By afternoon Gloria gathered all of the pirate history from the files into a tickler file and placed it all on my desk.

"You're the queen," I said.

Gloria sighed so loudly it made us all look. Lindle's desk looked like the grounds after the county fair.

"Think of this clutter as ideas coming to life." Lindle's brows made *v*'s above his eyes.

I called a meeting and announced Gloria's promotion. The Poe brothers, with faces as pallid as a fish's underbelly, peered at Gloria curiously but offered no comments. Lindle shook Gloria's hand and asked to be excused. Shaunda sighed but tried not to show jealousy. When they all disappeared into their cubicles, Gloria cleaned off the table where the men had shelled boiled peanuts.

"They don't like the idea," she said.

"Give them time to get used to it. Once they see you're as fair as I am, they'll relax. Their respect for you is more important than friendship right now."

"This is all my fault."

"It was the right decision and that's why we did it."

"You keep your cellular phone with you at all times in case of a mutiny," she said.

By Thursday we could all take a breath again. Shaunda took to the idea of Gloria's promotion first and invited her to lunch to celebrate.

But the Mustang was making a funny noise. Just to be sure, Gloria had a rental car delivered to the office for my trip. She left a few numbers on my desk with the names of recommended inns and motels on Nags Head. She also printed off an Internet map. I told her to pick a hotel and secure the reservation.

"The entire trip from here to Nags Head will be about three and a half hours. You'll take the ferry from Cedar Island. Wait, you told me you've done this before when you were young. Don't you think it is the longest stretch of nothing but water? Unless you see a boat or two. Oh, and pelicans. You'll see a lot of birds and such flapping around not being so far from the—what is it you call that—a bird sanctuary? But you nearly always have to show up with reservations for the Cedar Island ferry or you might get left behind. I took the liberty of making your ferry reservations. The ferry to Hatteras is shorter, no reservations needed whatsoever. Then just travel the highway up to Nags Head. Shaunda's taking me to lunch. Will you be gone when we get back?"

"The car is loaded down. Mason is staying over tonight with Dinah and the weekend with Dad. I'd take him with me, but he didn't want to miss a game. Maybe I'll journal. I'll grab a sandwich from Ruby's to go and see you all next week when I get back. You feel ready for the Tuesday crunch, I guess?"

"We can do this. I just have a feeling about it like it's a step for us in the right direction, you know, like with responsibility we grow and all that," said Shaunda.

Gloria gave me a hug.

I turned on my cellular phone right in front of her.

I took off for Cedar Island and allowed myself a chance to vent. I had waited for this quiet time and now would have it without interruption.

If anyone walked into my mind and joined me in the middle of what winds through my neural paths on road trips, they would call me certifiably nuts and start analyzing whether or not I hated my mother, or did I even realize I exhausted the topic of Joe's suicide with every person I ever knew. But if I spoke my thoughts aloud, I'd always be the one dampening the lively conversations with talk of death.

No one wants to hear it. I know it for a fact. Not the ones you like to run around with, anyway. It is the odd person, the woman you scarcely know who gets right in your face and say things like, "How are you doing? No, I mean, how are you *really* doing? Come, dear, now you can really tell me. I'm worried that you're holding it all in," although I was never certain what the "it" of the matter might actually be that I was nutting away. She wants to make you believe you've grown up knowing her your whole life, Great-aunt Henny Penny suddenly back in your life and brilliant. She treats you as if you've suddenly been put out for adoption and here she stands, this merciful angel with her twenty-two-liter urn of womanly balm ready to scoop you up in a basket with pink blankets and rescue you off the curb. "Tell me; I want to know," is code for "I see a person in pain and want to experiment with her hot buttons," as though she were the latest video game.

Truth be told, I don't hold in anything. I just organize pain, visiting with her in increments. "Oh, hello pain, so it's you! Well, come in and have a seat and we'll have a cup of tea." It is true I don't invite the neighbors in to watch. It is a private conversation, not one most civil people want to observe. I likened the moment to inviting your friends over to watch while you have your spleen removed. Now really! Who would want to come?

But as I meandered down past the least populated lanes of East Coast highway, I could not get the painful matter of the cross off my chest. Not the jewelry, the crucifixes that people wear for luck or tradition. But the splintered wood nailed together by men who did not consider the human suffering that would be laid upon its crossbeam. Pain. The kind that proper society would not consider polite dinner-table conversation. Pain as heavy as the world sinking into a man's chest until he became it—the cries of hungry, sick, angry, and hurting people needing an emergency bridge to God. Christ became the cries. The pain. The death. While He hung in vertical humiliation, He lifted His face to say my name as He swallowed my bitter pill, and said He was done so that I could cross over His lifeless body, clean.

Pain. I finally got it. The necessity for suffering, so that from the pyre of misery, eyes would be lifted up to see God's Son and emulate in a smaller worm-sized way His price.

I entered the harbor village of Beaufort, crying and undone. The town smelled of grilled fish and salt water. I set off for the ferry landing. The road made its crook to the left to wind ferry riders onto Highway 70. Within only a few miles the entire topography turned from rural trees to marsh grass. The stress ebbed away as the land narrowed on either side of the road to become wetland and a fusion of inward sea and fresh water known as Pamlico Sound.

I rolled down the windows to smell the sea water and hear the intermittent cry of gulls.

I called back amid the song of birds and sea, "You are God even when it hurts!"

The marsh grass was dark and thick and made underwater islands where fish nested and spawned. The highway became a winding high wire between motorists and Cedar Island, a crooked pencil line of artery. I wondered what exactly might hold up the roadway to keep it from floating out to sea, but something told me I knew. Then the land widened again and became rural neighborhoods in towns named Otway and Bettie and Stacy and Sealevel. Picket fences smiled in front of cottages with kitchen-garden patches, houses painted the color of grapes and daffodil next to tired-looking trailer homes with neglected lawns. A woman wearing her husband's shirt lifted an oversized watering can above her head and offered a drink to the potted geraniums that hung on rusted nails all along her covered porch. The floral baskets swayed like red petticoats hung out to dry. She was the only human I saw along the way.

But everywhere I looked was God.

Someone had taken scrap lumber and paint and nailed signs to trees all the way down Highway 70, or else many people had the same idea. The signs all said the same thing: JESUS LOVES YOU. I must have counted a dozen of them all the way out to Cedar Island.

Every time I read another one, the words sank deeper inside of me. Just the way I was without holding together anybody else's world, Jesus loved me.

I pulled onto the parking lot at Cedar Island. A line of cars had already formed a procession. A carload of adults and children pulled into line behind the Mustang. A young child with blond ringlets poked her head out of the minivan window and squealed when she saw a heron take flight. She made eye contact with anyone who looked at her and waved as though we were all about to embark on a great adventure.

I waved back at her and she laughed at what Mason sometimes called my silliest of grins.

The Island attendants finally allowed the cars to drive onto the ferry. After we parked on deck, the captain made ready and set us out across the sound. I locked up the Mustang and found a bench where I could journal. I wrote about everything that touched my senses, the stretches of ocean on either side of the ferry that cried how wide God is. The brown waters of the sound slapped lazily against the vessel, holding up the boat the way God holds up the universe.

I photographed an interesting-looking older man whose skin was browned by years spent in long stretches of daylight. His face told a story, but I could only guess it. I imagined he had spent his life aboard a shrimp boat. He watched fishermen dropping nets and spoke to another man next to him as though he possessed all of their thoughts. He chatted up the marine life that circulated in and around the estuaries and spawning grounds that emptied into the sound; fish like striped bass, carp, bream, and puppy drum. He spoke of how the tarpon returned to Oriental's shores in July to spawn, and the giant red drum that spawned on the lower Neuse and Pamlico Rivers.

After the first hour, the sun emerged from behind a cloud. It peeked out enough to scatter shimmering lights atop the surface of the water. Another hour passed and the white obelisk of Ocracoke's lighthouse came into sight. The ferry entered the channel called Teach's Hole, the place where Blackbeard lost his bragging rights when he died in a sea battle. The captain invited us to step back into our vehicles as the ferry entered the narrow passageway to the Silver Lake Harbor of Ocracoke Island.

I checked Gloria's notes. For lunch places, she wrote "check out the Pony Island Restaurant." A local who stood out on the park service dock gave it the thumbs-up although you cannot always trust locals in small villages. The lack of choices can broaden a discriminating palate.

None of the roads was marked with street signs, so I relied on a local map that invited visitors to look for landmarks. I passed the Anchorage Inn, the Ragpicker Too, the Jolly Roger, and the Pirate's Chest before I spotted the sign for the Pony Island Restaurant. The restaurant, an older building that preceded a motel by the same name, had only one vacant table. Several couples conversed across the tables near where the waitress seated me. Two women discussed the striped bass they had all caught and fried the night before and gave the impression they all camped along the water and bonded like tykes at a slumber party. *Campers who frequent Ocracoke congregate in packs and tend to meet year after year*, I wrote.

I observed them too long, unwilling to interact and spoil the reverie. One of the bass fisherwomen poked a camera in my face and asked if I would mind taking a photograph of the group. They collected around the table and primped for the first time all week.

"You, sir, to the right. Yes, you. If you could skooch in just a tad," I said. He misunderstood and tried to suck in a stomach that had stretched his T-shirt beyond its tailoring. I took two steps back, snapped the photo, and took a second one to satisfy them.

The waitress placed a sandwich platter atop my paper place mat. She filled my iced-tea glass again and dropped two more sweetener packets next to my plate.

Joe and I had never visited Ocracoke together. While I was taken in by the village architecture he would have liked the banter of the fishermen, the quiet coded language of the locals. I myself had not seen Ocracoke since a trip one weekend before Easter when my mother insisted my father escape from a cantata run amok. An organist who passed away some years past, Faith Justin, had decided the church needed an Easter cantata. She found just enough men to take the major biblical roles except for the part of Christ, who was played by a cousin of hers who had flaming red ears and a terrible case of acne. But the players all decided Faith was too domineering and that she favored the cousin who put in a poor showing as Christ. They called in Reverend Norville to quell the feud and soothe the afflicted emotions. We never heard anyone speak of cantatas again after that year.

The sky darkened outside the Pony Island. I phoned ahead to confirm my reservation at the First Colony Inn on Nags Head. Rain pattered against the windows, but only intermittently.

"You must have brought a storm with you," said the waitress.

"What time does Teach's Hole close?" I asked.

"Six this evening if that college student they hired doesn't take off early to tie one on."

The sign read TEACH'S HOLE—THE PIRATE SHOP. I picked up a history of pirates book, an eye patch for Mason, and a small bottle for collecting sand. A newlywed couple asked me to take their picture by the tall fake pirate.

The rain kept me from tripping through the woods where Blackbeard hid out. It didn't matter anyway because not even the faint aroma of history's cannons remained; nothing remained but trees.

But I found the wild mustangs herded onto a beach where they grazed. I scribbled notes about them that made little sense, except for a few metaphors that seemed to resonate.

The ferry trip to Hatteras was only a half-hour, and the sight of the candy-striped lighthouse made me long for Mason's eyes through which to see it. I passed right through Hatteras through the villages of Frisco and Buxton and up to Avon where the locals gathered at the Mad Crabber. Highway 12 into Nags Head was a coastal wonder of sand dunes and sea oats. The sun broke through during the twenty-minute drive through a feral landscape. The dunes, no longer the massive camel humps of sand and grass that blocked the view through Buxton, compressed to form gentler slopes. The Atlantic shined and tossed to the east while Pamlico Sound calmed and ebbed to the west.

Gloria's directions led me to the next highway and then I located the store called The Farmer's Daughter. The next turn down a two-lane road took me straight in to the First Colony Inn. She had found a quaint inn, lovely and historic. But I felt a need for a vast expanse of water out my window. I found a place called The Sea Oatel, a seaside inn recommended by the newlywed couple. I checked in and dragged my own luggage into the room.

While Ocracoke lured campers, Nags Head attracted shoppers. I fished a camera from the overnight bag along with an empty canvas bag with *The Charlotte Observer* imprinted on the side. A package of photos fell out. I did not pack them but had a feeling Mason stuck them into my toiletries case the night before. Placed inside the gold drugstore processing envelope, Mason had handpicked photos of himself with Hercules, one of him with his grandfather, and a dozen of him and the Arnetts in various ham-face poses. I remembered how he tucked reminders of himself into Joe's luggage whenever he would take the occasional business trip. Once Mason had taken a tea bag and written on the tag HERE'S A PICTURE OF ME AND HAVE A CUP OF TEA. He had taped a wallet-sized photo of himself to the tea bag. Joe had found the gesture cute, but it made me ache and smile all at once. Finding these photographs in my overnight bag made me wish I had taken him out of school and brought him along against his will.

A room attendant appeared and opened the sliding glass door to allow in the ocean breeze. She placed extra towels in the bathroom and departed without allowing me to tip her.

One of the photos left me curious. I did not remember when Mason and Colin had posed in front of the *Sparticus,* but recalled Ruth snapping photos at every turn that week, taking photographs of Colin and the children posed outside the boat, inside the boat, and sailing away. Mason's thick shock of boy bangs blew off his forehead and made him look all the more masculine, like the handsome man he would soon become. Colin, dressed in faded denims and a white cotton shirt, had placed his hand on Mason's shoulder, a gentle grip; not overly familiar but convivial.

When I saw Colin in the photo it made me wonder why I had not thrown my arms around his neck, pulled his big strapping self toward me, and kissed him right on the mouth. But Colin's preacherly posture made me think of my father, and that was such a hard thing to kiss in any way other than a polite peck on the cheek. Yet I thought of Colin a lot and how it would feel to just drop all of the decorum kneaded into me by Julia Norville and blow all caution to the wind. Colin had broken into our circle in his mellifluous way but not because his intent was to intrude, but to quietly appear and mend whomever he touched. He touched Mason, my father, even Dinah.

He might have touched me and I imagined in what way. First he tried to find the connection between Christ and me, and that seemed to be a priority, and well it should be. But I had to figure out the Christ equation on my own. At Candle Cove Presbyterian, my father had reluctantly married couples who in his estimation were spiritually out of sync. One led the other down the road to God while the other pedaled along pacifying the wishes of the spiritual mate just to get the hook set. I had done that with Joe—strung him along on what I thought was a spiritual journey while he pretended to go. But I felt like the spiritual lesser of Colin and me. Now I understood why.

Thunder rolled distantly, like a bear waking. According to the clock, ten minutes had passed since I had opened that packet of photographs. I laid aside the camera and the shopping bag. Everyone had evacuated the beach from the first storm. I passed through the open door and left my shoes on the patio. The air was a cocktail of oxygen and mist and distant salt. My feet bare, I walked in a slow progression down the shore. The water had finally warmed. The clouds were still tall boulders stacked above the Atlantic, but they separated into islands. I saw sky.

The thought came to me that some need a cause and it helps them over and through the dark places. At first glance, it occurred to me that Colin plowed into causes to ease the loss of his Eva. After all, everything that rose up around him had her touch on it as though she breathed it into being. But now I realized Colin's only cause seemed to be in making himself invisible. By doing that, it doubled who he was and what he was about, and suddenly it became very clear to me: Invisibility gave him his potency. Visibility had taken me down.

I bent one knee and then the other. Salt water flushed around my calves. I felt broken in two, a twig washed on shore. God helped me with our conversation. He took his time with me. We had our time together. Our hands locked. He washed my confessions from the shore and left nothing behind but the clean sheen of new tide.

Surrender is delicious.

Eighteen

THE SUNRISE ENCAPSULATED ALL THINGS GLORIOUS about the Atlantic. If America embodied one address, we occupied the country's eastern window, the keepers of dawn, the wardens of the first minute of day. To bask in that light before the rest of the country awoke tasted like a warm secret.

Just off the sandy porch of shoreline the bottle-nosed dolphins fed early. I took a mile run.

Gloria phoned to say she awoke at four with major acid so she figured she may as well make the most of it and work. She wrote an article for pregnant women who want to increase the intelligence of their unborn children.

"Perfect for you," I said.

"All the women in my Lamaze class will buy us out. Who doesn't want to birth, say, the next Albert Einstein?"

"Good idea! But I read to Mason from the womb, and he's no Einstein."

"It's something in certain foods called *choline*. Anyway, I want to fax it to you first so you can help me knock out the benign words and make it, how do you say, concise."

I gave her the hotel fax number.

"Oh, and I found a place called John's Drive-In and it's close to you, March. You have to try it for lunch. John's specialty is tuna boats, fried okra, and peanut butter shakes. I would donate a kidney to meet you for lunch."

"Can't wait," I said. I paused as if I wrote down everything she said.

I drove to the Grits and Grill for breakfast and made notes for the future. Brady did not make mention of restaurant facts for the pirate piece. An idea cooked in my mind: *The Haunted Lanes of Pamlico Sound.* I found an entire book full of the ghost stories of the area at a gift shop. We could offer a map of famous coastal ghosts, haunted accommodations, and places to eat for Halloween. I would pitch it to Brady.

The proprietor served me the house grits with biscuits, a side of the smokehouse meats, and homemade jam. It tasted like a meal fresh off a grandmother's cookstove, the strawberry jam still warm and glistening inside the open-mouthed biscuits.

I could never wind down on Fridays, an anomaly that had somehow been encoded into my psyche. Friday had always been *finesse* day for my father, the day he laid the finishing touch to his Sunday message. While the rest of the community prepared for leisure, Dad prepared for the flock. My mother and I rubbed Parson's Wood Soap over the historical wood at the church. Thelma ran overages of the church bulletin. We all turned the hymnals face out and stuffed offering envelopes into the wooden slots on the pew backs.

I could see my father's face, but somehow it turned into Colin. I imagined him in his study. Or crouched in Eva's prayer garden. I wondered if all the members of his flock assumed he had gotten on with life, unaware of the ache that does not pass. A grief that deep opens hollows too wide to fill. As far away as I tried to pull myself from him, I could not deny the connection we made when we looked into each other's eyes. A knowing. A blending of two pains I knew only served to deepen the crater.

Angst swept over me. If ever I embraced another love, I feared loss would come to call again. All of it became a stony, shingled shore in my dreams. It loomed in front of me, and I could not reach it. If I tried to run to Colin, I'd risk all new wounds. That is why I called myself a wreck, after all. Because of how I had to live in order to save myself. Alone, the island of March. The lonely savior of me disconnected from the shore. But desire wooed me into the tidal pool.

Colin had not allowed himself to become the poster child for grief. Instead he remained as a calm beacon. The more he helped others, the more it seemed to lift him out of the place that consumed me.

Instinctively, my fingers hovered over the directory in my palm mechanism. Colin Arnett's number blinked onto the screen. I mentally apologized to him for turning down a kind dinner invitation. I dialed his number, closed up the phone, and laid it aside. "Don't, March," I whispered.

The phone rang and my nerves coiled. It was Gloria with an idea.

"March, Ocracoke is sponsoring a kite festival in the morning and we thought how convenient that you happen to be in the vicinity. You want to get some shots in the morning before you leave? Closeups of the sky full of kites, the kid-and-dog shots?"

"Gloria, I need you to talk me out of something," I said.

"Don't say it. You met someone."

"It's crossed my mind that maybe I should drive on up to Raleigh. Catch a flight to Charlotte, maybe as soon as this weekend."

Background noise crackled through. The Poe brothers laughed wickedly over something that was between just the two of them.

"It's so unlike you, March."

"That's good. Keep talking like that."

"That's why I like it."

"You need me at the office."

"Shaunda and I are managing splendissimo in spite of what you might imagine."

"Mason hates staying with the Buckworths, though," I said.

"I took him to your dad's. They're out at the cottage. Fishing."

"Dad can't go fishing. It's too soon."

"Ellie the nurse got it in her head."

"I've been away too much."

"True, but I need the hours. Does this mean you can't do the kite shoot? Festivities begin in the morning. If I can get you a flight out Sunday, you can still catch the kite festival. Unless you think it's a bad idea."

"Or I could leave Saturday afternoon. I'd arrive in Charlotte in less than an hour," I said.

"I'll call you back." The phone went dead.

The flight from Raleigh on Saturday afternoon got delayed on the runway, and we sat for forty-five minutes while a shrieking infant tortured her adolescent-looking mother in the last seat. I stayed in the rest room up front as long as possible to nurse a throbbing headache. I checked my mascara twice, as though someone waited for me in Charlotte.

I checked Gloria's travel preparations. She'd arranged for a rental car to be waiting for me in Charlotte and threatened the man with her ancestor's ghost if he didn't find for me a nonsmoker's vehicle. She would be happy to see two rolls of film used up completely at the morning's kite festival.

Finally the jet taxied forward and I felt the lurch, the lift, and the squealing vacuum in my ears as the ground disappeared from under us.

Some of the clouds looked like charcoal etchings. We flew completely through them and left them behind at the state capitol.

I sat next to a woman, her body padded as soft as a marshmallow. She swathed herself in a polyester caftan that hung to the floor whenever she sat. Around her stack of black curls she wrapped a turban that matched the caftan exactly. She smiled and her whole face bloomed cherry red. I decided that if a seat remained empty, I should move and allow her to spread her luxury over two seats.

"I notice you use a palm gadget. Lately, they seem to be lower in cost, and I've been thinking perhaps I should invest in one," she said.

I handed it to her and showed her how it worked.

"All of my grands are on the Internet. They say you can take photos and zoom them up or whatever you call it and show off your pictures right then and there to your family and friends."

"How many grandchildren do you have?" The headache subsided slightly. Normally I sought out a nonverbal passenger, one who allowed me to sleep or read without commenting about every small nuance in the air. But I liked the sound of her voice, low like water burbling gently over a rock ledge.

"Six in all. Three here in Raleigh. I spend half my summer here, and we go to the beach. The other half I spend in Colorado and the mountains with my other grands."

She handed me the palm device and squeezed a canvas bag up from the floor.

I hoped she had it filled with traveling curiosities that would hold her attention. She fished around the bag and pulled out a half-eaten cinnamon roll wrapped carefully in wax paper. "I have all of the best magazines if you want something to read," she said. The cinnamon roll did not hold her interest so she pulled out a roll of hard candies. She had maintained dexterity in spite of her long acrylic nails dotted with daisies. With the middle of her upper finger and thumb she pinched the candies in just a way to lift them out, her other three fingers fanned daintily away from her.

"You live in Charlotte, then?" I said.

"Yes. Do you?" The thought enlivened her as though she had found a new friend.

"I live in Candle Cove. March Longfellow. I'm going to Charlotte on business." I stumbled on "business," as if it were a lie.

She sighed and her eyes looked as though someone had dabbed away the sheen. "I said I had three grands in Raleigh. But it isn't true anymore. It just seems unfair to leave Lula out and just say two. Let me show you the children's pictures."

I took the small album and turned the pages. Two little boys with stout bodies that looked as though their knit shirts would burst at the seams smiled from a blanket on the ground. The next photo showed a young girl attempting to cradle them in her lap. The third photo was of a grave decorated with so many flowers the town florist must have locked up and gone home that day because they all but ran out of flowers.

"That's Lula when she was only eight. Leukemia took her, but not until she was seventeen." She lowered her voice.

It occurred to me that the screaming infant had calmed in the rear of the plane. Some of the passengers had begun to fall asleep. I had never taken photos of Joe's grave, and it seemed distasteful to do so. Grandmother-of-Lula seemed bent on reliving her last memory of this child in the worst place a child should be.

"She held on for four years. Thought we might get to keep her, but that last bone-marrow transplant failed."

I dug a traveler's packet of tissues from my purse and handed it to her. For my sake, I flipped to the next photograph. A young woman with a youthful face and a prim nose sat next to a fountain. "Is this Lula?" I asked.

"Lula's mother. My daughter-in-law, Nancy. She and my son James met at Chapel Hill."

"No way! That's my old alma mater." It was a polite way to change the subject.

"Doesn't seem fair that a mother would outlive her child," she said.

"I lost my husband two years ago. Seems like the pain might soon ease, but you just learn to live with it."

"That's why you have to embrace it. It's been six years since we lost Lula."

From the way she spoke, I had assumed the child had died only months ago.

"It's forever fresh. But so is the good Lord's grace. It's new every day."

"I had hoped for a respite from the pain," I said. *Six years.*

"This is new for me, too. You know you fall into valleys in life, little problems in marriage, on the job, what have you. But when you lose a grandchild, the valley becomes your permanent abode. You don't climb out. Valleys have sunshine too, green grass, and growing things. It's not a walk in the park, mind you. But I've found an abundance of peace. Dear, do you know God?" she asked.

I nodded. Her hand slid on top of mine on the armrest. I had known him better in the last twenty-four hours than in my whole life put together.

"It's hard to imagine that God gives us pain as a gift. Doesn't seem the least bit fathomable at first. But it's like getting a new pair of glasses. You see life a little more clearly. Certainly you feel a lot closer to heaven," she said.

"You do. It's true. It's as though I once thought of heaven as far away. When I lost Joe, I spent more time thinking about things I can't see and certainly can't explain. It's as though I've decided I need to be ready, like I've got my passport stamped and ready for the trip."

The flight attendant appeared with the drink cart.

I asked my seatmate about her daughter-in-law.

"Lula was such a big part of Nancy's life. She was a bubbly kid, all denim and dirt bikes, who really loved God. Sometimes it seems as though that makes it harder to let her go."

"I suppose she tries to stay busy, keep her mind occupied with other things," I said.

"Actually, Nancy finds comfort in solitude and looks for quiet ways to remember Lula. She and James go away on Lula's birthday and take photos that remind them of the way she laughed. Lula was a regular comedienne. Never let us have a serious day. I didn't mean to get off on all of that. Tell me what you do for a living. I notice you've been holding that journal the whole trip."

I told her about the *Sentinel* and my work for the *Observer.*

"I've always wanted to own a little newspaper outfit. I was a journalist when I met Alfred. You must be on your way downtown, then," she said.

"Not actually."

"I'm almost positive I've seen your name then. Not that I eat out as much since my husband passed. I hate to eat alone."

I turned her attention to the cirrus clouds that had formed wisps outside the airplane window. The flight attendant almost sprinted back up the aisle to retrieve the litter while the other one announced that we should buckle our seat belts again.

"Such a short flight. I'm glad we met. By the way, I'm Geraldine Montague."

"Not Senator Alfred Montague's Geraldine?" I was shocked.

"God rest his soul." She stuffed magazines and candies back into her bag.

My face flushed.

"We're flying over his interstate right now." She pointed to a busy artery of throughway.

I craned to see it.

"Seems like they'd run out of bridges and interstates to dedicate. Alfred never knew he had an interstate named after him. I don't think he would have liked it. Maybe early in his young campaign years, but not later. He would have thought it ostentatious."

"I'm so glad we met," I said.

The landing gear dropped beneath us.

She snapped a business card out of her wide canvas purse and handed it to me. "I had these made up just for fun. Helps people remember me."

I wondered how anyone could forget Geraldine and her exotic turban.

May had blown its billows across the South and opened the door to the warm garden of summer. I stepped out into the heat with my bag and found the rental-car lot. Gloria's nagging had not produced a completely smoke-free car, but it was better than some I had rented.

Rush-hour traffic bunged the Charlotte highways like bumper cars at the county fair.

After forty-five minutes, I inched my way to the Cornelius exit, the middle village on Lake Norman. My stomach growled although the flight had stolen my appetite. I imagined Ruth scrambling around the kitchen preparing for the evening meal. Instead of interrupting their Saturday-night ritual, I stopped and had a sandwich at a Honey Baked Ham, stalled another hour at a home-decorating store called The Black Lion, and then drove up and down the stretch of lake near Colin's house. He lived on the peninsula, code for where elitists moved old lake houses off half-acre lots to build four-story walk-ups. Over coffee, Ruth had told me that Colin and Eva had snatched up the modest lake house when everyone else identified the lake as swamp living, before New Yorkers had spotted Lake Norman as a little slice of suburbia and developed it as a haven for millionaires. Eva found ways to stretch small living quarters into wide open spaces including a billiard and game room in the basement.

I toyed with an alibi.

If by chance Brady lingered in his office, I could connect with him about the pirate article, thereby giving me the proper business angle so that I could legitimately tell Colin I had breezed into town on business rather than let on that I wanted to beg another invitation from him. Several times I rehearsed the telling of it: *Hi, Colin. I'm in town on business with the* Charlotte Observer. *No. I'm meeting with Mr. Gallagher tomorrow about developing a column for possible syndication. . . .*

Brady's phone rang until it switched over to the operator who offered to forward me to his voice mail. I hung up.

From the rounded and curbed corner, Colin's house blended with the years-old trees, an emerald-green house that looked deceptively small from the street.

The airline ticket stub hung out of the front zippered pocket of my handbag. Though wrangled by Gloria on a budget ticket Web site, it was still treacherously expensive. I imagined writing it off my taxes come January and recalling the night I sat outside Colin's house to watch the sun slide into Lake Norman before I skulked home undetected.

Out of the foliage, a jeep appeared. Lights blazed in the dim glow of a young evening. I saw Ruth heading away from Colin's house, loaded down with Arnett children. I felt idiotic parked three blocks away; a stalker who waited for the sun to dissolve like sugar on the lake. Alibis raced through my mind. I dove for the recesses of the passenger-side floor and excavated through absolutely nothing. Ruth never saw me, and I realized that the car I sat in was completely foreign to her.

Colin was home alone. My bowels knotted around my throat.

I must say there are moments when imagination is a woman's darling friend. You can, as a writer, sit with your mind floating on a placid stream of consciousness and conjure scenes that come to life. Vivid only to you, they feed you with enough audacity to help you take paths you might otherwise avoid. I might do well to avoid them, but what I imagined sat upon the plate of my mind's eye, pleasing. Alluring but unsullied and enticing, I felt as comfortable speaking with him as I did my own father and saw the whole thing played out as plain as my own hands in front of me: The two of us conversed on his sofa an unsafe distance from one another. But the very idea, the danger of failure elicited in my thoughts caused me to pull right into the drive, pull back out, park, walk through the neighbor's backyard and stand a safe distance from Colin's rear patio. The only thing I had to catch sight of, I decided, was Colin himself moving about the house. After that, I assured myself, I would sidle back around to the front landing and ring his doorbell.

Through a set of tall windows, a candelabrum flickered on the dining table. I moved in closer because white window sheers obstructed a clear view. But for certain, Colin seated himself with his back to the window. He ate alone.

Not more than a half-minute passed when I caught sight of another person. She placed a water glass in front of Colin and another near the place setting next to him. Ruth had never mentioned a cook or a maid, but we did not discuss every detail of our everyday lives.

The woman lit candles, for Pete's sake! Her face radiated a confidence, a rare shade of self-assurance that shone through the window sheers. Tranquillity was her beauty as well as an auburn hair color she had purchased, in my estimation, at great cost. Colin entertained a dinner guest. Or from this distance it appeared she entertained him.

The airline ticket stub flapped against my leg. I shoved it deep into the purse pocket. My knees turned gelatinous. When I looked up again the woman had stopped halfway without completely taking her seat. She said something to Colin and both of them turned to look out the window toward me. I stepped sideways to hide my face, but twisted my ankle and toppled onto the lawn. Years ago, Eva must have gotten the idea in her head to install an automatic lawn sprinkler. It came on.

By the time I dug my shoe out of the bog that had formed near the window bed, Colin and his date disappeared to see what was the matter with the woman who swam about the back yard. But they found no one for I had already sprinted up the side yard and leaped into the rental car to speed toward the airport, and back to Candle Cove. Where I belonged.

The sky, black and ugly, overshadowed my six-hour drive back to the coast. Several times I attempted to call Gloria with the intent that I would bribe her into telling no one about my mad flight to Charlotte. I would pay her whatever she asked.

Nineteen

FIVE WEEKS PASSED SINCE I HAD TAKEN A ROLL through Colin Arnett's backyard lawn. The long gap in days that had passed since then had to equal the pure embarrassment I felt for having traipsed off to Lake Norman after a man. Julia Norville would have turned green around her feminine little gills if she had been privy to such things in Glory.

Gloria managed to pull snatches of information out of me until she had the humiliating whole. The fact that Colin never bothered to pursue me any further with phone calls annoyed her, but I never agreed with her outwardly. I pretended to only care about the newspaper business and in her estimable opinion that morphed me into a calculating machine incapable of feelings, while inwardly I fumed that Colin had not pursued me or at least called to find out if he was blind or if he had indeed witnessed my undoing in his very own backyard.

"So you aren't in the least bit put out?" asked Gloria.

I shook my head.

Gloria's stomach expanded seemingly with heliumlike velocity. By the end of June, her short frame heaved the extra weight around like an ant hefting an M&M. Eric the pet man's capacity to love a married woman amplified by the time Gloria crossed the doorstep to her second trimester. He brought by imported pickles and chocolate spoons to be stirred into the gourmet coffees left at night upon our doormat.

Phil Hammer, who enjoyed Eric's extravagant gifts lavished upon his wife, phoned her in the afternoon on some days to see what Eric had dropped secretly through the night drop or placed in the driver's seat of Gloria's Carman Ghia.

Summer once again visited our cove. I developed my journal entries about the island mustangs into a short piece. I slipped it through the fax machine one night so that it would be waiting on Brady's office floor when he came in the next morning.

Mason and Jerry Brevity took to sailing the *Sparticus* around the inlet every Friday in the early evenings while I came to a decision. I rehearsed gentle ways to ease Jerry on down the river. Jerry arrived with his usual bag of burgers that he passed out to me, invisibly stamped with obligation although his hints were becoming more blatant attempts to seal a commitment. I joined him on the shore for a ceremonial send-off, but grew weary of the way he tried to hold my hand or hook his arm through mine. "Jerry, we need to talk. I just don't know how we could ever be anything more than friends."

"It's that minister guy that's come between us," he said to me.

I held a finger over my lips, stepped toward the boat where Mason had already clambered aboard, and told my son to snap on his life jacket. I stopped Jerry before he boarded. "If you're spending time with Mason to be a nice man, I appreciate it. But, Jerry, whatever you hoped might happen, it just isn't happening for me."

It was Jerry's last voyage aboard the *Sparticus.* But that did not stop Mason from wanting to go out in her.

I took the dog for a walk on the beach one day. Mason was untying the boat alone. I threatened him with floggings and made him promise to never attempt to sail single-handedly no matter how calm the water.

"I'm not a little kid, and I know how to sail!" Mason battled with me once again.

"The *Sparticus* isn't a toy, and you know how I feel about taking it out again anyway. I wish we'd just left her in your grandfather's shed."

"It's not my fault Dad took her into a storm. You're punishing me for what he did, and I know it."

"Mason, don't make me say it."

"Say what?"

"That I'll sell her if you keep pushing me like this."

"You can't sell this boat! It's really mine anyway. You don't want it but you don't want me to have it." Mason charged down the shore kicking at seashells and jellyfish carcasses that had washed ashore.

Brady Gallagher accepted my pirate piece but rejected my mustang story ideas twice before I figured out he wanted no slices of island life, just the history. I could no more interest him in a story about the mustangs than I could entice him away from the trout in the spring. He did show an interest in the Pamlico ghosts. I developed it from two different angles and promised that I would personally visit the site of the headless lantern ghost at the railroad crossing at whatever place it happened, if indeed it happened. I would report it accordingly, in spite of my reservations.

I sat out on my father's dock and by lantern light read the meanderings of my journal while Mason night fished. Until he had the Buckworth twins to compete with, he had complained at the very mention of fishing. Now they headed for his grandfather's dock at least twice a week.

One evening off Nags Head, I had sloughed around the bog and listened to the spatter of sound fish upon the water's surface. I identified nothing, not even a long-legged bird that fed on fish in the shallows. But I had used the phrase *clean tide* every so often. I had truly encountered God at Nags Head. What came of it altered my perception of Christ, and now I served Him beyond words. I had written down a sentence taken from scripture. "This people honors me with their lips. But their heart is far from me." God was teaching me a better way. I honored Him now in my heart with more than tradition and talk.

Mason snagged three striped bass.

"You'll be wanting me to cook them, I gather," I said.

From a cord, he dangled them in front of me.

"Bass are supposed to be, what, broiled?"

He shrugged. "All's I can do is clean them. I know how. Grandpa taught me the best way to do it."

Five children who visited their grandparents up the shore ran along the sand with flashlights, searching for crab.

"Summer is too short," said Mason.

"We still have more summer left. Don't shortchange it with worry."

"Jerry says he has this special ingredient for bass."

I sighed. "Mason, I told you not to expect to see Jerry so often."

"I don't want to share these fishes anyway. Except with Grandpa," he said. He saw that pleased me.

I dug my phone out of my purse and hit the speed-dial button, Brady Gallagher's home phone number. I had manipulated it from him after my debacle in Charlotte. He answered as though he were waiting for my call.

"I got your pirate piece. Everyone has read it. You've got a star with your name on it in newspaper heaven."

I interrupted him while I had the nerve. "Brady, I've come to a decision."

"You'll marry me."

"I don't want to write travel pieces, or ghost stories."

He waited as though he felt I had more to say. I did.

"For the life of me, I don't know what it is that is churning up inside of me. But it smacks faintly of something deeper than what I've been doing."

"But does it smack of filthy lucre?"

"Everything doesn't have to be about money."

"Bite your tongue."

"When you go away to the mountains, you have time to reflect on your life. This doesn't move you in some way?" I asked.

"Oh, you're talking deep. Well, I've never confessed this to anyone, but when I'm standing out in the middle of that clear stream with nothing but me and the fish, it gives me pause. Like, someday they'll walk into my office and find me gone. A note will be taped to my chair."

"Sakes alive! What kind of note?"

"Don't be morbid. It will say, 'Brady's gone fishing.'"

"That's deep."

"Maybe I'll go so far as to say I've set aside a little money. I've had my eye on this mountain cabin for a while. Any day that owner's going to come down on his price and I'll scoop it up with my bag of money. It would be a shame not to share it with someone."

"Brady, some really lucky woman is going to think you've handed her the chance of a lifetime."

"Just not you." He read my silence. "Thank you for not saying something cliché."

He deserved better.

"So you're not interested in the column." His voice sounded flat.

"You'd think that I would at least figure out what I do want first before I go off the porch clubbing all of the things I don't want."

He did that breathing thing editors do when they don't know how to agree or disagree.

"I knew you'd understand." I promised we would get together soon for lunch. He hung up.

The tide was coming in and subtracting the shoreline from the walkers. *I hope I've done the right thing, God. You know what happens next, and I don't. And that is just fine with me.*

Gloria watched me appraisingly. Two mornings in a row, I had slipped into the office at dawn. Both times she found me sitting at my desk, writing in my journal.

"Here's your fan mail from yesterday. I don't know if you meant to overlook it, but one piece appears to be a check from the *Charlotte Observer.*"

"For the pirate piece. Oh good! It should be just enough to cover the new pair of shoes I ruined in Colin's backyard. Of course, the travel expense was a wash. One flight to Charlotte, two rental cars, a fairly decent ham sandwich, and a new pair of stockings."

I opened my journal and sat it next to my monitor. I typed some of it onto the screen to see how it looked in print.

"Let's see what else is in here. The rest are what looks to be the light bill and a letter from the President of the United States. He wants to do lunch with you next week, say Friday," she said.

"I realize you think I'm not listening to you, but I heard every word. I'll take the check." I turned around and snapped it out of her fingers.

She tightened the screws on the bill reminder with a Phillips screwdriver.

"You did a good job on your pregnancy series. The hospital bought extra copies to slip into their new mother gift package," I said.

"My feet are so swollen I had to wear sandals today. I hope you don't mind."

"I don't know. Might upset the dress code around here."

"If you don't want to tell me what you're doing here so early, March, you don't have to."

"Thank you."

She walked away, her face sullen.

"Oh, look," I waved and spoke with a strange jaded innocence. "This one's for you," I said. I stuck her envelope in the air.

We exchanged smiles.

She took it and opened it at her desk. Twice she blinked, then ran back to throw her arms around my neck.

"You're welcome. I figured you were the one who brought in the extra business. You deserve a bonus. But hide it. I don't want Lindle sniffing around for his bonus, like it's bonus day or something. I can't just toss out bonuses whenever I please."

"This will pay for a new crib," she said.

Later I called Phil and told him to stall her off on the crib. Shaunda had taken up a collection around the office. Instead of a baby shower, everyone opted for a new crib for Gloria and Phil. Not to be outdone, Eric filled a basket with stuffed pets and baby linens.

By the next day, my early mornings caught up with me.

"Subscriptions are down. Please, I need ideas, people," I said.

Shaunda raked sand in the wooden box on her desk, a Zen garden, though she wasn't a Buddhist. "I don't know how this reduces stress, but I'll give it a try."

Lindle lifted just high enough to show sleepy eyes over the top of his cubicle. "Don't look at me. I'm the ad guy," he said.

Gloria pressed cucumbers against her puffy eyes. "I need a massage. Do they do that for pregnant women?"

Wylie and Brendan ducked into the printing room.

"While you're in there, guys, please collect all those dirty coffee mugs. You could fill the pantry again with ceramics."

Gloria lifted my coffee mug and sniffed it. "You take a bossy pill or something?"

I just looked at her.

She watched the Poes skulk across the office with a box of clanking dishes.

"Just leave them by the sink, Wylie. I'll wash them for you," she said. She printed off the subscription list and handed it to me rather defensively.

Eric flounced in. He sported a completely new haircut although it was nothing more than a change of the part in his hair that made him look less like Opie Taylor and more like Andy.

"We're really busy, Eric," I said. Both of them ignored me, which made me feel more impatient.

Gloria blew out a breath.

He disregarded me and directed all of his attention on Gloria. "If you want me to stop by Saturday and paint the nursery, I checked my calendar and I am free. I still think lemon yellow is the best color since you want the baby's sex to remain a mystery until it's born."

"If you could discuss personal matters later, we might actually get some real work accomplished," I said.

Gloria fished a handful of paint samples out of her desk drawer. "You pick out the color then and just bring me the receipt."

Eric had already headed for the door and did not see the paint samples. "Frankly, I'm rooting for a girl and I hope she looks just like her mother," said Eric.

We watched him go.

"Gloria, a handful of female collegiates are home for the summer and while Eric moons over what will never be, and I say that with kindest concern, the parade passes him by. This doesn't bother you?"

"March, he's painting my nursery. Friends do nice things for one another," said Gloria. She yelled after him through the window. Like a happy sentinel, he stuck his head back through the doorway. She met him at the door, handed him the paint chips, and scooted him off to the animal farm.

"I have to head for Wharton's Pond. The Jaycees' summer duck races are today," said Shaunda.

"They train them to race?" Lindle asked, surprised.

"Rubber duckies, Lindle. As in, your mother put those little yellow toys in your bubble bath. You know, like a fund-raiser for the hospital children's fund?" Shaunda rubbed her finger over the painted daisy embedded in her manicure.

"I smell business people afoot. I'll go with you," Lindle said. He followed her out to her car.

"I need carbs. For the baby. I'll be right back." Gloria grabbed her knapsack of a purse and sauntered out behind them. The Poes tinkered around the sink. They commented about the amazing collection of mold and the awful shame of watching it glug down the drain. I held up the subscription list to the empty room. "So, any ideas, people, for increasing subscriptions?" Each of them scattered to the wind, confetti in a parade. *Okay, Lord, I'm still waiting on what's next. You're stretching me, right?*

Another silent answer.

Learning to wait was not an active image, but somehow I could feel God in it.

Gloria returned within the hour toting two bag lunches from Ruby's and a liter of soft drink.

"You didn't abandon me after all," I said.

"I got you the Reuben on rye, tortilla chips, and a sweet iced tea, extra ice."

"Are you mad at me for acting like the boss?"

"I like my job, March. The reason I like it is because you don't act like one."

"But if I don't take charge of the business it eats me alive."

"People are your business. The reason you do well is because everyone trusts you, they know you won't publish some left-wing propaganda mumbo jumbo, but that you will be fair and paint the world in living color."

"Am I fair?"

She set a paper plate in front of me and dropped a napkin onto my lap.

"Gloria, I'm sorry if I was rude to Eric."

"Eric eats Sunday dinner every weekend at my house after mass. Do you think Phil is worried? He and Eric are painting the nursery together."

"I should be taken out and shot, that's what."

"You take my salsa. It sends me to the throne room in a nanosecond."

"The Poes cleaned up the print room. I feel guilty about it."

"You shouldn't. Like you said, you're the boss."

"But I was harsh."

"That is true. But it was beginning to smell like my Uncle José's undershirts."

"I must have left my diplomacy at home this morning. When they get back from lunch I'll give them the afternoon off."

"I think you can't stop thinking about that preacher fellow."

"Nonsense." I used the remote to turn on the radio.

Dinah's otherwise live show had gone into reruns she called "The Best of Dinah." She introduced the show live, though. "Today's show teaches you how to make Valentine Cake, a dessert that is sure to please the main attraction in your life. I dedicate this show to a friend who shall remain anonymous, but who is as miserably in love as anyone I know."

I choked on my tea.

"Maybe she wasn't talking about you, March. You know, the whole world doesn't revolve around you. She knows you better than that anyway, that you have your head on straight and don't walk around in a stupor over some guy who is too lacking in persistence for you to care about."

"I find this is an exhausting conversation."

"But you do think about him. I wouldn't go so far as to say you're in love. That is just low for her to say it like that. If she's even talking about you. Do you want your pickle?"

"For all we know, the man is engaged and I am thankful and relieved to have my life uncomplicated by a long-distance relationship."

"I wonder if tuna contains choline. Or is it mercury? I can't remember anything today."

"But my attitude today has nothing to do with Colin. I'm writing a novel, if you have to know everything. It's beyond me how to start it, so I just began typing and it seems I have an opening to a chapter."

Gloria giggled.

"I shouldn't have told you."

"I'm happy as a clam for you. Finally, you're doing something for yourself for a change."

"I didn't think of it like that."

Gloria fished emeralds of pickle out of the tuna salad with a fork and ate them separate from the sandwich.

Dad called from the cottage to tell me the news: Bill Simmons invited a pastoral candidate in for a speaking engagement. He was from Pennsylvania. Colin's candidate had fizzled. He showed no interest in a small-town congregation.

Yolanda had picked up Mason and taken him to a movie. Dad said that before she came Mason had made them both turkey-and-lettuce sandwiches. He requested that I stock the cottage pantry with finer delicacies such as canned ham, cheddar, and bologna.

The Poes returned but would not hear of leaving for the day. They could not fathom at what moment I had offended them.

Brendan stepped out of the bathroom and pointed imperiously. "Help! The toilet is squealing again."

Gloria got out her wrench and worked her stomach between the toilet and the tight space of cabinet.

I handed her tools while she executed her magic.

"I've been thinking. If we know for certain that we are only going to attract a certain percentage of Candle Cove, then we need to expand our circulation all the way out to Cedar Island," she said.

"Why didn't I think of that? And I just came from there too. Lindle could approach the few stores along the way with an ad that targets the tourists, but include coupons for the locals who have to shop in those mom-and-pops along Highway 70 and in Beaufort." I ran for my pen and pad and wrote while Gloria and I brainstormed.

Shaunda returned with photographs from the duck race.

"Hop and shop at the mom-and-pop," said Gloria.

"They don't know we call them that, Gloria." I kept writing. "It isn't a compliment."

She gave her lyrics a melody.

"If anybody wants to know, I just sold a story to a newspaper in New York," said Shaunda.

"The *Times?* No way," said Gloria.

"Not the *Times.* But it isn't far from the Big Apple, and it wouldn't surprise me at all if this didn't lead to bigger things." Shaunda covered her egg roll from Ginger's with paper and placed it in the refrigerator.

"The phone again! Shaunda, will you please get it this time?" Gloria turned sideways to make more room for her stomach, but it did not help.

"March, it's for you. Someone by the name of Simone," said Shaunda.

I had visited Victoria Lane only once more since our first encounter before my trip to Ocracoke. "Simone? Is something wrong?"

"The family has been called in. Vicki is in a coma, and they don't expect her to last through the night." Simone sounded short of breath.

A nurse had placed several vases of flowers on a table outside Victoria Lane's window in ICU. I found Carla and Simone holding on to one another. An RN closed the curtain.

"I didn't make it," I said.

"Vicki just took a breath and was gone." Carla pulled a sweater about her shoulders.

I stepped into Vicki's room.

Herb had both hands clasped behind his neck. Both of us observed the stillness of a life just crossed over. He pulled the Gideon Bible out of his wife's hands. "I don't think they would mind if I kept this."

We left the room. I gave him my father's number and told him that Dad would like to speak with him. Together they could discuss the funeral arrangements.

I waited until I returned to the car. Then I pulled out a box of tissues and cried.

Before I picked up Mason, I dropped by the *Sentinel* to help Gloria lock up.

"I'm sorry about your friend." Gloria fastened the tool chest.

"Vicki's just not here anymore, that's all. Heaven is just another country." I waited until she left and then allowed myself to cry again. God had somehow used me to point the way to Him when I was just coming alive in my soul myself.

"You are a mystery sometimes, Father. You reveal yourself in ways that surprise me." I wondered what other mysteries and surprises lay beyond the valley.

Twenty

HERB LANE FOUND CHRIST. NO ONE HAILED IT AS AN overnight conversion. I compared it more to dawn. The light sends the night away and then incrementally reveals the source. Either you stay in bed or you embrace the sun. Herb embraced the Son.

First he showed up one Sunday and sat on the back pew. Bill Simmons joined him and invited him to stay for the church social. We did not see him again for two weeks. After that, he never missed a Sunday.

Herb could not keep quiet about his transformation. That made a few veterans of the faith green-eyed, but they painted their envy with condescension. He set to work carving little praying hands out of wood and passing them out to people so that each of us might remember the carpenter who set men free. Although not a soul seemed aware of the difference in their take on God and Herb's, I was grateful I finally did.

I placed the carving he gave to me on the kitchen windowsill beneath Charlotte's origami angels.

His sister-in-law Simone came into town for a visit, to help Herb box up Vicki's things. She brought her sons for a visit with their Uncle Herb on the weekend they didn't have to go and see their father.

Simone found a mouse in the attic and screamed until the next-door neighbor ran out into the yard. Herb did what everyone in Candle Cove did. He called Jerry. I am almost positive I saw the rat truck parked outside Herb's door for three nights in a row. Jerry must have been tending to other things besides rodents.

It was his time.

The pulpit committee settled on a candidate for the pastorate, the gentleman from Pennsylvania. From a video, the Reverend Frederick Tuck, a thin minister with a shoehorn-shaped posture, crooned the offertory with his wife, Lilly, while she played the organ. The Caudles and the Michaels forgave him the necessity of modern media techniques and applauded his time-honored views and oral execution of the sacraments. My father questioned the validity of offertory songs but agreed the sacraments and Tuck's immaculate views outweighed his one divergent practice. Bill and Irene Simmons lived for the day the telephone on their kitchen wall stopped resonating with impatient callers from the congregation. They found not even the teensiest flaw. Even as the candidate clambered into the rigors of the credentials committee and the meetings on the presbytery floor, we met and asked grace and guidance from above.

The fall sky appeared hard as glass to me, and I imagined our prayers hitting the ceiling of the earth and ricocheting off like tennis balls. When Reverend Tuck sermonized, a restless wind blew into my heart. It seemed a man could master the song and dance of church doctrine and still miss the calling. Every pastor, my mother said, was a watering hole, to some a crystal stream and others a neglectful algae pool. Not that Pastor Tuck with his simpering glances at his wife fell into any sour extreme. But some men lead while others just manage. Tuck was a maintainer if ever I saw one. I withheld my opinions, having found solace in quiet observance.

Bill and Irene Simmons hosted a dinner party for Dad in the fellowship hall Sunday evening after the service. But no one dared call it a going-away party. The children's club decorated the hall with crepe paper and a computer banner that said WE LOVE PASTOR NORVILLE surrounded by a border of hearts and cupids. Lorraine Bedinsky designed arrangements of diminutive potted mums with imaginative miniature spades and artsy-craftsy potter's tools. A youth with calligraphy ability designed small placards according to Lorraine's specifications. She placed the cards around the clay pots in such a way to indicate my father had gardened or tended the souls of men, the master cultivator, or some such metaphor that not everyone got, though Dad did. I saw him dab his eyes.

The only matter that kept me from the total enjoyment of the festivities, aside from the nagging worries about candidate Tuck, was the fact that early Monday I had to attend the trial of the two convicts that had held Yolanda at knife point. Since I was the key witness, the prosecuting attorney, Judd Neisen, placed my testimony at the crux of the trial. He called it open-and-shut, but I was well aware that the examination gave the New Jersey inmates another good gander at my face. In a town the size of Candle Cove, a good hiding place was nowhere to be found. But the boys' criminal trail stretched across four state lines, including a robbery spree all the way through the Chesapeake Bay that implicated them in four counties. Judd said the yellow Yanks faced a city full of witnesses for the next three years. By the time they peeked into the free light of day, their revenge list would be tethered to a foggy history.

Two little girls from the M&Ms, the Sunday night Memorization and More club, dragged my long-handled handbag across the floor.

"Your purse is chirping, Mrs. Longfellow," said one.

"My phone. Thanks, girls."

On the phone I heard a young woman sniff. She cleared her throat.

"May I help?" I asked.

"I'm Brady Gallagher's daughter, Jenny Owens. I just flew in from Dallas. It's Daddy. He's had a heart attack. They put him in intensive care here at Mercy Hospital. I know you're supposed to call people in instances like this, but I don't live here and he's not in a position to tell me whom I should call. I found his Christmas-card list and your name is at the top." Her voice had the sound of a young woman on her own for too long against her will. Her personality was not as well defined as her father's. She could not have been as educated or worldly-wise. I remember her small childhood portrait on his credenza, a plump girl whose deportment left uncomfortable inches between herself and her father with her round arms crossed in front of her.

"I'm Brady's friend. You did the right thing. How long is the list?"

"Five names long."

"Where is Brady?"

"At the Heart Center at Mercy."

"I don't suppose they've given you a prognosis."

"It's serious. My little brother, Will, just walked in. He lives in Kansas. I have to go."

Dad sat at the center of a ring of admirers. He sipped punch from a crystal mug kept full by Lorraine Bedinsky. If he ever noticed her admiration he did not indicate so. Her lack of loveliness would not have been the deterrent. My mother was a beautiful woman, but even women like her fade with years. Though even with cancer, Mother had never lost her splendor. Lorraine fluttered around my father while he acknowledged her with the same nod he might offer to a domestic.

He caught my eye and read the gloom in my thoughts.

"Pardon me." He dismissed himself from the well-wishers and joined me next to the punch bowl. "My daughter has a problem?"

"My newspaper friend, Brady Gallagher, Dad. He's had a heart attack."

"He's too young to join that club."

"Brady's forty-three. His eating habits would make you the king of health food. They've placed him in ICU in downtown Charlotte."

"Maybe you should go to Charlotte."

"I have to testify at that trial Monday. That's tomorrow morning. Judd said we could be tied up for days."

Dad clasped his hands around mine. "You'll have to send someone in your place. If you think about it for a bit, I'm sure you'll come up with a name." He joined the circle again.

Colin Arnett and I had not spoken for the length of the summer. Pastors could find admittance to ICU when even relatives could not. I felt desperate. I dialed his number.

It rang twice. He answered himself.

I hesitated. His voice sounded warm, expectant.

"Anyone there?"

"Colin, it's me, March. I have a problem. If I could handle it myself, believe me I would."

"March, I've been thinking about you. How are you?"

I was surprised. "I'm good. But I have a friend in need."

"What can I do to help?"

"Brady Gallagher, at the *Charlotte Observer*, he's had a heart attack. They rushed him by ambulance to Mercy Hospital. Near you, I think." My breath sucked in while I stifled a tear.

"He must mean a lot to you." Colin turned from the phone and scolded Troy and Luke for not taking their baths.

"Brady and I, we've been friends for years. Like Dinah and me."

"It's after eight. I'll call first and see if they'll allow me in. I know someone at Mercy. Does he have a pastor or a priest I should call?"

"No one."

"I'll go right away."

I expected him to hang up. But I heard him still breathing. Then a pause.

"I'd like to ask a favor of you, too," he said.

"Anything. I'm so appreciative of this, Colin. I know it's late. I know I haven't contacted you in a while."

"Thursday evening, I have to attend a banquet in Wilmington. It's an annual event. Your father and I first met at this ministers' banquet, two old widowed bachelors. The wife of one of our deacons is pressuring me to take her niece. I'd like to tell her I've made other arrangements. If you'd rather not go, I understand."

"Thursday night in Wilmington." I pretended to check my calendar. "Is it a formal affair?"

"Semiformal. But you look nice in anything. In my opinion."

I refrained from asking him if he saw me that night flitting around in his sprinkler system, wearing his lawn. "I believe I can go."

The next morning I climbed the stone steps to the courthouse. Fall trickled into the cove dropping summer temperatures to a bearable blister. Our fall provided its own tonic for the vacation weary, our shores a comfortable pillow for strangers, our streets a welcome mat. But climbing the steps to participate in a highly publicized trial made me feel anything but welcome. Photographers from newspapers and magazines snapped pictures of every person who entered the courthouse down to the hefty tax assessor who wiped jam from his bottom lip.

Judd Niesen met me at the door.

If Colin met with Brady or any of his family, he did not call later Sunday night to inform me of it. After the first court recess, I would call Mercy Hospital and see how Brady had fared through the night.

Judge Bernard Joiner presided over the trial, brother of the mayor whose heated mayoral race had dominated the front page of the *Sentinel* the entire summer. A news crew from a Raleigh television station pulled up at the base of the steps just as Judd whisked me inside.

Yolanda's excitement spilled over when she heard the TV news crew had arrived.

"March, my savior!" She hugged me and then stepped aside to allow her mother, Toni Goya, to shake my hand.

Toni never made eye contact, distracted by the camera crew. "We have not slept in a week, March. Worse than that is the absolute nightmare of this trial. Ever since these hideous men tried to abduct our baby girl, well, I can't tell you how it has disrupted our entire lives. I hope they put them away so far they can't find themselves, that's what. I'm just glad my Frank is in Washington State this week or I don't know what he would do the minute he saw them."

"I might need therapy," Yolanda said. The thought made her smile.

"He's not one to contend with." Toni Goya checked her face in the mirror of a powder compact. The whites of her eyes were pink, most likely from the neglected rest. Her teeth appeared a stark white, a product of expensive bleach trays.

Yolanda met the news crew at the door. Her attorney blew out a breath, stepped ahead of her to give the crew a "no comment until after the trial" statement, and led her down the hall and into a room. Toni followed them. I took a seat inside the courtroom.

If the accused man who had held the knife recognized me, he did not show it on his face. The only reaction I saw was when Yolanda and her mother entered the room. He shifted uncomfortably in his chair and leaned sideways to receive counsel from his attorney.

Yolanda's counselor must have scolded her for her candidness with the paparazzi. She seated herself somberly, her skirt falling prettily over her knees. Once or twice she allowed her eyes to regard the convict with disdain, careful that Judge Joiner failed to observe the reaction.

At exactly twelve, Joiner called for a recess for lunch. Yolanda met me out in the hall, asked if I carried a compact, and checked her rubescent cheeks thrice. I slipped away and ate alone in the courthouse cafeteria, exhausted by Yolanda's bubbly discourse on courtroom procedure and how she felt just every ounce of support from the jury issuing toward her like petals off a cherry tree, or some such. After several attempts to call Mercy, I finally reached a nurse who told me Brady was resting well, but she knew nothing about a visit from a pastor.

By the time Judd called me to the stand, it was thirty minutes after we had returned from lunch. Bill and Irene Simmons's daughter, Darlene, swore me in. She had a sweet demeanor that said she had been loved to death, but a pursy voice due to her size. Her squash-shaped frame filled up the straight-legged police trousers like bratwurst. She spoke to me in a manner that let everyone know we were acquaintances. That put me at ease somewhat.

Judd exercised precision in setting up the entire scenario of my part in the confrontation. "Would you point to the victim?"

I pointed to Yolanda, who allowed a small smile to dimple her cheek.

"Mrs. Longfellow, would you describe what you saw, please?" said Judd.

"Yolanda Goya has been my baby-sitter for many years. I was on the way home from the grocery store loaded down with corn and shrimp, and that's when I saw this hideous man put his hands on Yolanda."

Judd asked me to point out the criminal.

"Let the record show that the witness, March Longfellow, is pointing to the accused, Sam Jackson," said Judd. He asked me to continue.

"For the life of me, I could not think straight. If I called the police and just waited, well, then they might get away and take Yolanda with them. They say that once a person is kidnapped, her chances of making it home safely again are slight. So I told them they better stop what they were doing or something like that."

Jackson's attorney objected. Judge Joiner ordered me to say exactly what I said that day.

"I told them I was the police and to drop their weapon. I asked them to lay on the parking lot until our two cops, Harold and Bobby, arrived."

"Did you use a weapon, Mrs. Longfellow?"

"Not exactly."

"Describe how you apprehended the accused man, Samuel Jackson, and his partner, Eddy Fallon."

"With my son's water pistol."

Everyone laughed, and that really upset Judge Joiner. He had observed enough land-border arguments and sow-odor disputes to last his whole life. This trial was big publicity for our county, and he wanted it treated with importance.

"Were you questioned about the use of a weapon by the arresting officers, Mrs. Longfellow?" asked Judd.

"I gave it to them. Mason would really like it back." Bobby winked and gave me a thumbs-up as though he would handle the matter later.

Judd held up the water pistol. A tag dangled from it marked Exhibit B.

Joiner rapped the bench to quell the laughter again. "Mrs. Longfellow, I ask that you simply answer the prosecutor with a simple yes or no."

I tried.

The accused, Sam Jackson, stared at the tabletop the whole time. That helped settle my nerves.

After I finished my testimony, the judge called a recess until the next day.

I approached Judd. "I have to leave town early Thursday afternoon. Is that a problem?

"I'll let you know by Wednesday for certain, March. You did great today."

I had a headache. I hated the uncertainty of Judd's comment. I disappeared from the hall and down the courthouse steps before the news crew crowded around the victim and her family. Next door to the courthouse, a wedding party collected and waited for the bride and groom to appear from the old Methodist church. White wreaths with enormous satin bows hung on the centuries-old double doors of the church. I passed through the throng, a woman on a mission.

Madame Fergie's Boutique was having a sale. If heaven was in my favor, by Thursday I'd need a dress, semiformal.

On Thursday morning, Judd dismissed me entirely. At first, relief washed through me. But as soon as I descended the courthouse steps, I was nearly giddy. Then I thought about being alone with Colin and saying the stupidest things. So, by reason of insecurity, fear replaced giddiness. I was without any excuse for turning down Colin's invitation and glad about it.

Also petrified.

Yolanda stayed with Mason after school, and I gave them money for pizza and a rental movie.

Dad, if he formed any opinion at all about the meeting with Colin Arnett (I called it a meeting), offered none of it, and I did not share so much as a glimmer of the elation that was slowly overtaking me. I knew he would just stare at me smug, self-satisfied, and all at once the seer to this whole evening out.

The only route to Wilmington was the scenic coastal route. I traveled past Cape Carteret and Sneads Ferry until I connected with High-way 17. It was a picturesque route that allowed me to slip in Wilmington's back door, so to speak, and avoid the traffic that pa-raded in from Interstate 40.

I followed Colin's directions to the Hilton Riverside. A concierge directed me to a powder room where I changed for the evening and freshened up. A young woman just in town from Raleigh for a smaller dinner event wandered in to find a quiet place to take a prescription drug. She shook out two pills with her manicured fingers. Then she helped me with my dress zipper and with the hook and eye that is never easy to do alone.

She wore a shimmering teal calf-length sequined dress that had slits from calf to thigh. Her blond hair was upswept and then cascaded all around the back of her head in curls. She looked like a mermaid.

"I can never find a good black dress," she said to me.

If she was complimenting my own black creation from Madame Fergie's I could not tell.

"They all look the same, as though the buyers all think we women are in too big of a hurry to shop so we'll just take whatever. As if!"

"I actually took my time with this one," I said.

"That's what I'm trying to say. Always with the foot-in-mouth, my ex would say. Yours is so appealing with those sheer shoulders and sleeves. You have the shoulders for it. Well formed, like you don't have to do tricep weights or nothing. Not many girls could wear your dress. Nice choice."

What a relief! I had the mermaid's blessing.

The Hilton connected with an enormous floating dock. I left my day-wear and makeup kit in the Mustang and then took a walk near the ocean. The Ministerial Alliance banquet did not start for another hour, just enough time to have a full-blown anxiety attack. I wondered what Julia might say to her daughter right now. Might she offer me advice on table etiquette or how to sit, feet together, never crossing my legs? Or would she say how lovely I looked in black? Or disapprove of my moving on, away from Joe? Or with her new heavenly mind-set, somehow approve of Colin? Or approve of me?

A small orchestra rehearsed underneath snapping flags. The music soothed and wafted along the stream of early-evening breezes. I found a table and sat for a while to watch the tourists pad away only to emerge dressed for dancing and evening dinner parties. An older gentleman walked a younger lady half his age onto a yacht the size of a house. The moon appeared even though the daylight would dominate the harbor until well past eight o'clock. I followed the older yacht man and that giggling woman with my eyes and thought how mismatched the two of them looked. Colin was taller than Joe by at least three inches. People once commented how well matched Joe and I were. Until the walk on the beach I had not compared our heights. I wondered if people would look at Colin and me together and declare us mismatched.

I saw a flash of black coat. A gentleman seated himself at the table next to mine but I felt mesmerized by the yacht people.

I pulled out a stick of gum and chewed it.

Colin had asked me to meet him in the hotel lobby by seven. Thirty minutes to go. I felt awkward about that now. I imagined walking through the doors with a self-conscious smile to give the room a once-over only to find he was late. I would stand in the lobby, my high-heeled shoes gnawing at my feet while people I did not know swam around me as though I were a post in the shallows.

"I hate walking into parties too early. But here I am, too early. I must be nervous." The gentleman at the nearby table spoke. He sat alone with his back to me and it occurred to me that bewilderment seized this poor fellow enough to cause him to talk to himself. He turned around and smiled at me.

"Colin!" I think I swallowed my gum. "You should have joined me. I hope I didn't appear rude."

"You looked peaceful. I couldn't bring myself to disturb you."

Couples gathered around the orchestra to dance, men dressed in military dress uniforms and women in formals. The mermaid joined her lieutenant in a slow waltz.

"Your friend, Brady, he's going to be fine," he said casually, almost as though he assumed I knew.

"I keep missing him when I call. He's either sleeping or they've got him up and walking. They do that so fast nowadays." My eyes followed the progression of his movement, back relaxed against the chair, right foot and left hand tapping to the orchestral strains. "Thank you for coming to the aid of my friend. He knows nothing about God. I just thought you might help."

"We talked about God. Brady attended Sunday school as a kid."

"I never knew that."

"He might call me later." He turned slowly around in his chair, his leg crossed over his other knee. "The banquet inside will last a good two hours. I'll bet no one ordered an orchestra, either."

"One never knows. It's an interdenominational crowd."

"Have a go with me, March. The sun is going down."

"This isn't our party, Colin. Should we?"

He took my hand and led me onto the floating dock. We danced through the next three songs.

The sun disappeared and we could see the banquet hall filled with ministers and wives.

"We don't have to go inside." He said it while he looked right into my anxiety-laced eyes. "I'd rather not, come to think of it."

"But you came all this way for it," I answered, hoping he wouldn't listen to me.

"March, you can lay down your walls now. We don't have to play polite games."

Is that what I was doing? I felt his hand brush what the mermaid had termed my well-formed shoulder.

"We have to eat, I suppose. Wouldn't want to send you home hungry." He extended one hand as though he intended to lead me toward the hotel lobby.

First I laid my hand inside his. Then I screeched to a stop. "Colin, I want to finish what you just said to me. I have laid aside some walls since we spoke last. Some between God and me and some I had in place to ward off pain. You have to know that my timetable for healing is set at a different pace that yours."

I wanted to be next to him again, to dance. It is beyond me why I could not have said that instead.

"I know you came to Lake Norman that evening when I had a guest."

Oh, just great! "So you know I'm a fool." I said it matter-of-factly, as though I commented on the weather.

"I didn't want to see that woman. You have to understand the friends who badger me with eligible women friends. But I don't apologize for wanting a social life again."

"You weren't expecting me. I deserved to feel like an idiot." I hoped he would disagree with me as swiftly as possible.

"Please don't give excuses for me, March. Not that I did anything wrong. You know it and so do I. I didn't know you were coming and you—surprised me."

He didn't have to take it that far. "I wanted to surprise you. Are you saying that's wrong?"

"It isn't always a good idea. Not until you know someone better."

"It was a mistake." I felt a knot in my throat grow bigger than the one I got worrying over saying something stupid.

"So we both agree and that's that." He clasped his hands together as though he were in charge of punctuation, putting the big period at the end of our conversation.

"I feel as though we're having a fight, but we couldn't be because we don't know one another well enough and a quarrel would ruin the night. We have a moon out. Could we just dance again?" I asked. Marriage had its seesaws, but all of these undefined parameters spinning around Colin and me were complicated

The orchestra played "How Can I Remember?"

"I've made you uncomfortable. Let's start over. How about dinner? If I had stayed with the plan, we'd be inside cutting up our pâté and exchanging pleasantries right now."

He obviously didn't know what pâté was. I liked that in a man.

"Join me for dinner, please, March," he said, looking self-injected with regret.

I took his hand. Perhaps I was right about the bewildered man seated next to me.

"You're lovelier than I remember," he said. He kissed me. I felt his arms lift me, my toes pointed at the dock.

I tried to push away, to tell him I wasn't Eva, that I couldn't be as good as the angel he had lucked upon. He kissed me again while a tear ran down the side of my face.

"Do you want me to let you go, March?" He lowered me to the dock. When he saw the tear, he touched it and looked at his finger as though he had broken something.

"Colin, you don't know me or how easily I say the wrong things to the wrong people at the wrong time. I still live with my mother in my head telling me what to do. I can't be who you need."

"Will you listen to me for once? No one's asking you to be anyone but you. You don't have to step into Eva's shoes or your mother's or hold together anyone else's life. Just hold me, March. Hold me now. That's all I want."

We held each other, mismatched, while the moon cast spells upon the ocean.

Twenty-one

Brady Gallagher convalesced in his Charlotte apartment. The day nurse from Mercy Hospital promised to check on him since he lacked local family support. She dropped by every evening and brought him a meal. Then Brady suggested she stay and dine with him. He phoned me one evening early after she left for home.

"Tell me what to say, what to do, March. I don't want to blow it with this angel."

"You're smitten, Brady."

"Smitten, bitten. I'm supposed to go back to work Monday. But if I get well, she might disappear."

"Why do you think it's one-sided?"

"I have a history."

"Brady, you can count on one finger the relationships you've had since your divorce. If this nurse, this Elaine, is coming by every evening of her own free will, it is safe to assume there's the possibility of a spark between you. What is she saying to you? Is it all medical mumbo jumbo or has she asked you about yourself?"

"Elaine knows my life history. She knows more about me than I know about myself. She seems interested."

"Give it a chance to happen, Brady."

"See, that is exactly what I mean, that I won't give it the chance to just happen. That I'll rush her or wait too long. The timing thing is what turns me into Jell-O. I never had timing as a kid, not with girls. That is why I married Janelle from college. She wafted in from a wrong turn in Burlington and wound up working at the campus bookstore. She wasn't even a student, for Pete's sake! But she was available. That's all it took for me, availability."

"Trust Elaine. Be transparent. If it's meant to be, the slightest blunder on your part shouldn't scare her away. Get well. Ask her out on a real date, the kind where you pick up the tab."

"But what if the attraction is that she's one of those Florence Nightingales and once she realizes I'm healed, the magic is gone?"

"Then you admit you imagined it and move on."

"I like the fantasy better."

"You asked my advice."

"So how are things going with you and Billy Graham?"

"Colin would consider that a compliment, Brady. The Arnetts are coming into town tonight." I had counted down the days and even set the alarm on my Palm Pilot as though I might forget.

"I can joke, can't I? The good Reverend did me good that night. It just seems he lives the provincial life and you fancy a hint of danger." Brady had always put me on some glamorous pedestal.

"You've got it backwards. Colin isn't provincial. You don't know him."

"And you call me smitten."

Johnson walked crooked for a week before I took him to the vet. I found him leaning against a potted plant, an odd stance even for a cat with multiple phobias. The vet ran all sorts of tests, one where he aimed his tubby front portion toward a tabletop. Any cat, the vet said, would stretch its front paws toward the table to guard its body. Johnson only held out one paw. After accruing a two-hundred-dollar vet bill, the vet informed me our cat had a brain tumor.

From that point on, Johnson was treated with such newborn attention, it changed Hercules's behavior. He grew nervous and insecure, and every time I would pass him, he would clutch my feet in a strange scissors move as though he were trying to make me stay by his side. The dog had to either stay in a part of the house where he could not taunt the tabby or remain outdoors. Every time I drove the Mustang, Hercules stretched his long limbs across the back seat, the wind blowing the blond tufts around his ears and throat, just to meet his daily golden retriever quota of human contact.

But Colin and the Arnetts were coming to town. I met Colin and Ruth at the cottage with Hercules in tow.

"You've all had dinner, I presume," I said.

"I packed a picnic and we stopped at a rest stop along the highway," said Ruth.

Charlotte stroked Hercules along his back and pulled wads of hair from his shedding coat. "Where's Mason?"

"Here he comes." Mason ran dragging his book satchel behind. "If he doesn't finish his homework Friday night, it haunts him all weekend," I said.

"Charlotte and the boys have homework, too. But I'm too tired to care," said Ruth. "We'll do it in the morning before our swim."

"I'll help you all in with your things. Then I'm taking the dog for a run on the beach. He's been cooped up all day in our study. Our cat has a brain tumor of all things, and I have to keep them separated."

"My mother had a cat but we gave it to my aunt," said Troy.

"You boys run upstairs and take your bath together," said Colin.

"Your poor kitty. I'll walk your dog, Mrs. Longfellow." Charlotte slid her slight fingers through the leash handle and allowed it to slip over her forearm. She gripped the handle with her strong hand.

"We can go together if your father doesn't care." I waited for Colin's approval.

"You look pretty tousled, sister. Wouldn't you rather crawl into bed and get an early start?" He endeavored to coax Charlotte toward the cottage. She sidled toward me.

"We can all take the walk then," he said.

Rachel leaned against her Aunt Ruth, drowsy.

"The rest of us are going to bed," said Ruth.

We helped them in with the luggage and bags of food and toys.

A waxing moon drew out the tide. The lunar magnetism charmed us out onto the beach.

Mason invited Charlotte to take a run with him. I hurried to the Mustang and dug through the emergency bag in the trunk. I dug out two flashlights and brought along two foldable chairs. "Take this flashlight, will you, Charlotte? Your father will be less nervous." I encouraged her to unleash Hercules and allow him to run off his pent-up energy. She charged off after him and Mason. I aimed the other flashlight toward them. The gentle flow of low tidewater failed to wash her flip-flop imprints from the sand.

Colin tried to call after her.

"Let her go, Colin. She can keep up with Mason. Hercules will wear them both out and we can bed them down more easily tonight," I said, but in a ginger manner, not wanting Colin to think I tended to interfere. "Charlotte is so athletic."

"Athletic, artistic, tender, and rowdy. She's an anomaly."

"Or a gift. You realize, Colin, you can't keep her cooped up like I have to keep Johnson inside now. Charlotte is one of those girls bursting with health, her little motor on high speed. Somehow she'll find the way outside."

"Eva was better with Charlotte. She knew when to rein her in and when to let her go."

"Colin, you're a good father. I didn't mean to imply you aren't."

"Just overprotective." When he confessed it, it was the first time he had ever looked old, worn out by the lapping pangs of parenthood.

"It's our prerogative to feel guilty about our parenting."

"Yes, but you women have that nurturing mechanism. I'm blind to it. Don't they have 'Nurturing 101' in Braille for blind fathers?" He closed his eyes and felt around in the dark.

I handed Colin one of the chairs and we set them up. "Joe said one time that fathers teach their offspring to lead while mothers teach them how to live."

"I once taught them to lead, I think. But when Eva left me, I floundered. Charlotte is part Colin, part Eva. She is independent by nature. But I try and mold that nature and all I wind up doing is suffocating her."

"I just try to notice what draws Mason. He is drawn by baseball but he didn't want to try fishing. But he finally tried fishing and liked it. If I pushed him into fishing with his Grandpa, he might have resented it and hated it. But I'm not so balanced otherwise." I expected him to interrupt, but he just listened. "I can be a mother bear but with me it's not a noble thing, you know, where all of my friends sit on the sidelines cheering. You seem to have this magnetism about you that makes everyone who knows you admire you."

He laughed, of course.

"If I feel like my turf is being threatened, or Mason's for that matter, my fangs come out. It's not attractive at all."

"You don't look all that threatening."

"My mother-in-law would disagree."

"This is Joe's family that makes you feel this way—animalistic?"

"Joan Longfellow can bring out the worst in me, the way that woman drives her family. Case in point: Joe never felt comfortable in law. But Joe had one of those evenings where he started with a glass of wine but then finished off the whole bottle. I didn't know what was going wrong at the firm, but whatever the problem, it weighed on him. He didn't cry. I never saw him cry, but when he spoke, he had this deep anguish. He was trapped. It made me cry. He started confessing things, things such as he never wanted to be an attorney anyway. He wanted to be a social worker, help humanity, but Joan wouldn't hear of it. I told him to quit the practice. I never wanted the big house and the fancy cars. But Joan had this sick control over him. It made me resent her."

"She knows you know all of this?"

"That's why she hates me. I called her the next morning when he went to work. Before I called I had rehearsed it all in my head, you know, painted it all up with daisies and such, so I had it in my mind that Joan would really listen to me—another woman. I told her everything he said and she accused me of lying, of trying to manipulate Joe into quitting the practice."

Colin slid his fingers on top of mine. "Sounds as though Joe was never who he wanted to be."

"That's why we fought. The last thing I said to him was not the last thing I would have wanted to say. But I thought he was being weak. I hate that in anyone, but it made me the adversary. I was afraid he was going to pass all of this on to Mason, so I played the parent card all the time. Stand up to your mother, for Mason's sake, Joe. Not two weeks later the call came from the bank, the one that sent Joe running out of the house. But all I could think about was the bill collectors. I was more worried about humiliation or security than the pressure on Joe."

"You have a right to want to feel secure."

"My father struggled through much of my life to make our little church grow. He and my mother sacrificed a lot for the church. But somehow they always managed to pay the bills. So I feel maybe I was too hard on Joe about the phone call that morning about the unpaid bills."

"March, Joe put all of his eggs with that one big bank. Transactional attorneys can't do that, they have to take in enough clients to allow for a loss. Then he overspent. At least, that is what you have told me. He got in over his head. But he could have changed everything with one decision. He never took matters to God."

"Keep talking, Colin." His words lifted me away from the pulse of my emotions. The night was not so dark with Colin close by. He spoke with a soothing cadence, a poet imbued with the power to show me the better part of me, and how to forgive myself.

"Here I am now in charge of our money, and I'm not such a financial wizard myself," I said.

"You're faithful, March."

"Good old dependable March."

"I don't think it's out of style."

I turned my hand palm up so we could clasp hands. His middle finger slowly stroked my palm. "Have you always been a wise man?" I asked.

"It would have saved us a lot of pain, but, no, I haven't. It had to sort of develop. I became a minister later in life. I was in business, trying to live in both worlds—Eva's church world and my business crowd. I almost lost her."

"I can't imagine it."

"Eva's prayers and her patience were my salvation."

Charlotte and Hercules bounded toward us. Mason thundered behind them, panting.

"The call to the pulpit followed my surrender to the Lord. You know what I mean by surrender, I'm sure."

It was new, but I nodded.

"I fell in love with Christ and my wife fell in love with me again."

"Lots of jellyfish washed up on the shore, Daddy! They looked like bell jars," said Charlotte. She was out of breath. Hercules tried to use his weight against her. She shoved him back, picked up a thin piece of driftwood and hurled it. He scrambled across the sand to sniff it out in the dark.

"How do you know what a bell jar is?" Colin asked her.

"Read a book about it." She ran off after the dog and Mason.

"So that is why you're so good at bringing in the worldly set, Colin."

"We're all worldly, March. Who doesn't have the stench of the past on them?"

"So for the sake of your church crowd, you make it easy to come to Christ. Come as you are. That's the way it should be," I said.

Colin leaned toward me. "I'm not as good as you make me out to be, but I sure like seeing myself in your eyes, March." He kissed me, a quick brush of lips against mine just before the troops invaded.

"Mason taught Hercules to sit, but he won't do it for me," Charlotte reported back to her father.

"He knows whom to obey, Charlotte. His master." Colin put his left hand around her waist, but kept the other hand clasped firmly to mine. "Really, Charlotte, you've stayed up much later than your brothers and sister. Say 'goodnight' to Hercules and Mrs. Longfellow."

Charlotte threw her arms around me and held on to me for several minutes. It was a low tide and we had oceans of time.

Colin and I returned to the shore after we bedded down Charlotte and Mason. He told me he had to see me again, and I told him that it seemed crazy to move ahead but that I would if I could feel as though I was not being pulled into the tidewater of decision. He promised me there was no hurry, but as they left a few days later, I had to keep from running after them, tying my body to the bumper with a hyperactive golden retriever, a phobic cat, and Mason, and forgetting the life I had built here.

But something fashioned out of a storm has a way of becoming an anchor. So I let Colin pack up the children and Ruth believing all of what I said to him to be true. I swallowed the lump in my throat caused by my own uncertain declarations and quietly whispered while the Arnetts pulled away, *"Don't listen to me. I don't know what I'm saying."*

Colin and I took turns visiting the other's town in our long-distance romance. It was proving to be more and more difficult to be away from him. But I kept my nose to the church and the *Sentinel* and did what I always did—my job.

Baseball season faded and gave rise to soccer moms, all of us loaded down with kneepads and bottles of cold water iced down in summer coolers.

Dinah popped open a beach umbrella over our camp chairs. We lugged an ice chest to the players' side of the field and left it next to the coach's bench.

Mason played for his school, the CCCA Hawks. But this game was known locally simply as The Presbyterians against The Baptists.

Dinah's mother-in-law had placed the twins in Mason's school and the scent of blood was in the air. The Hawks warred in a slow simmer, though, their attack skills numbed by summer vacation. Mason took a defensive stance, the color of red defining his posture.

"Make me swear, Dinah, on my honor that I won't be the loudest soccer mom on the sidelines."

"I can promise you won't." She shrieked at Geraldine to hustle to her position.

The ref blew the whistle.

"Did I tell you I saw Ruth Arnett at Ruby's Saturday?" Dinah opened two bottles of water and handed one to me.

"She brought us all back lunch," I said.

"Ruth told me she is almost finished with her dissertation. What is she, a doctor or something?"

"It's a doctorate in math. She plans to teach college. Davidson is interviewing her."

"Don't you wish we had the sense to use our God-given abilities at that age? Now that I've wizened in my old age, I realize I've short-changed myself. Who said I had to settle here in Candle Cove? I might have liked Los Angeles."

"You got two talented girls in the swap, Dinah. Nothing is stopping you from completing your degree, what with all of the online courses available, what have you."

"I've hemmed myself in, so to speak, March."

"It's all in your mind."

Her finely tweaked brows lifted, soft brown pencil lines making a curve above the sheen on her face. "You ever think about starting over?"

Mason nailed the ball with his head and drove it straight toward the net. The Baptist stopped it in midair and punted it back into the game. A corporate sigh reverberated up and down the row of Hawk parents.

"You didn't answer me," she said.

"I'm sorry, could you please repeat the question?"

"You ever considered starting over again?"

"A month ago I might have said 'no.'"

Dinah shot forward on her chair. Geraldine rammed the ball toward the net but the goalie leaped in the air and stopped it. The row of parents groaned again.

"You've seen Colin, what, twice in four weeks?" Dinah asked.

"I don't belong in Lake Norman and he doesn't belong here."

"I knew it. By that, I mean that you're in love."

"If I so much as stepped a foot into Eva Arnett's shoes, you'd hear hissing all the way from Charlotte."

"His children seem to have taken a shine to you."

"It's not his children. It isn't even Mason who worries me. Eva was the Queen Mother at that church."

"You do seem to have your own little kingdom at Candle Cove Presbyterian, on a much smaller scale, of course."

The Baptists scored.

"I don't need a throne. That isn't what I meant at all. I just can't step into the shoes of perfection."

"You do a pretty mean job of it here."

I knew Dinah was blinded by friendship. "Nobody at his church, short of Ruth and Colin's children, is aware we're dating. Every matron in that place is trying to fix him up with her single niece or daughter. I act like it doesn't bother me, like this is all just an experiment." I hesitated and she looked at me. "But it bothers me. I'm starting to wish for things that will never be, like Colin taking over our little church, an act he says will never happen. So then I imagine what it would be like to live in his world and I start worrying about leaving Dad."

"You have given this some thought. Has Colin actually asked for a commitment?"

"We've not discussed anything but our past lives and child rearing. I think we're avoiding the subject altogether."

"But you love him."

"I never thought this would happen. He wants me to bring Mason up this weekend. He wants to introduce me to some of his church friends."

"Geraldine just kicked a goal!" Dinah leaped out of her chair and pranced up and down the sidelines.

I offered a thumbs-up to Mason who appeared dumbfounded.

Dinah settled back into her chair.

"Colin took me to Sonnets Saturday night. We shared fish and chips. And oysters. Did I tell you that? A jazz band played outdoors on the veranda. I don't know if I told you, but Colin's a good dancer."

"You told me about Wilmington. Do they allow pastors to do that sort of thing?"

"Who is *they?*"

"My mother's pastor would get excommunicated for dancing."

"I never saw my father and mother dance. Such a shame. But I don't know if it's, you know, church legal or not for pastors to dance these days. I'll ask Dad about it."

"Do they have good jazz in Lake Norman? Maybe it isn't an issue."

"See, even you are putting me in Lake Norman and not vice versa."

One of the boys on the Presbyterian team wildly kicked the ball out of bounds.

"Both teams are lousy. Geraldine, you get in the game or get out!" Dinah shouted so loud her drill sergeant demonstration raised the brows of the starchy booster club.

"Mason is so red-faced. They are desperate for shade on their side.

Maybe I'll put a bug in the ear of the Hammonds that the team needs an overhang. Marie Hammond and I once played tennis." I glanced toward the Hammonds at the end of the parents' row.

"Geraldine and Claudia are always red-faced. It's in our family tree."

The other team scored again.

"I'm sorry I've rattled on about all of this Colin business, Dinah. Here I am worrying about matters that haven't come up and most likely won't. Colin has only invited me to visit his church. That's all I'm going to do. I'll put on a visitor's badge and that will be the end of it."

She took my hand. "Look at you. You have a little pink hive on the palm of your hand. It's only Monday and you're having nerves. By Sunday you'll be coated in calamine lotion. But that's all right because you look good in pink," said Dinah.

I held up my right hand. In the center of my palm was a perfectly formed welt. "I never wanted to be my mother, Dinah. As the good reverend's daughter, I have slightly more license to be frank, to speak my mind. Those people will hang me out to dry."

"These aren't the fifties or the sixties or even the seventies, March. Who says you have to fit into some polyester mold?"

"Convention."

"If I were you, I'd just stay out of those conventions, that's what," said Dinah.

"Thanks, Dinah. You've solved everything." Here I kept telling myself that I would not show up at Lake Norman a bundle of nerves, that I would just be myself and not worry about whether or not I struck out or scored with the who's who of Colin's church. I wasn't trying to win any awards, I reminded myself; it wasn't about winning or being compared to Eva, or measuring up. If I just kept my thoughts on Colin, being supportive of him, I'd come out a winner in his eyes.

The Hawks lost, but only by a point. I hoped it wouldn't be a trend for my life in the upcoming days.

Twenty-two

Dad carried Arnie under his right arm like a rolled-up rug and stroked the white whiskers on his chin. "I can't just go off and leave him, March. Arnie's never known the inside of a kennel. He might think I've abandoned him. They keep them in cages, don't they?"

"Crates. Doggie crates. Like a den. The lady at the Pet Spa is always good to Hercules. It's a home away from home when I have to leave town," I said.

"Seems like it's been a while since I went out of town. Things are so unsettled at the church. What use am I to you all in Lake Norman anyway?"

"Colin invited you. He wants to return your kindnesses for allowing him so many stays at the cottage. The polite thing to do is accept."

"Or politely decline."

"Your doctor says you can travel. It would do you good to get out of here. You act as though the whole village will float away if you aren't here to anchor it to land."

"What about your cancerous cat?"

"Dinah is keeping Johnson. The vet has him on medication and she's going to keep an eye on him for me."

"Can't send Arnie to the Buckworths," Dad continued ruminating. "Forget that idea then. Those girls would make him nervous."

"I can ask Gloria if she'd mind taking the dachshund. He's no trouble, Dad."

He dropped Arnie onto the carpet and walked into the kitchen without the cane.

"You don't even show signs of a heart attack, Dad. Look at you. You're your old self. Take advantage of this time. Go somewhere with us."

"What do you do in Lake Norman, anyway?"

"Colin has a room, an atrium where he reads. It's shaded with a garden outside the glass."

"No one will try and make me get on a boat."

"I swear you won't be coerced to try anything new."

Dad had never learned to swim. He was an enigma to some. A man who hated the water yet lived by the sea.

"We'll go with the top down. Road trip," I said.

"I can't find the vanilla wafers. You had something to do with it, March. May as well confess."

"The laundry room, next to the grits."

I dreamed that Joe and I sat on the sofa, only I was sleeping while he watched me. The peaceful glow of morning gilded his lashes. He awakened me and two people were walking into our living room. The woman had red hair and was astoundingly beautiful. The man was round and dressed like Mafioso. But he stood back at a distance while she perched herself on the arm of our sofa with an air of propriety She said nothing to me but spoke to Joe and greeted him. He laughed nervously.

Angered that Joe had not allowed me to run upstairs to hide my pajama state, I asked him why he had let them in.

"I didn't," was all he said.

I looked up at the young woman. She pulled out a pistol, silver and feminine, and aimed it at Joe. They had come to rob us.

I could not bear to lose him, willing to die myself instead. I fought her and tried to ram her head against the kitchen bar. Joe said nothing. He watched like a man watching the minutes pass. Somehow I knew it was not a cowardly act. He could not lift a finger to hurt her.

I did not have the strength to knock her out and finally managed to wrest the gun from her manicured hands. She was as weak as me. Feeling that the pinstriped accomplice might jump me, I stepped back and fired. The girl died instantly and the fat guy ran off. At first I drank in the swell of triumph until the reality of this human death overtook my heart. Then I fell on the floor and sobbed deeply and hopelessly, just like I did when the policemen, Harold and Bobby, had told me my husband was gone.

When I woke up, the morning sun freckled my pillowcase with atoms of autumn gold. I could not understand if I had killed someone in my dreams or slain myself. It was odd the way my mind had painted me beautiful and Joe as a fat crook. And him as the guy who couldn't lift a finger to hurt me while we both robbed ourselves of a good life.

Dad had trouble deciding what hat to wear. Mason finally convinced him a baseball cap possessed the engineering to withstand the gusty streams of a convertible ride. Between the two of them, they added a whole duffle bag full of things easily left behind. But Dad would leave behind every bit of it to make room for Arnie. The dachshund wanted nothing to do with his travel crate, a pet accessory bought years ago by my mother and used once when she first brought him home. Twice I placed him in it, readjusted the soft doggie bed, and twice I took him out unable to bear the lugubrious cries he made. He sounded like an infant.

Mason settled him on the back car seat next to him and fed him gourmet liver snacks, five dollars for every quarter-pint.

Dad studied the map. He wanted to be certain that all of us who had traveled back and forth between the same two destinations for several months had not somehow missed a secret path.

Neighbors had gathered out on the lawns and waved at us as we drove past.

"Your neighbors are awfully friendly today, Dad. That's kind of odd, as though they've rolled out the red carpet. What did you do?"

"I've always said we have a good neighborhood," said Dad.

A carload of teenagers screeched to a halt and waved wildly out the open windows of someone's parent's Ford. A girl with braces blew me kisses and then held up both fists in a sanguine salute.

"Do we know them?" asked Mason.

"They look like some friends of Yolanda's. Maybe they're happy the trial is over and those New Jersey thugs were shipped up the river. I'll bet that's it," I said.

Dad watched Mason in the rearview mirror of his visor until we connected with I-40 south of Raleigh.

"Bringing along the dog was a good idea. Arnie keeps Mason company," he said.

By the time we reached the molasses-slow traffic of Greensboro it was lunch time.

"I wish we would have flown," I said.

"What, and miss the fall color?" Dad pulled out a paperback Tom Clancy novel.

"I forgot that you can sit for an hour alone just fifteen minutes outside of Greensboro. May as well stop here for lunch."

"My legs are tingling. I need to give them a stretch."

The leaves were mostly green along the coast. The closer we got to the Piedmont the more the trees turned to autumn bouquets. The brightness of the day made the leaves look translucent and membranous.

We found a hamburger hamlet with an outdoor patio. Arnie sat on Dad's feet and waited for munificent bites from his master's hand. Mason ordered a round of root beers for all, and we toasted to cooler weather.

"Bill Simmons said the new minister is jumping through all of the hoops. He has a bit of a tic, though. No, not a tic. I forget what you call his idiosyncrasy. It disturbs Grace and Hal Caudle, though. He cannot say his *s*'s without whistling. I've heard of men who whistle out of their nostrils, but this man distinctly does it with any word containing the letter *s*. I wish to goodness it wasn't pointed out to me, now. I feel like a dog hearing one of those dog whistles and no one around me can hear it. Just me. I can't even converse with the poor fellow without hearing it. Maybe if it isn't pointed out, everyone will be none the wiser. The elders should keep it among themselves. It's a dreadful thing to reveal about a man who is about to oversee a congregation."

"Mason, pass me that bowl of lemons, will you," I said.

"Don't tell me you've heard it too." The age spots along Dad's forehead made his face look like a speckled bean.

"It's best I don't have an opinion about the man. If this is his only flaw, then what's a small-town church to do but to hire him? He sent videos from Pennsylvania. Goodness knows everyone had the chance to listen for whistling consonants."

"Anything else?"

"I told you, I don't have an opinion."

"You said it's best you don't have an opinion, March."

"He's not of your caliber, Dad."

"Or Colin's." Dad handed Mason a straw.

"He's not even in the same boat as Colin. It's as though they're on completely different rivers with completely different maps."

"Not exactly. They both point to Christ."

"That's the objective anyway."

"But you don't have an opinion."

"No."

Leaves had begun to fall but only early loose foliage; it fell upon the Arnett lawn like yellow coasters. Colin had both garage doors open. He wore khaki Bermudas and a gray flannel sweatshirt with doeskin hiking boots. He might have looked like an advertisement for L. L.

Bean but his calves were too thick. If he had ever made it into films, his thick calves would be too distracting. I stared at his legs for the first time. I wanted to see how far my fingers would reach around them. I said a quick prayer for restraint.

He carried flattened boxes and overstuffed garbage bags out to the curb. All of the boxes had once held cling peaches. I imagined them standing in kitchen-help-high stacks in his church's pantry. Cling peaches exist for church socials crowning scoops of cottage cheese, the perfect cross between a dessert and a salad.

"We're taking the sailboat out to sail around the peninsula," he said. He opened my door and leaned forward with both arms becoming the gate between me and his lawn.

Dad sighed.

"Is it all right if Dad stays here?" I asked Colin.

"Ruth isn't going, either. You can keep her company, James. Or watch us from the shore at Jetton Park. We can help you set up a lawn chair. Jetton has a small beach."

Dad picked up his paperback and looked at me. "Where is that little glass room you were telling me about?"

Troy, the oldest and most agile of the boys at age seven, lugged a box of broken toys down the driveway and dropped them next to his father's heap. He had small knobby knees and an Adam's apple that protruded like a farm boy's. "She's here! We finally know someone famous."

Dad and I just looked at one another and blinked.

Ruth sat on a windowsill upstairs, buttocks out, and ran a squeegee down the window. When she saw us, her elegant knees lifted and she pulled herself inside. The window was only half washed.

"Troy, please show Reverend Norville into the house. He'd like to relax in the atrium," Colin told him.

"Are you all spending the night here?" Troy took my father's hand as though it were his duty to physically lead the decrepit old guy.

"We're staying at the old parsonage," I said.

Luke appeared in the doorway, sucking the life out of a blue Popsicle.

"My sister Charlotte was almost born right in the parsonage, right on the braided rug. You know, like having puppies." Luke waited as if he wanted to see whether or not I had already heard the story. When I did not respond, he said, "But my dad finally got up and drove Mom to the hospital."

"Wait until you're older, Luke. You'll find we men try to stick together," said Dad. He obliged Troy by allowing him to lead him all the way up the walk.

"Mrs. Longfellow, may I have your autograph?" asked Luke.

Mason compressed Arnie into the shape of a gherkin and followed them inside where Charlotte's shrill, eager greeting spilled out of the open doorway.

I returned to the car and fished out my purse.

"I didn't know I was courting a celebrity," said Colin. He met me at the car.

I picked crumbs of Cheetos off of my knit slacks.

Colin clasped both of my hands and pulled me out of the car. "Don't tell me you haven't seen a copy of *LIFE* magazine?"

I had not.

He retrieved his magazine off the top of a cling peaches box as though he had been reading it. He held it up. The cover story was "Hero Moms." Three women's faces, one of which was mine, were captured in a still-life frieze, our photographs forming a triangular ring. I had a pair of kiwi-colored sunglasses perched on the crown of my head. I remembered wearing them the day of Yolanda's trial. My expression read like a woman determined to lasso the villains of the world. I was pretty certain I was trying to mentally gather my grocery list, that pinch between the eyebrows simply a sign of my scattered memory trying to recall the inside of the pantry—iodized salt, Cheerios, brown sugar (or was it white?), and juice boxes for Mason's lunch. One of the other women was a Detroit mom who had donated a kidney to a child overseas, while the other lady had rescued an entire family from a burning car hit by a train in Toad Suck Ferry, Arkansas.

"I never saw this," I said.

"They didn't tell you?"

"A lot of cameras were popping all around me. I thought they were after Yolanda. I was trying to get out of the way, let her have her little moment in the limelight."

"*LIFE* just hit the stands this morning. I'll bet the local press is on a manhunt to find you. They'll want to interview you, too." Colin handed me the magazine.

"They'll find me gone, then. Good thing we brought Dad with us. This is embarrassing." I thumbed through the article and found adjectives like "heroic widow" and "courageous mother" next to my name. "This Detroit woman, Georgia Wallace, she donated a kidney to an orphan in Zimbabwe. This other lady, Flo Minirth, she rescued an entire family from a burning car with her own hands. Look at the bandages on her poor little parched hands. Mine should read 'March Longfellow pulled a water gun on two dweebs.'"

"You rush in where angels fear to tread. People want to admire you for it," said Colin before he added, "Some people are just admiration magnets."

"I'm an idiot and I can prove it. I'm not the hero type. It's just that somehow my gene pool has tanked me up with an overage of adrenaline. It gets the best of me. In my opinion, if you think heroically, you act heroically. You can't prove by me that I think at all. Mostly, I react."

We stood between the car and its open door, hands still clasped. Colin's eyes were two moons settling upon the gentle dunes of his face as he looked down at me.

"You left your socks at the cottage. I washed them. Want me to get them for you?" I asked.

"How kind of you. I think I'd rather kiss you."

"Your neighbor is out walking the dog. Is this a good idea? I mean, my father never kissed Mother out on the lawn like this." Surely he wouldn't listen to me.

Colin stooped like a crane getting at its fish and we kissed. I felt my powers slipping away, as though I were losing control of my monarchy.

Charlotte and I held hands on the shore at Jetton Park and waved at the sailors. My heart followed the fellows and Rachel around the waving line of peninsula while my feet remained on the sand. I don't believe they saw how I split in two on shore, frail and dichotomous, wanting to leap astern and grab a rope while panache nautical phrases spilled off of my tongue. When Charlotte heard that I don't do boats, she stayed on shore with me.

"Aunt Ruth is fixing a sandwich party for us tonight. At the parsonage," said Charlotte.

"We'll go back and help her then." I pulled a sweater around my shoulders.

"Everything is done. She's taking a nap. I cubed the cheese." When she said it, a blush reddened her entire face, like a girl who is not well-practiced at boasting.

We sat down together in the foldout camp chairs Colin had dragged out of his SUV. Charlotte pulled zippy plastic bags of sliced apples out of a small cooler and handed me a bag. "I dreamed last night that the angels took my mother to heaven, sort of like I got to watch the whole thing. I know why I dreamed it. Sometimes I worry about the walk from here to heaven, like, did my mother get lonely walking by herself to God. I think Jesus let me watch it all so that I wouldn't worry about her. Kind of like he pulled out the video of the whole thing and loaned it to me. Mother actually flew. I always wondered about, you know, will we fly because she told me that angels were different from humans, that we would not have angel's wings. She just lifted." Charlotte lifted her arms and pointed to the sky with one good hand and one disabled. It came to me that her flaw was what made her so perfect.

"I believe in angels too, Charlotte."

"Is your husband in heaven?"

"I don't know. He knew what it took to get there." Only because I had told him once. "I'd like to think that in those last few minutes when he realized he wasn't going to make it back that he took care of business, so to speak."

"My mother was very friendly. I'll bet she's already made your Joe feel right at home." Charlotte laid aside the apples and took off her shoes. She ran one big toe along the sand. "Usually, we do not have good sand for angels. Today it's soft." Then she lay down flat on the sand and spread her arms and legs back and forth just like Mason had done in Virginia in the cemetery snow.

"Making sand angels?" I asked.

"Have you ever made angels in the sand, Mrs. Longfellow? If we make them everywhere then more people will know."

"Know what, Charlotte?"

"That God cares for them and watches over them."

I joined her on the soggy shore of Lake Norman where we created whole families of celestials. As far as we knew the sand angels remained until the sun had set, turning the earthen impressions to gilded immortals.

Back in the eighties, a carpenter from Colin's church had assembled a large deck along the entire rear of the parsonage.

Ruth burned tiki torches around the perimeter of the deck and left all of the windows open to justify a fire in the fireplace of the old great room. Colin floated medallions of oranges in apple cider and warmed the batch over the fire until the whole room smelled like an orchard.

He and Ruth seated all the children around the kitchen table, mounding sandwiches and chips with dip in front of them, to keep them occupied. Troy made a moat with his potato chips and chocolate pudding. Ruth ate an anorexic portion of something she called vegetable jumble. Then she harnessed Arnie and coaxed him out the front door for a jog down Rio Oro.

"James, join me on the deck. It's a clear night," said Colin to Dad.

Dad threw on his corduroy jacket and then followed Colin out under the shadow of night and the stars.

Charlotte and I gathered up the paper plates smudged with mustard and other garnitures. Rachel nudged her way in between the open dishwasher door and her older sister, demanding a woman's share of the kitchen duties. I obliged her with the task of scooping up the plastic cups and dumping them into the almond porcelain sink.

Colin and I had spent all of twenty minutes together and even then it was in front of the next-door neighbor and his neurotic boxer. In the glow of the lawn lanterns Dad stretched out his arms like a clothesline cord. He heaved a sort of old-man sigh that said he was ready to turn in for the night. I pretended to gather the afghans up around the fireplace and then folded up on the recliner with my back to the men. Colin must not have noticed my antsy glance toward him. He kept talking to Dad, lowering his voice and filling the silence with a somber guys-only dialogue.

"It isn't easy to let go of a church," Dad told Colin. "Not when you've nurtured it from its inception. I worry that Candle Cove Presbyterian has such a limited outlook. It's hard to see beyond our own front porch when all you see are the same faces every week. I dreamed of a man who would take the church to the next level. I feel this new man needs more time with me. He needs a mentor."

"Speaking of letting go, James, I'd like to know how you feel about letting go of March and Mason."

I stared into the embers and felt like a spy curled beneath the mound of knitted throws. If Dad answered Colin, it tumbled out as a breathy whisper. Colin had not asked me about any sort of commitment but he must have known my worries about my father.

Their voices grew as soft as the glow of heat from the fireplace. I fell asleep and dreamed of tumbling into a cavern. I lay on the precipice of a cliff and stared into jagged bowels so deep and dark the bottom was fathomless. Below me was my father who clung to one of my hands. Above me was Colin who climbed out and wanted me to follow. I stretched to reach out to them both, but felt nothing between us but space. The one candle that lit the entire cavern dimmed and I felt the suffocating sense of gasping like a fish on the bank.

Colin dug me out of the afghans and awakened me. "You sounded like you were having a bad dream."

"Where's Dad?"

"He's gone upstairs to sleep. Mason's in bed too."

"Ruth? Your kids?" I climbed out of the recliner and saw my tangled reflection in a decorative mirror.

"Gone home. Except Charlotte. She's in your bed. I told her, okay, as long as she shares the blanket. We're all alone. Finally. But I won't stay long."

"You can if you want," I said while he pulled me to my feet.

"The kids have a fall break in three weeks. They want to come to Candle Cove again, and I told them we would. But the distance between us is . . ." He stopped so that I could fill in the blanks.

"Frustrating." I knew it was coming. "We discussed this already, that the distance would become a problem."

"March, you're all I think about. I'm looking for solutions here. That wasn't a complaint," Colin told me and then held me next to him, with both arms around my waist.

I could have thrown myself at him right at that moment and been done with it. "Colin, you don't have to feel as though this has to work out. There's no pressure from me." I had grown good at lying.

I heard Dad gargling in the upstairs bathroom.

"Over the next few weeks, March, I want you to think about us. How this could work out for both of us. For my family and yours." He stopped and looked toward the stairwell. Charlotte hovered at the top of the staircase in a white gown, all flannel and satin ribbon. The light above her head gave her crown an aura. She rubbed her eyes and floated back to her room as though she sleepwalked.

"She's checking on us." I moved my hands up both of his arms.

"Charlotte loves you, March. They all love you."

"I've never been good at starting at the beginning. It makes me feel impatient with myself." Somehow I knew this wasn't new to him, but I kept piecing together sentences hoping I would eventually make sense without chasing him out of my arms. "These people here at Church on the Lake have expectations of who you are and who Eva was. I just don't have any sort of way of turning myself into Eva. Socially, I'm not adept, and I can't keep my opinions to myself."

"And I'm not Joe, March. I'm not going to leave you stranded. Or emotionally bankrupt."

"Who said I was emotionally bankrupt? I'll admit, I've had to reshuffle my priorities." I tried hard not to sound defensive. "I was the epitome of a church lady, but not, as you say sometimes from your pulpit, so fully yielded in my heart to Christ. It was hard for me to admit I needed the Lord and easier to think that he needed me. Sometimes I was slow to admit I needed anyone for that matter." But "emotionally bankrupt" was just, well, severe. Said aloud, anyway.

"I think the question is, do you need me?"

"Only when I breathe, Colin. Or when it's storming. Or if the sky is completely clear and void of clouds, then I need you. Other than that, no."

"I don't want you to go home. Stay here in Lake Norman. Stay with me."

I buried my face against his chest and felt his breath against my neck.

He finally left without my answer.

The next morning, Colin did not embarrass us by asking us to stand in the middle of the service. Instead, after the dismissal, he led us himself to a church dinner in the large fellowship hall. It was catered by some barbecue catering group, and no one had to cook, not even Ruth. The youth group served and the older women stood behind them offering direction. Colin introduced me to members of his advisory board.

A younger woman who held an infant with cheeks as red as vermilion stuck out her hand and made an overboard effort to welcome me. She introduced herself as Laura Feines, the wife of Jack on Colin's board. She asked me a lot about myself and told me how she had been a college student staying in an apartment with two guys and three girls when Colin and Eva knocked on her door and invited her to a barbecue. "They didn't even try and get me to church, but just come and eat they said. And here I am now married to a board member. It's just the oddest way that God works."

I did not flinch at all when she mentioned Eva's name and she seemed to do so several times.

"Why don't you and your son join my family at our table?" she asked.

Mason had run off with Charlotte to the dessert table or some such so I picked up a plate of food and headed her way until Colin stopped me. "I have another person I want to introduce you to. He's special." He took me through the crowd of denim-clad people and led me right up to a young man who helped his young wife calm a newborn. "Ralph here is the son of the man who was with me from the beginning, Jonathan Henshaw. We lost Jon to a heart attack. Ralph, this is a friend, March Longfellow."

Ralph glanced up red-faced, apologetic that he could not quell the newborn mewl. "Nice to meet you, March. We go way back with the Arnetts. Colin and Eva were like second parents to me and my sister. Did you ever know Eva?"

"I never had the privilege," I said.

"If it wasn't for her, I don't even know if this church would exist." Ralph turned his back to us and lifted the infant out of the carriage. "Excuse me."

We politely dismissed ourselves.

"March, I'm sorry. Eva meant a lot to Ralph. He got into drugs and she coaxed him into rehab."

I could feel the ghost of Eva arising, but I didn't want to act defensive, as though I was just waiting for someone to breathe her name.

"Before I could tell him about you he was off into talk of Eva. That wasn't what I intended at all."

The more Colin apologized, the more I wanted to shrink up the size of a snail and slink away.

"Don't apologize. I wouldn't want everyone at Dad's church to just sweep the memory of my mother out with the newspaper."

An older woman with silver strands of hair glistening through her bangs interrupted. "Pastor Colin, I don't mean to be a tattletale, but your Charlotte has skipped the meal altogether and gone for the dessert." She pointed at the far corner of the hall.

Charlotte and Mason stacked towers of giant cookies onto their trays, no sight of a green salad or entrée between them both.

"Sakes, if she doesn't look just like that Eva leading that little boy around like she owns the place," said the lady who seemed to disappear into her memories.

Instead of waiting for Colin to explain that Eva had sat by this woman's bedside and breathed life back into her pneumonia-racked body, I simply said, "I'll go and get Mason and Charlotte and lead them back toward the real food line. Don't feel you have to introduce me to another person, Colin. I'll see those two get fed and then I'll just mingle."

His chest lifted and I could see flickers of anxiety in his face.

"Just watch. I'm quite the mingler." I turned away and began mentally packing up our luggage, Dad's new collection of books from Colin, and the dog's things. I wouldn't want to leave anything behind where it didn't belong.

Twenty-three

"If you and Pastor Arnett get married, will my last name change?" Mason asked in a rush, his words spilling out before he sneezed.

"Bless you, and use a tissue, Mason." I handed him a Kleenex. "No one said anything about marriage. Eat your Froot Loops." He grew less and less interested in breakfast each morning.

"I saw you kiss him. Do you miss Dad?"

"Are you going to eat your cereal, Mason?"

"I don't think Grandpa wants to move. We can't leave him here."

"We're not leaving Grandpa, we're not getting married. I can't remember if I gave Johnson his meds this morning."

"You did. He hacks every time you do. Do you love Pastor Arnett, Mom? I want to know, so stop beating out the bush." He dropped to the floor and began shoving pencils and dog-eared textbooks into his book satchel.

"Beating *around* the bush." I removed the bowl of colored sludge that was once his cereal. "I might love him, Mason. Is that a bad thing?"

"It's not. I just think it's going to be a big mess if you are. He calls a lot. The phone bill will be big, but you're nicer now."

"So I'm nicer. Don't forget your lunch." The phone rang. "Colin. I'm glad you called."

"I need to see you again," he said.

"When can you come?"

Mason lifted like a tortoise, his back straining to hold up the satchel. He craned his neck and stretched out his arms to adjust the straps. He studied my face and then lifted to kiss me. "You're a wreck, Mom, but a nicer wreck."

Colin read two calendar dates to me and we settled on one while I fretted over how this trip might be the one that scattered us in opposite directions.

The night the Arnetts arrived, an autumn cold had settled upon the cove, plunging temperatures to near freezing by bedtime. Mason emptied the Mustang's trunk of his belongings at the same time Ruth handed luggage and bagged possessions to Charlotte and the others to carry inside.

Our church school that Mason attended scheduled a fall break every October to make up for the long, tenuous stretch of school that ebbed into the first week of everyone else's summer. He seized the time off to spend the night in the cottage where he and Colin's boys stretched out sheets around the furniture and shoved flannel sleeping bags beneath their town of linen tents as near to the brick fireplace as Ruth would allow.

Colin and I stood against the cold wind and inspected the *Sparticus.*

"First thing in the morning I'll haul her back up to the shed after one last run around the harbor," said Colin. His words carried a weighty finality, as though he were resigning himself to the task. He watched the last Arnett drag a duffel bag into the house and close the door.

"I took the day off tomorrow. Gloria is helping me out," I said.

"I've missed you, March." He opened his navy pea jacket and wrapped it around me so that it swallowed up the both of us.

I laid my head against his chest until the warmth soothed the chill in my bones. "Colin, the new pastor is being installed. Dad is in such a gloom."

"Look at me, March."

I lifted my face out of the dark folds of his jacket.

He kissed me and I wanted to live forever curled inside the warm sanctuary of his arms.

"Colin, you're all I can think about. Gloria is near to killing me because I just start something, some PTA piece that screams to be written or somebody's aunt's obituary, and then I drift away and it's all on account of you." I felt ruined, with parts of me scattered along the sand.

"Walk with me," he said.

"No, I'd rather stand here with you like this."

"Let's walk." He led me a mile past the cottage and up an embankment where he seated himself in the cleft of a large rock. With one arm he pulled me up and drew me against him. "It's warmer here out of the wind."

"So this is where you hide when Ruth says she hasn't seen you all day." My back molded with the curve of his chest. "Colin, I've been thinking about what you asked me to think about." I pulled my head beneath his chin not wanting to see straight into the eyes that saw over pulpits into men's hearts.

"So have I and I wasn't being fair to you. I've realized, March, you never asked to be pursued, but that made me want to pursue you all the more. Your whole world is here and I've asked you to leave it, everything you call home. Then I expect you to live in a place filled with Eva, around people who have romanticized her memory."

I turned sideways and looked at him, my right hand against his chest. "You don't have to sound so apologetic. I don't know that you've officially asked me to leave it." I waited to see if he would.

"I want you to know that you don't have to answer anything, or do anything that makes you uncomfortable. Stand firm on that account, March. Never let anyone coerce you into choices that make you lose who you are."

I felt the pounding of his heart against my hand.

Colin turned his head and leaned toward me. We kissed, his breath warming me.

"If I ask you to leave everything that is you, that you've worked so hard to preserve and make your own, I'm asking you to leave behind who you are and become someone else. It's wrong. I don't want you to become someone else."

"So you're saying you don't want me to think about a life with you," I said.

"You're off the hook, March."

He thought I wanted to be released. "Is this how it ends then? You just cut me loose and I walk away?"

"I think you're one of those people who likes to set up hurdles and jump them when all you have to do is run."

I kept my eyes ahead on the dark ocean. "It's getting colder."

"Tell me what to say, March. I thought you'd want it this way. Can you imagine a life with me?"

"If I had known what would happen with Joe, would I have married him anyway? If you factor Mason into the equation, I have to say I would." I laid my head against his shoulder. "But it's like I have this ability now to see ahead and I hate it." I sat up and looked at him. "Is that caused by enduring the hard things?" He hesitated so I thought he probably knew the answer but waited. "I wish I couldn't predict what would happen to us."

"What makes you think you can?"

"Without a second thought, I could just take the life you seem willing to share with me. But when I stepped foot in your church, Colin, I knew they couldn't accept me."

"When I asked Eva to marry me, it seemed natural that she would say yes and that we would have a happy life. If I'd known about her cancer in advance, would I have avoided her just to avoid the pain?"

"I don't know. Would you have asked her, with the full knowledge of what you know now?"

"We aren't meant to know about pain in advance, any more than we can anticipate the thrilling moments like the one I just had when I kissed you. How else can we grow if we make choices knowing that all will be well and perfect? Look at all I acquired in the process: Rachel, Luke, Troy, and Charlotte. Without them I don't think I would have had the will to get out of bed the day after I buried my wife. By myself, I'm one grain of sand. But with my family, we are a shoreline built by the hand of Almighty God. That is how we hold back the tides, March. Not by escaping the storms, but by staying together through them. If we scatter, we are lost."

"Have I lost you?" The wind caught my words. Colin and I bowed our heads until the blustery cold died down.

"What did you say?" He tempered his words.

"I made hot chocolate. Let's go back to the cottage and I'll pour you a cup." I said it as brightly as possible. I had just lost all of my resolve to spill the hard things out in the open. But I would try and muster my thoughts again in the morning when the day's luminosity painted me objective and clever.

I would have tomorrow to say what I should say.

My phone rang sometime after six o' clock, just after the dawn arose with a storm on its back. Ruth sounded ill, her insides twisted around her heart.

"March, Rachel just woke me to tell me the boys, Luke and Mason, plus Charlotte took off in the *Sparticus.* A storm has moved in and they're all out in the middle of it. Sweet Jesus, have mercy!"

"Where is Colin?" I fumbled for my reading glasses.

"He's getting dressed. I've already called the Coast Guard but Colin says he's going out after them." She yelled something down the hall. "A neighbor has offered his boat, Colin says."

"Tell Colin I'm coming with him." I prayed all the way into the bathroom, started to brush my teeth, but then in my stupor came to myself and reconstructed my morning ritual so that I would be out the front door in five minutes. All I could see was Mason's face, his eyes the only shard of color in a black storm at sea. My motherly intuition concluded that Mason, on his own, might have never come up with the idea of sailing off in the *Sparticus* before dawn. Troy wouldn't, either. The culpability rested on the two of them jointly conspiring. I imagined them staying up past midnight daring one another, and then hatching the whole scheme to sail before dawn.

I then imagined Mason taking the helm and heading them back to the little dock by Sonnet's Fish and Chips, as though by willing him to do the right thing he would do it. I knew the owners who came early to start the salad bar would run out to them and wrap the kids in blankets and seat them around the table near the fireplace inside, laughing at how silly they had all been. Then the fantasy faded and Mason became Joe, and he fought the sea and wrestled the slapping waves refusing to turn back because he sought a more meaningful battle than the one that waited back home. He never cried out once, and I wondered how I knew that about him.

Several times I spoke Mason's name aloud in a fragile, ragged pleading to God to not let him slip from me or else I might not recover this time. Colin might not recover. We would have nothing between us but loss, and that is too much space between two people. I bargained all the way out to the beach, offering up my life for Mason's if the ocean had to be so hungry as to tear another piece from me, the one that gave me a reason to breathe.

A squad car flew past, all squealing tires and glaring lights.

A white, fragile paper angel tossed back and forth on a string, dangling from my rearview mirror. Upon the penciled-on angel toes were the initials "CA." Charlotte had made it for me along with a whole battalion of celestials that twirled comically in my kitchen window, down from my bathroom light fixture, and from the pull cord on a bedroom shade. Charlotte had surrounded me with angels and little-girl prayers. I knew why she had followed the boys onto the boat. She had gone off on her own crusade, the delicate sentry to her brother and my son. Through the kitchen window I saw that the cottage was filled with milling souls. Ruth traipsed back and forth cradling a pot of coffee while Rachel clung to her blouse.

I do not remember running up the rain-soaked path past the broken clay pots and across the deck stained by my mother.

"Colin, March is here!" Ruth handed the coffeepot to Dinah who had shown up barefaced, her hair pulled back in a ponytail.

Dinah's girls lay on the living-room floor cradling their pillows brought from home.

"I heard it on the police band, March. The whole town knows," said Dinah. She poured Bobby and Harold a cup of coffee.

"Have you heard anything?" I asked Ruth.

"Nothing from the Coast Guard. The neighbor is coming with the boat but I'd rather you all didn't go. Just look at that storm. It isn't safe, not for anyone!" Ruth said it to her brother.

"March, I don't know what to say." He grabbed me and held me. "The boys slipped out while we slept." Colin's eyes were red.

"Let's go, Colin. We'll find them."

"You on a boat, that's a laugh. You don't have to go, March. Maybe it's best you don't, that you wait here and answer the phone." Colin tied the hood of his rain slicker at his throat.

"Ruth and Dinah can take the calls. We're wasting time, Colin!"

Bobby took Ruth aside to gather facts and insert significance into the wait.

I felt Colin slip his hand into mine. He asked us all to bow for prayer. Harold and Bobby took off their caps and Dinah's daughters stopped their banter.

"We need you, God, need your guidance. Out of our weakness we lean on you. Please keep our children safe in your care. In Christ's name, amen," he said.

Colin and I barreled across the deck and ran for the dock. Dad's old neighbor, Vern Hottinger, clambered onto the dock and held the rope while we climbed aboard.

"She's a twenty-seven-footer, closed-bow, Reverend. She'll be fast and slice through the brine well enough, but the weather service is warning of ten- and twelve-foot swells in this torrent. Do you know how to operate a VHF radio?" Vern asked.

"I have one myself. Our thanks, Mr. Hottinger. We'd best shove off," said Colin. He helped me into the cabin.

Colin departed the banks at an angle. The craft nosed through the swells just as Vern said it would do, slamming the bow against the backs of the curls.

"None of this makes any sense, Colin. Mason has never taken the *Sparticus* without asking first. Then there's Charlotte who is just so well mannered and an obedient girl."

"Troy says they were up last night having popcorn wars and daring one another. They all thought Rachel was asleep but she heard the whole thing. When she woke up Charlotte was gone too."

The sky lowered all around us shrieking and roaring territorially around the misplaced humans.

"I didn't know you had experience driving a boat like this one," I said.

"Not exactly like this one." His thoughts seemed to disappear into the clamoring ocean ahead. "It's dark as coal out here. Times like this you realize the importance of knowing your coordinates."

"But you do know how to drive it?"

His mouth stretched into one of those superior smiles that men toss to women when they ask simple questions about plumbing parts. Only this was not a leaky toilet.

"I keep thinking that I didn't push Mason enough in his swim lessons. You know they start out as minnows and then progress up to trout, then dolphins, and then sharks. I can't even remember if he was a dolphin or a trout. But he stopped and started up his baseball again as though it didn't bother him that he never got his shark badge."

"Even a shark would have a hard time in this mess," he said.

"I read about experts who say you should sit down with your children and teach them, well, things about coping with real life. But it sounds like theory to me, you know, like how does that translate to something that prepares your child for danger? I don't know how to train him for disaster."

Colin kept staring into the storm and the waves while I babbled nervously.

"I mean, for gosh sakes! Does that mean we send them off to commando school? I can see him out in the middle of all of this scared and not knowing what to do and wondering why my voice is not breaking through and telling him 'Mason, do this' or 'Mason, do that.'"

"Mason is a good boy, March. You've done well by him."

The boat nosed up and smacked down so hard on the swell, it felt as though we were toppling. I grabbed tight and held on to the seat. The water never calmed for any space of time.

"Please God, help me see them!" said Colin.

The weather service broke through with another storm warning counseling all sea vessels to return to land.

I assumed Colin would ignore the warning. I proceeded to analyze my input in Mason's life, what would drive him out into this mess and how he might react in a crisis. It helped me to focus and not fall into the dark cavern of insanity. "I'm just worried. Mason has the ability to think, but he doesn't always practice it." I always saw those moms who came out of parent-teacher conferences smiling and hugging. But I always had this little twinge of anxiety about conferences. I knew the teacher would use words like *capable* and *potential,* which is code for he just doesn't try hard enough. I never heard that I did a good job as a mother and that all of my efforts shone through so clearly in the life of my child. I never understood why the teacher couldn't just validate me. I needed to be validated. "Somehow I missed out on all of these signals with Mason. I never saw this coming."

"Our kids made a mistake, March. We can't blame ourselves for this, although it wouldn't have hurt for me to put away the *Sparticus* last night. All the while I was teaching them to sail I never thought they would try this. But Mason is a good sailor. He knows what to do under normal circumstances." His words wilted.

"Colin, I see a light ahead."

"I see it." He changed gears and headed us toward the lights.

A large wave scooped us up and pushed us back, but Colin kept bearing down on the gas until we lurched ahead. "Thank God, it's the Coast Guard." He sounded the horn.

"That's the *Sparticus;* look!" I stood and clambered to see through the glass.

We pulled alongside the Coast Guard boat and saw Troy lifted from the *Sparticus.* He was rain-drenched and crying hysterically.

Colin dropped anchor.

"I don't see Mason and Charlotte, Colin. Where are they?" My knees felt weak and my hands trembled. I looked hard at the faces of the men who tried to calm Troy and question him. Colin leaped across the Coast Guard's vessel and grabbed his son. He pulled a blanket around him and shouted something at me. His words were snatched away by the wind. He pulled another soaked boy from the cabin and I saw that Mason was already safe inside. I cried and climbed out of Vern's vessel and allowed the crew to help me aboard.

Mason fell into my arms. "Mom, Charlotte tried to hang on, but she just couldn't! I tried, Troy and me tried really hard to help her, but it was her small hand that slipped. She lost her grip and we can't find her!" Mason wailed. "I'm so sorry. It's my fault!"

The Coast Guard searched the waters, their lights hovering over the ocean, motor trolling gently so as not to miss the smallest place a girl might be found.

Colin asked me to take the boys into the Coast Guard's cabin. He joined the crew in watching the searchlight. "Charlotte, angel! Charlotte, answer Daddy!"

I cried and held the boys. Troy buried his face in my shoulder. We held one another close and wept while Colin shouted at the storm.

Twenty-four

I KNOW NOTHING MORE COMFORTING THAN HOLDING my son next to me, but nothing more agonizing than watching a father look over the bow of a ship for a lost child. Colin looked flat in the dark next to the rescuers, all of them swaying in union like a row of paper dolls. The searchlights passed in front of them reflecting in the rain, which at times blew horizontally.

"How come they can't find Charlotte?" asked Troy. His whole body trembled, and it seemed I would never dry all of the rain and salt water from his hair.

"I don't know. It's such a big ocean, Troy," I told him, knowing I sounded like a lame adult.

Two of the men set up a commotion on deck. Three divers leaped into the water while two men held on to Colin to keep him from climbing overboard.

"Mason and Troy, I want you both to stay right here in your seats while I check on things out front." The wind blew me back and so I crouched and almost crawled up to the bow.

"I saw something, March, next to that buoy!" Colin pointed until the searchlight locked onto the buoy.

The divers fought the swells and bobbed in and out of sight until one of them grabbed onto the buoy. Another man broke the surface and waved wildly until he coaxed the searchlight his way.

"It's Charlotte," I whispered. They found her.

We watched them move her toward the boat against the wind and waves. She was strapped in a life vest, her eyes closed. They brought her aboard, a small doll-child wrapped in angel white. And still.

One of the Coast Guard crew members wrapped Charlotte in blankets. She never spoke or opened her eyes. Harold and Bobby had the ambulances waiting on shore. All three of the children were rushed to Holy Mary by the Sea Hospital.

I rode with Mason. He whispered the entire way as we drove past the beach cottages and the hundred-year-old homes along Durning Lane. Rain fell over the town, gray and pattering against the glass of the ambulance windows. The noontime lunch crowd had dis-appeared into the delis and coffee shops but I saw faces against the windows that turned into blurs of color and then flashed from sight.

Dinah stood with Dad just inside the emergency-room entrance. After we phoned home she had left immediately to fetch him and meet us at the hospital.

Charlotte was wheeled in first, but we could not see her for the flurry of attendants that surrounded her, lifted up her gurney, and literally ran with her through the open doors. The doors behind us were opened. I followed the parade through the doors, up the hall, and into the emergency room where each bed was divided by curtains.

A physician introduced himself to Colin then politely moved him aside, out of the way of the emergency-room nurses and a doctor who looked as young as Mason to me.

"Colin, let's wait here," I said. I gestured toward a group of three blue plastic chairs against the wall.

Colin hovered outside the flurry of movement around his daughter for a moment and then acquiesced to take a seat. Dad joined me on the other side.

"March, I just sat there next to her in the ambulance feeling as though I had nothing to offer her while the attendant intubated her. They called it aspiration pneumonia. I overheard the doctor say she has hypothermia, too," said Colin.

The young doctor moved down to Mason's bed while the older one took over Charlotte's care. I wanted to hover, but stayed next to Colin. "Mason looks so pale. When will they let me go to him?"

"Please, Lord, touch my little girl," Colin breathed out a prayer.

Dinah showed up with coffee.

"Thelma set the prayer chain in motion," said Dad. His fingers slid around my right hand.

"Mrs. Longfellow, we're ready for you," said the young child-of-a-physician.

"Finally. Come on, Dad. You come too." Dad followed me behind the curtain.

"We're treating Mason for shock. He's going to be fine but we'll keep him overnight just to make certain he doesn't develop pneumonia," said the doctor.

"What about Troy and Charlotte?" asked Mason.

"Troy is fine." Colin stopped there.

I kissed Mason first on his forehead and then directly on the mouth. When I stepped out from behind the curtain to tell Colin the good news, I saw him following the nurses out of the emergency room with Charlotte. He turned to me and his movements were mechanical, powered by rote rather than by reason. "They're moving her to ICU," he said and disappeared.

Dad and I opened the curtain between Troy and Mason so that they could see one another and know they were protected and safe.

The quiet humming outside of Intensive Care was like a large clock ticking, with each tick or tock carrying someone ahead into the next minute or carrying someone away. Holy Mary by the Sea Hospital, in its smallness, provided stoic efficiency with two nurses on duty. The reception desk was decorated with paper mobiles of orange-and-black Halloween motifs, hissing cats, and doe-eyed ghosts.

Colin paced outside of ICU calculating all of the things about him that were the sum total of a horrible father.

He had a stoop-shouldered posture, and I did not know whether I should touch him or leave him to himself. "If you get some food inside you, you'll feel better this afternoon," I said.

"I don't know about this place. If they could just get her stabilized and then get her back to a Charlotte hospital." Colin said it in a whisper. Then he signed another form the nurse handed to him.

"Did the doctor say what they think is wrong?"

"It's a concussion. Her breathing isn't right, either, and now she has a fever. It isn't good, and I have to get back down to Troy."

"Troy is fine. He and Mason are in the children's ward, maybe eating a little something by now."

"There is a children's ward here?"

"It's not fancy, but it isn't Dogpatch, either."

"March, I'm sorry. I don't mean to sound like your hospital is substandard, not big city enough or whatever. I'm not in my right mind. Where is James?"

"Dinah took him home. I told him he could come back tomorrow, but they're releasing Mason and Troy in the morning. Ruth took Luke and Rachel to the cafeteria for lunch. I think it finally stopped raining."

"Oh, I didn't realize it was lunchtime."

A nurse adjusted the oxygen mask over Charlotte's mouth. Her face looked oyster white with two bands of dark lashes that underlined her closed eyelids.

A candy striper clattered past and a nurse hushed her.

"Ms. March, is that you?" Yolanda whirled around with her hat barely pinned to a tousled half-ponytail. She wore a striped pinafore straight out of the fifties and a little white underblouse.

"Yolanda, I didn't expect to see you," I said.

"I'm a candy striper now. That whole kidnapping attempt thing changed my life. I've decided to dedicate my life to helping others. It's the least I can do considering, like, you know, I've been given a second chance and all. I would not be the least bit surprised if I didn't end up working with hungry children in a Third World country."

"You were almost kidnapped? You must be the girl March rescued in the story that they wrote about in *LIFE* magazine." Colin accepted a cup of coffee from the desk nurse.

"You saw it too?" Yolanda said it breathlessly, threw back her head, and declared, "Is there anyone who didn't see that piece? The whole town is forever changed, and it's all due to March."

I offered to add cream to Colin's coffee.

"But why are you here, Ms. March?" She looked at Colin. "Don't tell me you're the father of the little girl they rescued. Oh my word! Did you rescue that sweet precious little girl too?" Yolanda fiddled with the cap and poked more hair beneath it while she said to Colin, "I just would not put it past her at all."

"Yolanda, this is Reverend Arnett. Our children took an unexpected sailing trip and fell into some trouble. The Coast Guard actually rescued them," I said.

Colin clasped his hand around her trembling white fingers and greeted her, his words washed of any life.

"Mason—not Mason too?" Yolanda screeched.

"Mason's fine," I answered as quickly as was possible with Yolanda.

"Did he tell you how it happened?"

I nodded. He and Troy had argued over the fine points, but we came to something of a consensus. "Mason confessed some of it. He had gathered up the life vests but Troy denounced the need for them. Mason could not remember whether or not he had tossed them into the bow of the ship or if they just ended up there in a jumble." Charlotte had startled the boys with her appearance, still clothed in her angel-white gown but wearing a coat Ruth had purchased for her at the

Kmart. "Charlotte tried to talk them out of going, but machismo ruled the morning. Troy decided she had to go with them or risk being found out. That is how she wound up on board, sleepy-eyed and vulnerable."

A salmon-red sky had lured the trio out into deep waters. The raging storm was upon them before the first light appeared in the cottage window, when the darkening sky to the land dwellers was nothing more than a reason to lie in bed a few minutes more.

"But is Mason hurt?" asked Yolanda.

"No, Mason is going to be fine. He'll be released in the morning along with the pastor's son, Troy, and it wouldn't surprise me if they didn't let them go home tonight. Are you working in ICU? Because if you are, it would do a world of good if you could keep a watch out for little Charlotte here so Reverend Arnett can grab some lunch."

"I don't know if I should," said Colin.

"Little Charlotte! What a sweet name. Now you go get some food, Pastor, and I swear I'll send for you straightaway if there is any change. I practically raised Mason, so I am really a good one to sit with your angel." Yolanda trounced off toward Charlotte's bed.

Colin followed me, taking gangly reluctant strides backward with his back to the door.

When the elevator door opened, Jerry Brevity walked out with a basket of fruit piled a foot high. "Oh, thank goodness, I found you, March. They won't let you send flowers to ICU so I brought fruit. When my uncle was burned over forty percent of his body, the one thing my aunt appreciated was fruit and cheese. Ellen threw in a box of crackers too. How is Mason?" he asked.

"Oh. Fruit. How nice of you. Mason will get to go home tomorrow. He isn't in ICU. Jerry, this is Reverend Arnett. His little girl Charlotte is the one in ICU. Reverend Arnett, this is Jerry Brevity," I said. I couldn't remember if Colin knew about my sporadic life with Jerry, but Jerry most assuredly knew about Colin. It had seemed so simple to just drift, come-what-may, and not go into lengthy explanations either way.

"So you're the minister." Jerry stuck the fruit basket in my hands and turned and walked back into the elevator. "Going down?" He would not look at either of us, and his polite offer to hold the elevator door was sprinkled with a sharp tinny whine in his voice.

We stepped on and rode down with him, none of us speaking. After the old Holy Mary elevator lurched to a stop, the doors hesitated before opening, like always. Jerry sighed in a disgruntled groan twice before the doors finally jerked open. Jerry stepped off without saying another word to me and marched across the lobby and through the automatic doors at the entrance.

"I take it you're friends with Mr. Brevity." Colin held out his hands awkwardly, as though he wanted to relieve me of the weight of the basket but unsure if he was meddling.

"Jerry and I saw each other off and on."

"He knows about me?"

"The whole town knows about you, Colin. I don't have the luxury of privacy."

"I don't believe you've mentioned him." He hefted the basket. "Or was this the guy who took you to the sparkler boat parade? That's him, right?" It was the first time I had ever read sparks of jealousy on Colin's face. It was lovely to behold.

"I didn't think it was all that important."

"He had a rat embroidered on his lapel," he said flatly.

"They're having chicken fajitas in the cafeteria today. Would you prefer that or a burger?"

"If this Mr. Brevity is an issue with you, you should say so rather than letting me run around in circles wondering if I've done something wrong by moving toward an actual commitment."

"Jerry is not an issue." I wasn't sure if I wanted to calm his concern completely or give him food for thought.

"Fine."

"The cafeteria is this way," I said. I reeled in a smirk.

"But then everything else is of no consequence now anyway."

I don't believe he intended to sound harsh. Anger was the flagship for worry, I told myself. He wasn't angry with me, just the situation.

"I just want Charlotte back. I want her home where she belongs and everything back as it was."

He was taking too many jabs. I stepped back and allowed him to walk past and into the cafeteria.

He stopped and we looked at one another until I dropped my head, unable to retort with any womanly intelligence.

"I just can't muster an appetite, Colin. Please go ahead and join Ruth and Luke for lunch. I've got something I need to do." I tottered down the hallway and took a left into the gift shop. Colin might misinterpret my tears.

In one window, the shop attendant assembled an early Christmas display. I stared at the angels with feathered wings for so long the clerk asked if she could help me. "How much for the feathery angel whatnots?" I asked.

"Thirty-nine ninety-five, plus tax and you get a free Christmas wrap with that today." She wore a red gingham apron to usher in a little Yuletide spirit, but also had clasped on a Halloween pin, a battery-operated spider with a light-up orange nose that spread its spider legs every time the pull-string was yanked.

"I'll keep looking," I said. In an umbrella stand, someone had placed several packages. I pulled one out and saw it was a kite. The label displayed the full view of an angel. "How much are these?"

"Ten dollars. They're really left over from March. But the owner thought they might sell, what with the angel business picking up this time of year."

"I'll take one and the gift wrap."

"Gift wrap is three dollars and fifty cents. It's only free with one of those ceramic angels."

"I'll wrap it myself. Just bag it up then, if you will." I added a laptop checker game and two all-day suckers for the boys and a stuffed kitten with tufted ears for Charlotte when she woke up. The clerk clicked off the amounts on a computer. In the center of the Christmas display, a wig form had been transformed into a garish sequined hat display. Atop it was a plumed hat, and for a moment the wig form seemed to nag me like Joan. I could almost see the feathers waving in the little windowed cove at the hotel restaurant.

The clerk gave me the total and wrapped each piece with tissue paper even though I had not bought the ceramic thingy. I turned my back on Joan and her sequined eyelids and felt my soul turn into gelatin. She was Mason's grandmother, no matter what we thought of one another. Whatever the woman's transgressions, I had to make things right. I felt a Godlike thawing going on inside of me.

I found the boys perched in their beds behind hospital dinner trays. Troy was trying to engage Mason in a war with corn kernels from his lunch plate. But Mason stared straight ahead, his cheeks still pale.

"How about a checkers game?" I held up the bag, but both of the guys deflated. "I realize you were expecting a video game, but I swear you'll like this." I laid the suckers on each tray.

"Thanks, Mom," said Mason.

Troy reciprocated and then allowed the pillow to swallow his head. "This food is for people in jail."

"Mason, I want to ask you something. You know that big fight between Grandma and me? I think it's time we settled it."

"Just let her have the land?" His brows arched into pup tents above his eyes.

"Let's shake on it." We did.

"I'm in trouble, I guess." Mason rolled the sucker back and forth with one finger.

"I guess. We'll talk about it at home."

"Great. I'll look forward to that." He looked past me.

Colin appeared. His eyes conveyed resolve, as though he had been thinking things through again.

I turned my attention on Mason.

"Dad! Where have you been? Is Charlotte okay?" Troy tried to crawl out of his bed but Colin lifted him right back up into it.

"She's going to be fine." The circles under Colin's eyes made dark crescents like blue canoes, and I realized he was terrible at lying, which made him treacherously fascinating.

"I should have asked you if you have any candy issues, Colin," I said without a glance in his direction.

"Not at all." He kissed Troy. "I need to step out for just a minute, son, to talk with Ms. Longfellow."

"Don't think you have to, Colin. You need this time with your son. Anyone want to play checkers?"

Colin ambled around the foot of Mason's bed. "Please, March?"

"You go ahead and set up the checkers and I'll be back in a jiff," I told Mason.

Colin hesitated until a group of senior women in pink smocks walked past with salad trays. "March, sometimes you make me say things I don't mean."

"I make you?"

"You know I'm distracted right now. I just need to clear my head and then I'll say all of the right things. But just now when you walked away, I felt as though you were walking away from me, leaving me, not just without words, but leaving me period. I felt empty."

"I apologize for that," I said.

"Don't apologize! Just let me talk without a comment, if you don't mind."

I stared at him.

"Do you feel a part of my life, right now? Of the life that's up on the second floor and here in this room next to us?"

I opened my mouth, but all that came out was a whimper. I wiped the tears from my eyes and knew exactly, for once, what I had to say.

"March, Reverend Arnett, sir!" Yolanda skidded across the hall ahead and then ran toward us. "I am so glad I found you. This is awful! You've just got to come right this minute back up to ICU!"

Colin lost his breath.

"Yolanda, what on earth is wrong?" I asked.

"It's your little Charlotte, sir! She's gone into respiratory arrest." Yolanda burst into tears.

"We're coming, Yolanda," I said. I grasped Colin's hand. "Colin, let's get you upstairs."

A medical team surrounded Charlotte's pediatric bed. A doctor yelled at one of the nurses for her fumbling hands. The monitor beeped sporadically.

I waited several feet behind Colin. His shoulders were stooped. Whatever color had been in his face left him. He sobbed and all at once I could see him standing over Eva's bed. But I was not repelled by the image. I moved closer to him, took his hand, and pressed the side of my face against his arm. "Colin," I said, almost afraid to speak, to draw a father's attention from his little girl's bedside.

"March. I'm helpless to help her."

"I'm here, Colin."

He brought his arm around my shoulders and I cried with him. "To answer you earlier, of course I'm part of this, Colin." How could I not be? I was the least important person in the world now.

Twenty-five

NAGS HEAD IS A QUIET PLACE BETWEEN WINTER AND spring with plenty of places for children to run. Colin jogged along the water's edge holding the back of a kite while Mason, Troy, and Luke ran ahead to get the ten-dollar thing up in the air. The boys did not seem to mind the girlish smiling angel on the kite, only that it flew. Rachel ran behind them, galloping and tossing her hair like a mane. The angel soared and made loopy curls and zigs and zags at the ocean, but never did it nosedive altogether. It lifted and eventually folded out fully against the wind as though it would never come down. The kite reminded me of when Charlotte and I made sand angels along a bank that did not threaten to wash them away, only time. So different from the shoreline of an ocean.

We had spent the day before at Ocracoke, watching the local horsemen round up the wild mustangs that somehow had escaped their controlled areas and ventured into the village neighborhoods where they did not belong. I wrote about the ponies when I had first visited the Outer Banks alone, my spiritual trek back to the heart of God. I wrote until the words turned into pages of musings and then stories. Colin called it my "first novel", but I believed him to be too ambitious. But he knows that I know that about him.

The tide drew back and slapped against an outcropping of rocks beyond where the kids played. I know the ocean can swallow up things against your will, but it did not swallow up Troy, or Mason; nor did it swallow up Charlotte. Colin and I had gathered in the hospital chapel and breathed a prayer of gratitude for all of our many blessings and especially for our own little miracle girl the morning she woke up and asked for, of all things, water.

A squeal I likened to that of a wild ocean bird came from behind me and Charlotte leaped over our blanket and ran at the boys. "You put my kite back, you thieves, you! Get your grimy, boy hands off my angel!"

Colin accepted his defeat as a gentleman should and returned the ball of twine to its rightful owner. Charlotte lifted both hands high, her fingers fanning the wind, and she guided the kite in the beatific perfection that only a girl can give an object that dwells between the earth and the sky.

Colin walked toward me with his back to the shoreline and his face toward his miracle He settled beside me.

"Colin, this paragraph sounds terrible. Here, let me read it to you," I said.

"You've already read it to me and I like it. Stop trying to correct it as you write, March, and just let the words sing. You can't create perfection. Perfection arrives in thin layers, one atop another. It's like God remaking us until we take on the shape he intended."

"Why are you so wise?" I asked.

He rolled over on his stomach and faced me as I sat cross-legged. He touched my hand that rested on my knee. "Marry me, March."

"I already told you I would."

"You are lovely, lovely to look at." He ran his fingers along my nails as though he touched porcelain.

"If you're trying to flatter me, you cannot have another ice cream cone. I can't abide a fat husband."

"I don't know if I told you, but the minister just called. The chapel we wanted just came open. We won't have to marry at the hotel reception room after all."

"Colin, you don't say? I can't believe it. That is such a, well, an unbelievable place for a wedding. I'll call the photographer, the florist, and Dad. I hope he remembers to bring the wedding vows. First I'll call Dinah and ask her to meet him early and make certain he has everything. I'll bet he hasn't married anyone in a year. I know I'm forgetting so many things. But that isn't so awful, I guess."

"I'll call Mom and Dad. They should be here anytime. I'm glad Ruth is meeting them. I'm needing a little nap right about now." Colin checked his watch and flicked sand off of the face. "The realtor says we should meet him Monday morning." He rolled onto his back to follow the path of the angel kite overhead.

"But should we do that? You won't know if you want to pastor that church in Rocky Mount until after Sunday. Will Monday give you enough time to know for sure?"

"Have a little faith and then walk out on it. What have we here? A new bottle." He picked up the small, clear bottle with a tag around the neck that said "Nags Head."

"Mason made it."

"What are these inside it?"

"Seven stones. One for each of us. Enough for a whole shore."

Mason plopped down between Colin and me. "Save me from those crazy women!"

"Excuse me, sir. You're invading my space." Colin climbed over Mason and sat next to me. He kissed the tip of my nose right in the place where it freckled. "If the kids aren't exhausted, I am. I'm going to round them up." He called after them and then yelled when they scattered down both sides of the beach.

"It's going to be a noisy house," said Mason.

"I kind of like it," I said.

"Did that lady buy the *Sentinel?* Gloria said she's liquid, whatever that means."

"She was married to a senator once. Geraldine Montague. I met her on a flight to Charlotte and she wrote down my name, gave me her card. I just picked up the phone one day and asked her if she'd like to hear a business proposal. She likes this area. It's close to her grandchildren. She thinks of the *Sentinel* as a hobby. Gloria said she brought by paint samples yesterday. That's always a good sign."

"Grandpa says he doesn't think he's going to like Rocky Mount." Mason sounded just like Dad.

"Let him complain. The house we're looking at has plenty of places for him to read, and it's not near the water and that should satisfy him. Besides, he's keeping the cottage and that is what reminds him most of my mother."

"I looked at the atlas, and Rocky Mount is right in between where we live and where they live," Mason said.

I began rolling up the blanket and gathering the collection of plastic beach toys strewn around our little spot on the sand.

"I've been thinking about Grandma Joan, and she doesn't make sense."

"Toss me that sand pail, please, will you?" I asked.

"If she wanted Dad's land so badly, then why did she give it right back to me?"

"So I tried a little kindness. Don't look at me like that."

"You're turning into a wimp, Mom. I kind of like it." Mason clumped together an armload of sand toys and headed toward the parking lot with four squealing Arnetts on his heels. Colin opened the doors to let them clamber inside, a tangle of bare feet powdered with sand in every nook and cranny of every bend in every limb.

"Hold it! I want to take a picture," I said.

Colin groaned. Every Arnett child along with Mason clambered out of the vehicle and gathered around the tailgate posing like contortionists and body builders.

I considered the lovely sight of each one and how God used the small things to hold back life's tides.

Author's Note

IN THE MIDDLE OF WRITING *SANDPEBBLES*, OUR life took a tragic turn when three Huntersville policemen showed up at our door to tell us "Your daughter, Jessica, was in a terrible car accident. She didn't make it."

I say this to you, the reader, because some who hear of our tragedy may think that this sudden twist in our road fomented this story when, instead, our sudden loss caused the work already in progress to shift as I descended into a valley I did not want to travel. A valley that soon became a canyon.

In this canyon, I discovered many new things about pain and about the Lord: a deeper understanding of the Suffering Savior; how to offer real comfort to those in pain; and thirdly, a higher appreciation for the healing qualities of laughter. Within weeks after committing our angel girl eternally into the arms of Christ, the wonderful people from W Publishing and Women of Faith invited me along with the other fiction authors of this line to join them for a weekend of refreshing at the Nashville 2001 conference. I suddenly found myself surrounded by a unique sisterhood of authors and speakers who lifted my spirits, took me closer to the cross, and made me laugh until the pain was nothing but a soft pillow. I had taken a sabbatical from writing *Sandpebbles,* or anything for that matter, and did not know if I possessed the creative energy to return to my writing desk. But I realized that weekend that when I am an emotional wreck, Christ can handle all of my engine work. I returned home renewed and determined to write this story with a deeper understanding of pain and a hopeful measure of laughter. I had discovered a new elixir and wanted to share it with as many women as possible. And although laughter is addictive, you won't have to check into the Betty Ford Clinic when you overdo.

It was only a few months later that our nation was shaken by its own tragedy. Suddenly the world was reeling in the aftermath of a modern-day holocaust that affected every American somehow, some way. Through these dark days, God helped me realize that when pain takes up residence in my heart, hopelessness tries to wiggle through the door right behind her. And that is when I have to post an eviction notice—no hopelessness allowed.

Several weeks after our April tragedy, I noticed that my Bible promise desk calendar yet remained on the date of Jessica's death. April 27, 2001 was coincidentally decorated with her favorite flowers—daisies—and inscribed with this scripture: *"I waited patiently for the LORD to help me, and he turned to me and heard my cry. He lifted me out of the pit of despair, out of the mud and the mire. He set my feet on solid ground and steadied me as I walked along"* Psalm 40:1–2 NLT.

If you're up to your knees in life's mud and your pits have become canyons, this is my prayer for you—that Jesus Christ, who hears your cry, will lift you up onto His solid ground and keep you moving ahead, steady as you go, walking on Sonshine.

—Patricia Hickman

Acknowledgments

I WANT TO EXPRESS HOW GRATEFUL I AM TO THE following people for their advice and expert knowledge that lends accuracy to my story. Very warm thanks to Pastor Wade Malloy of Southlake Presbyterian Church for sharing facts about Presbyterian traditions and doctrines of faith. Additional thanks go to attorney Jeff Rothwell for providing me with legal facts and trial information. And thanks so much to John Bordsen, travel editor of the *Charlotte Observer,* who helped immensely in the early stages of *Sandpebbles* as I developed March Longfellow's eclectic newspaper career. Thanks to my wonderful friend, Shannon Anzivino, for lending the medical facts to this story as well as being a prayer warrior for this project. And to Deb Raney, massive thanks to you for assisting me in developing the quirky office staff and setting for the Candle Cove *Sentinel.* Your knowledge of small-town newspapers is as vital to this story as your own stories are to the CBA market.

I also want to thank the W Publishing Group family and the Women of Faith family for being a family to me during our trying year. Thank you for your patience in waiting for this story to finally come to its completion. Thank you, Debbie Wickwire, for being such a wonderful sister in the faith. Thank you, Stephen Arterburn, for your vision for this line of fiction. Thank you, Mary, Patsy, Barbara, Thelma, Marilyn, Sheila, and Luci (who is always last) for propping us up with your prayers and sharing your profound jewels of wisdom. Thank you to Mark Sweeney, Ami McConnell, Diane Eble, and the W editing staff and marketing team for your expert attention to detail and commitment to excellence in fiction. Thank you to Greg Johnson and Rick Christian of the best literary agency in the country and for being our friends. Lastly (but not leastly), thanks to my WOF Fictionette sisters, Angie, Terri, and Karen, and the ChiLibris family of writers for surrounding the Hickmans with your love and prayers. You have no idea . . . words just cannot express how deeply you touched our lives and helped us down the healing path.

Discussion Questions/ Study Guide

1. March Longfellow is a woman caught up in the busyness of life—motherhood, church, and career. She is religious but has missed the key to a close relationship with her Savior. Her relationship with her deceased husband lacked these same elements. Why is intimacy with God important?

2. Colin Arnett suffers through the grief process the same as March, yet he allows his weakness to become a strength while March fears her grief will make her bitter. Have you suffered loss in your life? Is it difficult to believe that in your weakness Christ can give you strength? Does loss make you angry with God?

3. The process of letting go and allowing change to come is difficult for March and even somewhat difficult for her pastor father, James Norville. But God uses change to refine us and mature us. Has God ever stretched you through change? What was your reaction?

4. Joan Longfellow might be perceived by some initially as the villain in the story. But by the story's end, March realizes Joan's antagonism toward her is an opportunity to show humility and the same forgiveness that Christ offered her. When villains come your way, what is your response?

5. March is outwardly confident, but inwardly she describes herself as a wreck. Human nature leads us to believe that we should put up a false front when faced with trials. But in the New Testament, Christ showed those around Him a different way to live. What would be the benefit of sharing your struggles with a trusted friend who has a committed prayer life?

6. March is trying to be both mother and father to her son, Mason. In her effort to shield him from her own internal pain, she alienates him instead. By her opening up to him in gentleness and vulnerability, he opens up to her and their relationship deepens to a more intimate level. If you are a parent or a child, do you have difficulty in sharing a concern with your family in love?

7. March feels inadequate in sharing her faith and is surprised and even jealous when Colin Arnett successfully plants a seed of faith with two of her very closest friends. But when she is cornered into sharing her faith with Vicky Lane based upon her own knowledge of the Bible, she realizes that the Spirit of God takes care of the results. Are you afraid that sharing your faith will make your friends uncomfortable? Do you know Christ as Savior? Would you like to?

8. When March finally "surrenders" her life to Christ, how did it change her? Do you believe that surrendering your life to Christ will take away from who you are or make you better?

9. In the midst of crisis, Colin led everyone to pray before launching out to try and solve the disaster himself. Making prayer a daily habit takes much practice before it becomes a natural part of your life. Before disaster strikes, have you considered making prayer a daily practice?

10. The elements of humor were used in this story as a healing balm for the deeper subject of grief. Do you seek out positive sources of laughter and encouraging influence to help you through dark periods? Do you surround yourself with positive friends who are mature in their faith? We encourage you to grab a couple of friends and attend a Women of Faith event. You will laugh. You will cry. You will be lifted up.

About the Author

An award-winning novelist and speaker, Patricia Hickman has published ten novels, including the critically acclaimed *Katrina's Wings*. Her works have been praised in such publications as *Affair de Coeur* magazine, *Romantic Times, Moody Magazine, Shine Magazine for Women* and *West Coast Review of Books*. Hickman has won two Silver Angel Awards for Excellence in Media and is a frequent guest on national radio programs. Patricia is married and the mother of three—two on earth and one in heaven. She makes her home in Huntersville, North Carolina.

A few of the latest inspirational fiction titles by Patricia Hickman

Katrina's Wings

The Touch

Coming in 2003—*Fallen Angels*

Please visit www.patriciahickman.com and e-mail any questions you may have about this story or a life of faith in Christ.

Additional Selections

When PanWorld flight 848 crashes into Tampa Bay killing all 261 people on board, journalist Peyton MacGruder is assigned to the story. Her discovery of a remnant of the tragedy—a simple note: "T—I love you...All is forgiven. Dad."—sends her on a quest to find its owner and the story behind it. In the process, Peyton uncovers lessons about love, forgiveness, and herself.

The decision has been made. After 23 years of marriage, John and Abby are getting a divorce. But before they can tell their family, their daughter announces that she is getting married, so they postpone their own announcement until after the wedding. But as the big day approaches, they wonder if the decision they've made is irreversible or if they can find once again what they've been missing for so many years, the joy of magnificent love, the time...to dance.

When Amanda's husband dies unexpectedly and her two step daughters are given over to their grandparents, Amanda desperately tries to keep ties with them through support money and letters—unbeknownst to them. Now she struggles to understand the wounds and scars of two girls she longs to know—trying to overcome their cynicism and doubt—and prove her love is genuine and her gifts come with no strings attached.

www.wpublishinggroup.com

A Division of Thomas Nelson, Inc.
www.ThomasNelson.com